Mary Jane Holmes

The Cameron Pride

Purified by Suffering

Mary Jane Holmes

The Cameron Pride
Purified by Suffering

ISBN/EAN: 9783743427501

Manufactured in Europe, USA, Canada, Australia, Japa

Cover: Foto ©Andreas Hilbeck / pixelio.de

Manufactured and distributed by brebook publishing software (www.brebook.com)

Mary Jane Holmes

The Cameron Pride

THE CAMERON PRIDE

OR

PURIFIED BY SUFFERING

𝕬 𝕹𝖔𝖛𝖊𝖑

BY

Mrs. MARY J. HOLMES

AUTHOR OF "TEMPEST AND SUNSHINE," "HUGH WORTHINGTON,"
"LENA RIVERS," ETC., ETC.

———

NEW YORK
HURST & COMPANY
PUBLISHERS

TO

MY BROTHER,

Kirke Dawes,

IN MEMORY OF THE OCTOBER DAY WHEN WE RAMBLED OVER THE

SILVERTON HILLS,

WHERE MORRIS AND KITTY LIVED,

THIS VOLUME

IS AFFECTIONATELY DEDICATED.

Brown Cottage, February 22, 1867.

CONTENTS.

THE CAMERON PRIDE;

OR, PURIFIED BY SUFFERING.

CHAPTER I.

THE FARM-HOUSE AT SILVERTON.

UNCLE EPHRAIM BARLOW was an old-fashioned man, clinging to the old-time customs of his fathers, and looking with but little toleration upon what he termed the "new-fangled notions" of the present generation. Born and reared amid the rocks and hills of the Bay State, his nature partook largely of the nature of his surroundings, and he grew into manhood with many a rough point adhering to his character, which, nevertheless, taken as a whole, was, like the wild New England scenery, beautiful and grand. None knew Uncle Ephraim Barlow but to respect him, and at the church in which he was a deacon, few would have been missed more than the tall, muscular man, with the long white hair, who, Sunday after Sunday, walked slowly up the middle aisle to his accustomed seat before the altar, and who regularly passed the contribution box, bowing involuntarily in token of approbation when a neighbor's gift was larger than its wont, and gravely dropping in his own ten cents—never more, never less, always ten cents—his weekly offering, which he knew amounted in a year to just five dollars and twenty cents. And still Uncle Ephraim was not stingy, as the Silverton poor could testify, for many a load of wood and bag of meal found entrance to the doors where cold and hunger would have otherwise been, while to his minister he was literally a holder up of the weary hands, and a comforter in the time of trouble.

His helpmeet, Aunt Hannah, like that virtuous woman

mentioned in the Bible, was one "who seeketh wool and flax, and worketh willingly with her hands, who riseth while yet it is night, and giveth meat to her household," while Miss Betsy Barlow, the deacon's maiden sister, was a character in her way, and bore no resemblance to those frivolous females to whom the Apostle Paul had reference when he condemned the plaiting of hair and the wearing of gold and jewels. Quaint, queer and simple-hearted, she had but little idea of any world this side of heaven, except the one bounded by the "huckleberry" hills and the crystal waters of Fairy Pond, which from the back door of the farm-house were plainly seen, both in the summer sunshine and when the intervening fields were covered with the winter snow.

The home of such a trio was, like themselves, ancient and unpretentious, nearly one hundred years having elapsed since the solid foundation was laid to a portion of the building. Unquestionably it was the oldest house in Silverton, for on the heavy oaken door of what was called the back room was still to be seen the mark of a bullet, left there by some marauders who, during the Revolution, had encamped in that neighborhood. George Washington, it was said, had spent a night beneath its roof, the deacon's mother pouring for him her Bohea tea and breaking her home-made bread. Since that time several attempts had been made to modernize the house. Lath and plaster had been put upon the rafters and paper upon the walls, wooden latches had given place to iron, while in the parlor, where Washington had slept, there was the extravagance of a porcelain knob, such, as Uncle Ephraim said, was only fit for gentry who could afford to be grand. For himself he was content to live as his father did; but young folks, he supposed, must in some things have their way, and so when his pretty niece, who had lived with him from childhood to the day of her marriage, came back to him a widow, bringing her two fatherless children and a host of new ideas, he good-humoredly suffered her to tear down some of his household idols and replace them with her own. And thus it was that the farm-house gradually changed its appearance, for young womanhood which has had one glimpse of the outer world will not settle down quietly amid fashions a century old. Lucy Lennox, when she returned to the farm-house, was not quite the same as when she went away. Indeed, Aunt Betsy in her guileless heart feared that she had actually fallen from grace, imputing the fall wholly to Lucy's predilection for a certain little book on whose back was written "Common Prayer," and at which Aunt Betsy scarcely dared to look, lest she should be guilty of the enormities practiced by the Romanists themselves. Clearer headed than his sister, the deacon read the black-bound book, finding therein much that was good, but wondering "why, when folks promised to renounce the pomps and vanities, they did not do so, instead of acting more stuck up than ever." Inconsistency was the underlying strata of the whole Episcopal Church, he said, and as Lucy had declared her preference for that church, he too, in a measure, charged her propensity for repairs to the same source with Aunt Betsy; but, as he could see no sin in what she did, he suffered hr in most things to have her way. But when she contemplated an attack upon the huge chimney occupying the centre of the building, he interfered; for there was nothing he liked better than the bright fire on the hearth when the evenings grew chilly and long, and the autumn rain was falling upon the roof. The chimney should stand, he said; and as no amount of coaxing could prevail on him to revoke his decision, the chimney stood, and with it the three fire-places, where, in the fall and spring, were burned the twisted knots too bulky for the kitchen stove. This was fourteen years ago, and in that lapse of time Lucy Lennox had gradually fallen in with the family ways of living, and ceased to talk of her cottage in western New York, where her husband had died and where were born her daughters, one of whom she was expecting home on the warm July day when our story opens.

Katy Lennox had been for a year an inmate of Canandaigua Seminary, whither she was sent at the expense of a distant relative to whom her father had been guardian, and who, during her infancy, had had a home with Uncle Ephraim, Mrs. Lennox having brought him with her when she returned to Silverton. Dr. Morris Grant he was now, and he had just come home from a three years' sojourn in Paris, and was living in his own handsome dwelling across the fields toward Silverton village, and half a mile or more from Uncle Ephraim's farm-house. He had written from Paris, offering to send his cousins, Helen and Kate, to any school their mother might select, and as Canandaigua was her choice, they had both gone thither the year before, but Helen, the eldest, had fallen sick within the first three months, and returned to Silverton, satisfied that the New England schools were good enough for her. This was Helen; but Katy was different. Katy was more susceptible of polish and refinement—so the mother thought; and as she arranged and rearranged the little parlor, lingering longest by the piano, Dr. Morris's gift, she drew bright pictures of her favorite child, wondering how the farm-house and its inmates would seem to her after all she must have seen during her weeks of travel since the close of the summer term. And then she wondered why cousin Morris was so annoyed when told that Katy had accepted an invitation to accompany Mrs. Woodhull and her party on a trip to Montreal and Lake George, taking Boston on her homeward route. Katy's movements were nothing to him, unless—and the little ambitious mother struck at random a few notes of the soft-toned piano as she thought how possible it was that the interest always manifested by staid, quiet Morris Grant for her light-hearted Kate was more than a brotherly interest, such as he would naturally feel for the daughter of one who had been to him a second father. But Katy was so much a child when he went away to Paris that it could not be. She would sooner think of Helen, who was more like him.

"It's Helen, if anybody," she said aloud, just as a voice near the window called out, "Please, Cousin Lucy, relieve me of these flowers. I brought them over in honor of Katy's return."

Blushing guiltily, Mrs. Lennox advanced to meet a tall, dark-looking man, with a grave, pleasant face, which, when he smiled, was strangely attractive, from the sudden lighting up of the hazel eyes and the glitter of the white, even teeth disclosed so fully to view.

"Oh, thank you, Morris! Katy will like them, I am

sure," Mrs. Lennox said, taking from his hand a bouquet of the choice flowers which grew only in the hothouse at Linwood. "Come in for a moment, please."

"No, thank you," the doctor replied. "There is a case of rheumatism just over the hill, and I must not be idle if I would retain the practice given to me. Not that I make anything but good will as yet, for only the Silverton poor dare trust their lives in my inexperienced hands. But I can afford to wait," and with another flash of the hazel eyes Morris walked away a pace or two, then, as if struck with some sudden thought, turned back, and fanning his heated face with his leghorn hat, said, hesitatingly, "By the way, Uncle Ephraim's last payment on the old mill falls due to-morrow. Tell him, if he says anything in your presence, not to mind unless it is perfectly convenient. He must be somewhat straitened just now, as Katy's trip cannot have cost him a small sum."

The clear, penetrating eyes were looking full at Mrs. Lennox, who for a moment felt slightly piqued that Morris Grant should take so much oversight of her uncle's affairs. It was natural, too, that he should, she knew, for there was a strong liking between the old man and the young, the latter of whom, having lived nine years in the family, took a kindly interest in everything pertaining to it.

"Uncle Ephraim did not pay the bills," Mrs. Lennox faltered at last, feeling intuitively how Morris's delicate sense of propriety would shrink from her next communication. "Mrs. Woodhull wrote that the expense should be nothing to me, and as she is fully able and makes so much of Katy, I did not think it wrong."

"Lucy Lennox! I am astonished!" was all Morris could say, as the tinge of wounded pride dyed his cheek.

Kate was a connection—distant, it is true; but his blood was in her veins, and his inborn pride shrank from receiving so much from strangers, while he wondered at her mother, feeling more and more convinced that what he had so long suspected was literally true. Mrs. Lennox was weak, Mrs. Lennox was ambitious, and for the sake of associating her daughter with people whom the world had placed above her she would stoop to accept that upon which she had no claim.

"Mrs. Woodhull was so urgent and so fond of Katy; and then I thought it well to give her the advantage of being with such people as compose that party, the very first in Canandaigua, besides some from New York," Mrs. Lennox began in self-defence, but Morris did not stop to hear more, and hurried off a second time, while Mrs. Lennox looked after him, wondering at the feeling which she could not understand. "If Katy can go with the Woodhulls and their set, I certainly shall not prevent it," she thought, as she continued her arrangement of the parlor, wishing that it was more like what she remembered Mrs. Woodhull's to have been, fifteen years ago.

Of course that lady had kept up with the times, and if her old house was finer than anything Mrs. Lennox had ever seen, what must her new one be, with all the modern improvements? and leaning her head upon the mantel, Mrs. Lennox thought how proud she should be could she live to see her daughter in similar circumstances to the envied Mrs. Woodhull, at that moment in the crowded car between Boston and Silverton, tired, hot, and dusty, and as nearly cross as a fashionable lady can be.

A call from Uncle Ephraim roused her, and going out into the square entry she tied his linen cravat, and then handing him the blue umbrella, an appendage he took with him in sunshine and in storm, she watched him as he stepped into his one-horse wagon and drove briskly away in the direction of the depot, where he was to meet his niece.

"I wish Cousin Morris had offered his carriage," she thought, as the corn-colored wagon disappeared from view. "The train stops five minutes at West Silverton, and some of those grand people will be likely to see the turn-out," and with a sigh as she doubted whether it were not a disgrace as well as an inconvenience to be poor, she repaired to the kitchen, where sundry savory smells betokened a plentiful dinner.

Bending over the sink, with her cap strings tucked back, her sleeves rolled up, and her short purple calico shielded from harm by her broad check apron, Aunt Betsy stood cleaning the silvery onions, and occasionally wiping her dim old eyes as the odor proved too strong for her.

At another table stood Aunt Hannah, deep in the mysteries of the light white crust which was to cover the tender chicken boiling in the pot, while in the oven bubbled and baked the custard pie, remembered as Katy's favorite, and prepared for her coming by Helen herself—plain-spoken, dark-eyed Helen—now out in the strawberry beds, picking the few luscious berries which almost by a miracle had been coaxed to wait for Katy, who loved them so dearly. Like her mother, Helen had wondered how the change would impress her bright little sister, for she remembered that even to her obtuse perceptions there had come a pang when after only three months abiding in a place where the etiquette of life was rigidly enforced, she had returned to their homely ways at Silverton, and felt that it was worse than vain to try to effect a change. But Helen's strong sense, with the help of two or three good cries, had carried her safely through, and her humble home among the hills was very dear to her now. But she was Helen, as the mother had said; she was different from Katy, who might be lonely and homesick, sobbing herself to sleep in her patient sister's arms, as she did on that first night in Canandaigua, which Helen remembered so well.

"It's better, too, now than when I came home," Helen thought, as with her rich, scarlet fruit she went slowly to the house. "Morris is here, and the new church, and if she likes she can teach ﹨ Sunday-school, though maybe she will prefer going with Uncle Ephraim. He will be pleased if she does," and pausing by the door, Helen looked across Fairy Pond in the direction of Silverton village, where the top of a slender spire was just visible— the spire of St. John's, built within the year, and mostly at the expense of Dr. Morris Grant, who, a zealous church-man himself, had labored successfully to instill into Helen's mind some of his own peculiar views, as well as to awaken in Mrs. Lennox's heart the professions which had lain dormant for as long a time as the little black bound book had lain on the cupboard shelf, forgotten and unread.

How the doctor's views were regarded by the Deacon's family we shall see, by and by. At present our story has to do with Helen, holding her bowl of berries by the rear door and looking across the distant fields. With one last glance at the object of her thoughts she re-entered the house, where her mother was arranging the square table for dinner, bringing out the white stone china instead of the mulberry set kept for every day use.

"We ought to have some silver forks," she said despondingly, as she laid by each plate the three tined forks of steel, to pay for which Helen and Katy had picked huckleberries on the hills and dried apples from the orchard.

"Never mind, mother," Helen answered cheerily: "if Katy is as she used to be she will care more for us than for silver, and I guess she is, for I imagine it would take a great deal to make her anything but a warmhearted, merry little creature."

This was sensible Helen's tribute of affection to the little, gay, chattering butterfly, at that moment an occupant of Uncle Ephraim's corn-colored wagon, and riding with that worthy toward home, throwing kisses to every barefoot boy and girl she met, and screaming with delight as the old familiar waymarks met her view.

"There is Aunt Betsy, with her dress pinned up as usual," she cried, when at last the wagon stopped before the door, and the four women came hurriedly out to meet her, almost smothering her with caresses, and then holding her off to see if she had changed.

She was very stylish in her pretty traveling dress of gray, made under Mrs. Woodhull's supervision, and nothing could be more becoming than her jaunty hat, tied with ribbons of blue, while the dainty kids, bought to match the dress, fitted her fat hands charmingly, and the little high-heeled boots of soft prunella were faultless in their style. She was very attractive in her personal appearance, and the mental verdict of the four females regarding her intently was something as follows: Mrs. Lennox detected unmistakable marks of the grand society she had been mingling in, and was pleased accordingly; Aunt Hannah pronounced her "the prettiest creeter she had ever seen;" Aunt Betsy decided that her hoops were too big and her clothes too fine for a Barlow; while Helen, who looked beyond dress, or style, or manner, straight into her sister's soft blue eyes, brimming with love and tears, decided that Katy was not changed for the worse. Nor was she. Truth-

ful, loving, simple-hearted and full of playful life she
had gone from home, and she came back the same, never
once thinking of the difference between the farm-house and
Mrs. Woodhull's palace, or if she did, giving the preference
to the former.

"It was perfectly splendid to get home," she said,
handing her gloves to Helen, her sun-shade to her mother,
her satchel to Aunt Hannah, and tossing her bonnet in
the vicinity of the water pail, from which it was saved by
Aunt Betsy, who put it carefully in the press, examining
it closely first and wondering how much it cost.

Deciding that "it was a good thumpin' price," she returned to the kitchen, where Katy, dancing and curvetting
in circles, scarcely stood still long enough for them to see
that in spite of boarding-school fare, of which she had
complained so bitterly, her cheeks were rounder, her eyes
brighter, and her figure fuller than of old. She had improved, but she did not appear to know it, or to guess
how beautiful she was in the fresh bloom of seventeen,
with her golden hair waving around her childish forehead,
and her deep blue eyes laughing so expressively with each
change of her constantly varying face. Everything animate
and inanimate pertaining to the old house, came in for
its share of notice. She kissed the kitten, squeezed the
cat, hugged the dog, and hugged the little goat, tied to his
post in the clover yard and trying so hard to get free. The
horse, to whom she fed handfuls of grass, had been already
hugged. She did that the first thing after strangling
Uncle Ephraim as she alighted from the train, and some
from the car window saw it, smiling at what they termed
the charming simplicity of an enthusiastic school-girl.
Blessed youth! blessed early girlhood, surrounded by a
halo of rare beauty! It was Katy's shield and buckler,
warding off many a cold criticism which might otherwise
have been passed upon her.

They were sitting down to dinner now, and the deacon's
voice trembled as, with the blessing invoked, he thanked
God for bringing back the little girl, whose head was for
a moment bent reverently, but quickly lifted itself up as
its owner, in the same breath with that in which the
deacon uttered his amen, declared how hungry she was,

and went into rhapsodies over the nicely cooked viands which loaded the table. The best bits were hers that day, and she refused nothing until it came to Aunt Betsy's onions, once her special delight, but now declined, greatly to the distress of the old lady, who having been on the watch for " quirks," as she styled any departure from long established customs, now knew she had found one, and with an injured expression withdrew the offered bowl, saying sadly, " You used to eat 'em raw, Catherine; what's got into you ? "

It was the first time Aunt Betsy had called a name so obnoxious to Kate, especially when, as in the present case, great emphasis was laid upon the *rine,* and from past experience Katy knew that her good aunt was displeased. Her first impulse was to accept the dish refused ; but when she remembered her reason for refusing she said, laughingly, " Excuse me, Aunt Betsy, I love them still, but—but—well, the fact is, I am going by and by to run over and see Cousin Morris, inasmuch as he was not polite enough to come here, and you know it might not be so pleasant."

" The land ! " and Aunt Betsy brightened. " If that's all, eat 'em. 'Tain't no ways likely you'll get near enough to him to make any difference—only turn your head when you shake hands."

But Katy remained incorrigible, while Helen, who guessed that her impulsive sister was contemplating a warmer greeting of the doctor than a mere shaking of his hands, kindly turned the conversation by telling how Morris was improved by his tour abroad, and how much the poor people thought of him.

" He is very fine looking, too," she said, whereupon Katy involuntarily exclaimed, " I wonder if he is as handsome as Wilford Cameron ? Oh, I never wrote about him, did I ? " and the little maiden began to blush as she stirred her tea industriously.

" Who is Wilford Cameron ? " asked Mrs. Lennox.

" Oh, he's Wilford Cameron, that's all ; lives on Fifth Avenue—is a lawyer—is very rich—a friend of Mrs. Woodhull, and was with us in our travels," Kate answered rapidly, the red burning on her cheeks so brightly that

Aunt Betsy innocently passed her a big feather fan, saying "she looked mighty hot."

And Katy was warm, but whether from talking of Wilford Cameron or not none could tell. She said no more of him, but went on to speak of Morris, asking if it were true, as she had heard, that he built the new church in Silverton.

"Yes, and runs it, too," Aunt Betsy answered, energetically, proceeding to tell "what goin's on they had, with the minister shiftin' his clothes every now and agin the folks all talkin' together. Morris got me in once," she said, "and I thought meetin' was let out half a dozen times, so much histin' round as there was. I'd as soon go to a show, if it was a good one, and I told Morris so. He laughed and said I'd feel different when I knew 'em better; but needn't tell me that prayers made up is as good as them as isn't, though Morris, I do believe, will get to Heaven a long ways ahead of me, if he is a 'Piscopal."

To this there was no response, and being launched on her favorite topic, Aunt Betsy continued:

"If you'll believe it, Helen here is one of 'em, and has got a sight of 'Piscopal quirks into her head. Why, she and Morris sing that talkin'-like singin' Sundays when the folks get up and Helen plays the accordeon."

"Melodeon, aunty, melodeon," and Helen laughed merrily at her aunt's mistake, turning the conversation again, and this time to Canandaigua, where she had some acquaintances.

But Katy was so much afraid of Canandaigua, and what talking of it might lead to, that she kept to Cousin Morris, asking innumerable questions about his house and grounds, and whether there were as many flowers there now as there used to be in the days when she and Helen went to say their lessons at Linwood, as they had done before Morris sailed for Europe.

"I think it right mean in him not to be here to see me," she said, poutingly, "and I am going over as quick as I eat my dinner."

But against this all exclaimed at once. She was too tired, the mother said, she must lie down and rest, while Helen suggested that she had not told them about her

trip, and Uncle Ephraim remarked that she would not
find Morris at home, as he was going that afternoon to
Spencer. This last settled it. Katy must stay at home;
but instead of lying down or talking about her journey,
she explored every nook and crevice of the old house and
barn, finding the nest Aunt Betsy had looked for in vain,
and proving to the anxious dame that she was right when
she insisted that the speckled hen had stolen her nest and
was in the act of setting. Later in the day, a neighbor
passing by spied the little maiden riding in the cart off
into the meadow, where she sported like a child among
the mounds of fragrant hay, playing her jokes upon the
sober deacon, who smiled fondly upon her, feeling how
much lighter the labor seemed because she was there with
him, a hindrance instead of a help, in spite of her efforts
to handle the rake skillfully.

"Are you glad to have me home again, Uncle Eph?"
she asked when once she caught him regarding her with
a peculiar look.

"Yes, Katy-did, very glad?" he answered; "I've missed
you every day, though you do nothing much but bother
me."

"Why did you look so funny at me just now?" Kate
continued, and the deacon replied: "I was thinking how
hard it would be for such a highty-tighty thing as you to
meet the crosses and disappointments which lie all along
the road which you must travel. I should hate to see your
young life crushed out of you, as young lives sometimes
are?"

"Oh, never fear for me. I am going to be happy all
my life long. Wilford Cameron said I ought to be," and
Katy tossed into the air a wisp of the new-made hay.

"I don't know who Wilford Cameron is, but there's no
ought about it," the deacon rejoined. "God marks out
the path for us to walk in, and when he says it's best, we
know it is, though some are straight and pleasant and
others crooked and hard."

"I'll choose the straight and pleasant then—why
shouldn't I?" Katy asked, laughing, as she seated herself
upon a rock near which the hay cart had stopped.

"Can't tell what path you'll take," the deacon answered.

" God knows whether you'll go easy through the world, or whether he'll send you suffering to purify and make you better."

" Purified by suffering," Katy said aloud, while a shadow involuntarily crept for an instant over her gay spirits.

She could not believe *she* was to be purified by suffering. She had never done anything very bad, and humming a part of a song learned from Wilford Cameron she followed after the loaded cart, returning slowly to the house, thinking to herself that there must be something great and good in the suffering which should purify at last, but hoping she was not the one to whom this great good should come.

It was supper-time ere long, and after that was over Katy announced her intention of going to Linwood whether Morris were there or not.

" I can see the housekeeper and the birds and flowers," she said, as she swung her straw hat by the string and started from the door.

" Ain't Helen going with you ? " Aunt Hannah asked, while Helen herself looked a little surprised.

But Katy would rather go alone. She had a heap to tell Cousin Morris, and Helen could go next time.

" Just as you like," Helen answered, good-naturedly, and so Katy went alone to call on Morris Grant.

CHAPTER II.

LINWOOD.

MORRIS had returned from Spencer, and in his dressing-gown and slippers was sitting by the window of his library, looking out upon the purple sunshine flooding the western sky, and thinking of the little girl coming so rapidly up the grassy lane in the rear of the house. He was going over to see her by and by, he said, and he pictured to himself how she must look by this time, hoping that he should not find her greatly changed, for Morris Grant's memories were very precious of the play-child who used to tease and worry him so much with her lessons poorly learned, and the never-ending jokes played off upon her teacher. He had thought of her so often when across the sea, and, knowing her love of the beautiful, he had never looked upon a painting or scene of rare beauty that he did not wish her by his side sharing in the pleasure. He had brought her from that far-off land many little trophies which he thought she would prize, and which he was going to take with him when he went to the farm-house. He never dreamed of her coming there to-night. She would, of course, wait for him, to call upon her first. How then was he amazed when, just as the sun was going down and he was watching its last rays lingering on the brow of the hill across the pond, the library door was opened wide and the room suddenly filled with life and joy, as a graceful figure, with reddish golden hair, bounded across the floor, and winding its arms around his neck gave him the hearty kiss which Katy had in her mind when she declined Aunt Betsy's favorite vegetable.

Morris Grant was not averse to being kissed, and yet the fact that Katy Lennox had kissed him in such a way awoke a chill of disappointment, for it said that to her he was the teacher still, the elder brother, whom, as a child, she had loaded with caresses.

"Oh, Cousin Morris!" she exclaimed, "why didn't you come over at noon, you naughty boy! But what a splendid-looking man you've got to be, though! and what do you think of me?" she added, blushing for the first time, as he held her off from him and looked into the sunny face.

"I think you wholly unchanged," he answered, so gravely that Katy began to pout as she said, "And you are sorry, I know. Pray what did you expect of me, and what would you have me be?"

"Nothing but what you are—the same Kitty as of old," he answered, his own bright smile breaking all over his sober face.

He saw that his manner repelled her, and he tried to be natural, succeeding so well that Katy forgot her first disappointment, and making him sit by her on the sofa, where she could see him distinctly, she poured forth a volley of talk, telling him, among other things, how much afraid of him some of his letters made her—they were so serious and so like a sermon.

"You wrote me once that you thought of being a minister," she added. "Why did you change your mind? It must be splendid, I think, to be a young clergyman— invited to so many tea-drinkings, and having all the girls in the parish after you, as they always are after un-married ministers."

Into Morris Grant's eyes there stole a troubled light as he thought how little Katy realized what it was to be a minister of God—to point the people heavenward and teach them the right way. There was a moment's pause, and then he tried to explain to her that he hoped he had not been influenced either by thoughts of tea-drinkings or having the parish girls after him, but rather by an honest desire to choose the sphere in which he could accomplish the most good.

"I did not decide rashly," he said, "but after weeks of anxious thought and prayer for guidance I came to the conclusion that in the practice of medicine I could find perhaps as broad a field for good as in the church, and so I decided to go on with my profession—to be a physician of the poor and suffering, speaking to them of Him who came to save, and in this way I shall not labor in vain. Many would seek another place than Silverton and its vicinity, but something told me that my work was here, and so I am content to stay, feeling thankful that my means admit of my waiting for patients, if need be, and at the same time ministering to the wants of those who are needy."

Gradually, as he talked, there came into his face a light born only from the peace which passeth understanding, and the awe-struck Katy crept closer to his side and grasp-ing his hand in hers, said softly, "Dear cousin, what a good man you are, and how silly I must seem to you, thinking you cared for tea-drinkings, or even girls, when, of course, you do not."

"Perhaps I do," the doctor replied, slightly pressing the warm, fat hand holding his so fast. "A minister's or a doctor's life would be dreary indeed if there was no one to share it, and I have had my dreams of the girls, or girl, who was some day to brighten my home."

He looked fully at Katy now, but she was thinking of something else, and her next remark was to ask him rather abruptly "how old he was?"

"Twenty-six last May," he answered, while Katy continued, "You are not old enough to be married yet. Wilford Cameron is thirty."

"Where did *you* meet Wilford Cameron?" Morris asked, in some surprise, and then the story which Katy had not told, even to her sister, came out in full, and Morris tried to listen patiently while Katy explained how, on the very first day of the examination, Mrs. Woodhull had come in, and with her the grandest, proudest-looking man, who the girls said was Mr. Wilford Cameron, from New York, a fastidious bachelor, whose family were noted for their wealth and exclusiveness, keeping six servants, and living in the finest style; that Mrs. Woodhull, who all through the year had been very kind to Katy, came to her after school and invited her home to tea; that she had gone and met Mr. Cameron; that she was very much afraid of him at first, and was not sure that she was quite over it now, although he was so polite to her all through the journey, taking so much pains to have her see the finest sights, and laughing at her enthusiasm.

"Wilford Cameron with you in your trip?" Morris asked, a new idea dawning on his mind.

"Yes, let me tell you," and Katy spoke rapidly. "I saw him that night, and then Mrs. Woodhull took me to ride with him in the carriage, and then—well, I rode alone with him once down by the lake, and he talked to me just as if he was not a grand man and I a little school-girl. And when the term closed I stayed at Mrs. Woodhull's and he was there. He liked my playing and liked my singing, and I guess he liked me—that is, you know—yes, he liked me *some*," and Katy twisted the fringe of her shawl, while Morris, in spite of the pain tugging at his heart strings, laughed aloud as he rejoined, "I have no doubt he did; but go on—what next?"

"He said more about my joining that party than anybody, and I am very sure *he* paid the *bills*."

"Oh, Katy," and Morris started as if he had been stung. "I would rather have given Linwood than have you thus indebted to Wilford Cameron, or any other man."

"I could not well help it. I did not mean any harm," Katy said timidly, explaining how she had shrunk from the proposition which Mrs. Woodhull thought was right, urging it until she had consented, and telling how kind Mr. Cameron was, and how careful not to remind her of her indebtedness to him, attending to and anticipating every want as if she had been his sister.

"You would like Mr. Cameron, Cousin Morris. He made me think of you a little, only he is prouder," and Katy's hand moved up Morris's coat sleeve till it rested on his shoulder.

"Perhaps so," Morris answered, feeling a growing resentment towards one who it seemed to him had done him some great wrong.

But Wilford was not to blame, he reflected. He could not help admiring the bright little Katy—and so conquering all ungenerous feelings, he turned to her at last, and said,

"Did my little Cousin Kitty like Wilford Cameron?"

Something in Morris's voice startled Katy strangely; her hand came down from his shoulder, and for an instant there swept over her an emotion similar to what she had felt when with Wilford Cameron she rambled along the shores of Lake George, or sat alone with him on the deck of the steamer which carried them down Lake Champlain. But Morris had always been her brother, and she did not guess that she was more to him than a sister, so she answered frankly at last, "I guess I did like him a little. I couldn't help it, Morris. You could not either, or any one. I believe Mrs. Woodhull was more than half in love with him herself, and she talked so much of his family; they must be very grand."

"Yes, I know those Camerons," was Morris's quiet remark.

"What! You don't know Wilford?" Katy almost screamed, and Morris replied, "Not Wilford, no; but the mother and the sisters were in Paris, and I met them many times."

"What were they doing in Paris?" Katy asked, and Morris replied that he believed the immediate object of their being there was to obtain the best medical advice for a little orphan grand-child, a bright, beautiful boy, to whom some terrible accident had happened in infancy, preventing his walking entirely, and making him nearly helpless. His name was Jamie, Morris said, and as he saw that Katy was interested, he told her how sweet-tempered the little fellow was, how patient under suffering, and how eagerly he listened when Morris, who at one time attended him, told him of the Saviour and his love for little children.

"Did he get well?" Katy asked, her eyes filling with tears at the picture Morris drew of Jamie Cameron, sitting all day long in his wheel chair, and trying to comfort his grand-mother's distress when the torturing instruments for straightening his poor back were applied.

"No, he died one lovely day in October, and they buried him beneath the bright skies of France," Morris said, and then Katy asked about the mother and sisters. "Were they proud, and did he like them much?"

"They were very proud," Morris said; "but they were always civil to him," and Katy, had she been watching, might have seen a slight flush on his cheek as he told her of the stately woman, Wilford's mother, of the haughty Juno, a beauty and a belle, and lastly of Arabella, whom the family nicknamed Bluebell, from her excessive fondness for books, and her contempt for the fashionable life her mother and sister led.

It was evident that neither of the young ladies were wholly to Morris's taste, but of the two he preferred Bluebell, for though imperious and self-willed, she had some heart, some principle, while Juno had none. This was Morris's opinion, and it disturbed little Katy, as was very perceptible from the nervous tapping of her foot upon the carpet and the working of her hands.

"How would *I* appear by the side of those ladies?" she suddenly asked, her countenance changing as Morris replied that it was almost impossible to think of her as associated with the Camerons, she was so wholly unlike them in every respect.

"I don't believe I shocked Wilford so very much," Katy rejoined, reproachfully, while again a heavy pain shot through Morris's heart, for he saw more and more how Wilford Cameron was mingled with every thought of the young girl, who continued: "And if he was satisfied, his mother and sisters will be. Any way, I don't want you to make me feel how different I am from them."

There was tears now on Katy's face, and casting aside all selfishness, Morris wound his arm around her, and smoothing her golden hair, just as he used to do when she was a child and came to him to be soothed, he said, very gently,

"My poor Kitty, you do like Wilford Cameron; tell me honestly—is it not so?"

"Yes, I guess I do," and Katy's voice was a half sob. "I could not help it, either, he was so kind, so—I don't know what, only I could not help doing what he bade me. Why, if he had said, 'Jump overboard, Katy Lennox,' I should have done it, I know—that is, if his eyes had been upon me, they controlled me so absolutely. Can you imagine what I mean?"

"Yes, I understand. There was the same look in Bell Cameron's eye, a kind of mesmeric influence which commanded obedience. They idolize Wilford, and I dare say he is worthy of their idolatry. One thing at least is in his favor—the crippled Jamie, for whose opinion I would give more than all the rest, seemed to worship his Uncle Will; talking of him continually, and telling how kind he was, sometimes staying up all night to carry him in his arms when the pain in his back was more than usually severe. So there must be a good, kind heart in Wilford Cameron, and if my Cousin Kitty likes him, as she says she does, and he likes her as I believe he must, why, I hope——"

Morris Grant could not finish the sentence, for he did *not* hope that Wilford Cameron would win the gem he had so long coveted as his own.

He might give Kitty up because she loved another best. He was generous enough to do that, but if he did it, she must never know how much it cost him, and lest he should betray himself he could not to-night talk with her longer of Wilford Cameron. It was time too for Kitty to go home, but she did not seem to remember it until Morris suggested to her that her mother might be uneasy if she stayed away much longer, and so they went together across the fields, the shadows all gone from Katy's heart, but lying so dark and heavy around Morris Grant, who was glad when he could leave Katy at the farm-house door and go back alone to the quiet library, where only God could witness the mighty struggle, it was for him to say, "Thy will be done." And while he prayed, Katy, in her humble bedroom, with her head nestled close to Helen's neck, was telling her of Wilford Cameron, who, when they went down the rapids and she had cried with fear, had put his arm around her trying to quiet her, and who once again, on the mountain overlooking Lake George, had held her hand a moment, while he pointed out a splendid view seen through the opening trees. And Helen, listening, knew that Katy's heart was lost, and that for Wilford Cameron to deceive her now would be a cruel thing.

CHAPTER III.

WILFORD CAMERON.

The day succeeding Katy Lennox's return to Silverton was rainy and cold for the season, the storm extending as far westward as the city of New York, and making Wilford Cameron shiver as he stepped from the Hudson River cars into the carriage waiting for him, first greeting pleasantly the white-gloved driver, who, closing the carriage door, mounted to his seat and drove his handsome bays in the direction of No. — Fifth Avenue. And Wilford, leaning back among the cushions, thought how pleasant it was to be home again, feeling glad, as he frequently did, that the home was in every particular unexceptionable. The Camerons, he knew, were an old and highly respectable family, while it was his mother's pride that, go back as far as one might, on either side there could not be found a single blemish, or a member of whom to be ashamed. On the Cameron side there were millionaires, merchant princes, bankers, and stockholders, professors and scholars, while on hers, the Rossiter side, there were LL. D.'s and D. D.'s, lawyers and clergymen, authors and artists, beauties and bells, the whole forming an illustrious line of ancestry, admirably represented and sustained by the present family of Camerons, occupying the brown-stone front, corner of ——street and Fifth Avenue, where the handsome carriage stopped, and a tall figure ran quickly up the marble steps. There was a soft rustle of silk, an odor of delicate perfume, and from the luxurious chair before the fire kindled in the grate, a lady rose and advanced a step or two towards the parlor door. In another moment she was kissing the young man bending over her and saluting her as mother, kissing him quietly, properly, as the Camerons always kissed. She was very glad to have Wilford home again, for he was her favorite child; and brushing the rain-drops from his coat she led him to the fire, offering him her own easy-chair, and starting herself in quest of another. But Wilford held her back, and making her sit down, he drew an ottoman beside her, and then asked her first how she had been, then where his sisters were, and if his father had come home—for there was a father, a quiet, unassuming man, who stayed all day in Wall street, seldom coming home in time to carve at his own dinner table, and when he was at home, asking for nothing except to be left by his fashionable wife and daughters to himself, free to smoke and doze over his evening paper in the seclusion of his own reading-room.

As Wilford's question concerning his sire had been the last one asked, so it was the last one answered, his mother parting his dark hair with her jeweled hand, and telling him first that, with the exception of a cold taken at the Park on Saturday afternoon, she was in usual health—second, that Juno was spending a few days in Orange, and that Bell had gone to pass the night with her particular friend, Mrs. Meredith, the most bookish woman in New York.

"Your father," the lady added, "has not yet returned; but as the dinner is ready I think we will not wait."

She touched a silver bell beside her, and ordering dinner to be sent up at once, went on to ask her son concerning his journey and the people he had met. But Wilford, though intending to tell her all, would wait till after dinner. So, offering her his arm, he led her out to where the table was spread, widely different from the table prepared for Katy Lennox among the Silverton hills, for where at the farm-house there had been only the homely wares common to the country, with Aunt Betsy's onions served in a bowl, there was here the finest of damask, the choicest of china, the costliest of cut-glass, and the heaviest of silver, with the well-trained waiter gliding in and out. himself the very personification of strict table etiquette, such as the Barlows had never dreamed about. There was no fricasseed chicken here, or flaky crust, with pickled beans and apple-sauce; no custard pie with strawberries and rich, sweet cream, poured from a blue earthen pitcher; but there were soups, and fish, and roasted meats, and dishes with French names and taste, and dessert elaborately gotten up, and served with the utmost precision, and Mrs. Cameron presiding over all with lady-like decorum, her soft glossy silk of brown, with her rich lace and diamond pin in perfect keeping with herself and her surroundings. And opposite to her Wilford sat, a tall, dark, handsome man, of thirty or thereabouts—a man, whose polished manners betokened at once a perfect knowledge of the world, and whose face, to a close observer, indicated how little satisfaction he had as yet found in the world. He had tried its pleasures, drinking the cup of freedom and happiness to its very dregs, and though he thought he liked it, he often found himself dissatisfied and reaching after something which should make life more real, more worth the living for. He had traveled all over Europe twice, had visited every spot worth visiting in his own country, had been a frequenter of every fashionable resort in New York, from the skating-pond to the theatres, had been admitted as a lawyer, had opened an office on Broadway, acquiring some reputation in his profession, had looked at more than twenty girls with the view of making them his wife, and found, as he believed, alike fickle, selfish, artificial and hollow-hearted. In short, while thinking far more of family, and accomplishments, and style, than he ought, he was yet heartily tired of the butterflies who flitted so constantly around him, offering to be caught if he would but stretch out his hand to catch them. This he would not do, and disgusted with the world as he saw it in New York, he had gone to the the Far West, roaming awhile amid the solitude of the broad prairies, and finding there much that was soothing to him, but not discovering the fulfillment of the great want he was craving until com-

ing back to Canandaigua, he met with Katy Lennox. He
had smiled wearily when asked by Mrs. Woodhull to go
with her to the examination then in progress at the Seminary.   There was nothing there to interest him, he
thought, as Euclid and Algebra, French and Rhetoric were
bygone things, while young school-misses, in braided hair
and pantalettes, were shockingly insipid.   Still, to be
polite to Mrs. Woodhull, a childless, fashionable woman,
who patronized Canandaigua generally and Katy Lennox
in particular, he consented, and soon found himself in the
crowded room, the cynosure of many eyes as the whisper
ran round that the fine-looking man with Mrs. Woodhull
was Wilford Cameron, from New York, brother to the
proud, dashing Juno Cameron, who once spent a few weeks
in town.   Wilford knew they were talking about him, but
he did not care, and assuming as easy an attitude as possible, he leaned back in his chair, yawning indolently until
the class in Algebra was called, and Katy Lennox came
tripping on the stage, a pale blue ribbon in her golden
hair, and her simple dress of white relieved by no ornament except the cluster of wild flowers fastened in her belt
and at her throat.   But Katy needed no ornaments to make
her more beautiful than she was at the moment when,
with glowing cheeks and sparkling eyes, she first burst
upon Wilford's vision, a creature of rare, bewitching beauty,
such as he had never dreamed about.

Wilford had met his destiny, and he felt it in every
throb of blood which went rushing through his veins.

"Who is she?" he asked of Mrs. Woodhull, and that
lady knew at once whom he meant, even though he had
not designated her.

An old acquaintance of Mrs. Lennox when she lived in
East Bloomfield, Mrs. Woodhull had petted Katy from the
first day of her arrival in Canandaigua with a letter of
introduction to herself from the ambitious mother, and
being rather inclined to match-making, she had had Katy
in her mind when she urged Wilford to accompany her
to the Seminary.   Accordingly, she answered him at once,
"That is Katy Lennox, daughter of Judge Lennox, who
died in East Bloomfield a few years ago."

"Pretty, is she not?"

Wilford did not answer her. He had neither eye nor ear for anything save Katy, acquitting herself with a good deal of credit as she worked out a rather difficult problem, her dimpled white hand showing to good advantage against the deep black of the board; and then her voice, soft-toned and silvery, as a lady's voice should be, thrilled in Wilford's ear, awaking a strange feeling of disquiet, as if the world would never again be quite the same to him that it was before he met that fair young girl now passing from the room.

Mrs. Woodhull saw that he was interested. It was time he was settled in life. With the exception of wealth and family position, he could not find a better wife than Katy, and she would do what she could to bring the marriage about. Accordingly, having first gained the preceptress's consent, Katy was taken home with her to dinner. And this was how Wilford Cameron came to know little Katy Lennox, the simple-hearted child, who blushed so prettily when first presented to him, and blushed again when he praised her recitations, but who after that forgot the difference in their social relations, laughing and chatting as merrily in his presence as if she had been alone with Mrs. Woodhull. This was the great charm to Wilford. Katy was so wholly unconscious of herself or what he might think of her, that he could not sit in judgment upon her, and he watched her eagerly as she sported, and flashed, and sparkled, filling the room with sunshine, and putting to rout the entire regiment of blues which had been for months harassing the city-bred young man.

If there was any one thing in which Katy excelled, it was music, both vocal and instrumental, a taste for which had been developed very early, and fostered by Morris Grant, who had seen that his cousin had every advantage which Silverton could afford. Great pains had been given to her style of playing while in Canandaigua, so that as a performer upon the piano she had few rivals in the seminary, while her birdlike voice filled every nook and corner of the room, where, on the night after her visit to Mrs. Woodhull, a select exhibition was held, Katy shining as the one bright star, and winning golden laurels for beauty, grace, and perfect self-possession, from others than Wilford Cameron, who was one of the invited auditors.

Juno herself could not equal that, he thought, as Katy's fingers flew over the keys, executing a brilliant and difficult piece without a single mistake, and receiving the applause of the spectators easily, naturally, as if it were an every day occurrence. But when by request she sang " Comin' through the Rye," Wilford's heart, if he had any before, was wholly gone, and he dreamed of Katy Lennox that night, wondering all the ensuing day how his haughty mother would receive that young school-girl as her daughter, wife of the son whose bride she fancied must be equal to the first lady in the land. And if Katy were not now equal she could be made so, Wilford thought, wondering if Canandaigua were the best place for her, and if she would consent to receive a year or two years' tuition from *him,* provided her family were poor. He did not know as they were, but he would ask, and he did, feeling a pang of regret when he heard to some extent how Katy was circumstanced. Mrs. Woodhull had never been to Silverton, and so she did not know of Uncle Ephraim, and his old-fashioned sister; but she knew that they were poor—that some relation sent Katy to school; and she frankly told Wilford so, adding, as she detected the shadow on his face, that one could not expect everything, and that a girl like Katy was not found every day. Wilford admitted all this, growing more and more infatuated, until at last he consented to join the traveling party, provided Katy joined it too, and when on the morning of their departure for the Falls he seated himself beside her in the car, he could not well have been happier, unless she had really been his wife, as he so much wished she was.

It was a most delightful trip, and Wilford was better satisfied with himself than he had been before in years. His past life was not all free from error, and there were many sad memories haunting him, but with Katy at his side, seeing what he saw, admiring what he admired, and doing what he bade her do, he gave the bygones to the wind, feeling only an intense desire to clasp the young girl in his arms and bear her away to some spot where with her pure fresh life all his own he could begin the world anew, and retrieve the past which he had lost. This was when he was with Katy. Away from her he could remem-

ber the difference in their position, and prudential motives
began to make themselves heard. Never but once had he
taken an important step without consulting his mother,
and the trouble in which that had involved him warned
him to be more cautious a second time. And this was
why Katy came back to Silverton unengaged, leaving her
heart with Wilford Cameron, who would first seek advice
from his mother ere committing himself by word. He had
seen the white-haired man waiting for her when the train
stopped at Silverton, but standing there as he did, with
his silvery locks parted in the centre, and shading his
honest, open face, Uncle Ephraim looked like some patri-
arch of old rather than a man to be despised, and Wilford
felt only respect for him until he saw Katy's arms wound
so lovingly around his neck as she called him Uncle Eph.
That sight grated harshly, and Wilford felt glad that he
was not bound to her by any pledge. Very curiously he
looked after the couple, witnessing the meeting between
Katy and old Whiting, and guessing rightly that the corn-
colored vehicle was the one sent to transport Katy home.
He was very moody for the remainder of the route between
Silverton and Albany, where he parted with his Canandaigua friends, they going on to the westward, while he
stopped all night in Albany, where he had some business
to transact for his father.

He was intending to tell his mother everything, except
that he paid Katy's bills. He would rather keep that to
himself, as it might shock his mother's sense of propriety
and make her think less of Katy; so after dinner was over,
and they had returned to the parlor, he opened the subject
by asking her to guess what took him off so suddenly with
Mrs. Woodhull.

The mother did not know—unless—and a strange light
gleamed in her eye, as she asked if it were some girl.

"Yes, mother, it was," and without any reservation Wilford frankly told the story of his interest in Katy Lennox.

He admitted that she was poor and unaccustomed to
society, but he loved her more than words could express.

"Not as I loved Genevra," he said, and there came a
look of intense pain into his eyes as he continued. "That
was the passion of a boy of nineteen, stimulated by secrecy,

but this is the love of a mature man of thirty, who feels that he is capable of judging for himself."

In Wilford's voice there was a tone warning the mother that opposition would only feed the flame, and so she offered none directly, but heard him patiently to the end, and then quietly questioned him of Katy and her family, especially the last. What did he know of it? Was it one to detract from the Cameron line, kept untarnished so long? Were the relatives such as he never need blush to own even if they came there into their drawing-rooms as they would come if Katy did?

Wilford thought of Uncle Ephraim as he had seen him upon the platform at Silverton, and could scarcely repress a smile as he pictured to himself his mother's consternation at beholding that man in her drawing-room. But he did not mention the deacon, though he acknowledged that Katy's family friends were not exactly the Cameron style. But Katy was young: Katy could be easily moulded, and once away from her old associates, his mother and sisters could make of her what they pleased.

"I understand, then, that if you marry her you do not marry the family," and in the handsome matronly face there was an expression from which Katy would have shrunk, could she have seen it and understood its meaning.

"No, I do not marry the family," Wilford rejoined emphatically, but the expression of his face was different from his mother's, for where she thought only of herself, not hesitating to trample on all Katy's love of home and friends, Wilford remembered Katy, thinking how he would make amends for separating her wholly from her home as he surely meant to do if he should win her. "Did I tell you," he continued, "that her father was a judge? She must be well connected on that side. And now, what shall I do?" he asked playfully. "Shall I propose to Katy Lennox, or shall I try to forget her?"

"I should not do either," was Mrs. Cameron's reply, for she knew that trying to forget her was the surest way of keeping her in mind, and she dared not confess to him how determined she was that Katy Lennox should never be her daughter if she could prevent it.

If she could not, then as a lady and a woman of policy,

she should make the most of it, receiving Katy kindly and doing her best to educate her up to the Cameron ideas of style and manner.

"Let matters take their course for awhile," she said, "and see how you feel after a little. We are going to Newport the first of August, and perhaps you may find somebody there infinitely superior to this Katy Lennox. That's your father's ring. He is earlier than usual to-night. I would not tell him yet, till you are more decided," and the lady went hastily out into the hall to meet her husband.

A moment more and the elder Cameron appeared—a short, square-built man, with a face seamed with lines of care and eyes much like Wilford's, save that the shaggy eyebrows gave them a different expression. He was very glad to see his son, though he merely shook his hand, asking what nonsense took him off around the Lakes with Mrs. Woodhull, and wondering if women were never happy unless they were chasing after fashion. The elder Cameron was evidently not of his wife's way of thinking, but she let him go on until he was through, and then, with the most unruffled mien, suggested that his dinner would be cold. He was accustomed to that and so he did not mind, but he hurried through his lonely meal to-night, for Wilford was home, and the father was always happier when he knew his son was in the house. Contrary to his usual custom, he spent the short summer evening in the parlor, talking with Wilford on various items of business, and thus preventing any further conversation concerning Katy Lennox. It took but a short time for Wilford to fall back into his old way of living, passing a few hours of each day in his office, driving with his mother, sparring with his imperious sister Juno, and teasing his blue sister Bell, but never after that first night breathing a word to any one of Katy Lennox. And still Katy was not forgotten, as his mother sometimes believed. On the contrary, the very silence he kept concerning her increased his passion, until he began seriously to contemplate a trip to Silverton. The family's removal to Newport, however, diverted his attention for a little, making him decide to wait and see what Newport might have in store for him.

But Newport was dull this season, though Juno and Bell both found ample scope for their different powers of attraction, and his mother was always happy when showing off her children and knowing that they were appreciated, but with Wilford it was different. Listless and taciturn, he went through with the daily routine, wondering how he had ever found happiness there, and finally, at the close of the season, casting all policy and prudence aside, he wrote to Katy Lennox that he was coming to Silverton on his way home, and that he presumed he should have no difficulty in finding his way to the farm-house.

CHAPTER IV.

PREPARING FOR THE VISIT.

KATY had waited very anxiously for a letter from Wilford, and as the weeks went by and nothing came, a shadow had fallen upon her spirits and the family missed something from her ringing laugh and frolicsome ways, while she herself wondered at the change which had come over everything. Even the light household duties she used to enjoy so much, were irksome to her and she enjoyed nothing except going with Uncle Ephraim into the fields where she could sit alone while he worked nearby, or to ride with Morris as she sometimes did when he made his round of calls. She was not as good as she used to be, she thought, and with a view of making herself better she took to teaching in Morris and Helen's Sunday School, greatly to the distress of Aunt Betsy, who groaned bitterly when both her nieces adopted the "Episcopal quirks," forsaking entirely the house where, Sunday after Sunday, her old-fashioned leghorn, with its faded ribbon of green was seen, bending down in the humble worship which God so much approves. But teaching in Sunday-school, taken by itself, could not make Katy better, and the old restlessness remained until the morning when, sitting on the grass beneath the apple-tree, she read that Wilford Cameron was coming; then everything was changed and Katy never forgot the brightness of that day when the robins sang so merrily above her head, and all nature seemed to sympathize with her joy. There was no shadow around her now, nothing but hopeful sunshine, and with a bounding step she sought out Helen to tell her the good news. Helen's first remark, however, was a chill upon her spirits.

"Wilford Cameron coming here? What will he think of us, we are so unlike him?"

This was the first time Katy had seriously considered the difference between her surroundings and those of Wilford Cameron, or how it might affect him. But Aunt Betsy, who had never dreamed of anything like Wilford's home, comforted her, telling her, "if he was any kind of a chap he wouldn't be looking round, and if he did, who cared? She guessed they were as good as he, and as much thought of by the neighbors."

Wilford's lettter had been delayed so that the morrow was the day appointed for his coming, and never was there a busier afternoon at the farm-house than the one which followed the receipt of the letter. Everything not spotlessly clean before was made so now, Aunt Betsy, in her petticoat and short gown, going down upon her knees to scrub the back door-sill, as if the city guest were expected to notice that. On Aunt Hannah and Mrs. Lennox devolved the duty of preparing for the wants of the inner man, while Helen and Katy bent their energies to beautifying their home and making the most of their plain furniture.

The "spare bed-room," kept for company, was only large enough to admit the high-post bed, a single chair, and the old-fashioned wash-stand, with the hole in the top for the bowl, and a drawer beneath for towels; and the two girls held a consultation as to whether it would not be better to dispense with the parlor altogether, and give that room to their visitor. But this was vetoed by Aunt Betsy, who, having finished the back door-sill, had now come round to the front, and with her scrubbing-brush in one hand and her saucer of sand in the other, held forth upon the foolishness of the girls.

"Of course, if they had a beau, they'd want a t'other room, else where would they do their sparkin'?"

That settled it. The parlor must remain as it was, Katy said, and Aunt Betsy went on with her scouring, while Helen and Katy consulted together how to make the huge feather-bed more like the mattresses to which Wilford must be accustomed. Helen's mind being the more suggestive, solved the problem first, and a large comfortable was brought from the box in the garret and folded carefully over the bed, which, thus hardened and flattened, "seemed like a mattress," Katy said, for she tried it, feeling quite well satisfied with the room when it was finished. And certainly it was not uninviting, with its strip of bright carpeting upon the floor, its vase of flowers upon the stand, and its white-fringed curtain sweeping back from the narrow window.

"I'd like to sleep here myself," was Katy's comment, while Helen offered no opinion, but followed her sister into the yard, where they were to sweep the grass and prune the early September flowers.

This afforded Aunt Betsy a chance to reconnoitre and criticise, which last she did unsparingly.

"What have them children been doin' to that bed? Put on a quilt, as I'm alive! It would break my back to lie there, and this *Carmon* is none of the youngest, accordin' to their tell; nigh onto thirty, if not turned. It will make his bones ache, of course. I am glad I know better than to treat visitors that way. The comforter may stay, but I'll be bound I'll make it softer!" And stealing up the stairs, Aunt Betsy brought down a second feather-bed, much lighter than the one already on, but still large enough to suggest the thought of smothering. This she had made herself, intending it as a part of Katy's "setting out," should she ever marry; and as things now seemed tending that way, it was only right, she thought, that Mr. Carmon, as she called him, should begin to have the benefit of it. Accordingly *two* beds, instead of one, were placed beneath the comfortable, which Aunt Betsy permitted to remain.

"I'm mighty feared they'll find me out," she said, taking great pains in the making of her bed, and succeeding so well that when her task was done there was no perceptible difference between Helen's bed and her own, except that the latter was a few inches higher than the former, and more nearly resembled a pincushion in shape.

There was but little chance for Aunt Betsy to be de-

tected, for Helen, supposing the room to be in order, had
dismissed it from her mind, and was training a rose over a
frame, while Katy was on her way to Linwood in quest
of various little things which Mrs. Lennox considered
indispensable to the entertainment of a man like Wilford
Cameron. Morris was out on his piazza, enjoying the
fine prospect he had of the sun shining across the pond,
on the Silverton hill, and just gilding the top of the little
church nestled in the valley. At sight of Katy he rose
and greeted her with the kind, brotherly manner now
habitual with him, for he had learned to listen quite
calmly while Katy talked to him, as she often did, of
Wilford Cameron, never trying to conceal from him how
anxious she was for some word of remembrance, and often
asking if he thought Mr. Cameron would ever write to her.
It was hard at first for Morris to listen, and harder still
to keep back the passionate words of love trembling on his
lips—to refrain from asking her to take him in Cameron's
stead—him who had loved her so long. But Morris had
kept silence, and as the weeks went by there came insensibly
into his heart a hope, or rather conviction, that Wilford
Cameron had forgotten the little girl who might in time
turn to him, gladdening his home just as she did every
spot where her fairy foosteps trod. Morris did not fully
know that he was hugging this fond dream until he felt
the keen pang which cut like a dissector's knife as Katy,
turning her bright, eager face up to him, whispered softly,
" He's coming to-morrow—he surely is; I have his letter
to tell me so."

Morris could not see the sunshine upon the distant
hills, although it lay there just as purple and warm as it
had a moment before. There was an instant of darkness,
in which the hills, the pond, the sun setting, and Katy
seemed a great way off to Morris, trying so hard to be
calm, and mentally asking for help to do so. But Katy's
hat, which she swung in her hand, had become entangled
in the vines encircling one of the pillars of the piazza,
and so she did not notice him until all traces of his agitation were past, and he could talk with her concerning
Wilford; then playfully lifting her basket he asked what
she had come to get.

This was not the first time the great house had rendered a like service to the little house, and so Katy did not blush when she explained that her mother wanted Morris's forks, and salt-cellars, and spoons, and would he be kind enough to bring the caster over himself, and come to dinner to-morrow at two o'clock, and would he go for Mr. Cameron? The forks, and salt-cellars, and spoons, and caster were cheerfully promised, while Morris consented to go for the guest; and then Katy came to the rest of her errand, the part distasteful to her, inasmuch as it concerned Uncle Ephraim—honest, unsophisticated Uncle Ephraim, *who would come to the table in his shirt sleeves!* This was the burden of her grief—the one thing she dreaded most, because she knew how such an act was looked upon by Mr. Cameron who, never having lived in the country a day in his life, except as he was either guest or traveler, could not make due allowance for these little departures from refinement, so obnoxious to people of his training.

"What is it, Katy?" Morris asked, as he saw how she hesitated, and guessed her errand was not all told.

"I hope you will not think me foolish or wicked," Katy began, her eyes filling with tears, as she felt that she might be doing Uncle Ephraim a wrong by admitting that in any way he could be improved. "I certainly love Uncle Ephraim dearly, and *I* do not mind his ways, but —but—Mr. Cameron may—that is, oh, Cousin Morris, *did* you ever notice how Uncle Ephraim will persist in coming to the table in his shirt sleeves?"

"*Persist* is hardly the word to use," Morris replied, smiling comically, as he readily understood Katy's misgivings. "Persist would imply his having been often remonstrated with for that breach of etiquette; whereas I doubt whether the idea that it was not in strict accordance with politeness was ever suggested to him."

"Maybe not," Katy answered. "It was never necessary till now, and I feel so disturbed, for I want Mr. Cameron to like him, and if he does that I am sure he won't."

"Why do you think so?" Morris asked, and Katy replied, "He is so particular, and was so very angry at a little hotel between Lakes George and Champlain, where

we took our dinner before going on the boat. There was
a man along—a real good-natured man, too, so kind to
everybody—and, as the day was warm, he carried his coat
on his arm, and sat down to the table right opposite me.
Mr. Cameron was *so* indignant, and said such harsh things,
which the man heard I am sure, for he put on his coat
directly, and I saw him afterward on the boat, sweating
like rain, and looking so sorry, as if he had been guilty
of something wrong. I am sure, though, he had not?"

This last was spoken interrogatively, and Morris replied:
"There is nothing wrong or wicked in going without
one's coat. Everything depends upon the circumstances
under which it is done. For *me* to appear at table in
my shirt-sleeves would be very rude, but for an old man
like Uncle Ephraim to do so is a very different thing.
Still, Mr. Cameron may see from another standpoint.
But I would not distress myself. That love is not worth
much which would think the less of you for anything *outré*
which Uncle Ephraim may do. If Mr. Cameron cannot
stand the test of seeing your relatives as they are, he
is not worth the long face you are wearing," and Morris
pinched her cheek playfully.

"Yes, I know," Katy replied, "but if you only could
manage Uncle Eph, I should be so glad."

Morris had little hope of breaking a habit of years, but
he promised to try if an opportunity should occur, and
as Mrs. Hull, the housekeeper, had by this time gathered
up the articles required for the morrow, Morris took the
basket in his own hands and went with Katy across the
fields.

"God bless you, Katy, and may Mr. Cameron's visit
bring you as much happiness as you anticipate," he said,
as he set her basket upon the door-step and turned back
without entering the house.

Katy noticed the peculiar tone of his voice, and again
there swept over her the same thrill she had felt when
Morris first said to her, "And did Katy like this Mr.
Cameron?" but so far was she from guessing the truth
that she only feared she might have displeased him by
what she had said of Uncle Ephraim. Perhaps she *had*
wronged him, she thought, and the good old man, rest-

ing from his hard day's toil, in his accustomed chair, with
not only his coat, but his vest and boots cast aside, little
guessed what prompted the caresses which Katy lavished
upon him, sitting in his lap and parting his snowy hair,
as if thus she would make amends for any injury done.
Little Katy-did he called her, looking fondly into her
bright, pretty face, and thinking how terrible it would be
to see that face shadowed with pain and care. Somehow,
of late, Uncle Ephraim was always thinking of such a
calamity as more than possible for Katy, and when that
night she knelt beside him, his voice was full of pleading
earnestness as he prayed that God would keep them all
in safety, and bring to none of them more grief or pain
than was necessary to fit them for himself. And Katy,
listening to him, remembered the talk down in the meadow,
when she sat on the rock beneath the butternut tree. But
the world, while it held Wilford Cameron, as he seemed
to her now, was too full of joy for her to dread what the
future might have in store for her, and so she arose from
her knees, thinking only how long it would be before to-
morrow noon, wondering if Wilford would surely be there
next time their evening prayers were said, and if he would
notice Uncle Ephraim's shocking grammar!

CHAPTER V.

WILFORD'S VISIT.

WILFORD had made the last change of cars, and when
he stopped again it would be at Silverton. He did not
expect any one to meet him, but as he remembered the man
whom he had seen greeting Katy, he thought it not
unlikely that he might be there now, laughing to himself
as he pictured his mother's horror, could she see him riding
along in the corn-colored vehicle which Uncle Ephraim
drove. But that vehicle was safe at home beneath the
shed, while Uncle Ephraim was laying a stone wall upon
the huckleberry hill, and the handsome carriage waiting
at Silverton depot was certainly unexceptionable; while in
the young man who, as the train stopped and Wilford
stepped out upon the platform, came to meet him, asking
if he were Mr. Cameron, Wilford recognized the true

gentleman, and his spirits rose at once as Morris said to him, "I am Miss Lennox's cousin, deputed by her to take charge of you for a time."

Wilford had heard of Dr. Morris Grant and of his kindness to poor little Jamie, who died in Paris; he had heard too that his proud sister Juno had tried her powers of coquetry in vain upon the grave American; but he had no suspicion that his new acquaintance was the one until Morris mentioned having met his family in France and inquired after their welfare.

After that the conversation became very familiar, and the ride seemed so short that Wilford was surprised when, as they turned a corner in the sandy road, Morris pointed to the farm-house, saying: "We are almost there—that is the place."

"*That!*" and Wilford's voice indicated his disappointment, for in all his mental pictures of Katy Lennox's home he had never imagined anything like this.

Large, rambling and weird-like, with something lofty and imposing, just because it was so ancient, was the house he had in his mind, and he could not conceal his chagrin as his eye took in the small, low building, with its high windows and tiny panes of glass, paintless and blindless, standing there alone among the hills. Morris understood it perfectly; but without seeming to notice it, remarked, "It is the oldest house probably in the country, and should be invaluable on that account. I think we Americans are too fond of change and too much inclined to throw aside all that reminds us of the past. Now I like the farm-house just because it is old and unpretentious."

"Yes, certainly," Wilford answered, looking ruefully around him at the stone wall, half tumbled down, the tall well-sweep, and the patch of sun-flowers in the garden, with Aunt Betsy bending behind them, picking tomatoes for dinner, and shading her eyes with her hand to look at him as he drove up.

It was all very rural, no doubt, and very charming to people who liked it, but Wilford did *not* like it, and he was wishing himself safely in New York when a golden head flashed for an instant before the window and then disappeared as Katy emerged into view, waiting at the door to receive him and looking so sweetly in her dress of white with the scarlet geranium blossoms in her hair that Wilford forgot the homeliness of the surroundings, thinking only of her and how soft and warm was the little hand he held as she led him into the parlor. He did not know she was so beautiful, he said to himself, and he feasted his eyes upon her, forgetful for a time of all else. But afterwards, when Katy left him for a moment, he had time to observe the well-worn carpet, the six cane-seated chairs, large stuffed rocking-chair, the fall-leaf table, with its plain wool spread, and lastly the really expensive piano, the only handsome piece of furniture the room contained, and which he rightly guessed must have come from Morris.

"What *would* Juno or Mark say?" he kept repeating to himself half shuddering as he recalled the bantering proposition to accompany him made by Mark Ray, the only young man whom he considered fully his equal in New York.

Wilford knew these feelings were unworthy of him, and he tried to shake them off, listlessly turning over the books upon the table—books which betokened in some one both taste and talent of no low order.

"Mark's favorite," he said, lifting up a volume of Schiller; and turning to the fly-leaf he read, "Helen Lennox, from Cousin Morris," just as Katy returned with her sister, whom she presented to the stranger.

Helen was prepared to like him because Katy did, and her first thought was that he was very fine looking; but when she met his cold, proud eyes, and knew how closely he was scrutinizing her, there arose in her heart a feeling of dislike which she could never wholly conquer. He was very polite to her, but something in his manner annoyed and irritated her, it was so cool, so condescending, as if he endured her merely because she was Katy's sister, nothing more.

"Rather pretty, more character than Katy, but odd and self-willed, with no kind of style," was Wilford's running comment on Helen as he took her in from the plain arrangement of her dark hair to the fit of her French calico and the cut of her linen collar.

Fashionable dress would improve her very much, he thought, turning with a feeling of relief to Katy, whom nothing could disfigure, and who was now watching the door eagerly for the entrance of her mother. That lady had spent a good deal of time at her toilet, and she came in at last, flurried, fidgety, and very red, both from exercise and the bright-hued ribbons streaming from her cap and sadly at variance with the color of the dress. Wilford noticed the discrepancy at once, and noticed too how little style there was about the nervous woman greeting him so deferentially, and evidently regarding him as something infinitely superior to herself. Wilford had looked with indifference on Helen, but it would take a stronger word to express his opinion of the mother. Morris, who remained to dinner, was in the parlor now, and in his presence Wilford felt more at ease, more as if he had found an affinity. Uncle Ephraim was not there, having eaten his bowl of milk and gone back to his stone wall, so that upon Morris devolved the duties of host, and he courteously led the way to the little dining-room, where the table was loaded with the good things Aunt Hannah had prepared, burning and browning her wrinkled face, which nevertheless smiled pleasantly upon the stranger presented as Mr. Cameron.

About Aunt Hannah there was something naturally lady like, and Wilford recognized it at once; but when it came to Aunt Betsy, of whom he had never heard, he felt for a moment as if by being there in such promiscuous company he had somehow fallen from the Camerons' high estate. By way of pleasing the girls and doing honor to their guest, Aunt Betsy had donned her very best attire, wearing the slate-colored pongee dress, bought twenty years before, and actually sporting a set of Helen's cast-off hoops, which being too large for the dimensions of her scanty skirt, gave her anything but the graceful appearance she intended.

"Oh, auntie!" was Katy's involuntary exclamation, while Helen bit her lip with vexation, for the *hoop* had been an afterthought to Aunt Betsy just before going in to dinner.

But the good old lady never dreamed of shocking anyone with her attempts at fashion; and curtsying very low to Mr. Cameron, she hoped for a better acquaintance, and then took her seat at the table, just where each movement could be distinctly seen by Wilford, scanning her so intently as scarcely to hear the reverent words with which Morris asked a blessing upon themselves and the food so abundantly prepared. They could hardly have gotten through that first dinner without Morris, who adroitly led the conversation into channels which he knew would interest Mr. Cameron, and divert his mind from what was passing around him, and so the dinner proceeded quietly enough, Wilford discovering, ere its close, that Mrs. Lennox had really some pretensions to a lady, while Helen's dress and collar ceased to be obnoxious, as he watched the play of her fine features and saw her eyes kindle as she took a modest part in the conversation when it turned on books and literature.

Meanwhile Katy kept very silent, but when, after dinner was over and Morris was gone, she went with Wilford down to the shore of the pond, her tongue was loosed, and he found again the little fairy who had so bewitched him a few weeks before. And yet there was a load upon his heart, a shadow upon his brow, for he knew now that between Katy's family and his there was a social gulf which never could be crossed by either party. He might bear Katy over, it was true, but would she not look longingly back to her humble home, and might he not sometimes be greatly chagrined by the sudden appearing of some one of this low-bred family who did not seem to realize how ignorant they were, or how far below him in the social scale? Poor Wilford! he winced and shivered when he thought of Aunt Betsy, in her antiquated pongee, and remembered that she was a near relative of the little maiden sporting so playfully around him, stealing his heart away in spite of his family pride, and making him more deeply in love than ever. It was very pleasant down by the pond, and Wilford kept Katy there until the sun was going down and they heard in the distance the tinkle of a bell as the deacon's cows plodded slowly homeward. Supper was waiting for them, and with his appetite sharpened by his walk, Wilford found no cause of complaint

against Aunt Hannah's viands, though he smiled mentally
as he accepted the piece of apple pie Aunt Betsy offered
him, saying, by way of recommendation, that "she made
the crust but *Catherine* peeled and sliced the apples."

The deacon had not returned from his work, and Wilford did not see him until he came suddenly upon him,
seated in the wood-shed door, resting after the labor of
the day. "The young man was welcome to Silverton,"
he said, "but he must excuse him from visitin' much that
night, for the cows was to milk and the chores to do, as
he never kep' no boy." The "chores" were done at last,
just as the clock pointed to half-past eight, the hour for
family worship. Unaccustomed as Wilford was to such
things, he felt the influence of the deacon's voice as he
read from the word of God, and involuntarily found himself kneeling when Katy knelt, noticing the deacon's grammar it is true, but still listening patiently to the lengthy
prayer, which included him together with the rest of mankind.

There was no chance of seeing Katy alone, that night,
and so full two hours before his usual custom Wilford retired to the little room to which the deacon conducted him,
saying, as he put down the lamp, "You'll find it pretty
snug quarters, I guess, for such a close, muggy night as
this."

And truly they were snug quarters, Wilford thought,
as he surveyed the dimensions of the room; but there was
no alternative, and a few moments found him in the centre
of the two feather beds, neither Helen nor Katy having
discovered the addition made by Aunt Betsy, and which
came near being the death of the New York guest. To
sleep was impossible, and never for a moment did Wilford
lose his consciousness or forget to accuse himself of being
an idiot for coming into that heathenish neighborhood
after a wife when in New York there were so many girls
ready and waiting for him.

"I'll go back to-morrow morning," he said, striking a
match he consulted his Railway Guide to find when the first
train passed Silverton, feeling comforted to know that only
a few hours intervened between him and freedom.

But alas for Wilford! He was but a man, subject **to**

man's caprices, and when next morning he met Katy Lennox, looking in her light muslin as pure and fair as the white blossoms twined in her wavy hair, his resolution began to waver. Perhaps there was a decent hotel in Silverton; he would inquire of Dr. Grant; at all events he would not take the first train, though he might the next; and so he stayed, eating fried apples and beefsteak, but forgetting to criticise, in his appreciation of the rich thick cream poured into his coffee, and the sweet, golden butter, which melted in soft waves upon the flaky rolls. Again Uncle Ephraim was absent, having gone to mill before Wilford left his room, nor was he visible to the young man until after dinner, for Wilford did not go home, but drove instead with Katy in the carriage which Morris sent round, excusing himself from coming on the plea of being too busy, but saying he would join them at tea, if possible. Wilford's mind was not yet fully made up, so he concluded to remain another day and see more of Katy's family. Accordingly, after dinner, he bent his energies to cultivating them all, from Helen down to Aunt Betsy, who proved the most transparent of the four. Arrayed again in the pongee, but this time without the hoop, she came into the parlor, bringing her calico patch-work, which she informed him was pieced in the " herrin' bone pattern " and intended for Katy : telling him further, that the feather bed on which he slept was also a part of " Catherine's setting out," and was made from feathers she picked herself, showing him as proof a mark upon her arm, left there by the gray goose, which had proved a little refractory when she tried to draw a stocking over its head.

Wilford groaned and Katy's chance for being Mrs. Cameron was growing constantly less and less as he saw more and more how vast was the difference between the Barlows and himself. Helen, he acknowledged, was passable, though she was not one whom he could ever introduce into New York society; and he was wondering how Katy chanced to be so unlike the rest, when Uncle Ephraim came up from the meadow, and announced himself as ready now to *visit,* apologizing for his apparent neglect, and seeming so absolutely to believe that his company was desirable, that Wilford felt amused, wondering again what Juno, or even Mark Ray, would think of the rough old man, sitting with his chair tipped back against the wall, and going occasionally to the door to relieve himself of his tobacco juice, for chewing was one of the deacon's weaknesses. His pants were faultlessly clean, and his vest was buttoned nearly up to his throat, but his coat was hanging on a nail out by the kitchen door, and, to Katy's distress and Wilford's horror, he sat among them in his shirt sleeves, all unconscious of harm or of the disquiet awakened in the bosom of the young man, who on that point was foolishly fastidious, and who showed by his face how much he was annoyed. Not even the presence of Morris, who came about tea time, was of any avail to lift the cloud from his brow, and he seemed moody and silent until supper was announced. This was the first opportunity Morris had had of trying his powers of persuasion upon the deacon, and now, at a hint from Katy, he said to him in an aside, as they were passing into the dining-room : " Suppose, Uncle Ephraim, you put on your coat for once. It is better than coming to the table so."

" Pooh," was Uncle Ephraim's innocent rejoinder, spoken loudly enough for Wilford to hear, " I shan't catch cold, for I am used to it ; besides that, I never could stand the racket this hot weather."

In his simplicity he did not even suspect Morris's motive, but imputed it wholly to concern for his health. And so Wilford Cameron found himself seated next to a man who wilfully trampled upon all rules of etiquette, shocking him in his most sensitive points, and making him thoroughly disgusted with the country and country people generally. All but Morris and Katy—he *did* make an exception in their favor, leaning most to Morris, whom he admired more and more, as he became better acquainted with him, wondering how he could content himself to settle down quietly in Silverton, when he would surely die if compelled to live there for a week. Something like this he said to Dr. Grant, when that evening they sat together in the handsome parlor at Linwood, for Morris kindly invited him to spend the night with him.

" I stay in Silverton, first, because I think I can do more good here than elsewhere, and secondly, because I really like the country and the country people; for, strange and uncouth as they may seem to you, who never lived among them, they have kinder, truer hearts beating beneath their rough exteriors, than are often in the city."

"This was Morris's reply, and in the conversation which ensued Wilford Cameron caught glimpses of a nobler, higher phase of manhood than he had thought existed, feeling an unbounded respect for one who, because he believed it to be his duty, was, as it seemed to him, wasting his life among people who could not appreciate his character, though they might idolize the man. But this did not reconcile Wilford one whit the more to Silverton. Uncle Ephraim had completed the work commenced by the two feather beds, and at breakfast, next morning, he announced his intention of returning to New York that day. To this Morris offered no objection, but asked to be remembered to the mother and sisters, and then invited Wilford to stop altogether at Linwood when he came again to Silverton.

"Thank you; but it is hardly probable that I shall be here very soon," Wilford replied, adding, as he met the peculiar glance of Morris's eye, "I found Miss Katy a delightful traveling acquaintance, and on my way from Newport thought I would renew it and see a little of rustic life."

Poor Katy! how her heart would have ached could she have heard those words and understood their meaning, just as Morris did, feeling a rising indignation for the man with whom he could not be absolutely angry, he was so self-possessed, so pleasant and gentlemanly, while better than all, was he not virtually giving Katy up? and if he did might she not turn at last to him?

These were Morris's thoughts as he walked with Wilford across the fields to the farm-house, where Katy met them with her sunniest smile, singing to them, at Wilford's request, her sweetest song, and making him half wish he could revoke his hasty decision and tarry a little longer. But it was now too late for that, the carriage which would take him to the depot was already on its way from Linwood; and when the song was ended he told her of his intentions to leave on the next train, feeling a pang when he saw how the blood left her cheek and lip, and then came surging back as she said timidly, " Why need you leave so soon? "

" I have already outstayed my time. I thought of going yesterday, and my partner, Mr. Ray, will be expecting me," Wilford replied, laying his hand upon Katy's hair, while Morris and Helen stole quietly from the room.

Thus left to himself, Wilford continued, " Maybe I'll come again sometime. Would you like to have me? "

" Yes," and Katy's blue eyes were lifted pleadingly to the young man, who had never loved her so well as at that very moment when resolving to cast her off.

For a moment Wilford was strongly tempted to throw all pride aside, and ask that young girl to be his; but thoughts of his mother, of Juno and Bell, and more than all, thoughts of Uncle Ephraim and his sister Betsy, arose in time to prevent it, and so he only kissed her forehead caressingly as he said good-bye, telling her that he should not soon forget his visit to Silverton, and then, as the carriage drove up, going out to where the remainder of the family were standing together and commenting upon his sudden departure.

It was not sudden, he said, trying to explain. He really had thought seriously of going yesterday, and feeling that he had something to atone for, he tried to be unusually gracious as he shook their hands, thanking them for their kindness, but seeming wholly oblivious to Aunt Betsy's remark that " she hoped to see him again, if not at Silverton, in New York, where she wanted dreadfully to visit, but never had on account of the 'bominable prices charged to the taverns, and she hadn't no acquaintances there."

This was Aunt Betsy's parting remark, and, after Katy, Aunt Betsy liked Wilford Cameron better than any one of the group which watched him as he drove from their door. Aunt Hannah thought him too much stuck up for farmers' folks; Mrs. Lennox, whose ambition would have accounted him a most desirable match for her daughter, could not deny that his manner towards them, though polite in the extreme, was that of a superior to people greatly beneath him; while Helen, who saw clearer than the rest, read him aright, and detected the struggle between his pride and his love for poor little Katy, whom she found sitting on the floor, just where Wilford left her standing, her head resting on the chair and her face hidden in her hands as she sobbed quietly, hardly knowing why she cried or what to answer when Helen asked what was the matter.

"It was so queer in him to go so soon," she said; "just as if he were offended about something."

"Never mind, Katy," Helen said, soothingly. "If he cares for you he will come back again. He could not stay here always, of course; and I must say I respect him for attending to his business, if he has any. He has been gone from home for weeks, you know."

This was Helen's reasoning; but it did not comfort Katy, whose face looked white and sad, as she moved listlessly about the house, almost crying again when she heard in the distance the whistle of the train which was to carry Wilford Cameron away and end his first visit to Silverton.

CHAPTER VI.

IN THE SPRING.

KATY LENNOX had been very sick, and the bed where Wilford slept had stood in the parlor during the long weeks while the obstinate fever ran its course; but she was better now, and sat nearly all day before the fire, sometimes trying to crochet a little, and again turning over the books which Morris had bought to interest her—Morris, the kind physician, who had attended her so faithfully, never leaving her while the fever was at its height, unless it was necessary, but staying with her day and night, watching her symptoms carefully, and praying so earnestly that she might not die, not, at least, until some token had been given that again in the better world he should find her, where partings were unknown and where no Wilford Camerons could contest the prize with him. Not that he was greatly afraid of Wilford now; that fear had mostly died away just as the hope had died from Katy's heart that she would ever meet him again.

Since the September morning when he left her, she had

not heard from him except once, when in the winter Morris had been to New York, and having a few hours' leisure on his hands had called at Wilford's office, receiving a most cordial reception, and meeting with Mark Ray, who impressed him as a man quite as highly cultivated as Wilford, and possessed of more character and principle. This call was not altogether of Morris's seeking, but was made rather with a view to pleasing Katy, who, when she learned that he was going to New York, had said inadvertently, " Oh, I do so hope you'll meet with Mr. Cameron, for then we shall know that he is neither sick nor dead, as I have sometimes feared."

And so Morris had sought his rival, feeling repaid for the effort it had cost him, when he saw how glad Wilford seemed to meet him. The first commonplaces over, Wilford inquired for Katy. Was she well, and how was she occupying her time this winter?

" Both Helen and Katy are pupils of mine," Morris replied, " reciting their lessons to me every day when the weather will admit of their crossing the fields to Linwood. We have often wondered what had become of you, that you did not even let us know of your safe arrival home," he added, looking Wilford fully in the eye, and rather enjoying his confusion as he tried to apologize.

He had intended writing, but an unusual amount of business had occupied his time. " Mark will tell you how busy I was," and he turned appealingly to his partner, in whose expressive eyes Morris read that Silverton was not unknown to him.

But if Wilford had told him anything derogatory of the farm-house or its inmates, it did not appear in Mr. Ray's manner, as he replied that Mr. Cameron had been very busy ever since his return from Silverton, adding, " From what Cameron tells me of your neighborhood, there must be some splendid hunting and fishing there, and I had last fall half a mind to try it."

This time there was something comical in the eyes turned so mischievously upon Wilford, who colored scarlet for an instant, but soon recovered his composure, and invited Morris home with him to dinner.

" I shall not take a refusal," he said, as Morris began

to decline. "Mother and the young ladies will be delighted to see you again. Mark will go with us, of course."

There was something so hearty in Wilford's invitation that Morris did not again object, and two hours later found him in the drawing room at No.—Fifth Avenue, receiving the friendly greetings of Mrs. Cameron and her daughters, each of whom vied with the other in their polite attentions to him.

Morris did not regret having accepted Wilford's invitation to dinner, as by this means he saw the home which had well nigh been little Katy Lennox's. She would be sadly out of place here with these people, he thought, and he looked upon all their formality and ceremony, and then contrasted it with what Katy had been accustomed to. Juno would kill her outright, was his next mental comment, as he watched that haughty young lady, dividing her coquetries between himself and Mr. Ray, who being every way desirable, both in point of family and wealth, was evidently her favorite. She had colored scarlet when first presented to Dr. Grant, and her voice had trembled as she took his offered hand, for she remembered the time when her liking had not been concealed, and was only withdrawn at the last because she found how useless it was to waste her affections upon one who did not prize them.

When Wilford first returned from Silverton he had, as a sure means of forgetting Katy, told his mother and sister something of the farm-house and its inmates; and Juno, while ridiculing both Helen and Katy, had felt a fierce pang of jealousy in knowing they were cousins to Morris Grant, who lived so near that he could, if he liked, see them every day. In Paris Juno had suspected that somebody was standing between her and Dr. Grant, and with the quick insight of a smart, bright woman, she guessed that it was one of these cousins—Katy most likely, her brother having described Helen as very commonplace, —and for a time she had hated poor, innocent Katy most cordially for having come between her and the only man for whom she had ever really cared. Gradually, however, the feeling died away, but was revived again at sight of Morris Grant, and at the table she could not forbear saying to him,

" By the way, Dr. Grant, why did you never tell us of those charming cousins, when you were in Paris? Brother Will describes one of them as a little water-lily, she is so fair and pretty. Katy, I think, is her name. Wilford, isn't it Katy Lennox whom you think so beautiful, and with whom you are more than half in love?"

" Yes, it *is* Katy," and Wilford spoke sternly, for he did not like Juno's bantering tone, but he could not stop her, and she went on,

" Are they your own cousins, Dr. Grant?"

" No, they are removed from me two or three degrees, their father having been only my second cousin."

The fact that Katy Lennox was not nearly enough related to Dr. Grant to prevent his marrying her if he liked, did not improve Juno's amiability, and she continued to ask questions concerning both Katy and Helen, the latter of whom she persisted in thinking was strong-minded, until Mark Ray came to the rescue, diverting her attention by adroitly complimenting her in some way, and so relieving Wilford and Morris, both of whom were exceedingly annoyed.

" When Will visits Silverton again I mean to go with him," she said to Morris at parting, but he did not tell her that such an event would give him the greatest pleasure. On the contrary, he merely replied,

" If you do you will find plenty of room at Linwood for those four trunks which I remember seeing in Paris, and your brother will tell you whether I am a hospitable host or not."

Biting her lip with chagrin, Juno went back to the drawing-room, while Morris returned to his hotel, accompanied by Wilford, who passed the entire evening with him, appearing somewhat constrained, as if there was something on his mind which he wished to say; but it remained unspoken, and there was no allusion to Silverton until, as Wilford was leaving, he said,

" Remember me kindly to the Silverton friends, and say I have not forgotten them."

And this was all there was to carry back to Katy, who on the afternoon of Morris's return from New York was at Linwood, waiting to pour his tea and make his toast, she pretended, though the real reason was shining all over her tell-tale face, which grew so bright and eager when Morris said,

"I dined at Mr. Cameron's, Kitty."

But the brightness gradually faded as Morris described his call and then repeated Wilford's message.

"And that was all," Katy whispered sorrowfully as she beat the damask cloth softly with her fingers, shutting her lips tightly together to keep back her disappointment.

When Morris glanced at her again there was a tear on her long eye-lashes, and it dropped upon her cheek, followed by another and another, but he did not seem to see it, and talked of New York and the fine sights in Broadway until Katy was able to take part in the conversation.

"Please don't tell *Helen* that you saw Wilford," she said to Morris as he walked home with her after tea, and that was the only allusion she made to it, never after that mentioning Wilford's name or giving any token of the love still so strong within her heart, and waiting only for some slight token to waken it again to life and vigor.

This was in the winter, and Katy had been very sick since then, while Morris had come to believe that Wilford was forgotten, and when, as she grew stronger, he saw how her eyes sparkled at his coming, and how impatient she seemed if he was obliged to hurry off, hope whispered that she would surely be his, and his usually grave face wore a look of happiness which his patients noticed, feeling themselves better after one of his cheery visits. Poor Morris! he was little prepared for the terrible blow in store for him, when one day early in April he started, as usual, to visit Katy, saying to himself, "If I find her alone, perhaps I'll ask if she will come to Linwood this summer;" and Morris paused a moment beneath a beechwood tree to still the throbbings of his heart, which beat so fast as he thought of going home from his weary work and finding Kate there, his little wife—whom he might caress and love all his affectionate nature would prompt him to. He knew that in some points she was weak, but then she was very young, and there was about her so much of purity, innocence, and perfect beauty, that few men, however strong their intellect, could withstand her, and Morris felt

that in possessing her he should have all he needed to make
this life desirable. She would improve as she grew older,
and it would be a most delightful task to train her into
what she was capable of becoming. Alas for Dr. Morris!
He was very near the farm-house now, and there were
only a few minutes between him and the cloud which would
darken his horizon so completely. Katy was alone, sitting
up in her pretty dressing gown of blue, which was so
becoming to her pure complexion. Her hair, which had
been all cut away during her long sickness, was growing
out again somewhat darker than before, and lay in rings
upon her head, making her look more childish than ever.
But to this Morris did not object. He liked to have her a
child, and he thought he had never seen her so beautiful
as she was this morning, when, with glowing cheek and
dancing eyes, she greeted him as he came in.

" Oh, Dr. Morris! " she began, holding up a letter she
had in her hand, " I am so glad you've come! Wilford
has not forgotten me. He has written, and he is coming
again, if I will let him; I *am* so glad! Ain't you? Seeing
you knew all about it, and never told Helen, I'll let you
read the letter."

And she held it toward the young man leaning against
the mantel and panting for the breath which came so
heavily.

Something he said apologetically about being *snow blind,*
for there was that day quite a fall of soft spring snow;
and then, with a mighty effort which made his heart
quiver with pain, Morris was himself once more, and took
the letter in his hand.

" Perhaps I ought not to read it," he said, but Katy
insisted, and thinking to himself, " It will cure me sooner
perhaps," he read the few lines Wilford Cameron had
written to his " dear little Katy."

That was the way he addressed her, going on to say
that circumstances which he could not explain to her had
kept him silent ever since he left her the previous autumn;
but through all he never for a moment had forgotten her,
thinking of her the more for the silence he had maintained.
" And now that I have risen above the circumstances," he
added, in conclusion, " I write to ask if I may come to

Silverton again? If I may, just drop me one word, 'come,' and in less than a week I shall be there. Yours very truly, W. Cameron."

Morris read the letter through, feeling that every word was separating him further and further from Katy, to whom he said, "You will answer this?"

"Yes, oh yes; perhaps to-day."

"And you will tell him to come?"

"Why,—what else should I tell him?" and Katy's blue eyes looked wonderingly at Morris, who hardly knew what he was doing, or why he said to her next, "Listen to me, Katy. You know why Wilford Cameron comes here a second time, and what he will probably ask you ere he goes away: but, Katy, you are not strong enough yet to see him under so exciting circumstances, and, as your physician, I desire that you tell him to wait at least three weeks before he comes. Will you do so, Katy?"

"That is just as Helen talked," Katy answered mournfully. "She said I was not able."

"And will you heed us?" Morris asked again, while Katy after a moment consented, and glad of this respite from what he knew to a certainty would be, Morris dealt out her medicine, and for an instant felt her rapid pulse, but did not retain her hand within his own, nor lay his other upon her head, as he had sometimes done.

He could not do that now, so he hurried away, finding the world into which he went far different from what it had seemed an hour ago. Then all was bright and hopeful; but now, alas! a darker night was gathering round him than any he had ever known, and the patients visited that day marveled at the whiteness of his face, asking if he were ill. Yes, he answered them truly, and for two days he was not seen again, but remained at home alone, where none but his God was witness to what he suffered; but when the third day came he went again among his sick, grave, quiet and unchanged in outward appearance, unless it was that his voice, always so kind, had now a kinder tone and his manner was tenderer, more sympathizing. Inwardly, however, there was a change, for Morris Grant had lain himself upon the sacrificial altar, willing to be and to endure whatever God should appoint, knowing that all would eventually be for his good. To the farm-house he went every day, talking most with Helen now, but never forgetting who it was sitting so demurely in the arm-chair, or flitting about the room, for Katy was gain-ing rapidly. Love perhaps had had nothing to do with her dangerous illness, but it had much to do with her re-covery, and those not in the secret wondered to see how she improved, her cheeks growing round and full and her eyes shining with returning health and happiness.

At Helen's instigation Katy had deferred Wilford's visit four weeks instead of three, but in that time there had come two letters from him, so full of anxiety and sympathy for "his poor little Katy who had been so sick," that even Helen began to think that he was not as proud and heart-less as she supposed, and that he did love her sister after all.

"If I supposed he meant to deceive her I should wish I was a man to cowhide him," she said to herself, with flashing eye, as she heard Katy exulting that he was com-ing "to-morrow."

This time he would stop at Linwood, for Katy had asked Morris if he might, while Morris had told her yes, feeling his heart-wound throb afresh, as he thought how hard it would be to entertain his rival. Of himself Morris could do nothing, but with the help he never sought in vain he could do all things, and so he gave orders that the best chamber should be prepared for his guest, bidding Mrs. Hull see that no pains were spared for his entertainment, and then with Katy he waited for the day, the last one in April, which would bring Wilford Cameron a second time to Silverton.

CHAPTER VII.

WILFORD'S SECOND VISIT.

WILFORD CAMERON had tried to forget Katy Lennox, both for his sake and her own, for he foresaw that she could not be happy with his family, and he came to think it might be a wrong to her to transplant her into a soil so wholly unlike that in which her habits and affections had taken root.

His father once had abruptly asked him if there was any truth in the report that he was about to marry and make a fool of himself, and when Wilford had answered " No," he had replied with a significant

" Umph ! Old enough, I should think, if you ever intend to marry. Wilford," and the old man faced square about, " I know nothing of the girl, except what I gathered from your mother and sisters. You have not asked my advice. I don't suppose you want it, but if you do, here it is. If you love the girl and she is respectable, marry her if she is poor as poverty and the daughter of a tinker; but if you don't love her, and she's as rich as a nabob, for thunder's sake keep away from her."

This was the elder Cameron's counsel, and Katy's cause rose fifty per cent. in consequence. Still Wilford was sadly disquieted, so much so that his partner, Mark Ray, could not fail to observe that something was troubling him, and at last frankly asked what it was. Wilford knew he could trust Mark, and he confessed the whole, telling him far more of Silverton than he had told his mother, and then asking what his friend would do were the case his own.

Fond of fun and frolic, Mark laughed immoderately at Wilford's description of Aunt Betsy bringing her " herrin'-bone " patch work into the parlor, and telling him it was a part of Katy's " settin' out," but when it came to her hint for an invitation to *visit* New York, the amused young man roared with laughter, wishing so much that he might live to see the day when poor Aunt Betsy Barlow stood ringing for admittance at No. — Fifth Avenue.

" Wouldn't it be rich, though, the meeting between your Aunt Betsy and Juno ? " and the tears fairly poured down the young man's face.

But Wilford was too serious for trifling, and after his merriment had subsided, Mark talked with him candidly of Katy Lennox, whose cause he warmly espoused, telling Wilford that he was far too sensitive with regard to family and position.

" You are a good fellow on the whole, but too out-rageously proud," he said. " Of course this Aunt Betsy in her *pongee,* whatever that may be, and the uncle in his shirt sleeves, and this mother whom you describe as weak and ambitious, are objections which you would rather should not exist; but if you love the girl, take her, family and all. Not that you are to transport the whole colony of Barlows to New York," he added, as he saw Wilford's look of horror, "but make up your mind to endure what cannot be helped, resting yourself upon the fact that your position is such as cannot well be affected by any marriage you might make, provided the wife were right."

This was Mark Ray's advice, and it had great weight with Wilford, who knew that Mark came, if possible, from a better line of ancestry than himself. And still Wilford hesitated, waiting until the winter was over, before he came to the decision which, when it was reached, was firm as a granite rock. He had made up his mind at last to marry Katy Lennox if she would accept him, and he told his mother so in presence of his sisters, when one evening they were all kept at home by the rain. There was a sudden uplifting of Bell's eyelashes, a contemptuous shrug of her shoulders, and then she went on with the book she was reading, wondering if Katy was at all inclined to literature, and thinking if she were that it might be easier to tolerate her. Juno, who was expected to say the sharpest things, turned upon him with the exclamation,

"If you can stand those two feather beds, you can do more than I supposed," and as one means of showing her disapproval, she quitted the room, while Bell, who had taken to writing articles on the follies of the age, soon followed her sister to elaborate an idea suggested to her mind by her brother's contemplated marriage.

Thus left alone with her son, Mrs. Cameron tried all her powers of persuasion upon him. But nothing she said influenced him in the least, seeing which she suddenly confronted him with the question, "Shall you tell her *all?* A husband should have no secrets of that kind from his wife."

Wilford's face was white as ashes, and his voice trembled as he replied, "Yes, mother, I shall tell her all; but, oh! you do not know how hard it has been for me to bring my mind to that, or how sorry I am that we ever kept that secret—when Genevra died——"

" Hush—h ! " came warningly from the mother as Juno reappeared, the warning indicating that Genevra was a name never mentioned, except by mother and son.

As Juno remained, the conversation was not resumed, and the next morning Wilford wrote to Katy Lennox the letter which carried to her so much of joy, and to Dr. Grant so much of grief. To wait four weeks, as Katy said he must, was a terrible trial to Wilford, who counted every moment which kept him from her side. It was all owing to Dr. Grant and that perpendicular Helen, he knew, for Katy in her letter had admitted that the waiting was wholly their suggestion; and Wilford's thoughts concerning them were anything but complimentary, until a new idea was suggested, which drove every other consideration from his mind.

Wilford was naturally *jealous,* but that fault had once led him into so deep a trouble that he had struggled to overcome it, and now, at its first approach, after he thought it dead, he tried to shake it off—tried not to believe that Morris cared especially for Katy. But the mere possibility was unendurable, and in a most feverish state of excitement he started again for Silverton.

As before, Morris was at the station, his cordial greeting and friendly manner disarming him from all anxiety in that quarter, and making him resolve anew to trample the demon jealousy under his feet, where it could never rise again. Katy's life should not be darkened by the green monster, he thought, and her future would have been bright indeed had it proved all that he pictured it as he drove along with Morris in the direction of the farmhouse.

Katy was waiting for him, and he did not hesitate to kiss her more than once as he kept her for a moment in his arms, and then held her off to see if her illness had left any traces upon her. It had not, except it were in the increased delicacy of her complexion and the short hair now growing out in silky rings. She was very pretty in her short hair, but Wilford felt a little impatient as he saw how childish it made her look, and thought how long it would take for it to attain its former length. He was already appropriating her to himself, and devising ways of improving her. In New York, with Morris Grant standing before his jealous gaze, he could see no fault in Katy, and even now, with her beside him, and the ogre jealousy gone, he saw no fault in *her;* it was only her hair, and that would be remedied in time; otherwise she was perfect, and in his delight at meeting her again he forgot to criticise the farm-house and its occupants, as he had done before.

They were very civil to him—the mother overwhelmingly so, and Wilford could not help detecting her anxiety that all should be settled this time. Helen, on the contrary, was unusually cool, confirming him in his opinion that she was strong-minded and self-willed, and making him resolve to remove Katy as soon as possible from her influence. When talking with his mother he had said that if Katy told him "yes," he should probably place her at some fashionable school for a year or two; but on the way to Silverton he had changed his mind. He could not wait a year, and if he married Katy at all, it should be immediately. He would then take her to Europe, where she could have the best of teachers, besides the advantage of traveling; and it was a very satisfactory picture he drew of the woman whom he should introduce into New York society as his wife, Mrs. Wilford Cameron. It is true that Katy had not yet said the all-important word, but she was going to say it, and when late that afternoon they came from the walk he had asked her to take, she had listened to his tale of love and was his promised wife. Katy was no coquette; whatever she felt she expressed, and she had frankly confessed to Wilford her love for him, telling him how the fear that he had forgotten her had haunted her all the long winter; and then with her clear, truthful blue eyes looking into his, asking him why he had not sent her some message if as he said, he loved her all the time.

For a moment Wilford's lip was compressed and a flush overspread his face, as, drawing her closer to him, he replied, "My little Katy will remember that in my first note I spoke of certain circumstances which had prevented my writing earlier. I do not know that I asked her not to seek to know those circumstances; but I ask it now.

Will Katy trust me so far as to believe that all is right between us, and never allude to these circumstances?"

He was kissing her fondly, and his voice was so winning that Katy promised, and then came the hardest, the trying to tell her *all*, as he had said to his mother he would. Twice he essayed to speak, and as often something sealed his lips, until at last he began, "You must not think me perfect, Katy, for I have faults, and perhaps if you knew my past life you would wish to revoke your recent decision and render a different verdict to my suit. Suppose I unfold the blackest leaf for your inspection?"

"No, no, oh no," and Katy playfully stopped his mouth with her hand. "Of course you have some faults, but I would rather find them out by myself. I could not hear anything against you now. I am satisfied to take you as you are."

Wilford felt his heart throb wildly with the feeling that he was deceiving the young girl; but if she would not suffer him to tell her, he was not to be censured if she remained in ignorance. And so the golden moment fled, and when he spoke again he said, "If Katy will not now read the leaf I offered to show her, she must not shrink in horror, if ever it does meet her eye."

"I won't, I promise," Kate answered, a vague feeling of fear creeping over her as to what the reading of that mysterious page involved. But this was soon forgotten, as Wilford, remembering his suspicions of Dr. Grant, thought to probe her a little by asking if she had ever loved any one before himself.

"No, never," she answered. "I never dreamed of such a thing until I saw you, Mr. Cameron;" and Wilford believed the trusting girl, whose loving nature shone in every lineament of her face, upturned to receive the kisses he pressed upon it, resolving within himself to be to her what he ought to be.

"By the way," he continued, "don't call me Mr. Cameron again, as you did just now. I would rather be your Wilford. It sounds more familiar;" and then he told her of his projected tour to Europe, and Katy felt her pulses quicken as she thought of London, Paris and Rome, as places which her plain country eyes might yet look upon.

But when it came to their marriage, which Wilford said
must be within a few weeks—she demurred, for this arrangement was not in accordance with her desires; and
she opposed her lover with all her strength, telling him
she was so young, not eighteen till July, and she knew so
little of housekeeping. He must let her stay at home until
she learned at least the art of making bread!

Poor, ignorant Katy! Wilford could not forbear a smile
as he thought how different were her views from his, and
tried to explain that the art of bread-making, though very
desirable in most wives, was *not* an essential accomplish-
ment for his. Servants would do that; besides he did not
intend to have a house of his own at once; he should take
her first to live with his mother, where she could learn
what was necessary much better than in Silverton.

Wilford Cameron expected to be obeyed in every important matter by the happy person who should be his wife,
and as he possessed the faculty of enforcing perfect obedience without seeming to be severe, so he silenced Katy's
arguments, and when they left the shadow of the butternut
tree she knew that in all human probability six weeks'
time would find her on the broad ocean alone with Wilford
Cameron. So perfect was Katy's faith and love that she
had no fear of Wilford now, but as his affianced wife walked
confidently by his side, feeling fully his equal, nor once
dreaming how great the disparity his city friends would
discover between the fastidious man of fashion and the unsophisticated country girl. And Wilford did not seek to
enlighten her, but suffered her to talk of the delight it
would be to live in New York, and how pleasant for mother
and Helen to visit her, especially the latter, who would
thus have a chance to see something of the world.

"When I get a house of my own I mean she shall live
with me all the while," she said, stooping to gather a tuft
of wild blue-bells growing in a marshy spot.

Wilford winced a little, but he would not so soon tear
down Katy's castles, and so he merely remarked, as she
asked if it would not be nice to have Helen with them,

"Yes, very nice; but do not speak of it to her yet, as it
will probably be some time before she will come to us."

And so Helen never suspected the honor in store for her

as she stood in the doorway anxiously waiting for her sister, who she feared would take cold from being out so long. Something though in Katy's face made her guess that to her was lost forever the bright little sister whom she loved so dearly, and fleeing up the narrow stairway to her room, she wept bitterly as she thought of the coming time when she would occupy that room alone, and know that never again would a little golden head lie upon her neck just as it had lain, for there would be a new love, a new interest between them, a love for the man whose voice she could hear now talking to her mother in the peculiar tone he always assumed when speaking to any one of them excepting Morris or Katy.

"I wish it were not wrong to hate him," she exclaimed passionately; "it would be such a relief; but if he is only kind to Katy, I do not care how much he despises us," and bathing her face, Helen sat down by her window, wondering, if Mr. Cameron took her sister, when it would probably be. "Not this year or more," she said, "for Katy is so young;" but on this point she was soon set right by Katy herself, who, leaving her lover alone with her mother, stole up to tell her sister the good news.

"Yes, I know; I guessed as much when you came back from the meadows," and Helen's voice was very unsteady in its tone as she smoothed the soft rings clustering around her sister's brow.

"Crying, Helen! oh, don't. I shall love you just the same, and you are coming to live with us," Katy said, forgetting Wilford's instructions in her desire to comfort Helen, who broke down again, while Katy's tears were mingled with her own.

It was the first time Katy had thought what it would be to leave forever the good, patient sister, who had been so kind, treating her like a petted kitten and standing between her and every hardship.

"Don't cry, Nellie," she said, "New York is not far away, and I shall come so often, that is, after we return from Europe. Did I tell you we are going there first, and Wilford will not wait, but says we must be married the 10th of June?—that's his birthday—thirty—and he is telling mother now."

" So soon—oh Katy ! and you so young ! " was all Helen
could say, as with quivering lip she kissed her sister's hand
raised to wipe her tears away.

" Yes, it is soon, and I am young: but Wilford is in
such a hurry; he don't care," Katy replied, trying to comfort Helen, and begging of her not to cry so hard.

" No, Wilford did not care how much he wrung the
hearts of Katy's family by taking her from them at once,
and by dictating to a certain extent the way in which he
would take her.   There must be no invited guests, he said;
no lookers-on, except such as chose to go to the church
where the ceremony would be performed, and from which
place he should go directly to the Boston train.   It was
his wish, too, that the matter should be kept as quiet as
possible, and not be generally discussed in the neighborhood, as he disliked being a subject for gossip.   And Mrs.
Lennox, to whom this was said, promised compliance with
everything, or if she ventured to object she found herself
borne down by a stronger will than her own, and weakly
yielded, her manner fully testifying to her delight at the
honor conferred upon her by this high marriage of her
child.   Wilford knew just how pleased she was, and her
obsequious manner annoyed him far more than Helen's
blunt straightforwardness, when, after supper was over,
she told him how averse she was to his taking Katy so soon,
adding still further that if it must be, she saw no harm
in inviting a few of their neighbors.   It was custo-
mary, it would be expected, she said, while Mrs. Lennox,
emboldened by Helen's boldness, chimed in, " at least *your*
folks will come; I shall be glad to meet your mother."

Wilford was very polite to them both; very good-humored, but he kept to his first position, and poor Mrs.
Lennox saw fade into airy nothingness all her visions of
roasted fowls and frosted cake trimmed with myrtle and
flowers, with hosts of the Silverton people there to admire
and partake of the marriage feast.   It was too bad and so
Aunt Betsy said, when, after Wilford had gone to Linwood, the family sat together around the kitchen stove,
talking the matter over.

" Yes, it was too bad, when there was that white hen-
turkey she could fat up so easy before June, and she knew

how to make 'lection cake that would melt in your mouth, and was enough sight better than the black stuff they called weddin' cake. She meant to try what *she* could do with Mr. Carmon."

And next morning when he came again she did try, holding out as inducements why he should be married the night before starting for Boston, the "white hen-turkey, the 'lection cake, and the gay old times the young folks would have playing snap-and-catchem; or if they had a mind, they could dance a bit in the kitchen. She didn't believe in it, to be sure—none of the Orthodox did; but as Wilford was a 'Piscopal, and that was a 'Piscopal quirk, it wouldn't harm for once."

Wilford tried not to show his disgust, and only Helen suspected how hard it was for him to keep down his utter contempt. She saw it in his eyes, which resembled two smouldering volcanoes as they rested upon Aunt Betsy during her harangue.

"Thank you, madam, for your good intentions, but I think we will dispense with the turkey and the cake," was all he said, though he did smile at the old lady's definition of dancing, which for once she might allow.

Even Morris, when appealed to, decided with Wilford against Mrs. Lennox and Aunt Betsy, knowing how unequal he was to the task which would devolve on him in case of a bridal party at the farm-house. In comparative silence he heard from Wilford of his engagement offering no objection when told how soon the marriage would take place, but congratulating him so quietly, that if Wilford had retained a feeling of jealousy, it would have disappeared; Morris was so seemingly indifferent to everything except Katy's happiness. But Wilford did not observe closely, and failed to detect the hopeless look in Morris's eyes, or the whiteness which settled about his mouth as he fulfilled the duties of host and sought to entertain his guest. Those were dark hours for Morris Grant, and he was glad when at the end of the second day Wilford's visit expired, and he saw him driven from Linwood round to the farm-house, where he would say his parting words to Katy and then go back to New York.

CHAPTER VIII.

GETTING READY TO BE MARRIED.

Miss Helen Lennox, Silverton, Mass."
This was the superscription of a letter, postmarked New
York, and brought to Helen within a week after Wilford's
departure. It was his handwriting, too; and wondering
what he could have written to her, Helen broke the seal,
starting as there dropped into her lap a check for five
hundred dollars.

" What does it mean?" she said, her cheek flushing with
anger and insulted pride as she read the following brief
lines:

"New York, May 8th.

" Miss Helen Lennox: Please pardon the liberty I
have taken in enclosing the sum of $500 to be used by you
in procuring whatever Katy may need for present neces-
sities. Presuming that the country seamstresses have not
the best facilities for obtaining the latest fashions, my
mother proposes sending out her own private dressmaker,
Mrs. Ryan. You may look for her the last of the week.

"Yours truly,   Wilford Cameron."

It would be impossible to describe Helen's indignation
as she read this letter, which roused her to a pitch of
anger such as Wilford Cameron had never imagined when
he wrote the offensive lines. He had really no intention of
insulting her. On the contrary, the gift of money was
kindly meant, for he knew that Uncle Ephraim was poor,
while the part referring to the dressmaker was wholly
his mother's proposition, to which he had acceded, knowing
how much confidence Juno had in her taste, and that
whatever she might see at the farm-house would remain
a secret with her, or at most be confined to the ears of his
mother and sisters. He wished Katy to look well, and
foolishly fancying that no country artiste could make her
look so, he consented to Mrs. Ryan's going, never dreaming

of the effect it would have upon Helen, whose first impulse was to throw the check into the fire. Her second, however, was soberer. She would not destroy it, nor tell any one she had it, but Morris—*he* should know the whole. Accordingly, she repaired to Linwood, finding Morris at home, and startling him with the vehemence of her anger as she explained the nature of her errand.

"If I disliked Wilford Cameron before, I hate him now. Yes, hate him," she said, stamping her little foot in fury.

"Why, Helen!" Morris exclaimed, laying his hand reprovingly on her shoulder; "is this the right spirit for one who professes better things? Stop a moment and think."

"I know it is wrong," Helen answered, "but somehow since he came after Katy, I have grown so hard, so wicked toward Mr. Cameron. He seems so proud, so unapproachable. Say, Cousin Morris, do you think him a good man, that is, good enough for Katy?"

"Most people would call him too good for her," Morris replied. And, in a worldly point of view, she is doing well. Cameron, I believe, is better than three-fourths of the men who marry our girls. He is very proud: but that results from his education and training. Looking only from a New York stand-point he misjudges country people, but he will appreciate you by and by. Do not begin by hating him so cordially."

"Yes, but this money. Now, Morris, we do not want him to get Katy's outfit. I would rather go without clothes my whole life. Shall I send it back?"

"I think that the best disposition to make of it," Morris replied. "As your brother, I can and will supply Katy's needs."

"I knew you would, Morris. And I'll send it to-day, in time to keep that dreadful Mrs. Ryan from coming; for I won't have any of Wilford Cameron's dressmakers in the house."

Morris could not help smiling at Helen's energetic manner, as she hurried to his library and taking his pen wrote to Wilford Cameron as follows:

SILVERTON, May 9th, 18—.

MR. WILFORD CAMERON:—I give you credit for the kindest of motives in sending the check which I now return to you, with my compliments. We are not as poor as you suppose, and would almost deem it sacrilege to let another than ourselves provide for Katy so long as she is ours. And furthermore, Mrs. Ryan's services will not be needed, so it is not worth her while to make a journey here for nothing.   Yours,

HELEN LENNOX.

Helen felt better after this letter had gone, wondering often how it would be received, and if Wilford would be angry. She hoped he would, and his mother too. "The idea of sending that Ryan woman to us, as if we did not know anything!" and Helen's lip curled scornfully as she thus denounced the Ryan woman, whose trunk was packed with paper patterns and devices of various kinds when the letter arrived, saying she was not needed. Being a woman of few words, she quietly unpacked her patterns and went back to the work she was engaged upon when Mrs. Cameron proposed her going into the country. Juno, on the contrary, flew into a violent passion to think their first friendly advances should be thus received. Bell laughed immoderately, saying she liked Helen Lennox's spirit, and wished her brother had chosen her instead of the other, who, she presumed, was a milk and water thing, even if Mrs. Woodhull did extol her so highly. Mrs. Cameron felt the rebuke keenly, wincing under it, and saying "that Helen Lennox must be a very rude, ill-bred girl," and hoping her son would draw the line of division between his wife and her family so tightly that the sister could never pass over it. She had received the news of her son's engagement without opposition, for she knew the time for that was past. Wilford would marry Katy Lennox, and she must make the best of it, so she offered no remonstrance, but, when they were alone, she said to him, "Did you tell her? Does she know it all?"

"No, mother," and the old look of pain came back into

Wilford's face. "I meant to do so, and I actually began, but she stopped me short, saying she did not wish to hear my faults, she would rather find them out herself. Away from her it is very easy to think what I will do, but when the trial comes I find it hard, we have kept it so long; but I shall tell her yet; not till after we are married though, and I have made her love me even more than she does now. She will not mind it then. I shall take her where I first met Genevra, and there I will tell her. Is that right?"

"Yes, if you think so," Mrs. Cameron replied.

Whatever it was which Wilford had to tell Katy Lennox, it was very evident that he and his mother looked at it differently, he regarding it as a duty he owed to Katy not to conceal from her what might possibly influence her decision, while his mother only wished the secret told in hopes that it would prevent the marriage; but now that Wilford had deferred it till after the marriage, she saw no reason why it need be told at all. At least Wilford could do as he thought best, and she changed the conversation from Genevra to Helen's letter, which had so upset her plans. That her future daughter-in-law was handsome she did not doubt, but she, of course, had no manner, no style, and as a means of improving her in the latter respect, and making her presentable at the altar and in Boston, she had proposed sending out *Ryan;* but that project had failed, and Helen Lennox did not stand very high in the Cameron family, though Wilford in his heart felt an increased respect for her independent spirit, notwithstanding that she had thwarted his designs.

"I have another idea," Mrs. Cameron said to her daughters that afternoon, when talking with them upon the subject. "Wilford tells me Katy and Bell are about the same size and figure, and Ryan shall make up a traveling suit proper for the occasion. Of course there will be no one at the wedding for whom we care, but in Boston, at the Revere, it will be different. Cousin Harvey boards there, and she is very stylish. I saw some elegant grey poplins, of the finest lustre, at Stewart's yesterday. Suppose we drive down this afternoon."

This was said to Juno as the more fashionable one of

the sisters, but Bell answered quickly, "Poplin, mother, on Katy? It will not become her style, I am sure, though suitable for many. If I am to be fitted, I shall say a word about the fabric. Get a little checked silk, as expensive as you like. It will suit her better than a heavy poplin."

Perhaps Bell was right, Mrs. Cameron said; they would look at both, and as the result of this looking, two dresses, one of the finest poplin, and one of the softest, richest, plaided silk, were given the next day into Mrs. Ryan's hands, with injunctions to spare no pains or expense in trimming and making both. And so the dress-making for Katy's bridal was proceeding in New York, in spite of Helen's letter; while down in Silverton, at the farm-house, there were numerous consultations as to what was proper and what was not, Helen sometimes almost wishing she had suffered Mrs. Ryan to come. Katy would look well in anything, but Helen knew there were certain styles preferable to others, and in a maze of perplexity she consulted with this and that individual, until all Silverton knew what was projected, each one offering the benefit of her advice until Helen and Katy were nearly distracted. Aunt Betsy suggested a blue delaine and round cape, offering to get it herself, and actually purchasing the material with her own funds, saved from drying apples. That would answer for one dress, Helen said, but not for the wedding; and she was becoming more undecided, when Morris came to the rescue, telling Katy of a young woman who had for some time past been his patient, but who was now nearly well and was anxious to obtain work again. She had evidently seen better days, he said; was very lady-like in her manner, and possessed of a great deal of taste, he imagined; besides that, she had worked in one of the largest shops in New York. "As I am going this afternoon over to North Silverton," he added, in conclusion, "and shall pass Miss Hazelton's house, you or Helen might accompany me and see for yourself."

It was decided that Helen should go, and about four o'clock she found herself ringing at the cottage over whose door hung the sign, "Miss M. Hazelton, Fashionable Dressmaker." She was at home, and in a few moments Helen was talking with Marian Hazelton, whose face showed signs of recent illness, but was nevertheless very attractive, from its peculiarly sad expression and the soft liquid eyes of dark blue, which looked as if they were not strangers to tears. At twenty she must have been strikingly beautiful; and even now, at thirty, few ladies could have vied with her had she possessed the means for gratifying her taste and studying her style. About the mouth, so perfect in repose, there was when she spoke a singularly sweet smile, which in a measure prepared one for the low, silvery voice, which had a strange note of mournful music in its tone, making Helen start as it asked, " Did you wish to see me? "

" Yes; Dr. Grant told me you could make dresses, and I drove round with him to secure your services, if possible, for my sister, who is soon to be married. We would like it so much if you could go to our house instead of having Katy come here."

Marian Hazelton was needing work, for there was due more than three months' board, besides the doctor's bill, and so, though it was not her custom to go from house to house, she would, in this instance, accommodate Miss Lennox, especially as during her illness her customers had many of them gone elsewhere, and her little shop was nearly broken up. " Was it an elaborate trousseau she was expected to make? " and she bent down to turn over some fashion plates lying upon the table.

" Oh, no! we are plain country people. We cannot afford as much for Katy as we would like; besides, I dare say Mr. Cameron will prefer selecting most of her wardrobe himself, as he is very wealthy and fastidious," Helen replied, repenting the next instant the part concerning Mr. Cameron's wealth, as that might look like boasting to Miss Hazelton, whose head was bent lower over the magazine as she said, " Did I understand that the gentleman's name was Cameron? "

" Yes, Wilford Cameron, from New York," Helen answered, holding up her skirts and s-s-kt-ing at the kitten which came running toward her, evidently intent upon springing into her lap.

Fear of cats was Helen's weakness, if weakness it can be called, and in her efforts to frighten her tormentor

she did not look again at Miss Hazelton until startled by
a gasping cry and heavy fall. Marian had fainted, and
Helen was just raising her head from the floor to her lap
when Morris appeared, relieving her of her burden, of
whom he took charge until she showed signs of life. In
her alarm Helen forgot entirely what they were talking
about when the faint came on, and her first question put
to Marian was, "Were you taken suddenly ill? Why
did you faint?"

There was no answer at first; but when she did speak
Marian said, "I am still so weak that the least exertion
affects me, and I was bending over the table; it will soon
pass off."

If she was so weak she was not able to work, Helen said,
proposing that the plan be for the present abandoned,
but to this Marian would not listen; and her great eager
eyes had in them so scared a look that Helen said no
more on that subject, but made arrangements for her
coming to them at once. Morris was to leave his patient
some medicine, and while he was preparing it, Helen had
time to notice her more carefully, admiring her ladylike
manners, and thinking her smile the sweetest she had ever
seen. Greatly interested in her, Helen plied Morris with
questions of Miss Hazelton during their ride home, asking
what he knew of her.

"Nothing, except that she came to North Silverton a
year ago, opening her shop, and by her faithfulness, and
pleasant, obliging manners, winning favor with all who
employed her. Previous to her sickness she had a few
times attended St. Paul's at South Silverton, that being
the church of her choice. Had Helen never observed
her?"

No, Helen had not. And then she spoke of her fainting, telling how sudden it was, and wondering if she was
subject to such turns. Marian Hazelton had made a
strong impression on Helen's mind, and she talked of
her so much that Katy waited her appearance at the
farm-house with feverish anxiety. It was evening when
she came, looking very white, and seeming to Helen as
if she had changed since she saw her first. In her eyes
there was a kind of hopeless, weary expression, while

her smile made one almost wish to cry, it was so sad, and yet so strangely sweet. Katy felt its influence at once, growing very confidential with the stranger, who, during the half hour in which they were accidentally left alone, drew from her every particular concerning her intended marriage. Very closely the dark blue eyes scrutinized little Katy, taking in first the faultless beauty of her face, and then going away down into the inmost depths of her character, as if to find out what was there.

"Pure, loving innocent, and unsuspecting," was Marian Hazelton's verdict, and she followed wistfully every movement of the young girl as she flitted around the room, chatting as familiarly with the dressmaker as if she were a friend long known instead of an entire stranger.

"You look very young to be married," Miss Hazelton said to her once, and shaking back her short rings of hair Katy answered, "Eighteen next Fourth of July; but Mr. Cameron is thirty."

"Is he a widower?" was the next question, which Katy answered with a merry laugh. "Mercy, no! I marry a widower! How funny! I don't believe he ever cared a fig for anybody but me. I mean to ask him."

"I would," and the pale lips shut tightly together, while a resentful gleam shot for a moment across Marian's face; but it quickly passed away, and her smile was as sweet as ever as she at last bade the family good night and repaired to the little room where Wilford Cameron once had slept.

A long time she stood before the glass, brushing her dark abundant hair, and intently regarding her own features, while in her eyes there was a hard, terrible look, from which Katy Lennox would have shrunk in fear. But that too passed, and the eyes grew soft with tears as she turned away, and falling on her knees moaned sadly, "I never will—no, I never will. God help me to keep the promise. Were it the other one—Helen—I might, for she could bear it; but Katy, that child—no, I never will," and as the words died on her lips there came struggling up from her heart a prayer for Katy Lennox's happiness, as fervent and sincere as any which had ever been made for her since she was betrothed.

They grew to liking each other rapidly, Marian and
Katy, the latter of whom thought her new friend greatly
out of place as a dressmaker, telling her she ought to
marry some rich man, calling her Marian altogether, and
questioning her very closely of her previous life. But
Marian only told her that she was born in London; that
she learned her trade on the Isle of Wight, near to the
Osborne House, where the royal family sometimes came,
and that she had often seen the present Queen, thus trying
to divert Katy's mind from asking what there was besides
that apprenticeship to the Misses True on the Isle of
Wight. Once indeed she went farther, saying that her
friends were dead; that she had come to America in hopes
of doing better than she could at home; that she had
stayed in New York until her health began to fail, and then
had tried what country air would do, coming to North
Silverton because a young woman who worked in the same
shop was acquainted there, and recommended the place.
This was all Katy could learn, and Marian's heart history,
if she had one, was guarded carefully.

They had decided at last upon the wedding dress,
which Helen reserved the right to make herself. Miss
Hazelton must fit it, of course, but to her belonged the
privilege of making it, every stitch; Katy would think
more of it if she did it all, she said; but she did not confess how the bending over the dress, both early and late,
was the escape-valve for the feeling which otherwise would
have found vent in passionate tears. Helen was very
wretched during the pleasant May days she usually enjoyed
so much, but over which now a dark pall was spread,
shutting out all the brightness and leaving only the
terrible certainty that Katy was lost to her forever—bright,
frolicsome Katy, who, without a shadow on her heart,
sported amid the bridal finery, unmindful of the anguish
tugging at the hearts of both the patient women, Marian
and Helen, who worked on so silently, reserving their tears
for the night-time, when Katy was dreaming of Wilford
Cameron. Helen was greatly interested in Marian, but
never guessed that her feelings, too, were stirred to their
very depths as the bridal preparations progressed. She
only knew how wretched she was herself, and how hard

it was to fight her tears back as she bent over the silk, weaving in with every stitch a part of the clinging love which each day grew stronger for the only sister, who would soon be gone, leaving her alone. Only once did she break entirely down, and that was when the dress was done and Katy tried it on, admiring its effect and having a second glass brought that she might see it behind.

"Isn't it lovely?" she exclaimed; "and the more valuable because you made it. I shall think of you every time I wear it," and the impulsive girl wound her arms around Helen's neck, kissing her lovingly, while Helen sank into a chair and sobbed aloud, "Oh, Katy, darling Katy! you won't forget me when you are rich and admired, and can have all you want? You will remember us here at home, so sad and lonely? You don't know how desolate it will be, knowing you are gone, never to come back again, just as you go away."

In an instant Katy was on her knees before Helen, whom she tried to comfort by telling her she should come back,—come often, too, staying a long while; and that when she had a city home of her own she should live with her for good, and they would be so happy.

"I cannot quite give Wilford up to please you," she said, when that gigantic sacrifice suggested itself as something which it was possible Helen might require of her; "but I will do anything else, only please don't cry, darling Nellie—please don't cry. It spoils all my pleasure," and Katy's soft hands wiped away the tears running so fast over her sister's face.

After that Helen did not cry again in Katy's presence, but the latter knew she wanted to, and it made her rather sad, particularly when she saw reflected in the faces of the other members of the family the grief she had witnessed in Helen. Even Uncle Ephraim was not as cheerful as usual, and once when Katy came upon him in the woodshed chamber, where he was shelling corn, she found him resting from his work and looking from the window far off across the hills, with a look which made her guess he was thinking of her, and stealing up beside him she laid her hand upon his wrinkled face, whispering softly, "Poor Uncle Eph, are you sorry, too?"

He knew what she meant, and the aged chin quivered, while a big tear dropped into the tub of corn as he replied. "Yes, Katy-did—very sorry."

That was all he said, and Katy, after smoothing his silvery hair a moment, kissed his cheek and then stole away, wondering if the love to which she was going was equal to the love of home, which, as the days went by, grew stronger and stronger, enfolding her in a mighty embrace, which could only be severed by bitter tears and fierce heart-pangs, such as death itself sometimes brings. In that household there was, after Katy, no one glad of that marriage except the mother, and she was only glad because of the position it would bring to her daughter. But among them all Morris suffered most, and suffered more because he had to endure in secret, so that no one guessed the pain it was for him to go each day where Katy was, and watch her as she sometimes donned a part of her finery for his benefit, asking him once if he did not wish he were in Wilford's place, so as to have as pretty a bride as she should make. Then Marian Hazelton glanced up in time to see the expression of his face, a look whose meaning she readily recognized, and when Dr. Grant left the farm-house that day, another than himself knew of his love for Katy, drawing her breath hurriedly as she thought of taking back the words, "I never will,"—of revoking that decision and telling Katy what Wilford Cameron should have told her long before. But the wild wish fled, and Wilford's secret was safe, while Marian watched Morris Grant with a pitying interest as he came among them, speaking always in the same kind, gentle tone, and trying so hard to enter into Katy's joy.

"His burden is greater than mine. God help us both," Marian said, as she resumed her work.

And so amid joy and gladness, silent tears and breaking hearts, the preparations went on until all was done, and only three days remained before the eventful tenth. Marian Hazelton was going home, for she would not stay at the farm-house until all was over, notwithstanding Katy's entreaties were joined to those of Helen.

"Perhaps she would come to the church," she said,

"though she could not promise;" and her manner was so strange that Katy wondered if she could have offended her, and at last said to her timidly, as she stood with her bonnet on, waiting for Uncle Ephraim, "You are not angry with me for anything, are you?"

"Angry with *you!*" and Katy never forgot the glitter of the tearful eyes, or their peculiar expression as they turned upon her. "No, oh, no; I could not be angry with you, and yet, Katy Lennox, some in my position would *hate* you, contrasting your prospects with their own; but I do not; I love you; I bless you, and pray that you may be happy with your husband; honor him, obey him if need be, and above all, never give him the slightest cause to doubt you. You will have admirers, Katy Lennox. In New York others than your husband will speak to you words of flattery, but don't you listen. Remember what I tell you; and now, again, God bless you."

She touched her lips to Katy's forehead, and when they were withdrawn there were great tears there which she had left! Marian's tears on Katy's brow; and it was very meet that just before her bridal day Wilford Cameron's bride should receive such baptism from Marian Hazelton.

CHAPTER IX.

BEFORE THE MARRIAGE.

On the morning of the 9th day of June, 18—, Wilford Cameron stood in his father's parlor, surrounded by the entire family, who, after their unusually early breakfast, had assembled to bid him good-bye, for Wilford was going for his bride, and it would be months, if not a year, ere he returned to them again. They had given him up to his idol, asking only that none of the idol's family should be permitted to cross their threshold, and also that the idol should not often be allowed the privilege of returning to the place from whence she came. These restrictions had emanated from the female portion of the Cameron family, the mother, Juno and Bell. The father, on the contrary, had sworn roundly as he would sometimes swear at what he called the contemptible pride of his wife and daughters. Katy was sure of a place in his heart just because of the pride which was building up so high a wall between her and her friends, and when at parting he held his son's hand in his, he said,

"I charge you, Will, be kind to that young girl, and don't for Heaven's sake go to cramming her with airs and nonsense which she does not understand. Tell her I'll be a father to her; her own, you say, is dead, and give her this as my bridal present."

He held out a small box containing a most exquisite set of pearls, such as he fancied would be becoming to the soft, girlish beauty Wilford had described. Something in his father's manner touched Wilford closely, making him resolve anew that if Kitty were not happy as Mrs. Cameron it should not be his fault. His mother had said all she wished to say, while his sisters had been gracious enough to send their love to the bride, Bell hoping she would look as well in the poplin and little plaid as she had done. Either was suitable for the wedding day, Mrs. Cameron said, and she might take her choice, only Wilford must see that she did not wear with the poplin the gloves and belt intended for the silk; country people had so little taste, and she did want Katy to look well, even if she were not there to see her. And with his brain a confused medley of poplins and plaids, belts and gloves, pearls and Katy, Wilford finally tore himself away, and at three o'clock that afternoon drove through Silverton village, past the little church, which the Silverton maidens were decorating with flowers, pausing a moment in their work to look at him as he went by. Among them was Marian Hazelton, but she only bent lower over her work, thus hiding the tear which dropped upon the delicate buds she was fashioning into the words, "Joy to the Bride," intending the whole as the center of the wreath to be placed over the altar where all could see it.

"The handsomest man I ever saw," was the verdict of most of the girls as they came back to their work, while Wilford drove on to the farm-house where Katy had been so anxiously watching for him.

When he came in sight, however, and she knew he was actually there, she ran away to hide her blushes, and the feeling of awe which had come suddenly over her for the man who was to be her husband. But Helen bade her go back, and so she went coyly in to Wilford, who met her with loving caresses, and then put upon her finger the superb diamond which he said he had thought to send as a pledge of their engagement, but had finally concluded to wait and present himself. Katy had heard much of diamonds, and seen some in Canandaigua; but the idea that she, plain Katy Lennox, would ever wear them, had never entered her mind; and now, as she looked at the brilliant gem sparkling upon her hand, she felt a thrill of something more than joy at that good fortune which had brought her to diamonds. Vanity, we suppose it was—such vanity as was very natural in her case, and she thought she should never tire of looking at the precious stone; but when Wilford showed her next the plain broad band of gold, and tried it on her third finger, asking if she knew what it meant, the true woman spoke within her, and she answered tearfully,

"Yes, I know, and I will try to prove worthy of what I shall be to you when I wear that ring for good."

Katy was very quiet for a moment as she sat with her head nestled against Wilford's bosom, but when he observed that she was looking tired, and asked if she had been working hard, the quiet fit was broken, and she told him of the dress "we had made," the *we* referring solely to Helen and Marian, for Katy had hardly done a thing. But it did not matter; she fancied she had, and she asked if he did not wish to see her dresses. Wilford knew it would please Katy, and so he followed her into the adjoining room, where they were spread out upon tables and chairs, with Helen in their midst, ready to pack them away. Wilford thought of Mrs. Ryan and the check, but he shook hands with Helen very civilly, saying to her playfully,

"I suppose you are willing I should take your sister with me this time."

Helen could not answer, but turned away to hide her face, while Katy showed one dress after another, until

she came to the silk, which, with a bright blush, she told
him "was the very thing itself—the one intended for
to-morrow," and asked if he did not like it.

Wilford could not help telling her yes, for he knew she
wished him to do so, but in his heart he was thinking
bad thoughts against the wardrobe of his bride elect—
thoughts which would have won for him the title of *hen·
huzzy* from Helen, could she have known them. And yet
Wilford did not deserve that name. He had been accustomed all his life to hearing dress discussed in his mother's
parlor, and in his sister's boudoir, while for the last
five weeks he had heard at home of little else than the
probable *tout ensemble* of Katy's wardrobe, bought and
made in the country, his mother deciding finally to write
to her cousin, Mrs. Harvey, who boarded at the Revere,
and have her see to it before Katy left the city. Under
these circumstances, it was not strange that Wilford did
not enter into Katy's delight, even after she told him how
Helen had made every stitch of the dress herself, and that
it would on that account be very dear to her. This
was a favorable time for getting the poplin off his mind,
and with a premonitory *ahem* he said, "Yes, it is very
nice. no doubt; but," and here he turned to Helen,
"after Mrs. Ryan's services were declined, my mother determined to have two dresses fitted to sister Bell, who I
think is just Katy's size and figure. I need not say," and
his eyes still rested on Helen, who gave him back an un-
flinching glance, "I need not say that no pains have been
spared to make these garments everything they should be
in point of quality and style. I have them in my trunk,
and," turning now to Katy, "it is my mother's special
request that one of them be worn to-morrow. You could
take your choice, she said—either was suitable. I will
bring them for your inspection."

He left the room, while Helen's face resembled a
dark thunder-cloud, whose lightnings shone in her flashing
eyes as she looked after him and then back to
where Katy stood, bewildered and wondering what was
wrong.

"Who is Mrs. Ryan?" she asked. "What does he
mean?" but before Helen could command her voice to

explain, Wilford was with them again, bringing the dresses, over which Katy nearly went wild.

She had never seen anything as elegant as the rich heavy poplin or the soft lustrous silk, while even Helen acknowledged that there was about them a finish which threw Miss Hazelton's quite in the shade.

"Beautiful!" Katy exclaimed; "and trimmed so exquisitely! I do so hope they will fit!"

"I dare say they will," Wilford replied, enjoying her appreciation of his mother's gift. "At all events they will answer for to-morrow, and any needful alterations can be made in Boston. Which will you wear?"

"Oh, I don't know. I wish I could wear both. Helen, which shall I?" and Katy appealed to her sister, who could endure no more, but hid her head among the pillows of the bed and cried.

Katy understood the whole, and dropping the silk to which she inclined the most, she flew to Helen's side and whispered to her, "Don't, Nellie, I won't wear either of them. I'll wear the one you made. It was mean and vain in me to think of doing otherwise."

During this scene Wilford had stolen from the room, and with him gone Helen was capable of judging candidly and sensibly. She knew the city silk was handsomer and better suited for Wilford Cameron's bride than the country plaid, and so she said to Katy, "I would rather you should wear the one they sent. It will become you better. Suppose you try it on," and in seeking to gratify her sister, Helen forgot in part her own cruel disappointment, and that her work of days had been for naught. The dress fitted well, though Katy pronounced it too tight and too long. A few moments, however, accustomed her to the length, and then her mother, Aunt Hannah, and Aunt Betsy, came to see and admire, while Katy proposed going out to Wilford, but Helen kept her back, Aunt Betsy remarking under her breath, that "she didn't see for the life on her how Catherine could be so free and easy with that man when just the sight of him was enough to take away a body's breath."

"More free and easy than she will be by and by," was Helen's mental comment as she proceeded quietly to pack the trunk which Morris had brought for the voyage across the sea, dropping into it many a tear as she folded away one article after another, and wondered under what circumstances she should see them again if she saw them ever.

Helen was a Christian girl, and many a time had she prayed in secret that He who rules the deep would keep its waters calm and still while her sister was upon them, and she prayed so now, constantly, burying her face once in her hands, and asking that Katy might come back to them unchanged, if possible, and asking next that God would remove from her heart all bitterness towards the bridegroom, who was to be her brother, and whom, after that short, earnest prayer, she found herself liking better. He loved Katy, she was sure, and that was all she cared for, though she did wish he would release her before twelve o'clock on that night, the last she would spend with them for a long, long time. But Wilford kept her with him in the parlor, kissing away the tears which flowed so fast when she recalled the prayer said by Uncle Ephraim, with her kneeling by him as she might never kneel again. He had called her by her name, and his voice was very sad as he commended her to God, asking that he would "be with our little Katy wherever she might go, keeping her in all the *mewandering* scenes of life, and bringing her at last to his own heavenly home."

Wilford himself was touched, and though he noticed the deacon's pronunciation, he did not even smile, and his manner was very respectful, when, after the prayer was over and they were alone a moment, the white-haired deacon felt it incumbent upon him to say a few words concerning Katy.

"She's a young, rattle-headed creature, not much like your own kin, I guess; but, young man, she is as dear as the apple of our eyes, and I charge you to treat her well. She has never had a crossways word spoke to her all her life, and don't you be the first to speak it, nor let your folks browbeat her."

As they were alone, it was easier for Wilford to be humble and conciliatory, and he promised all the old man required, and then went back to Katy, who was going into raptures over the beautiful little watch which Morris had sent over as her bridal gift from him. Even Mrs. Cameron herself could have found no fault with this, and Wilford praised it as much as Katy could desire, noticing the inscription, " Katy, from Cousin Morris, June 10th, 18—," wishing that after the " Katy " had come the name Cameron, and wondering if Morris had any design in omitting it. Wilford had not yet presented his father's gift, but he did so now, and Katy's tears dropped upon the pale, soft pearls as she whispered, " I shall like your father. I never thought of having things like these."

Nor had she; but she would grow to them very soon, while even the family gathering round and sharing in her joy began to realize how great a lady their Katy was to be. It was late that night ere anybody slept, if sleep at all they did, which was doubtful, unless it were the bride, who, with Wilford's kisses warm upon her lips, crept up to bed just as the clock was striking twelve, nor awoke until it was again chiming six, and over her Helen bent, a dark ring about her eyes and her face very white as she whispered, " Wake, Katy darling, this is your wedding day."

CHAPTER X.

MARRIAGE AT ST. JOHN'S.

THERE were more than a few lookers-on to see Katy Lennox married, and the church was literally jammed for full three-quarters of an hour before the appointed time. Back by the door, where she commanded a full view of the middle aisle, Marian Hazelton sat, her face as white as ashes, and her eyes gleaming strangely wild from beneath the thickly dotted veil she wore over her hat. Doubts as to her wisdom in coming there were agitating her mind, but something kept her sitting just as others sat waiting for the bride until the sexton, opening wide the doors, and assuming an added air of consequence, told the anxious spectators that the party had arrived— Uncle Ephraim and Katy, Wilford and Mrs. Lennox, Dr. Morris and Helen, Aunt Hannah and Aunt Betsy—that was all, and they came slowly up the aisle, while countless eyes were turned upon them, every woman noticing Katy's dress sweeping the carpet with so long a trail, and knowing by some queer female instinct that it was city-made, and not the handiwork of Marian Hazelton, panting for breath in that pew near the door, and trying to forget herself by watching Dr. Grant. She could not have told what Katy wore; she would not have sworn that Katy was there, for she saw only two, Wilford and Morris Grant. She could have touched the former as he passed her by, and she did breathe the odor of his garments while her hands clasped each other tightly, and then she turned to Morris Grant, growing content with her own pain, so much less than his as he stood before the altar with Wilford Cameron between him and the bride which should have been his. How pretty she was in her wedding garb, and how like a bird her voice rang out as she responded to the solemn question,

"Will you have this man to be thy wedded husband," etc.

Upon Uncle Ephraim devolved the duty of giving her away, a thing which Aunt Betsy denounced as a " 'Piscopal quirk," classing it in the same category with dancing. Still if Ephraim had got it to do she wanted him to do it well, and she had taken some pains to study that part of the ceremony, so as to know when to, nudge her brother in case he failed of coming up to time.

"Now, Ephraim, now; they've reached the quirk," she whispered, audibly, almost before Katy's " I will " was heard, clear and distinct; but Ephraim did not need her prompting, and his hand rested lovingly upon Katy's shoulder as he signified his consent, and then fell back to his place next to Hannah. But when Wilford's voice said, " I, Wilford, take thee Katy to be my wedded wife," there was a slight confusion near the door, and those sitting by said to those in front that some one had fainted. Looking round, the audience saw the sexton leading Marian Hazleton out into the open air, where, at her request, he left her, and went back to see the closing of the ceremony which made Katy Lennox a wife. Morris's carriage was at the door, and the newly married pair moved slowly out, Katy smiling upon all, kissing her hand to some and whispering a good-bye to others, her diamonds flashing in the light and her rich silk rustling as she walked, while at her side was Wilford, proudly erect, and holding his head so high as not to see one of the crowd around him, until, arrived at the vestibule, he stopped a moment and was seized by a young man with curling hair, saucy eyes, and that air of ease and assurance which betokens high breeding and wealth.

"Mark Ray!" was Wilford's astonished exclamation, while Mark Ray replied,

"You did not expect to see me here, neither did I expect to come until last night, when I found myself in the little village where you know Scranton lives. Then it occurred to me that as Silverton was only a few miles distant I would drive over and surprise you, but I am too late for the ceremony, I see," and Mark's eyes rested admiringly upon Katy, whose graceful beauty was fully equal to what he had imagined.

Very modestly she received his congratulatory greeting, blushing prettily when he called her by the new name she had not heard before, and then, at a motion from Wilford, entered the carriage waiting for her. Close behind her came Morris and Helen, the former quite as much astonished at meeting Mark as Wilford had been. There was no time for conversation, and hurriedly introducing Helen as Miss Lennox, Morris followed her into the carriage with the bridal pair, and was driven to the depot, where they were joined by Mark, whose pleasant good-humored sallies did much towards making the parting more cheerful than it would otherwise have been. It was sad enough at the most, and Katy's eyes were very red, while Wilford was beginning to look chagrined and impatient, when at last the train swept round the corner and the very last good-bye was said. Many of the village people were there to see Katy off, and in the crowd Mark had no means of distinguishing the Barlows from the others, except it were by the fond caresses given to the bride. Aunt Betsy he had observed from all the rest, both from the hanging of her pongee and the general quaintness of her attire, and thinking it just possible that it might be the lady of herrin' bone memory, he touched Wilford's arm as she passed them by, and said,

"Tell me, Will, quick, who is that woman in the poke bonnet and short, slim dress?"

Wilford was just then too much occupied in his efforts to rescue Katy from the crowd of plebeians who had seized upon her to hear his friend's query, but Helen heard it, and with a cheek which crimsoned with anger, she replied,

"That, sir, is my aunt, Miss Betsy Barlow."

"I beg your pardon, I really do. I was not aware——" Mark began, lifting his hat involuntarily, and mentally cursing himself for his stupidity in not observing who was near to him before asking personal questions.

With a toss of her head Helen turned away, forgetting her resentment in the more absorbing thought that Katy was leaving her.

The bell had rung, the heavy machinery groaned and creaked, and the long train was under way, while from an open window a little white hand was thrust, waving its handkerchief until the husband quietly drew it in, experiencing a feeling of relief that all was over, and that unless he chose his wife need never go back again to that vulgar crowd standing upon the platform and looking with tearful eyes and aching hearts after the fast receding train.

For a moment Mark talked with Morris Grant, explaining how he came there, and adding that on the morrow he too intended going on to Boston, to remain for a few days before Wilford sailed; then, feeling that he must in some way atone for his awkward speech regarding Aunt Betsy, he sought out Helen, still standing like a statue and watching the feathery line of smoke rising above the distant trees. Her bonnet had partially fallen from her head, revealing her bands of rich brown hair and the smooth broad forehead, while her hands were locked together, and a tear trembled on her dark eye-lashes. Taken as a whole she made a striking picture standing apart from the rest and totally oblivious to them all, and Mark gazed at her a moment curiously; then, as her attitude changed and she drew her hat back to its place, he advanced toward her, making some pleasant remark about the morning and the appearance of the country generally. He knew he could not openly apologize, but he made what amends he could by talking to her so familiarly that Helen almost forgot how she hated him and all others who like him lived in New York and resembled Wilford Cameron. It was Mark who led her to the carriage which Morris said was waiting. Mark who handed her in, smoothing down the folds of her dress, and then stood leaning against the door, chatting with Morris, who thought once of asking him to enter and go back to Linwood. But when he remembered how unequal he was to entertaining any one that day, he said merely,

"On your way from Boston, call and see me. I shall be glad of your company then."

"Which means that you do not wish it now," Mark laughingly rejoined, as, offering his hand to both Morris and Helen, he touched his hat and walked away.

CHAPTER XI.

AFTER THE MARRIAGE.

WHY did you invite him to Linwood?" Helen began. "I am sure we have had city guests enough. Oh, if Wilford Cameron had only never come, we should have had Katy now," and the sister-love overcame every other feeling, making Helen cry bitterly as they drove back to the farm-house.

Morris could not comfort her then, and so in silence he left her and went on his way to Linwood. It was well for him that there were many sick ones on his list, for in attending to them he forgot himself in part, so that the day with him passed faster than at the farm-house, where life and its interests seemed suddenly to have stopped. Nothing had power to rouse Helen, who never realized how much she loved her young sister until now, when she listlessly put to rights the room which had been theirs so long, but which was now hers alone. It was a sad task picking up that disordered chamber, bearing so many traces of Katy, and Helen's heart ached terribly as she hung away the little pink calico dressing-gown in

which Katy had looked so prettily, and picked up from
the floor the pile of skirts lying just where they had
been left the previous night; but when it came to the
little half-worn slippers which had been thrown one here
and another there as Katy danced out of them, she could
control herself no longer, and stopping in her work sobbed
bitterly, " Oh, Katy, Katy, how can I live without you ! "
But tears could not bring Katy back, and knowing this,
Helen dried her eyes ere long and joined the family below, who like herself were spiritless and sad.

It was some little solace to them all that day to follow
Katy in her journey, saying, she is at Worcester, or
Framingham, or Newton, and when at noon they sat down
to their dinner in the tidy kitchen they said, " She is in
Boston," and the saying so made the time which had
elapsed since the morning seem interminable. Slowly the
hours dragged, and at last, before the sun-setting, Helen,
who could bear the loneliness of home no longer, stole
across the fields to Linwood, hoping in Morris's compan-
ionship to forget her own grief in part. But Morris was
a sorry comforter then. He had ministered as usual
to his patients that day, listening to their complaints and
answering patiently their inquiries; but amid it all he
walked as in a maze, hearing nothing except the words,
" I, Katy, take thee, Wilford, to be my wedded husband,"
and seeing nothing but the airy little ·figure which stood
up on tiptoe for him to kiss its lips at parting. His work
for the day was over now, and he sat alone in his library
when Helen came hurriedly in, starting at sight of his
face, and asking if he was ill.

" I have had a hard day's work," he said. " I am
always tired at night," and he tried to smile and appear
natural. " Are you very lonely at the farm-house? " he
asked, and then Helen broke out afresh, mourning sometimes for Katy, and again denouncing Wilford as proud
and heartless.

" Positively, Cousin Morris, he acted all the while he
was in the church as if he were doing something of which
he was ashamed; and then did you notice how impatient
he seemed when the neighbors were shaking hands with
Katy at the depot, and bidding her good-bye? He looked

as if he thought they had no right to touch her, she was so much their superior, just because she had married *him*, and he even hurried her away before Aunt Betsy had time to kiss her. And yet the people think it such a splendid match for Katy, because he is so rich and generous. Gave the clergyman fifty dollars and the sexton five, so I heard; but that does not help him with me. I know it's wicked, Morris, but I find myself taking real comfort in hating Wilford Cameron.

"That is wrong, Helen, all wrong," and Morris tried to reason with her; but his arguments this time were not very strong, and he finally said to her, inadvertently, "If *I* can forgive Wilford Cameron for marrying our Katy, you surely ought to do so, for he has hurt *me* the most."

"*You*, Morris! you, you!" Helen kept repeating, standing back still further and further from him, while strange, overwhelming thoughts passed like lightning through her mind as she marked the pallid face, where was written since the morning more than one line of suffering, and saw in the brown eyes a look such as they were not wont to wear. "Morris, tell me—tell me truly—did you love my sister Katy?" and with an impetuous rush Helen knelt beside him, as, laying his head upon the table he answered,

"Yes, Helen. God forgive me if it were wrong. I *did* love your sister Katy, and love her yet, and that is the hardest to bear."

All the tender pitying woman was roused in Helen, and like a sister she smoothed the locks of damp, dark hair, keeping a perfect silence as the strong man, no longer able to bear up, wept like a very child. For a time Helen felt as if bereft of reason, while earth and sky seemed blended in one wild chaos as she thought, "Oh, why couldn't it have been? Why didn't you tell her in time?" and at last she said to him, "If Katy had known it! Oh, Morris, why didn't you tell her? She never guessed it, never! If she had—if she had," Helen's breath came chokingly, "I am very sure—yes, I know *it might have been!*"

"Of all sad words of tongue or pen,
The saddest are these—it might have been."

Morris involuntarily thought of these lines, but they only mocked his sorrow as he answered Helen, " I doubt if you are right; I hope you are not. Katy loved me as her brother, nothing more, I am confident. Had she waited till she was older, God only knows what might have been, but now she is gone and our Father will help me to bear, will help us both, if we ask him, as we must."

And then, as only he could do, Morris talked with Helen until she felt her hardness towards Wilford giving way, while she wondered how Morris could speak so kindly of one who was his rival.

" Not of myself could I do it," Morris said; " but I trust in One who says ' As thy day shall thy strength be,' and He, you know, never fails."

There was a fresh bond of sympathy now between Morris and Helen, and the latter needed no caution against repeating what she had discovered. The secret was safe with her, and by dwelling on what " might have been " she forgot to think so much of what *was,* and so the first days after Katy's departure were more tolerable than she had thought it possible for them to be. At the close of the fourth there came a short note from Katy, who was still in Boston at the Revere, and perfectly happy, she said, going into ecstasies over her husband, the best in the world, and certainly the most generous and indulgent. " Such beautiful things as I am having made," she wrote, " when I already had more than I needed, and so I told him, but he only smiled a queer kind of smile as he said ' Very true; you do not need them.' I wonder then why he gets me more. Oh, I forgot to tell you how much I like his cousin, Mrs. Harvey, who boards at the Revere, and whom Wilford consults about my dress. I am somewhat afraid of her, too, she is so grand, but she pets me a great deal and laughs at my speeches. Mr. Ray is here, and I think him splendid.

" By the way, Helen, I heard him tell Wilford that you had one of the best shaped heads he ever saw, and that he thought you decidedly good looking. I must tell you now of the only thing which troubles me in the least, and I shall get used to that, I suppose. It is so strange Wilford never told me a word until she came. Think of little Katy Lennox with a waiting-maid, who jabbers French half the time, for she speaks that language as well as her own, having been abroad with the family once before. That is why they sent her to me; they knew her services would be invaluable in Paris. Her name is Esther, and she came the day after we did, and brought me such a beautiful mantilla from Wilford's mother, and the loveliest dress. Just the pattern was fifty dollars, she said.

"The steamer sails in three days, and I will write again before that time, sending it by Mr. Ray, who is to stop over one train at Linwood. Wilford has just come in, and says I have written enough for now, but I must tell you he has bought me a diamond pin and ear-rings, which Esther, who knows the value of everything, says never cost less than five hundred dollars.

"Your loving,
KATY CAMERON."

"Five hundred dollars!" and Aunt Betsy held up her hands in horror, while Helen sat a long time with the letter in her hand, cogitating upon its contents, and especially upon the part referring to herself, and what Mark Ray had said of her.

Every human heart is susceptible of flattery, and Helen's was not an exception. Still with her ideas of city men she could not at once think favorably of Mark Ray, just for a few complimentary words which might or might not have been in earnest, and she found herself looking forward with nervous dread to the time when he would stop at Linwood, and of course call on her, as he would bring a letter from Katy.

Very sadly to the inmates of the farm-house rose the morning of the day when Katy was to sail, and as if they could really see the tall masts of the vessel which was to bear her away, the eyes of the whole family were turned often to the eastward with a wistful, anxious gaze, while on their lips and in their hearts were earnest prayers for the safety of that ship and the precious freight it bore. But hours, however sad, will wear themselves away, and so the day went on, succeeded by the night, until that too had passed and another day had come, the second of Katy's ocean life. At the farm-house the work was all done up, and Helen in her neat gingham dress, with her bands of brown hair bound about her head, sat sewing, when she was startled by the sound of wheels, and looking up saw the boy employed to carry packages from the express office, driving to their door with a trunk, which he said had come that morning from Boston.

In some surprise Helen hastened to unlock it with the key which she found appended to it. The trunk was full, and over the whole a linen towel was folded, while on the top of that lay a letter in Katy's hand-writing, directed to Helen, who, sitting down upon the floor, broke the seal and read aloud as follows:

> Boston, June—, Revere House
> "Nearly midnight.

"My Dear Sister Helen:—I have just come in from a little party given by one of Mrs. Harvey's friends, and I am *so* tired, for you know I am not accustomed to such late hours. The party was very pleasant indeed, and everybody was so kind to me, especially Mr. Ray, who stood by me all the time, and who somehow seemed to help me, so that I knew just what to do, and was not awkward at all. I hope not, at least for Wilford's sake.

"You do not know how grand and dignified he is here in Boston among his own set; he is so different from what he was in Silverton that I should be afraid of him if I did not know how much he loves me. He shows that in every action, and I am perfectly happy, except when I think that to-morrow night at this time I shall be on the sea, going away from you all. Here it does not seem far to Silverton, and I often look towards home, wondering what you are doing, and if you miss me any. I wish I could see you once before I go, just to tell you all how much I love you—more than I ever did before, I am sure.

"And now I come to the trunk. I know you will be surprised at its contents, but you cannot be more so than I was when Wilford said I must pack them up and send them back—all the dresses you and Marion made."

"No, oh no!" and Helen felt her strength leave her

wrists in one sudden throb as the letter dropped from her hand, while she tore off the linen covering and saw for herself that Katy had written truly.

She could not weep then, but her face was white as marble as she again took up the letter and commenced at the point where she had broken off.

"It seems that people traveling in Europe do not need many things, but what they have must be just right, and so Mrs. Cameron wrote for Mrs. Harvey to see to my wardrobe, and if I had not exactly what was proper she was to procure it. It is very funny that she did not find a single proper garment among them all, when we thought them so nice. They were not just the style, she said, and that was very desirable in Mrs. Wilford Cameron. Somehow she tries to impress me with the idea that *Mrs. Wilford Cameron* is a very different person from little Katy Lennox, but I can see no difference except that I am a great deal happier and have Wilford all the time.

"Well, as I was telling you, I was measured and fitted, and my figure praised, until my head was nearly turned, only I did not like the horrid stays they put on me, squeezing me up and making me feel so stiff. Mrs. Harvey says no lady does without them, expressing much surprise that I had never worn them, and so I submit to the powers that be; but every chance I get here in my room I take them off and throw them on the floor, where Wilford has stumbled over them two or three times.

"This afternoon the dresses came home, and they do look beautifully, while every one has belt, and gloves, and ribbons, and sashes, and laces or muslins to match—fashionable people are so particular about these things. I have tried them on, and except that I think them too tight, they fit admirably, and *do* give me a different air from what Miss Hazelton's did. But I really believe I like the old ones best, because *you* helped to make them; and when Wilford said I must send them home, I went where he could not see me and cried, because—well, I hardly know why I cried, unless I feared you might feel badly. Dearest Helen, don't, will you? I love you just as much, and shall remember you the same as if I wore the dresses. Dearest sister, I can fancy the look that will come on your face, and I wish I could be present to kiss it away. Imagine me there, will you? with my arms around your neck, and tell mother not to mind. Tell her I never loved her so well as now, and that when I come home from Europe I shall bring her ever so many things. There is a new black silk for her in the trunk, and one for each of the aunties, while for you there is a lovely brown, which Wilford said was just your style, telling me to select as nice a silk as I pleased, and this he did, I think, because he guessed I had been crying. He asked what made my eyes so red, and when I would not tell him he took me with him to the silk store and bade me get what I liked. Oh, he is the dearest, kindest husband, and I love him all the more because I am the least bit afraid of him.

"And now I must stop, for Wilford says so. Dear Helen, dear all of you, I can't help crying as I say good-bye. Remember little Katy, and if she ever did anything bad, don't lay it up against her. Kiss Morris and Uncle Ephraim, and say how much I love them. Darling sister, darling mother, good-bye."

This was Katy's letter, and it brought a gush of tears from the four women remembered so lovingly in it, the mother and the aunts stealing away to weep in secret, without ever stopping to look at the new dresses sent to them by Wilford Cameron. They were very soft, very handsome, especially Helen's rich golden brown, and as she looked at it she felt a thrill of satisfaction in knowing it was hers, but this quickly passed as she took out one by one the garments she had folded with so much care, wondering when Katy would wear each one and where she would be.

"She will never wear them, never—they are not fine enough for her now!" she exclaimed, and as she just then came upon the little plaid, she laid her head upon the trunk lid, while her tears dropped like rain in among the discarded articles condemned by Wilford Cameron.

It seemed to her like Katy's grave, and she was sobbing bitterly, when a step sounded outside the window, and a voice called her name. It was Morris, and lifting up her head Helen said passionately,

"Oh, Morris, look! he has sent back all Katy's clothes, which you bought and I worked so hard to make. They were not good enough for his wife to wear, and so he insulted us. Oh, Katy, I never fully realized till now how wholly she is lost to us!"

"Helen, Helen," Morris kept saying, trying to stop her, for close behind him was Mark Ray, who heard her distinctly, and glancing in, saw her kneeling before the trunk, her pale face stained with tears, and her dark eyes shining with excitement.

Mark Ray understood it at once, feeling indignant at Wilford for thus unnecessarily wounding the sensitive girl, whose expression, as she sat there upon the floor, with her face upturned to Morris, haunted him for months. Mark was sorry for her—so sorry that his first impulse was to go quietly away, and so spare her the mortification of knowing that he had witnessed that little scene; but it was now too late. As she finished speaking her eye fell on him, and coloring scarlet she struggled to her feet, and covering her face with her hands wept still more violently. Mark was in a dilemma, and whispered softly to Morris, "I think I will leave. You can tell her all I had to say;" but Helen heard him, and mastering her agitation, she said to him,

"Please, Mr. Ray, don't go—not yet at least, not till I have asked you of Katy. Did you see her off? Has she gone?"

Thus importuned Mark Ray came in, and sitting down where his boot almost touched the new brown silk, he very politely began to answer her rapid questions, putting her entirely at her ease by his pleasant, affable manner, and making her forget the littered appearance of the room, as she listened to his praises of her sister, who, he said, seemed so very happy, and attracted universal admiration wherever she went. No allusion whatever was made to the trunk during the time of Mark's stay, which was not long. If he took the next train to New York, he had but an hour more to spend, and feeling that Helen would rather he should spend it at Linwood he soon arose to go. Offering his hand to Helen, there passed from his eyes into hers a look which had over her a strangely quieting influence, and prepared her for a remark which otherwise might have seemed out of place.

"I have known Wilford Cameron for years; he is my best friend, and I respect him as a brother. In some things he may be peculiar, but he will make your sister a kind husband. He loves her devotedly, I know, choosing her from the throng of ladies who would gladly have taken her place. I hope you will like him for *my* sake as well as Katy's."

His warm hand unclasped from Helen's, and with another good-bye he was gone, without seeing either Mrs. Lennox, Aunt Hannah or Aunt Betsy. This was not the time for extending his acquaintance, he knew, and he went away with Morris, feeling that the farm-house, so far as he could judge, was not exactly what Wilford had pictured it. But then he came for a wife, and I did not," he thought, while Helen's face came before him as it looked up to Morris, and he wondered, were he obliged to choose between the sisters, which he should prefer. During the few days passed in Boston he had become more than half in love with Katy himself, almost envying his friend the pretty little creature he had won. She was very beautiful and very fascinating in her simplicity, but there was something in Helen's face more attractive than mere beauty, and Mark said to Morris as they walked along,

"Miss Lennox is not much like her sister."

"Not much, no; but Helen is a splendid girl—more strength of character, perhaps, than Katy, who is younger than her years even. She has always been petted from babyhood; it will take time or some great sorrow to show what she really is."

This was Morris's reply, and the two then proceeded on in silence until they reached the boundary line between Morris's farm and Uncle Ephraim's, where they found the deacon mending a bit of broken fence, his coat lying on a pile of stones, and his wide, blue cotton trowsers hanging loosely around him. When told who Mark was, and that he brought news of Katy, he greeted him cordially, and sitting down upon his fence listened to all Mark had to say. Between the old and young man there seemed at once a mutual liking, the former saying to himself as Mark went on, and he resumed his work,

"I most wish it was this chap with Katy on the sea. I like his looks the best," while Mark's thoughts were,

"Will need not be ashamed of that man, though I don't suppose *I* should really want him coming suddenly in among a drawing-room full of guests."

Morris did not feel much like entertaining Mark, but Mark was fully competent to entertain himself, and thought the hour spent at Linwood a very pleasant one, half wishing for some excuse to tarry longer; but there was none, and so at the appointed time he bade Morris good-bye and went on his way to New York.

CHAPTER XII.

FIRST MONTHS OF MARRIED LIFE.

If Katy's letters, written, one on board the steamer and another from London, were to be trusted, she was as nearly perfectly happy as a young bride well can be, and the people at the farm-house felt themselves more and more kindly disposed towards Wilford Cameron with each letter received. They were going soon into the northern part of England, and from thence into Scotland, Katy wrote from London, and two weeks after found them comfortably settled at the inn at Alnwick, near to Alnwick Castle. Wilford had seemed very anxious to get there, leaving London before Katy was quite ready, and hurrying across the country until Alnwick was reached. He had been there before, years ago, he said, but no one seemed to recognize him, though all paid due respect to the distinguished looking American and his beautiful young wife. An entrance into Alnwick Castle was easily obtained, and Katy felt that all her girlish dreams of grandeur and magnificence were more than realized here in this home of the Percys, where ancient and modern styles of architecture and furnishing were so blended together. She would never tire of that place, she thought, but Wilford's taste led him elsewhere, and he took more delight in wandering around St. Mary's church, which stood upon a hill commanding a view of the castle and of the surrounding

country for miles away. Here Katy also came, rambling
with him through the village grave-yard where slept the
dust of centuries, the grey, mossy tomb-stones bearing
date backward for more than a hundred years, their quaint
inscriptions both puzzling and amusing Katy, who studied
them by the hour.

One quiet summer morning, however, when the heat
was unusually great, she felt too listless to wander about,
and so sat upon the grass, listening to the birds as they
sang above her head, while Wilford, at some distance from
her, stood leaning against a tree and thinking sad, re-
gretful thoughts, as his eye rested upon the rough headstone at his feet.

" Genevra Lambert, aged 22," was the lettering upon
it, and as he read it a feeling of reproach was in his
heart, while he said, " I hope I am not glad to know that
she is dead."

He had come to Alnwick for the sole purpose of finding
that humble grave—of assuring himself that after life's
fitful fever, Genevra Lambert slept quietly, forgetful of
the wrong once done to her by him. It is true he had not
doubted her death before, but as seeing was believing, so
now he felt sure of it, and plucking from the turf above
her a little flower growing there, he· went back to Katy
and sitting down beside her with his arm around her
waist, tried to devise some way of telling her what he had
promised himself he would tell her there in that very
yard, where Genevra was buried. But the task was harder
now than before. Katy was so happy with him, trusting
his love so fully that he dared not lift the veil and read to
her that page hinted at once in Silverton, when they sat
beneath the butternut tree, with the fresh young grass
springing around them. Then she was not his wife, and
the fear that she would not be if he told her all had kept
him silent, but now she was his alone; nothing could undo
that, and there, in the shadow of the grey old church
through whose aisles Genevra had been borne out to where
the rude headstone was gleaming in the English sunlight,
it seemed meet that he should tell the sad story. And Katy
would have forgiven him then, for not a shadow of regret
had darkened her life since it was linked with his, and in

her perfect love she could have pardoned much. But Wilford did not tell. It was not needful, he made himself believe—not necessary for her ever to know that once he met a maiden called Genevra, almost as beautiful as she, but never so beloved. *No, never.* Wilford said that truly, when that night he bent over his sleeping Katy, comparing her face with Genevra's, and his love for her with his love for Genevra.

Wilford was very fond of his girlish wife, and very proud of her, too, when strangers paused, as they often did, to look back after her. Thus far nothing had arisen to mar the happiness of his first weeks of married life, except the letters from Silverton, over which Katy always cried, until he sometimes wished that the family could not write. But they could and they did; even Aunt Betsy inclosed in Helen's letter a note, wonderful both in orthography and composition, and concluding with the remark that "she would be glad when Catherine returned and was settled in a home of her own, as she would then have a new place to visit."

There was a dark frown on Wilford's face, and for a moment he felt tempted to withhold the note from Katy, but this he could not do then, so he gave it into her hands, watching her as with burning cheeks, she read it through, and asking her at its close why she looked so red.

"Oh, Wilford," and she crept closely to him, "Aunt Betsy spells so queerly, that I was wishing you would not always open my letters first. Do all husbands do so?"

It was the only time Katy had ventured to question a single act of his, submitting without a word to whatever was his will. Wilford knew that his father would never have presumed to break a seal belonging to his mother, but he had broken Katy's, and he should continue breaking them, so he answered, laughingly,

"Why, yes, I guess they do. My little wife has surely no secrets to hide from me?"

"No secrets," Katy answered, "only I did not want you to see Aunt Betsy's letter, that's all."

"I did not marry Aunt Betsy—I married you," was Wilford's reply, which meant far more than Katy guessed.

With three thousand miles between him and his wife's

relatives, Wilford could endure to think of them; but whenever letters came to Katy bearing the Silverton postmark, he was conscious of a far different sensation from what he experienced when the postmark was New York and the handwriting that of his own family. But not in any way did this feeling manifest itself to Katy, who, as she always wrote to Helen, was very, very happy, and never more so, perhaps, than while they were at Alnwick, where, as if he had something for which to atone, he was unusually kind and indulgent, caressing her with unwonted tenderness, and making her ask him once if he loved her a great deal more now than when they were first married.

"Yes, darling, a great deal more," was Wilford's answer, as he kissed her upturned face, and then went for the last time to Genevra's grave; for on the morrow they were to leave the neighborhood of Alnwick for the heather blooms of Scotland.

There was a trip to Edinburgh, a stormy passage across the Straits of Dover, a two months' sojourn in Paris, and then they went to Rome, where Wilford intended to pass the winter, journeying in the spring through different parts of Europe. He was in no haste to return to America; he would rather stay where he could have Katy all to himself, away from her family and his own. But it was not so to be, and not very long after his arrival at Rome there came a letter from his mother apprising him of his father's dangerous illness, and asking him to come home at once. The elder Cameron had not been well since Wilford left the country, and the physician was fearful that the disease had assumed a consumptive form, Mrs. Cameron wrote, adding that her husband's only anxiety was to see his son again. To this there was no demur, and about the first of December, six months from the time he had sailed, Wilford arrived in Boston, having taken a steamer for that city. His first act was to telegraph for news of his father, receiving in reply that he was better; the alarming symptoms had disappeared, and there was now great hope of his recovery.

"We might have stayed longer in Europe," Katy said, feeling a little chill of disappointment—not that her father-in-law was better, but at being called home for nothing, when her life abroad was so happy and free from care.

Somehow the atmosphere of America seemed different from what it used to be. It was colder, bluer, the little lady said, tapping her foot uneasily and looking from her windows at the Revere out upon the snowy streets, through which the wintry wind was blowing in heavy gales.

"Yes, it is a heap colder," she siged, as she returned to the large chair which Esther had drawn for her before the cheerful fire, charging her disquiet to the weather, but never dreaming of imputing it to her husband, who was far more its cause than was the December cold.

He, too, though glad of his father's improvement, was sorry to have been recalled for nothing to a country which brought his old life back again, with all its forms and ceremonies, and revived his dread lest Katy should not acquit herself as was becoming Mrs. Wilford Cameron. In his selfishness he had kept her almost wholly to himself, so that the polish she was to acquire from her travels abroad was not as perceptible as he could desire. Katy was Katy still, in spite of London, Paris, or Rome. To be sure there was about her a little more maturity and self-assurance, but in all essential points she was the same: and Wilford winced as he thought how the free, impulsive manner which, among the Scottish hills, where there was no one to criticize, had been so charming to him, would shock his lady mother and sister Juno. And this it was which made him moody and silent, replying hastily to Katy when she said to him, " Please, Wilford, telegraph to Helen to be with mother at the West depot when we pass there to-morrow. The train stops five minutes, you know, and I want to see them so much. Will you, Wilford? "

She had come up to him now, and was standing behind him, with her hands upon his shoulder; so she did not see the expression of his face as he answered quickly.

" Yes, yes."

A moment after he quitted the room ,and it was then that Katy, standing before the window, charged the day with what was strictly Wilford's fault. Returning at last to her chair she went off into a reverie as to the new

home to which she was going and the new friends she was
to meet, wondering what they would think of her, and if
they would like her. Once she had said to Wilford,

" Which of your sisters shall I like best? "

And Wilford had answered her by asking,

" Which do you like best, *books* or going to parties in
full dress? "

" Oh, parties and dress," Katy had said, and Wilford
had then rejoined,

" You will like Juno best, for she is all fashion and
gayety, while Blue-Bell prefers her books and the quiet
of her own room."

Katy felt afraid of Bell, and in fact, now that they
were so near, she felt afraid of them all, notwithstanding
Esther's assurances that they could not help loving her.
During the six months they had been together Esther had
learned to feel for her young lady that strong affection
which sometimes exists between mistress and servant.
Everything which she could do for her she did, smoothing
as much as possible the meeting which she also dreaded,
for though the Camerons were too proud to express before
her their opinion of Wilford's choice, she had guessed it
readily, and pitied the young wife brought up with ideas
so different from those of her husband's family. More
accustomed to Wilford's moods than Katy, she saw that
something was the matter, and it prompted her to unusual
attentions, stirring the fire into a cheerful blaze and bring-·
ing a stool for Katy, who, in blissful ignorance of her
husband's real feelings, sat waiting his return from the
telegraph office whither she supposed he had gone, and
building pleasant pictures of to-morrow's meeting with her
mother and Helen, and possibly Dr. Morris, if not Uncle
Ephraim himself.

So absorbed was she in her reverie as not to hear
Wilford's step as he came in, but when he stood behind
her and took her head playfully between his hands, she
started up, feeling that the weather had changed; it was
not as cold and dreary in Boston as she imagined, and
laying her head on Wilford's shoulder, she said,

" You went out to telegraph, didn't you? "

He had gone out with the intention of telegraphing as

she desired, but in the hall below he had met with an old acquaintance who talked with him so long that he entirely forgot his errand until Katy recalled it to his mind, making him feel very uncomfortable as he frankly told her of his forgetfulness.

"It is too late now," he added, "besides you could only see them for a moment, just long enough to make you cry—a thing I do not greatly desire, inasmuch as I wish my wife to look her best when I present her to my family, and with red eyes she couldn't, you know."

Katy knew it was settled, and choking back the tears, she tried to listen, while Wilford, having fairly broken the ice with regard to his family, told her how anxious he was that she should make a good first impression upon his mother. Did Katy remember that Mrs. Morey whom they met at Paris, and could she not throw a little of *her air* into her manner, that is, could she not drop her girlishness when in the presence of others and be a little more dignified? When alone with him he liked to have her just what she was, a loving, affectionate little wife, but the world looked on such things differently. Would Katy try?

Wilford when he commenced had no definite idea as to what he should say, and without meaning it he made Katy moan piteously.

"I don't know what you mean. I would do anything if I knew how. Tell me, how *shall* I be dignified?"

She was crying so hard that Wilford, while mentally calling himself a fool and a brute, could only try to comfort her, telling her she need not be anything but what she was—that his mother and sisters would love her just as he did—and that daily association with them would teach her all that was necessary.

Katy's tears were stopped at last; but the frightened, anxious look did not leave her face, even though Wilford tried his best to divert her mind. A nervous terror of her new relations had gained possession of her heart, and nearly the entire night she lay awake, pondering in her mind what Wilford had said, and thinking how terrible it would be if he should be disappointed in her after all. The consequence of this was that a very white

tired face sat opposite Wilford next morning at the breakfast served in their private parlor; nor did it look much
fresher even after they were in the cars and rolling out of
Boston. But when Worcester was reached, and the old
home way-marks began to grow familiar, the color came
stealing back, until the cheeks burned with an unnatural
red, and the blue eyes fairly danced as they rested on the
hills of Silverton.

"Only three miles from mother and Helen! Oh, if I
could go there!" Katy thought, working her fingers nervously; but the express train did not pause there, and it
went so swiftly by the depot that Katy could hardly distinguish who was standing there, whether friend or stranger.

But when at last they came to West Silverton, and the
long train slowly stopped, the first object she saw was
Dr. Morris, driving down from the village. He had no
intention of going to the depot, and only checked his
horse a moment, lest it should prove restive if too near
the engine; but when a clear young voice called from the
window, "Morris! oh, Cousin Morris! I've come!" his
heart gave a great throb, for he knew whose voice it was
and whose the little hand beckoning to him. He had
supposed her far away beneath Italian skies, for at the
farm-house no intelligence had been received of her intended return, and in much surprise he reined up to the
rear-door, and throwing his lines to a boy, went forward
to where Katy stood, her face glowing with delight as
she flew into his arms, wholly forgetful of the last night's
lecture on dignity, and also forgetful of Wilford, standing close beside her. He had not tried to hold her back
when, at the sight of Morris, she sprang away from him;
but he followed after, biting his lip, and wishing she had
a little more discretion. Surely it was not necessary to
nalf strangle Dr. Grant as she was doing, kissing his
hand after she had kissed his face a full half dozen times,
and all the people looking on. But Katy did not care
for people. She only knew that Morris was there—the
Morris whom, in her great happiness abroad, she had
perhaps slighted by not writing directly to him but once.
In Wilford's sheltering care she had not felt the need of
this good cousin, as she used to do; but she was so glad

to see him, wondering why he looked so thin and sad. Was he sick? she asked, with a pitying look, which made him shiver as he answered,

"No, not sick, though tired, perhaps, as I have at present an unusual amount of work to do."

And this was true—he was unusually busy. But that was not the cause of his thin face, which others than Katy remarked. Helen's words, "It might have been,' spoken to him on the night of Katy's bridal, had never left his mind, much as he had tried to dislodge them. Some men can love a dozen times; but it was not so with Morris. He could overcome his love so that it should not be a sin, but no other could ever fill the place where Katy had been; and as he looked along the road through life he felt that he must travel it alone. Truly, if Katy were not yet passing through the fire, he was, and it had left its mark upon him, purifying as it burned, and bringing his every act into closer submission to his God. Only Helen and Marian Hazelton interpreted aright that look upon his face, and knew it came from the hunger of his heart, but they kept silence; while others said that he was working far too hard, urging him to abate his unwearied labors, for they would not lose their young physician yet. But Morris smiled his patient, kindly smile on all their fears and went his way, doing his work as one who knew he must render strict account for the popularity he was daily gaining, both in his own town and those around. He could think of Katy now without a sin, but he was not thinking of her when she came so unexpectedly upon him, and for an instant she almost bore his breath away in her vehement joy.

Quick to note a change in those he knew, he saw that her form was not quite so full, nor her cheeks so round; but she was weary with the voyage, and knowing how sea-sickness will wear upon one's strength, Morris imputed it wholly to that, and believed she was, as she professed to be, perfectly happy.

"Come, Katy, we must go now," Wilford said, as the bell rang its first alarm, and the passengers, some with sandwiches and some with fried cakes in their hands, ran back to find their seats.

"Yes, I know, but I have not asked half I meant to. Oh, how I want to go home with you, Morris," Katy exclaimed, again throwing her arms around the doctor's neck as she bade him good bye, and sent fresh messages of love to the friends at home, who, had they known she was to be there at that time, would have walked the entire distance for the sake of looking once more into her dear face.

"I intended to have brought them heaps of things," she said, "but we came home so suddenly I had no time. Here, take Helen this. Tell her it is *real*," and the impulsive creature drew from her finger a small diamond set in black enamel, which Wilford had bought in Paris.

"She did not need it; she had two more, and she was sure Wilford would not mind," she said, turning to him for his approbation.

But Wilford did mind, and his face indicated as much, although he tried to be natural as he replied, "Certainly, send it if you like."

In her excitement Katy did not observe it, but Morris did, and he at first declined taking it, saying Helen had no use for it, and would be better pleased with something not half as valuable. Katy, however, insisted, appealing to Wilford, who, ashamed of his first emotion, now seemed quite as anxious as Katy herself, until Morris placed the ring in his purse, and then bade Katy hasten or she would certainly be left. One more wave of the hand, one more kiss thrown from the window, and the train moved on, Katy feeling like a different creature for having seen some one from home.

"I am so glad I saw him—so glad I sent the ring, for now they will know I am the same Katy Lennox, and I think Helen sometimes feared I might get proud with you," she said, while Wilford pulled her rich fur around her, smiling to see how bright and pretty she was looking since that meeting with Dr. Grant. "It was better than medicine," Katy said, when beyond Springfield he referred to it a second time, and leaning her head upon his shoulder she fell into a refreshing sleep, from which she did not waken until New York was reached, and Wilford, lifting her gently up, whispered to her, "Come, darling, we are home at last."

CHAPTER XIII.

KATY'S FIRST EVENING IN NEW YORK.

THE elder Cameron was really better, and more than once he had regretted recalling his son, who he knew had contemplated a longer stay abroad. But that could not now be helped. Wilford had arrived in Boston, as his telegram of yesterday announced—he would be at home to-day; and No.—Fifth Avenue was all the morning and a portion of the afternoon the scene of unusual excitement, for both Mrs. Cameron and her daughters wished to give the six months' wife a good impression of her new home. At first they thought of inviting company to dinner, but to this the father objected. "Katy should not be troubled the first day," he said; "it was bad enough for her to meet them all; they could ask Mark if they chose, but no one else."

And so only Mark Ray was invited to the dinner, gotten up as elaborately as if a princess had been expected instead of little Katy, trembling in every joint when, about four P. M., Wilford awoke her at the depot and whispered, "Come, darling, we are home at last."

"Why do you shiver so?" he asked, wrapping her cloak around her, and almost lifting her from the car.

"I don't—know. I guess—I'm cold," and Katy drew a long breath as she thought of Silverton and the farm-house, wishing that she was going into its low-walled kitchen, instead of the handsome carriage, where the cushions were so soft and yielding, and the whole effect so grand.

"What would our folks say?" she kept repeating to herself as she drove along the streets, where they were beginning to light the street lamps, for the December day was dark and cloudy. It seemed so like a dream, that she, who once had picked huckleberries on the Silverton hills, and bound coarse heavy shoes to buy herself a pink gingham dress, should now be riding in her carriage toward the home which she knew was magnificent; and Katy's tears fell like rain as, nestling close to Wilford, who asked what was the matter, she whispered, "I can hardly believe that it is I—it is so unreal."

"Please don't cry," Wilford rejoined, brushing her tears away. "You know I don't like your eyes to be red."

With a great effort Katy kept her tears back, and was very calm when they reached the brown-stone front, far enough up town to save it from the slightest approach to plebeianism. In the hall the chandelier was burning, and as the carriage stopped a flame of light seemed suddenly to burst from every window as the gas heads were turned up, so that Katy caught glimpses of rich silken curtains and costly lace as she went up the steps, clinging to Wilford and looking ruefully around for Esther, who had disappeared through the basement door. Another moment and they stood within the marbled hall, Katy conscious of nothing definite—nothing but a vague atmosphere of refined elegance, and that a richly-dressed lady came out to meet them, kissing Wilford quietly and calling him her son; that the same lady turned to her saying kindly, "And this is my new daughter?"

Then Katy came to life, and did that, at the very thought of which she shuddered when a few months' experience had taught her the temerity of the act—she wound her arms impulsively around Mrs. Cameron's neck, rumpling her point lace collar, and sadly displacing the coiffure of the astonished lady, who had seldom received so genuine a greeting as that which Katy gave her, kissing her lips and whispering softly, "I love you now, because you are Wilford's mother, but by and by because you are mine. And you *will* love me some because I am his wife."

Wilford was horrified, particularly when he saw how startled his mother looked as she tried to release herself and adjust her tumbled head-gear. It was not what he had hoped, nor what his mother had expected, for she was unaccustomed to such demonstrations; but under the circumstances Katy could not have done better. There was a tender spot in Mrs. Cameron's heart, and Katy touched it, making her feel a throb of affection for the childish creature suing for her love.

"Yes, darling, I love you now," she said, removing Katy's clinging arms and taking care that they should not enfold her a second time. "You are tired and cold," she continued; "and had better go at once to your rooms. I will send Esther up. There is plenty of time to dress for dinner," and with a wave of her hand she dismissed Katy up the stairs, noticing as she went the exquisite softness of her fur cloak; but thinking it too heavy a garment for her slight figure, and noticing, too, the graceful ankle and foot which the little high-heeled gaiter showed to good advantage. "I did not see her face distinctly, but she has a well-turned instep and walks easily," was the report she carried to her daughters, who, in their own room over Katy's, were dressing for dinner.

"She will undoubtedly make a good dancer, then, unless, like Dr. Grant, she is too blue for that," Juno said, while Bell shrugged her shoulders, congratulating herself that she had a mind above such frivolous matters as dancing and well-turned insteps, and wondering if Katy cared in the least for books.

"Couldn't you see her face at all, mother?" Juno asked.

"Scarcely; but the glimpse I did get was satisfactory. I think she is pretty."

And this was all the sisters could ascertain until their toilets were finished, and they went down into the library, where their brother waited for them, kissing them both affectionately, and complimenting them on their good looks.

"I wish we could say the same of you," Juno answered, playfully pulling his moustache; "but upon my word, Will, you are fast settling down into an oldish married man, even turning gray," and she ran her fingers through his dark hair, where there was now and then a thread of silver. "Disappointed in your domestic relations, eh?" she continued, looking him archly in the face.

Wilford was rather proud of his good looks, and during his sojourn aboard, Katy had not helped him any in overcoming this weakness, but on the contrary, had fed his

vanity by constant flattery. And still he was himself conscious of not looking quite as well as usual just now, for
the sea voyage had tired him as well as Katy, but he did
not care to be told of it, and Juno's ill-timed remarks
roused him at once, particularly as they reflected somewhat on Katy.

"I assure you I am not disappointed," he answered,
"and the six months of my married life have been the hap-
piest I ever knew. Katy is more than I expected her to
be."

Juno elevated her eyebrows slightly, but made no direct
reply, while Bell began to ask about Paris and the places
he had visited.

Meanwhile Katy had been ushered into her room, which
was directly over the library, and separated from Mrs.
Cameron's only by a range of closets and presses, a portion of which were to be appropriated to her own use.
Great pains had been taken to make her rooms attractive,
and as the large bay window in the library below extended
to the third story, it was really the pleasantest chamber in
the house. To Katy it was perfect, and her first exclamation was one of delight.

"Oh, how pleasant, how beautiful!" she cried, skipping
across the soft carpet to the warm fire blazing in the grate.
"A bay window, too, when I like them so much. I shall
be happy here."

But happy as she was, Katy could not help feeling tired,
and she sank into one of the luxurious easy-chairs, wishing
she could stay there all the evening instead of going down
to that formidable dinner with her new relations. How
she dreaded it, especially when she remembered that Mrs.
Cameron had said there would be plenty of time to *dress*
—a thing which Katy hated, the process was so tiresome,
particularly to-night. Surely her handsome traveling
dress, made in Paris, was good enough, and she was about
settling in her own mind to venture upon wearing it, when
Esther demolished her castle at once.

"Wear your traveling habit!" she exclaimed, "when
the young ladies, especially Miss Juno, are so particular
about their dinner costume. There would be no end to
the scolding I should get for suffering it," and she began

good-naturedly to remove her mistress's collar and pin, while Katy, standing up, sighed as she said, " I wish I was in Silverton to-night. I could wear anything there. What must I put on? How I dread it! " and she began to shiver again.

Fortunately for Katy, Esther had been in the family long enough to know just what they regarded proper, a? by this means the dress selected was sure to please. It was very becoming to Katy, and having been made in Paris was not open to criticism.

" Very pretty indeed," was Mrs. Cameron's verdict, when at half-past five she came in to see her daughter, kissing her cheek and stroking her head, wholly unadorned except by the short, silken curls which could not be coaxed to grow faster than they chose, and which had sometimes annoyed Wilford, they made his wife seem so young beside him. Mrs. Cameron was annoyed, too, for she had no idea of a head except as it was connected with a hairdresser, and her annoyance showed itself as she asked,

" Did you have your hair cut on purpose? "

But when Katy explained, she answered pleasantly,

" Never mind, it is a fault which will mend every day, only it makes you look like a child."

" I am eighteen and a half," Katy said, feeling a lump rising in her throat, for she guessed that her mother-in-law was not quite pleased with her hair.

For herself, she liked it, it was so easy to brush and fix. She should go wild if she had to submit to all Esther had told her of hair-dressing and what it involved.

Mrs. Cameron had asked if she would not like to see Mr. Cameron, the elder, before going down to dinner, and Katy had answered that she would; so as soon as Esther had smoothed a refractory fold and brought her handkerchief, she followed to the room where Wilford's father was sitting. He might not have felt complimented could he have known that something in his appearance reminded Katy of Uncle Ephraim. He was not nearly as old or as tall, nor was his hair as white, but the resemblance, if there were any, lay in the smile with which he greeted Katy, calling her his youngest child, and drawing her closely to him.

It was remarked of Mr. Cameron that since their baby-hood he had never kissed one of his own children; but when Katy, who looked upon such a salutation as a matter of course, put up her rosy lips, making the first advance, he kissed her twice. Hearty, honest kisses they were, for the man was strongly drawn towards the young girl, who said to him timidly,

"I am glad to have a father—mine died before I could remember him. May I call you so?"

"Yes, yes; God bless you, my child," and Mr. Cameron's voice shook as he said it, for neither Bell nor Juno were wont to address him just as Katy did—Katy, standing close to him, with her hand upon his shoulder and her kiss fresh upon his lips.

She had already crept a long way into his heart, and he took her hand from his shoulder and holding it between his own, said to her,

"I did not think you were so small or young. You are my little daughter, my baby, instead of my son's wife. How do you ever expect to fulfill the duties of Mrs. Wilford Cameron?"

"It's my short hair, sir. I am not so young," Katy answered, her eyes filling with tears as she began to wish back the thick curls Helen cut away when the fever was at its height.

"Never mind, child," Mr. Cameron rejoined playfully. "Youth is no reproach; there's many a one would give their right hand to be young like you. Juno for instance, who is—"

"Hus-band!" came reprovingly from Mrs. Cameron, spoken as only she could speak it, with a prolonged buzzing sound on the first syllable, and warning the husband that he was venturing too far.

"It is time to go down if Mrs. Cameron sees the young ladies before dinner," she said, a little stiffly; whereupon her better half startled Katy with the exclamation,

"Mrs. Cameron! Thunder and lightning! wife, call her Katy, and don't go into any nonsense of that kind."

The lady reddened, but said nothing until she reached the hall, when she whispered to Katy, apologetically,

"Don't mind it. He is rather irritable since his illness, and sometimes makes use of coarse language."

Katy had been a little frightened at the outburst, but she liked Mr. Cameron notwithstanding, and her heart was lighter as she went down to the library, where Wilford met her at the door, and taking her on his arm led her in to his sisters, holding her back as he presented her, lest she should assault them as she had his mother. But Katy felt no desire to hug the tall, queenly girl whom Wilford introduced as Juno, and whose black eyes seemed to read her through as she offered her hand and very daintily kissed her forehead, murmuring something about a welcome to New York. Bell came next, broad-faced, plainer-looking Bell, who yet had many pretentions to beauty, but whose manner, if possible, was frostier, cooler than her sister's. Of the two Katy liked Juno best, for there was about her a flash and sparkle very fascinating to one who had never seen anything of the kind, and did not know that much of this vivacity was the result of patient study and practice. Katy would have known they were high bred, as the world defines high breeding, and something in their manner reminded her of the ladies she had seen abroad, ladies in whose veins lordly blood was flowing. She could not help feeling uncomfortable in their presence, especially as she felt that Juno's black eyes were on her constantly. Not that she could ever meet them looking at her, for they darted away the instant hers were raised, but she knew just when they returned to her again, and how closely they were scanning her.

"Your wife looks tired, Will. Let her sit down," Bell said, herself wheeling the easy-chair nearer to the fire, while Wilford placed Katy in it; then, thinking she would get on better if he were not there, he left the room, and Katy was alone with her new sisters.

Juno had examined her dress and found no fault with it, simply because it was Parisian made; while Bell had examined her head, deciding that there might be something in it, though she doubted it, but that at all events short hair was very becoming to it, showing all its fine proportions, and half deciding to have her own locks cut away. Juno had a similar thought, wondering if it were the Paris fashion, and if she would look as young in proportion as Katy did were her hair worn on her neck.

With their brother's departure the tongues of both the girls were loosened, and standing near to Katy they began to question her of what she had seen, Juno asking if she did not hate to leave Italy, and did not wish herself back again. Wholly truthful, Katy answered, "Oh, yes, I would rather be there than home."

"Complimentary to us, very," Bell murmured audibly in French, blushing as Katy's eyes were lifted quickly to hers, and she knew she was understood.

If there was anything which Katy liked more than another in the way of study, it was French. She had excelled in it at Canandaigua, and while abroad had taken great pains to acquire a pure pronunciation, so that she spoke it with a good deal of fluency, and readily comprehended Bell.

"I did not mean to be rude," she said, earnestly. "I liked Italy so much, and we expected to stay longer; but that does not hinder my liking to be here. I hope I did not offend you."

"Certainly not; you are an honest little puss," Bell replied, placing her hand caressingly upon the curly head laying back so wearily on the chair. "Here in New York we have a bad way of not telling the whole truth, but you will soon be used to it."

"Used to not telling the truth! Oh, I hope not!" and this time the blue eyes lifted so wonderingly to Bell's face had in them a startled look.

"Simpleton!" was Juno's mental comment, while Bell's was, "I like the child," as she continued to smooth the golden curls and wind them round her finger, wondering if Katy had a taste for metaphysics, that being the last branch of science which she had taken up.

"I suppose you find Will a pattern husband," Juno said after a moment's pause, and Katy replied, "There never could be a better, I am sure, and I have been very happy."

"Has he never said one cross word to you in all these

six months?" was Juno's next question, to which Katy answered truthfully, "Never."

"And lets you do as you please?"

"Yes, just as I please," Katy replied, while Juno continued, "He must have changed greatly then from what he used to be; but marriage has probably improved him. He tells you all his *secrets,* too, I presume?"

Anxious that Wilford should appear well in every light, Katy replied at random, "Yes, if he has any."

"Well, then," and in Juno's black eyes there was a wicked look, "perhaps you will tell me who was or is the original of that picture he guards so carefully."

"What picture?" and Katy looked up inquiringly, while Juno, with a little sarcastic laugh, continued: "Oh, he has not told you then. I thought he would not, he was so angry when he saw me with it three or four years ago. I found it in his room where he had accidentally left it, and was looking at it when he came in. It was the picture of a young girl who must have been very beautiful, and I did not blame Will for loving her if he ever did, but he need not have been so indignant at me for wishing to know who it was. I never saw him so angry or so much disturbed. I hope you will ferret the secret out and tell me, for I have a great deal of curiosity, fancying that picture had something to do with his remaining so long a bachelor. I do not mean that he does not love you," she added, as she saw how white Katy grew. "It is not to be expected that a man can live to be thirty without loving more than one. There was Sybil Grey, a famous belle, whom I thought at one time he would marry; but when Judge Grandon offered she accepted, and Will was left in the lurch. I do not really believe he cared though, for Sybil was too much of a flirt to suit his jealous lordship, and I will do him the justice to say that however many fancies he may have had, he likes you the best of all;" and this Juno felt constrained to say because of the look in Katy's face, which warned her that in her thoughtlessness she had gone too far and pierced the young wife's heart with a pang as cruel as it was unnecessary.

Bell had tried to stop her, but she had rattled on until

now it was too late, and she could not recall her words, however much she might wish to do so. "Don't tell Will," she was about to say, when Will himself appeared, to take Katy out to dinner. Very beautiful and sad were the blue eyes which looked up at him so wistfully, and nothing but the remembrance of Juno's words, "He likes you best of all," kept Katy from crying outright, when he took her hand, and asked if she was tired.

"Let us try what dinner will do for you," he said, and in silence Katy went with him to the dining-room, where the glare and the ceremony bewildered her, bringing a homesick feeling as she thought of Silverton, and the plain tea-table, graced with the mulberry set instead of the costly china before her.

Never had Katy felt so embarrassed as she did when seated for the first time at dinner in her husband's home, with all those criticising eyes upon her. She had been very hungry, but her appetite was gone and she almost loathed the rich food offered her, feeling so glad when the dinner was ended, and Wilford took her to the parlor, where she found Mark Ray waiting for her. He had been obliged to decline Mrs. Cameron's invitation to dinner, but had come as early as possible after it, and Katy was delighted to see him, for she remembered how he had helped her during that week of gayety in Boston, when society was so new to her. As he had been then, so he was now, and his friendly manner put Katy as much at her ease as it was possible for her to be in the presence of Wilford's mother and sisters.

"I suppose you have not seen your sister Helen? You know I called there," Mark said to Katy; but before she could reply, a pair of black eyes shot a keen glance at luckless Mark, and Juno's sharp voice said quickly, "I did not know you had the honor of Miss Lennox's acquaintance."

Mark was in a dilemma. He had kept his call at Silverton to himself, as he did not care to be questioned about Katy's family; and now, when it accidentally came out, he tried to make some evasive reply, pretending that he had spoken of it, and Juno had forgotten. But Juno knew better, and from that night dated a strong feeling of dislike for Helen Lennox, whom she affected to despise, even though she could be jealous of her. Wisely changing the conversation, Mark asked Katy to play, and as she seldom refused, she went at once to the piano, astonishing both Mrs. Cameron and her daughters with the brilliancy of her performance. Even Juno complimented her, saying she must have taken lessons very young.

"When I was ten," Katy answered. "Cousin Morris gave me my first exercise himself. He plays sometimes."

"Yes, I knew that," Juno replied. "Does your sister play as well as you?"

Katy knew that Helen did not, and she answered frankly, "Morris thinks she does not. She is not as fond of it as I am." Then feeling that she must in some way make amends for Helen, she added, "But she knows a great deal more than I do about *books*. Helen is very smart."

There was a smile on every lip at this ingenuous remark, but only Mark and Bell liked Katy the better for it. Wilford did not care to have her talking of her friends, and he kept her at the piano, until she said her fingers were tired and begged leave to stop.

It was late ere Mark bade them good night; so late that Katy began to wonder if he would never go, yawning once so perceptibly that Wilford gave her a reproving glance, which sent the hot blood to her face and drove from her every feeling of drowsiness. Even after he had gone the family were in no haste to retire, but sat chatting with Wilford until the city clock struck twelve and Katy was nodding in her chair.

"Poor child, she is very tired," Wilford said, apologetically, gently waking Katy, who begged them to excuse her, and followed her husband to her room, where she was free to ask him what she must ask before she could ever be quite as happy as she had been before.

Going up to the chair where Wilford was sitting before the fire, and standing partly behind him, she said timidly, "Will you answer me one thing truly?"

Alone with Katy, Wilford felt all his old tenderness returning, and drawing her into his lap he asked her what it was she wished to know.

"*Did* you love anybody three or four years ago, or ever

—that is, love them well enough to wish to make them your wife?"

Katy could feel how Wilford started, as he said, " What put that idea into your head? Who has been talking to you?"

"Juno," Katy answered. "She told me she believed that it was some other love which kept you a bachelor so long. Was it, Wilford?" and Katy's lips quivered in a grieved kind of way as she put the question.

" Juno be——"

Wilford did not say what, for he seldom swore, and never in a lady's presence. So he said instead,

" It was very unkind in Juno to distress you with matters about which she knew nothing."

" But did you?" Katy asked again. " Was there not a Sybil Grey, or some one of that name?"

At the mention of Sybil Grey, Wilford looked relieved, and answered her at once.

" Yes, there was a Sybil Grey, Mrs. Judge Grandon now, and a dashing widow. Don't sigh so wearily," he continued, as Katy drew a gasping breath. " Knowing she was a widow I chose you, thus showing which I preferred. Few men live to be thirty without more or less fancies, which under some circumstances might ripen into something stronger, and I am not an exception. I never loved Sybil Grey, nor wished to make her my wife. I admired her very much. I admire her yet, and among all my acquaintances there is not one upon whom I would care to have you make so good an impression as upon her, nor one whose manner you could better imitate."

" Oh, will she call? Shall I see her?" Katy asked, beginning to feel alarmed at the very thought of Sybil Grey, with all her polish and manner.

" She is spending the winter in New Orleans with her late husband's relatives. She will not return till spring," Wilford replied. " But do not look so distressed, for I tell you solemnly that I never loved another as I love you. Do you believe me?"

" Yes," and Katy's head drooped upon his shoulder.

She was satisfied with regard to Sybil Grandon, only hoping she would not have to meet her when she came home.

But the picture. Whose was that? Not Sybil's certainly, else Juno would have known. The picture troubled her, but she dared not speak of it, Wilford had seemed so angry at Juno. Still she would probe him a little further, and so she continued,

"I do believe you, and if I ever see this Sybil I will try to imitate her; but tell me, if after her, there was among your friends *one* better than the rest, one almost as dear as I am, one whom you sometimes remember even now— is she living, or is she dead?"

Wilford thought of that humble grave far off in St. Mary's churchyard, and he answered quickly,

"If there ever was such an one, she certainly is *not* living. Are you satisfied?"

Katy answered that she was, but perfect confidence in her husband's affection had been terribly shaken, and Katy's heart was too full to sleep even after she had retired. Visions of Sybil Grey, blended with visions of another whom she called the "dead fancy," flitted before her mind, as she lay awake, while hour after hour went by, until tired nature could endure no longer, and just as the great city was waking up and the rattle of wheels was beginning to be heard upon the pavements, she fell away to sleep.

CHAPTER XIV.

EXTRACTS FROM BELL CAMERON'S DIARY.

NEW YORK, December.

AFTER German Philosophy and Hamilton's Metaphysics, it is a great relief to have introduced into the family an entirely new element—a character the dissection of which is at once a novelty and a recreation. It is absolutely refreshing, and I find myself returning to my books with increased vigor after an encounter with that unsophisticated, innocent-minded creature, our sister-in-law Mrs. Wilford Cameron. Such pictures as Juno and I used to draw of the stately personage who was one day coming to us as Wilford's wife, and of whom even mother was to stand in awe. Alas, how hath our idol fallen! And still I rather like the little creature, who, the very first night,

nearly choked mother to death, giving her lace streamers
a most uncomfortable twitch, and actually kissing *father*
—a thing I have not done since I can remember.   But
then the Camerons are all a set of icicles, encased in a
refrigerator at that.   If we were not, we should thaw out,
when Katy leans on us so affectionately and looks up at
us so wistfully, as if pleading for our love.   Wilford does
wonders; he used to be so grave, so dignified and silent,
that I never supposed he would bear having a wife meet
him at the door with cooing and kisses, and climbing into
his lap right before us all.   Juno says it makes her sick,
while mother is dreadfully shocked; and even Will sometimes seems annoyed, gently shoving her aside and telling
her he is tired.

After all, it is a query in my mind whether it is not
better to be like Katy than like Sybil Grandon, about
whom Juno was mean enough to tell her the first day of
her arrival.

"Very pretty, but shockingly insipid," is Juno's verdict
upon Mrs. Wilford, while mother says less, but looks a
great deal more, especially when she talks about "my
folks," as she did to Mrs. Gen. Reynolds the first time she
called.   Mother and Juno were so annoyed, while Will
looked like a thunder cloud, when she spoke of Uncle
Ephraim saying so and so.   He was better satisfied with
Katy in Europe, where he was not known, than he is here,
where he sees her with other people's eyes.   One of his
weaknesses is a too great reverence for the world's opinion,
as held and expounded by our very fashionable mother, and
as in a quiet kind of way she has arrayed herself against
poor Katy, while Juno is more open in her acts and say-
ings, I predict that it will not be many months before he
comes to the conclusion that he has made a *mésalliance,*
a thing of which no Cameron was ever guilty.

I wonder if there is any truth in the rumor that Mrs.
Gen. Reynolds once taught a district school, and if she
did, how much would that detract from the merits of her
son, Lieutenant Bob.   But what nonsense to be writing
about him.   Let me go back to Katy, to whom Mrs. Gen.
Reynolds took at once, laughing merrily at her *naïve*
speeches, as she called them—speeches which made Will

turn black in the face, they betrayed so much of rustic
life and breeding. I fancy that he has given Katy a few
hints, and that she is beginning to be afraid of him, for
she watches him constantly when she is talking, and she
does not now slip her hand into his as she used to when
guests are leaving and she stands at his side; neither is
she so demonstrative when he comes up from the office at
night, and there is a look upon her face which was not
there when she came. They are "*toning* her down,"
mother and Juno, and to-morrow they are actually going
to commence a systematic course of training preparatory
to her début into society, said début to occur on the night
of the——, when Mrs. Gen. Reynolds gives the party talked
about so long. I was present when they met in solemn
conclave to talk it over, mother asking Will if he had any
objections to Juno's instructing his wife with regard to
certain things of which she was ignorant. Will's forehead
knit itself together at first, and I half hoped he would veto
the whole proceeding, but after a moment he replied,

"No, provided Katy is willing. Her feelings must not
be hurt."

"Certainly not," mother said. "Katy is a dear little
creature, and we all love her very much, but that does
not blind us to her deficiencies, and as we are anxious
that she should fill that place in society which Mrs. Wilford Cameron ought to fill, it seems necessary to tone her
down a little before her first appearance at a party."

To this Will assented, and then Juno went on to enu-
merate her deficiencies, which, as nearly as I can remember,
are these: She laughs too much and too loud; is too enthusiastic over novelties; has too much to say about Silverton and "my folks;" quotes Uncle Ephraim and sister
Helen too often, and is even guilty at times of mentioning
a certain Aunt Betsy, who must have floated with the ark,
and snuffed the breezes of Ararat. She does not know
how to enter, or cross, or leave a room properly, or receive
an introduction, or, in short, to do anything according to
New York ideas, as understood by the Camerons, and so
she is to be taught—*toned down,* mother called it—dwelling upon her high spirit as something vulgar, if not absolutely wicked. How father would have sworn, for he calls

her his little sunbeam, and says he never should have gained so fast if she had not come with her sunny face, and lively, merry laugh, to cheer his sick room. Katy has a fast friend in him. But mother and Juno—well, I shall be glad if they do not annihilate her altogether, and I am surprised that Will allows it. I wonder if Katy is really happy with us. She says she is, and is evidently delighted with New York life, clapping her hands when the invitation to Mrs. Reynolds's party was received, and running with it to Wilford as soon as he came home. It is her first big party, she says, she having never attended any except that little sociable in Boston, and those insipid school-girl affairs at the seminary. I may be conceited—Juno thinks I am—but really and truly, Bell Cameron's private opinion of herself is that at heart she is better than the rest of her family, and so I pity this little sister of ours, while at the same time I am exceedingly anxious to be present whenever Juno takes her in hand, for I like to see the fun. Were she at all bookish, I should avow myself her champion, and openly defend her; but she is not, and so I give her into the hands of the Philistines, hoping they will, at least, spare her hair, and not worry her life out on that head. It is very becoming to her, and several young ladies have whispered their intention of trying its effect upon themselves, so that Katy may yet be a leader of the fashion.

CHAPTER XV.

TONING DOWN.—BELL'S DIARY CONTINUED.

Such fun as it was to see mother and Juno training Katy, showing her how to enter the parlor, how to arrange her dress, how to carry her hands and feet, and how to sit in a chair—Juno going through with the performance first, and then requiring Katy to imitate her. Had I been Katy I should have rebelled, but she is far too sweet-tempered and anxious to please, while I suspect that fear of my lord Wilford had something to do with it, for when the drill was over, she asked so earnestly if we thought he would be ashamed of her, and there were tears in her great blue eyes as she said it. Hang Wilford! Hang the whole of them; I am not sure I shall not yet espouse her cause myself, or else tell father, who will do it so much better.

Dec. —*th.*—Another drill, with Juno commanding officer, while the poor little *private* seemed completely worried out. This time there were open doors, but so absorbed were mother and Juno as not to hear the bell, and just as Juno was saying, "Now imagine me Mrs. Gen. Reynolds, to whom you are being presented," while Katy was bowing almost to the floor, who should appear but Mark Ray, stumbling square upon that ludicrous rehearsal, and, of course, bringing it to an end. No explanation was made, nor was any needed, for Mark's face showed that he understood it, and it was as much as he could do to keep from roaring with merriment; I am sure he pitied Katy, for his manner towards her was very affectionate and kind, and when she left the room he complimented her highly, repeating many things. he had heard in her praise from those who had seen her both in the street and here at home. Juno's face was like a thunder-cloud, for she is as much in love with Mark Ray as she was once with Dr. Grant, and is even jealous of his praise of Katy. Glad am I that I never yet saw the man who could make me jealous, or for whom I cared a pin. There's Bob Reynolds up at West Point. I suppose I do think his epaulettes very becoming to him, but his hair is too light, and he cannot raise whiskers big enough to cast a shadow on the wall, while I know he looks with contempt upon females who write, even though their writings never see the light of day; thinks them strong-minded, self-willed, and all that. He is expected to be present at the party, but I shall not go. I prefer to stay at home and finish that article entitled, "Women of the Present Century," suggested to my mind by my sister Katy, who stands for the picture I am drawing of a pretty woman, with more heart than brains, contrasting her with such an one as Juno, her opposite.

January 10.—The last time I wrote in my journal was just before the party, which is over now, the long talked of affair at which Katy was the reigning belle. I don't know *how* it happened, but happen it did, and Juno's glory faded before that of her rival, whose ringing laugh frequently penetrated to every room, and made more than one look up in some surprise. But when Mrs. Humphreys said, " It's that charming little Mrs. Cameron, the prettiest creature I ever saw, her laugh is so refreshing and genuine," the point was settled, and Katy was free to laugh as loudly as she pleased.

She did look beautifully, in lace and pearls, with her short hair curling in her neck. She would not allow us to put so much as a bud in her hair, showing, in this respect, a willfulness we never expected; but as she was perfectly irresistible, we suffered her to have her way, and when she was dressed, sent her in to father, who had asked to see her. And now comes the strangest thing in the world.

" You are very beautiful, little daughter," father said, " I almost wish I was going with you to see the sensation you are sure to create."

Then straight into his lap climbed Katy, *father's* lap, where none of us ever sat, I am sure, and began to coax him to go, telling him she should appear better if he were there, and that she should need him when Wilford left her, as of course he must a part of the time. And father actually dressed himself and went. But Katy did not need him after the people began to understand that Mrs. Wilford Cameron was the rage. Even Sybil Grey in her palmiest days never received such homage as was paid to the little Silverton girl, whose great charm was her perfect enjoyment of everything, and her perfect faith in what people said to her. Juno was nothing and I worse than nothing, for I *did* go after all, wearing a plain black silk, with high neck and long sleeves, looking, as Juno said, like a Sister of Charity.

Lieut. Bob was there, his light hair lighter than ever, and his chin as smooth as my hand. He likes to dance and I do not, but somehow he persisted in staying where I was, notwithstanding that I said my sharpest things in hopes to get rid of him. He left me at last to dance with Katy, who makes up in grace and airiness what she lacks in knowledge. Once upon the floor she did not lack for partners, but I verily believe danced every set, growing prettier and fairer as she danced, for hers is a complexion which does not get red and blowsy with exercise.

Mark Ray was there too, and I saw him smile comically when Katy met the people with that bow she was making at the time he came so suddenly upon us. Mark is a good fellow, and I really think we have him to thank in a measure for Katy's successful début. He was the first to take her from Wilford, walking with her up and down the hall by way of reassuring her, and once as they passed me I heard her say,

"I feel so timid here—so much afraid of doing something wrong—something countrified."

"Never mind," he answered. "Act yourself just as you would were you at home in Silverton, where you are known. That is far better than affecting a manner not natural to you."

After that Katy brightened wonderfully. The stiffness which at first was perceptible passed off, and she was Katy Lennox, queening it over all the city belles, drawing after her a host of gentlemen, and between the sets holding a miniature court at one end of the room, where the more desirable of the guests crowded around, flattering her until her little head ought to have been turned if it was not. To do her justice she bore her honors well, and when we were in the carriage and father complimented her upon her success, she only said,

"If I pleased you all I am glad."

So many calls as we had the next day, and so many invitations as there are now on our table for Mrs. Wilford Cameron, while our opera box between the scenes is packed with beaux, until one would suppose Wilford might be jealous; but Katy takes it so quietly and modestly, seeming only gratified for his sake, that I really believe he enjoys it more than she does. At all events he persists in her going even when she would rather stay at home, so if she is spoiled the fault will rest with him.

February—th.—Poor Katy! Dissipation is beginning to wear upon her, for she is not accustomed to our late hours, and sometimes falls asleep while Esther is dressing her. But go she must, for Wilford wills it so, and she is but an automaton to do his bidding.

Why can't mother let her alone, when everybody seems so satisfied with her? Somehow she does not believe that people are as delighted as they pretend, and so she keeps training and tormenting her until I do not wonder that Katy sometimes hates to go out, lest she shall unconsciously be guilty of an impropriety. I pitied her last night when, after she was ready for the opera, she came into my room where I was indulging in the luxury of a loose dressing gown, with my feet on the sofa. At first I think she liked Juno best, but latterly she has taken to me, and now sitting down before the fire into which her blue eyes looked with a steady stare, she said,

"I wish I might stay here with you to-night. I have heard this opera before, and it will be so tiresome. I get so sleepy while they are singing, for I never care to watch the acting. I did at first when it was new, but now it seems insipid to see them make believe, while the theatre is worse yet," and she gave a weary yawn.

In less than three months she had exhausted fashionable life, and I looked at her in astonishment, asking what would please her if the opera did not. What would she like?

Turning her eyes full upon me, she exclaimed,

"I do like it some, I suppose, only I get so tired. I like to ride, I like to skate, I like to shop, and all that, but oh, you don't know how I want to go home to mother and Helen. I have not seen them for so long; but I am going in the spring—going in May. How many days are there in March and April? Sixty-one," she continued; "then I may safely say that in eighty days I shall see mother, and all the dear old places. It is not a grand home like this. You, Bell, might laugh at it; Juno would, I am sure, but you do not know how dear it is to me, or how I long for a sight of the huckleberry hills and the rocks where Helen and I used to play."

Just then Will called to say the carriage was waiting, and Katy was driven away, while I sat thinking of her, and the devoted love with which she clings to her home and friends, wondering if it were the kindest thing which could have been done, transplanting her to our atmosphere, so different from her own.

March 1st.—As it was in the winter, so it is now; Mrs. Wilford Cameron is the rage—the bright star of society, which quotes and pets and flatters, and even laughs at her by turns; and Wilford, though still watchful, lest she should do something *outré,* is very proud of her, insisting upon her accepting invitations, sometimes two for one evening, until the child is absolutely worn out, and said to me once when I told her how well she was looking and how pretty her dress was, "Yes, pretty enough, but I am so tired. If I could lie down on mother's bed, in a shilling calico, just as I used to do!"

Mother's bed seems at present to be the height of her ambition—the thing she most desires; and as Juno fancies it must be the *feathers* she is sighing for, she wickedly suggests that Wilford either buy a feather bed for his wife, or else send to Aunty Betsy for the one which was to be Katy's setting out! They go to housekeeping in May, and on Madison Square, too. I think Wilford would quite as soon remain with us, for he does not fancy change; but Katy wants a home of her own, and I never saw anything more absolutely beautiful than her face when father said to Wilford that No— Madison Square was for sale, advising him to secure it. But when mother intimated that there was no necessity for the two families to separate at present—that Katy was too young to have the charge of a house—there came into her eyes a look of such distress that it went straight to father's heart, and calling her to him, he said,

"Tell me, sunbeam, what is your choice—to stay with us, or have a home of your own?"

Katy was very white, and her voice trembled as she replied,

"You have been kind to me here, and it is very pleasant; but I guess—I think—I'm sure—I should like the housekeeping best. I am not so young either. Nineteen in July, and when I go home next month I can learn so much of Aunt Betsy and Aunt Hannah."

Mother looked at Wilford then; but he was looking into the fire with an expression anything but favorable to that visit home, fixed now for April instead of May. But Katy has no discernment, and believes she is actually going to learn how to make apple dumplings and pumpkin pies. In spite of mother the house is bought, and now she is gone

all day deciding how it shall be furnished, always leaving
Katy out of the question, as if she were a cipher, and only
consulting Wilford's choice. They will be happier alone, I
know. Mrs. Gen. Reynolds says that it is the way for
young people to live; that her son's wife shall never come
home to her, for of course their habits could not be alike;
and then she looked queerly at me, as if she knew I was
thinking of Lieutenant Bob and who his wife might be.

Sybil Grandon is coming in April or May, and Mrs.
Reynolds wonders *will* she flirt as she used to do. Just
as if Bob would care for a widow! There is more danger from Will, who thinks Mrs. Grandon a perfect para-
gon, and who is very anxious that Katy may appear well
before her, saying nothing and doing nothing which shall
in any way approximate to Silverton and the *shoes* which
Katy told Esther she used to bind when a girl. Will need
not be disturbed, for Sybil Grandon was never half as
pretty as Katy, or half as much admired. Neither need
Mrs. Gen. Reynolds fret about Bob, as if he would care for
her. Sybil Grandon indeed!

CHAPTER XVI.

KATY.

MUCH which Bell had written of Katy was true. She
had been in New York nearly four months, drinking deep
draughts from the cup of folly and fashion held so constantly to her lips; but she cloyed of it at last, and what
at first had been so eagerly grasped, began, from daily
repetition, to grow insipid and dull. To be the belle of
every place, to know that her dress, her style, and even
the fashion of her hair was copied and admired, was gratifying to her, because she knew it pleased her husband,
who was never happier or prouder than when, with Katy
on his arm, he entered some crowded parlor and heard the
buzz of admiration as it circled round, while Katy smiled
and blushed like a little child, wondering at the attentions
lavished upon her, and attributing them mostly to her
husband, whose position she understood, marveling more
and more that he should have chosen her to be his wife.
That he had so honored her made her love him with a

strange kind of grateful, clinging love, which as yet would acknowledge no fault in him, no wrong, no error; and if ever a shadow did cloud her heart she was the one to blame, not Wilford; he was right—he had idol she worshiped—he the one for whose sake she tried to drop her country ways and conform to the rules his mother and sister taught, submitting with the utmost good nature to what Bell called the *drill*, but never losing that natural, playful, airy manner which so charmed the city people and made her the reigning belle. As Marian Hazelton had predicted, others than her husband had spoken words of praise in Katy's ear; but such was her nature that the shafts of flattery glanced aside, leaving her unharmed, so that her husband, though sometimes disquieted, had no cause for jealousy, enjoying Katy's success far more than she did herself, urging her out when she would rather have stayed at home, and evincing so much annoyance if she ventured to remonstrate, that she gave it up at last and floated on with the tide.

Mrs. Cameron had at first been greatly shocked at Katy's want of propriety, looking on aghast when she wound her arms around Wilford's neck, or sat upon his knee; but to the elder Cameron the sight was a pleasant one, bringing back sunny memories of a summer-time years ago, when *he* was young, and a fair bride had for a few brief weeks made this earth a paradise to him. But fashion had entered his Eden—that summer time was gone, and only the dun leaves of autumn lay where the buds which promised so much had been. The girlish bride was a stately matron now, doing nothing amiss, but making all her acts conform to a prescribed rule of etiquette, and frowning majestically upon the frolicsome, impulsive Katy, who had crept so far into the heart of the eccentric man that he always found the hours of her absence long, listening intently for the sound of her bounding footsteps, and feeling that her coming to his household had infused into his veins a better, healthier life than he had known for years. Katy was very dear to him, and he felt a thrill of pain when first the *toning down* process commenced. He had heard them talk about it, and in his wrath he had hurled a cut-glass goblet upon the marble hearth, breaking it in atoms, while he called them a pair of precious fools, and Wilford a bigger one because he suffered it. So long as his convalescence lasted, he was some restraint upon his wife, but when he was well enough to resume his duties in his Wall Street office, there was nothing in the way, and Katy's education progressed accordingly. For Wilford's sake Katy would do anything, and she submitted to much which would otherwise have been excessively annoying. But she was growing tired now, and it told upon her face, which was whiter than when she came to New York, while her figure was, if possible, slighter and more airy; but this only enhanced her loveliness, Wilford thought, and so he paid no heed to her complaints of weariness, but kept her in the circle which welcomed her so warmly, and would have missed her so much.

Little by little it had come to Katy that she was not quite as comfortable in her husband's family as she would be in a house of her own. The constant watch kept over her by Mrs. Cameron and Juno irritated and fretted her, making her wonder what was the matter, and why she should so often feel lonely and desolate when surrounded by every luxury which wealth could purchase. "It is *his folks,*" she always said to herself when cogitating upon the subject. "Alone with Wilford I shall feel as light and happy as I did in Silverton."

And so Katy caught eagerly at the prospect of a release from the restraint of No.—, seeming so anxious that Wilford, almost before he was aware of it himself, became the owner of one of the most desirable situations on Madison Square. Of all the household after Katy, Juno was perhaps the only one glad of the new house. It would be a change for herself, for she meant to spend much of her time on Madison Square, where everything was to be on the most magnificent style. Fortunately for Katy, she knew nothing of Juno's intentions and built castles of her new home, where mother could come with Helen and Dr. Grant. Somehow she never saw Uncle Ephraim, nor his wife, nor Aunt Betsy there. She knew how out of place they would appear, and how they would annoy Wilford; but surely to her mother and Helen there could be no objection, and when she first went over the house she designated this room as mother's, and another one as Helen's, thinking how each should be fitted up with direct reference to their tastes, Helen's containing a great many books, while her mother's should have easy-chairs and lounges, with a host of drawers for holding things. And Wilford heard it all, making no reply, but considering how he could manage best so as to have no scene, for he had not the slightest intention of inviting either Mrs. Lennox or Helen to visit him, much less to become a part of his household. That he did not marry Katy's relatives was a fact as fixed as the laws of the Medes and Persians, and Katy's anticipations were answering no other purpose than to divert her mind for the time being, keeping her bright and cheerful.

Very pleasant indeed were the pictures Katy drew of the new house where Helen was to come, but pleasanter far were her pictures of that visit to Silverton, to occur in April. Poor Katy! how much she thought about that visit when she should see them all and go with Uncle Ephraim down into the meadows, making believe she was Katy Lennox still—when she could climb the ladder in the barn after new-laid eggs, or steal across the fields to Linwood, talking with Morris as she used to talk in the days which seemed so long ago. Morris she feared was not liking her as well as of old, thinking her very frivolous and silly, for he had only written her one short note in reply to the letter she had sent, telling him of the parties she had attended, and the gay, happy life she led, for to him she would not then confess that in her cup of joy there was a single bitter dreg. All was bright and fair, she said, and Morris had replied that he was glad, "But do not forget that *death* can find you even amid your splendor, or that after death the judgment comes, and then what shall it profit you if you gain the whole world and lose your own soul."

These words had rung in Katy's ears for many a day, following her to the dance and to the opera, where even the music was drowned by the echo of the words, "lose your own soul." But the sting grew less and less, till Katy no longer felt it, and now was only anxious to talk with Morris and convince him that she was not as thoughtless as he might suppose, that she still remembered his teachings, and the little church in the valley, preferring it to the handsome, aristocratic house where she went with the Camerons once on every Sunday.

"One more week and then it is April," she said to Wilford one evening after they had retired to their room, and she was talking of Silverton. "I guess we'd better go about the tenth. Shall you stay as long as I do?"

Wilford bit his lip, and after a moment replied,

"I have been talking with mother, and we think April is not a good time for you to be in the country; it is so wet and cold, and I want you here to help order our furniture."

"Oh, Wilford!" and Katy's voice trembled, for from past experience she knew that for Wilford to object to her plans was equivalent to a refusal, and her heart throbbed with disappointment as she tried to listen while Wilford urged many reasons why she should not go, convincing her at last that of all times for visiting Silverton, spring was the worst; that summer or autumn were better, and that it was her duty to remain where she was until such time as he saw fit for her to do otherwise.

This was the meaning of what he said, and though his manner was guarded, and his words kind, they were very conclusive, and with one gasping sob Katy gave up Silverton, charging it more to Mrs. Cameron than to Wilford, and writing next day to Helen that she could not come just then, but that after she was settled they might surely expect her.

With a bitter pang Helen read this letter to the three women who had anticipated Katy's visit so much, and each of whom cried quietly over her disappointment, while Uncle Ephraim went back to his work that afternoon with a heavy heart, for now his labor was not lightened by thoughts of Katy's being there so soon.

"Please God she may come to us sometime," he said, pausing beneath the butternut in the meadow, and remembering just how Katy looked on that first day of her return from Canandaigua, when she sat on the flat stone while he piled up his hay and talked with her of different paths through life, one of which she must surely tread.

She had said, "I will choose the straight and pleasant,"

and some would think she had; but Uncle Ephraim was
not so sure, and leaning against a tree, he asked silently
that whether he ever saw his darling again or not, God
would care for her and keep her unspotted from the
world.

CHAPTER XVII.

THE NEW HOUSE.

It was a cruel thing for Wilford Cameron to try to
separate Katy from the hearts which loved her so much;
and, as if he felt reproached, there was an increased tenderness in his manner towards her, particularly as he saw
how sad she was for a few days after his decision. But
Katy could not be sorry long, and in the excitement of
settling the new house her spirits rallied, and her merry
laugh trilled like a bird through the rooms where the work-
men were so busy, and where Mrs. Cameron was the real
superintendent, though there was sometimes a show of
consulting Katy, who nevertheless was a mere cipher in
the matter. In everything the mother had her way, until
it came to the room designed for Helen, and which Mrs.
Cameron was for converting into a kind of smoking or
lounging room for Wilford and his associates. Katy must
not expect him to be always as devoted to her as he had
been during the winter, she said. He had a great many
bachelor friends, and now that he had a house of his own,
it was natural that he should have some place where they
could spend an hour or so with him without the restraint
of ladies' society, and this was just the room—large, airy,
quiet, and so far from the parlors that the odor of the
smoke could not reach them.

Katy had submitted to much without knowing that she
was submitting; but something Bell had dropped that
morning had awakened a suspicion that possibly she was
being ignored, and the wicked part of Helen would have
enjoyed the look in her eye as she said, not to Mrs. Cameron, but to Wilford, " I have from the very first decided
this chamber for Helen, and I cannot give it up for a
smoking room. You never had one at home. Why did
you not, if it is so necessary?"

Wilford could not tell her that his mother would as soon have brought into her house one of Barnum's shows, as to have had a room set apart for smoking, which she specially disliked; neither could he at once reply at all, so astonished was he at this sudden flash of spirit. Mrs. Cameron was the first to rally, and in her usual quiet tone she said, "I did not know that your sister was to form a part of your household. When do you expect her?" and her cold gray eyes rested steadily upon Katy, who never before so fully realized the distance there was between her husband's friends and her own. But as the worm will turn when trampled on, so Katy, though hitherto powerless to defend herself, roused in Helen's behalf, and in a tone as quiet and decided as that of her mother-in-law, replied, "She will come whenever I write for her. It was arranged from the first. Wasn't it, Wilford?" and she turned to her husband, who, unwilling to decide between a wife he loved and a mother whose judgment he considered infallible, affected not to hear her, and stole from the room, followed by Mrs. Cameron, so that Katy was left mistress of the field.

After that no one interfered in her arrangement of Helen's room, which, with far less expense than Mrs. Cameron would have done, she fitted up so cosily that Wilford pronounced it the pleasantest room in the house, while Bell went into ecstasies over it, and even Juno might have unbent enough to praise it, were it not for Mark Ray, who, from being tacitly claimed by Juno, was frequently admitted to their counsels, and had asked the privilege of contributing to Helen's room a handsome volume of German poetry, such as he fancied she might enjoy. So long as Mark's attentions were not bestowed in any other quarter Juno was comparatively satisfied, but the moment he swerved a hair's breadth from the line she had marked out, her anger was aroused; and now, remembering his commendations of Helen Lennox, she hated her as cordially as one jealous girl can hate another whom she has not seen, making Katy so uncomfortable, without knowing what was the matter, that she hailed the morning of her exit from No.—— as the brightest since her marriage.

It was a very happy day for Katy, and when she first

sat down to dinner in her own home, her face shone with a joy which even the presence of her mother-in-law could not materially lessen. She would rather have been alone with Wilford, it is true, but as her choice was not consulted she submitted cheerfully, proudly taking her rightful place at the table, and doing the honors so well that Mrs. Cameron, in speaking of it to her daughters, acknowledged that Wilford had little to fear if Katy always appeared as much at ease as she did that day. A thought similar to this passed through the mind of Wilford, who was very observant of such matters, and that night, after his mother was gone, he warmly commended Katy, but spoiled the pleasure his commendations would have given by telling her next, as if one thought suggested the other, that Sybil Grandon had returned, that he saw her on Broadway, accepting her invitation to a seat in her carriage which brought him to his door. She had made many inquiries concerning Katy, expressing a great curiosity to see her, and saying that as she drove past the house that morning, she was strongly tempted to waive all ceremony and run in, knowing she should be pardoned for the sake of Auld Lang Syne, when she was privileged to take liberties with the Camerons. All this Wilford repeated to Katy, but he did not tell her how at the words Auld Lang Syne, Sybil had turned her fine eyes upon him with an expression which made him color, for he knew she was referring to the time when her name and his were always coupled together.

Katy had dreaded the return of Sybil Grandon, of whom she had heard so much, and now that she had come, she felt for a moment a terror of meeting her which she tried to shake off, succeeded at last, for perfect faith in Wilford was to her a strong shield of defence, and her only trouble was a fear lest she should fall in the scale of comparison which might be instituted between herself and Mrs. Grandon, who after a few days ceased to be a bugbear, Wilford never mentioning her again, and Katy only hearing of her through Juno and Bell, the first of whom went into raptures over her, while the latter styled her a silly, coquettish widow, who would appear much better to have worn her weeds a little longer, and not throw herself quite

so soon into the market. That she should of course meet
her some time, Katy knew, but she would not distress herself till the time arrived, and so she dismissed her fears,
or rather lost them in the excitement of her new dignity
as mistress of a house.

In her girlhood Katy had evinced a taste for housekeeping, which now developed so rapidly that she won the
respect of all the servants, from the man who answered the
bell to the accomplished cook, hired by Mrs. Cameron, and
who, like most accomplished cooks, was sharp and cross and
opinionated, but who did not find it easy to scold the blithe
little woman who every morning came flitting into her
dominions, not asking what they would have for dinner, as
she had been led to suppose she would, but *ordering* it with
a matter of course air, which amused the usually overbearing Mrs. Phillips. But when the little lady, rolling her
sleeves above her dimpled elbows and donning the clean
white apron which Phillips was reserving for afternoon,
announced her intention of surprising Wilford, with a pudding such as Aunt Betsy used to make, there were signs
of rebellion, Phillips telling her bluntly that she couldn't
be bothered—that it was not a lady's place in the kitchen
under foot—that the other Mrs. Cameron never did it, and
would not like it in Mrs. Wilford.

For a moment Katy paused and looked straight at Mrs.
Phillips; then said, quietly, " I have only six eggs here—
the recipe is ten. Bring me four more, please."

There was something in the blue eyes which compelled
obedience, and the dessert progressed without another word
of remonstrance. But when the door bell rang, and word
came down that there were ladies in the parlor—Juno,
with some one else—Phillips would not tell her of the
flour on her hair; and as Katy, after casting aside her
apron and putting down her sleeves, only glanced hastily
at herself in the hall mirror as she passed it, she appeared
in the parlor with this mark upon her curls, and greatly
to her astonishment was presented to "Mrs. Sybil
Grandon," Juno explaining, that as Sybil was anxious to
see her, and they were passing the house, she had presumed upon her privilege as a sister and brought her in.

For a moment the room turned dark, it was so sudden,

so unexpected, and she so unprepared; but Sybil's familiar manner quieted her, and she was able at last to look
fully at her visitor, finding her *not* as handsome as she
expected, nor as young, but in all other respects she had
not perhaps been exaggerated.   Cultivated and self-possessed, she was very pleasing in her manner, making Katy
feel wholly at ease by a few well-timed compliments, which
had the merit of seeming genuine, so perfect was she in
the art of deception.

To Katy she was very gracious, admiring her house, admiring herself, admiring everything, until Katy wondered
how she could ever have dreaded to meet her, laughing and
chatting as familiarly as if the fashionable woman were
not criticising every movement, and every act, and every
feature of her face, wondering most at the *flour* upon her
hair!

Juno wondered, too, but knowing Katy's domestic pro-
pensities, suspected the truth, and feigning some errand
with Phillips, she excused herself for a moment and de-
scended to the kitchen, where she was not long in hearing
about Katy's "queer ways, coming where she was not
needed, and making country puddings after some heathenish aunt's rule."

"Was it Aunt Betsy?" Juno asked, her face betoken-
ing its disgust when told that she was right, and her
manner on her return to the parlor was very frigid towards
Katy, who had discovered the flour on her hair, and was
laughing merrily over it, telling Sybil how it happened—
how cross Phillips was—and lastly, how "our folks" often
made the pudding, and that was why she wished to surprise Wilford with it.

There was a sarcastic smile upon Sybil's lip as she wished
Mrs. Cameron success and then departed, leaving Katy to
finish the dessert, which, when ready for the table, was certainly very inviting, and would have tempted the appetite
of any man who had not been listening to gossip not wholly
conducive to his peace of mind.

On his way home Wilford had stopped at his father's,
where Juno was relating the particulars of her call upon
his wife, and as she did not think it necessary to stop for
him, he heard of Katy's misdoings, and her general ap-

pearance in the presence of Sybil Grandon, whom she entertained with a description of " our folks' " favorite dishes, together with Aunt Betsy's recipes. This was the straw too many, and since his marriage Wilford had not been as angry as he was while listening to Juno, who reported Sybil's verdict on his wife, " A domestic little body and very pretty."

Wilford did not care to have his wife domestic; he did not marry her for that, and in a mood anything but favorable to the light, delicate dessert Katy had prepared with so much care, he went to his luxurious home, where Katy ran as usual to meet him, her face brimming with the surprise she had in store for him, and herself so much excited that she did not at first observe the cloud upon his brow, as he moodily answered her rapid questions. When the important moment arrived, and the dessert was brought on, he promptly declined it, even after her explanation that she made it herself, urging him to try it for the sake of pleasing her, if nothing more. But Wilford was not hungry then, and even had he been, he would have chosen anything before a pudding made from a recipe of Betsy Barlow, so the dessert was untasted even by Katy herself, who, knowing now that something had gone wrong, sat fighting back her tears until the servant left the room, when she timidly asked, " What is it, Wilford? What makes you seem so——" She would not say *cross,* and so substituted " queer," while Wilford plunged at once into the matter by saying, " Juno tells me she called here this afternoon with Mrs. Grandon."

" Yes, I forgot to mention it," Katy answered, feeling puzzled to know why that should annoy her husband; but his next remarks disclosed the whole, and Katy's tears flowed fast as Wilford asked what she supposed Mrs. Grandon thought, to see his wife looking as if fresh from the flour barrel, and to hear her talk about Aunt Betsy's recipes and *" our folks."* " That is a bad habit of yours, Katy," he continued, " one of which I wish you to break yourself. if possible. I have never spoken to you directly on the subject before, but it annoys me exceedingly, inasmuch as it is an indication of low breeding."

There was no answer from Katy, whose heart was **too**

full to speak, and so Wilford went on, " Our servants were selected by mother with a direct reference to your youth and inexperience, and it is not necessary for you to frequent the kitchen, or, indeed, to go there oftener than once a week. Let them come to you for orders, not you go to them. Neither need you speak quite so familiarly to them, treating them almost as if they were your equals. Try to remember your true position—that whatever you may have been you are now Mrs. Wilford Cameron, equal to any lady in New York."

They were in the library now, and the soft May breeze came stealing through the open window, stirring the fleecy curtains and blowing across the tasteful bouquet which Katy had arranged; but Katy was too wretched to care for her surroundings. It was the first time Wilford had ever spoken to her in just this way, and his manner hurt her more than his words, making her feel as if she were an ignorant, ill-bred creature, whom he had raised to a position she did not know how to fill. It was cruel thus to repay her attempts to please, and so, perhaps, Wilford thought, as with folded arms he sat looking at her weeping so bitterly upon the sofa; but he was too indignant to make any concession then, and he suffered her to weep in silence until he remembered that his mother had requested him to bring her round that evening, as they were expecting a few of Juno's friends, and among them Sybil Grandon. If Katy went he wished her to look her best, and he unbent so far as to try to check her tears. But Katy could not stop, and she wept so passionately that Wilford's anger subsided, leaving only tenderness and pity for the wife he soothed and caressed, until the sobbing ceased, and Katy lay passively in his arms, her face so white, and the dark rings about her eyes showing so distinctly that Wilford did not press her when she declined his mother's invitation. He could go, she said, urging so many reasons why he should that, for the first time since their marriage, he left her alone, and went where Sybil Grandon smiled her sunniest smile, and put forth her most persuasive powers to keep him at her side, expressing so much regret that he did not bring " his charming little wife, who completely won her heart, she was so child-like and simple-hearted, laughing

so merrily when she discovered the flour on her hair, but
not seeming to mind it in the least. Really, she did not
see how it happened that he was fortunate enough to win
such a domestic treasure. Where did he find her?"

If Sybil Grandon meant this to be complimentary, it
was not received as such. Wilford, almost grating his
teeth with vexation as he listened to it, and feeling doubly
mortified with Katy, whom he found waiting for him,
when at a late hour he left the society of Sybil Grandon
and repaired to his home.

To Katy the time of his absence had seemed an age,
for her thoughts had been busy with the past, gathering
up every incident connected with her married life since
she came to New York, and deducing from them the conclusion that "Wilford's folks" were ashamed of her, and
that Wilford himself might perhaps become so if he were
not already. That would be worse than death itself, and
the darkest hours she had ever known were those she spent
alone that night, sobbing so violently as to bring on a
racking headache, which showed itself upon her face and
touched Wilford at once.

Sybil Grandon was forgotten in those moments of contrition, when he ministered so tenderly to his suffering
wife, whom he felt that he had wronged. But he could
not tell her so then. It was not natural for him to confess
his errors. There had always been a struggle between his
duty and his pride when he had done so, and now the
latter conquered, especially as Katy, grown more calm,
began to take the censure to herself, lamenting her short-
comings, and promising to do better, even to the imitating
of Sybil Grandon, if that would make him forget the past
and love her as before.

Wilford could accord forgiveness far more graciously
than he could ask it, and so peace was restored, and
Katy's face next day looked bright and happy when seen
in her new carriage, which took her down Broadway to
Stewart's, where she encountered Sybil Grandon, and with
her Juno Cameron.

From the latter Katy instinctively shrank, but she could
not resist the former, who greeted her so familiarly that
Katy readily forgave her the pain of which she had been

the cause, and spoke of her to Wilford without a pang
when he came home to dinner. Still she could not overcome her dread of meeting her, and she grew more and
more averse to mingling in society, where she might do
many things to mortify her husband or his family, and
thus provoke a scene she hoped never again to pass through.

"Oh, if Helen were only here!" she thought, as she
began to experience a sensation of loneliness she had never
felt before.

But Helen was not there, nor coming there at present.
One word from Wilford had settled that, convincing Katy
that it was better to wait until the autumn, inasmuch as
they were going so soon to Saratoga and Newport, places
which Katy dreaded, after she knew that Mrs. Cameron
and Juno were to be of the party, and probably Sybil
Grandon. Katy did not dislike the latter, but she was
never easy in her presence, while she could not deny to
herself that since Sybil's return Wilford had not been
quite the same as before. In company he was more attentive than ever, but at home he was sometimes moody and
silent, while Katy strove in vain to ascertain the cause.

They were not as happy in the new home as she had
expected to be, but the fault did not lie with Katy. She
performed her part and more, taking upon her young
shoulders the whole of the burden which her husband
should have helped her to bear. The easy, indolent life
Wilford had led so long as a petted son of a partial mother
unfitted him for care, and he was as much a boarder in his
own home as he had even been in the hotels in Paris,
thoughtlessly requiring of Katy more than he should have
required, so that Bell was not far from right when in her
journal she described her sister-in-law as "a little servant
whose feet were never supposed to be tired, and whose
wishes were never consulted." It is true Bell had put it
rather strongly, but the spirit of what she said was right,
Wilford seldom considering Katy, or allowing her wishes
to interfere with his own plans; while accustomed to every
possible attention from his mother, he exacted the same
from his wife, whose life was not one of unmixed happiness, notwithstanding that every letter home bore assurances to the contrary.

CHAPTER XVIII.

MARIAN HAZLETON.

THE last days of June had come, and Wilford was beginning to make arrangements for removing Katy from the city before the warmer weather. To this he had been urged by Mark Ray's remarking that Katy was not looking as well as when he first saw her, one year ago. " She has grown thin and pale," he said. " Had Wilford remarked it? "

Wilford had not. She complained much of headache, but that was only natural. Still he wrote to the Mountain House that afternoon to secure rooms for himself and wife, and then at an earlier hour than usual went home to tell her of the arrangement. Katy was out shopping, Esther said, and had not yet returned, adding, " There is a note for her up stairs, left by a woman who I guess came for work."

That a woman should come for work was not strange, but that she should leave a note seemed rather too familiar; and when on going to the library he saw it upon the table, he took it in his hand and examined the superscription closely, holding it up to the light and forgetting to open it in his perplexity and the train of thought it awakened.

" They are singularly alike," he said, and still holding the note in his hand he opened a drawer of his writing desk, which was always kept locked, and took from it a *picture* and a bit of soiled paper, on which was written, " I am *not* guilty, Wilford, and God will never forgive the wrong you have done to me."

There was no name or date, but Wilford knew whose hand had penned those lines, and he sat comparing them with the " Mrs. Wilford Cameron " which the strange woman had written. Then opening the note, he read that, having returned to New York, and wishing employment either as seamstress or dressmaker, Marian Hazelton had ventured to call upon Mrs. Cameron, remembering her promise to give her work if she should desire it.

"Who is Marian Hazelton?" Wilford asked himself as he threw down the missive. "Some of Katy's country friends, I dare say. Seems to me I have heard that name. She certainly writes as Genevra did, except that this Hazelton's is more decided and firm. Poor Genevra!"

There was a pallor about Wilford's lips as he said this, and taking up the picture he gazed for a long time upon the handsome, girlish face, whose dark eyes seemed to look reproachfully upon him, just as they must have looked when the words were penned, "God will never forgive the wrong you have done to me."

"Genevra was mistaken," he said. "At least if God has not forgiven, he has prospered me, which amounts to the same thing;" and without a single throb of gratitude to Him who had thus prospered him, Wilford laid Genevra's picture and Genevra's note back with the withered grass and flowers plucked from Genevra's grave, just as Katy's ring was heard and Katy herself came in.

As thoughts of Genevra always made Wilford kinder towards his wife, so now he kissed her white cheek, noticing that, as Mark had said, it was whiter than last year in June. But mountain air would bring back the roses, he thought, as he handed her the note.

"Oh, yes, from Marian Hazelton," Katy said, glancing first at the name and then hastily reading it through.

"Who is Marian Hazelton?" Wilford asked, and Katy replied by repeating all she knew of Marian, and how she chanced to know her at all. "Don't you remember Helen wrote that she fainted at our wedding, and I was so sorry, fearing I might have overworked her?"

Wilford did remember something about it, and then dismissing Marian from his mind, he told Katy of his plan for taking her to the Mountain House a few weeks before going to Saratoga.

"Would you not like it?" he asked, as she continued silent, with her eyes fixed upon the window opposite.

"Yes," and Katy drew a long and weary breath. I shall like any place where there are birds, and rocks, and trees, and real grass, such as grows of itself in the country; but Wilford," and Katy crept close to him now, "if I

might go to Silverton, I should get strong so fast! You
don't know how I long to see home once more. I dream
about it nights and think about it days, knowing just
how pleasant it is there, with the roses in bloom and the
meadows so fresh and green. May I go, Wilford? May
I go home to mother?"

Had Katy asked for half his fortune, just as she asked
to go home, Wilford would have given it to her; but
Silverton had a power to lock all the softer avenues of
his heart, and so he answered that the Mountain House
was preferable, that the rooms were engaged, and that as
he should enjoy it so much better he thought they would
make no change.

Katy did not cry, nor utter a word of remonstrance;
she was learning that quiet submission was better than
useless opposition, and so Silverton was again given up.
But there was one consolation. Seeing Marian Hazelton
would be almost as good as going home, for had she not
recently come from that neighborhood, bringing with her
the odor from the hills and freshness from the woods?
Perhaps, too, she had lately seen Helen or Morris at
church, and had heard the music of the organ which
Helen played, and the singing of the children just as it
sometimes came to Katy in her dreams, making her start
in her sleep and murmur snatches of the sacred songs
which Dr. Morris had taught. Yes, Marian could tell
her of all this, and very impatiently Katy waited for the
morning when she started for No.—Fourth Street, with
the piles of sewing intended for Marian.

It was a fault of Marian's not to remain long contented
in any place. Tiring of the country, she had returned to
the city, and thinking she might succeed better alone, had
hired a room far up the narrow stairway of a high, som-
bre-looking building, and then from her old acquaintances,
of whom she had several in the city, she had solicited work.
More than once she had passed the handsome house on
Madison Square where Katy lived, walking slowly, and
contrasting it with her *one* room, which was not wholly
uninviting, for where Marian went there was always an
air of comfort; and Katy, as she crossed the threshold,
uttered an exclamation of delight at the cheerful, airy

aspect of the apartment, with its bright ingrain carpet, its simple shades of white, its chintz-covered lounge, its one rocking-chair, its small parlor stove, and its pots of flowers upon the broad window sill.

"Oh Marian," she exclaimed, tripping across the floor. and impulsively throwing her arms around Miss Hazelton's neck, "I am so glad to meet some one from home. It seems almost like Helen I am kissing," and her lips again met those of Marian Hazelton, amid her joy at finding Katy unchanged, wondered what the Camerons would say to see their Mrs. Wilford kissing a poor seamstress whom they would have spurned.

But Katy did not care for *Camerons* then, or even think of them, as in her rich basquine and pretty hat, with emeralds and diamonds sparkling on her fingers, she sat down by Marian.

"Tell me of Silverton; you don't know how I want to go there; but Wilford does not think it best, at present. Next fall I am surely going, and I picture to myself just how it will look: Morris's garden, full of the autumnal flowers—the ripe peaches in our orchard, the grapes ripening on the wall, and the long shadows on the grass, just as I used to watch them, wondering what made them move so fast, and where they could be going. Will it be unchanged, Marian? Do places seem the same when once we have left them?" and Katy's eager eyes looked wistfully at Marian, who replied, "Not always—not often, in fact; but in your case they may. You have not been long away."

"Only a year," Katy said. "I was as long as that in Canandaigua; but this past year is different. I have seen so much, and lived so much, that I feel ten years older than I did last spring, when you and Helen made my wedding dress. Darling Helen! When did you see her last?"

"I was there five weeks ago," Marian replied; "I saw them all, and told them I was coming to New York."

"Do they miss me any? Do they talk of me? Do they wish me back again?" Katy asked, and Marian replied, "They talked of little else, that is your own family. Dr. Morris, I think, did not mention your name. He has

grown very silent and reserved," and Marian's eyes were
fixed inquiringly upon Katy, as if to ascertain how much
she knew of the cause for Morris's reserve.

But Katy had no suspicion, and only replied, "Perhaps he is vexed that I do not write to him oftener, but
I can't. I think of him a great deal, and respect him
more than any living man, except, of course, Wilford;
but when I try to write, something comes in between me
and what I wish to say, for I want to convince him that
I am *not* as frivolous as he thinks I am. I have *not* forgotten the Sunday school, nor the church service; but in
the city it is so hard to be good, and the service and
music seem all for show, and I feel so hateful when I see
Juno and Wilford's mother putting their heads down on
velvet cushions, knowing as I do that they both are
thinking either of their own bonnets or those just in
front."

"Are you not a little uncharitable?" Marian asked,
laughing in spite of herself at the picture Katy drew of
fashion trying to imitate religion in its humility.

"Perhaps so," Katy answered. "I grow bad from looking behind the scenes, and the worst is that I do not care,
and then Katy went back again to the farm-house asking
numberless questions and reaching finally the *business*
which had brought her to Marian's room.

There were spots on Marian's neck, and her lips were
white, as she grasped the bundles tossed into her lap—
the yards and yards of lace and embroidery, linen, and
cambric, which she was expected to make for the wife of
Wilford Cameron; and her voice was husky as she asked
directions or made suggestions of her own.

"It's because she has no such joy in expectation. I
should feel so, too, if I were thirty and unmarried," Katy
thought, as she noticed Marian's agitation, and tried to
divert her mind by talking of Europe and the places she
had visited.

"By the way, you were born in England? Were you
ever at Alnwick?" Katy asked, and Marian replied, "Once,
yes. I've seen the castle and the church. Did you go
there—to St. Mary's, I mean?"

"Oh, yes, and I was never tired of that old churchyard.

Wilford liked it, too, and we wandered by the hour among the sunken graves and quaint headstones."

" Do you remember any of the names upon the stones? Perhaps I may know them?" Marian asked; but Katy did not remember any, or if she did, it was not " Genevra Lambert, aged 22." And so Marian asked her no more questions concerning Alnwick, but talked instead of London and other places, until three hours went by, and down in the street the coachman chafed and fretted at the long delay, wondering what kept his mistress in that neighborhood so long. Had she friends, or had she come on some errand of mercy? The latter most likely, he concluded, and so his face was not quite so cross when Katy at last appeared, looking at her watch and exclaiming at the lateness of the hour.

Katy was very happy that morning, for seeing Marian had brought Silverton near to her, and airy as a bird she ran up the steps of her own dwelling, where the door opened as by magic, and Wilford himself confronted her, asking, with the tone which always made her heart beat, where she had been, and he waiting for her two whole hours. " Surely it was not necessary to stop so long with a seamstress," he continued when she tried to explain. " Ten minutes would suffice for directions," and he could not imagine what attraction there was in Miss Hazelton to keep her there three hours, and then the real cause of his vexation came out. He had come expressly for the carriage to take her and Sybil Grandon to a picnic up the river, whither his mother, Juno and Bell, had already gone. Mrs. Grandon must wonder why he stayed so long, and perhaps give up going. Could Katy be ready soon? and Wilford walked rapidly up and down the parlor with a restless motion of his hands which always betokened impatience. Poor Katy! how the brightness of the morning faded, and how averse she felt to joining that picnic, which she knew had been in prospect for some time, and had fancied she should enjoy! But not to-day, with that look on Wilford's face, and the feeling that he was vexed. Still she could think of no reasonable excuse, and so an hour later found her driving into the country with Sybil Grandon, who received her apologies with as much good-natured grace as if she too had not worked herself into a passion at the delay, for Sybil had been very cross and impatient; but all this vanished when she met Wilford and saw that he was disturbed and irritated. Soft, and sweet, and smooth was she both in word and manner, so that by the time the grove was reached Wilford's ruffled spirits had been soothed, and he was himself again, ready to enjoy the pleasures of the day as keenly as if no harsh word had been said to Katy, who, silent and unhappy, listened to the graceful badinage between Sybil and her husband, thinking how differently his voice had sounded when addressing her only a little while before.

"Pray put some animation into your face, or Mrs. Grandon will think we have been quarreling," Wilford whispered, as he lifted his wife from the carriage, and with a great effort Katy tried to be gay and natural.

But all the while she was fighting back her tears and wishing she were away. Even Marian's room, looking into the dingy court, was preferable to that place, and she was glad when the long day came to an end, and with a fearful headache she was riding back to the city.

The next morning was dark and rainy; but in spite of the weather Katy found her way to Marian's room, this time taking the—avenue cars, which left her independent as regarded the length of her stay. About Marian there was something more congenial than about her city friends, and day after day found her there, watching while Marian fashioned into shape the beautiful little garments, the sight of which had a strangely quieting influence upon Katy, sobering her down and maturing her more than all the years of her life had done. Those were happy hours spent with Marian Hazelton, and Katy felt it keenly when Wilford at last interfered, telling her she was growing quite too familiar with that sewing woman, and her calls must be discontinued, except, indeed, such as were necessary to the work in progress.

With one great gush of tears, when there was no one to see her, Katy gave Marian up, writing her a note, in which were sundry directions for the work, which would go on even after she had left for the Mountain House, as she intended doing the last of June. And Marian guessed at more than Katy meant she should, and with a bitter sigh laid it in her basket, and then resumed the work, which seemed doubly monotonous now that there was no more listening for the little feet tripping up the stairs, or for the bird-like voice which had brought so much of music and sunshine to her lonely room.

CHAPTER XIX.

SARATOGA AND NEWPORT.

FOR three weeks Katy had been at the Mountain House, growing stronger every day, until she was much like the Katy of one year ago. But their stay among the Catskills was ended, and on the morrow they were going to Saratoga, where Mrs. Cameron and her daughters were, and where, too, was Sybil Grandon, the reigning belle of the United States. So Bell had written to her brother, bidding him hasten on with Katy, as she wished to see "that chit of a widow in her proper place." And Katy had been weak enough for a moment to feel a throb of satisfaction in knowing how effectually Sybil's claims to belle-ship would be put aside when she was once in the field; even glancing at herself in the mirror as she leaned on Wilford's shoulder, and feeling glad that mountain air and mountain exercise had brought the roses back to her white cheeks and the brightness to her eyes. But Katy wept passionate tears of repentance for that weakness, when an hour later she read the letter which Dr. Grant had sent in answer to one she had written from the Mountain House, confessing her short-comings, and lamenting that the evils and excesses which shocked her once did not startle her now. To this letter Morris had replied as a brother might write to an only sister, first expressing pleasure at her happiness, and then reminding her of that other life to which this is only a preparation, and beseeching her so to use the good things of this world, given her in such profusion, as not to lose the life eternal.

This was the substance of Morris's letter, which Katy read with streaming eyes, forgetting Saratoga as Morris's solemn words of warning and admonition rang in her ears, and shuddering as she thought of losing the life

eternal, of going where Morris would never come, nor
any of those she loved the best, unless it were Wilford,
who might reproach her with having dragged him there
when she could have saved him.

"Keep yourself unspotted from the world," Morris had
said, and she repeated it to herself, asking "how shall I
do that? how can one be good and fashionable too?"

Then laying her head upon the rock where she was
sitting, Katy tried to pray as she had not prayed in
months, asking that God would teach her what she ought
to know and keep her unspotted from the world. But at
the Mountain House it is easier to pray that one be kept
from temptation than it is at Saratoga, which this summer was crowded to overflowing, its streets presenting a
fitting picture of Vanity Fair, so full were they of show
and gala dress. At the United States, where Mrs. Cameron
stopped, two rooms, for which an enormous price was paid,
had been reserved for Mr. and Mrs. Wilford Cameron, and
this of itself would have given them a certain éclat, even
if there had not been present many who remembered the
proud, fastidious bachelor, and were proportionately anxious to see his wife. *She came, she saw, she conquered;*
and within three days after her arrival Katy Cameron
was the acknowledged belle of Saratoga, from the United
States to the Clarendon. And Katy, alas, was not quite
the same as she who on the mountain ridge had sat with
Morris's letter in her hand, praying that its teachings
might not be forgotten. Saratoga seemed different to her
from New York, and she plunged into its gaieties, never
pausing, never tiring, and seldom giving herself time to
think; much less to pray, as Morris had bidden her do.
And Wilford, though hardly able to recognize the usually
timid Katy in the brilliant woman who led rather than
followed, was sure of her faith to him, and so was only
proud and gratified to see her bear off the palm from
every competitor, while Juno, though she quarreled with
the shadow into which she was so completely thrown,
enjoyed the éclat cast upon their party by the presence of
Mrs. Wilford, who had passed beyond her criticism. Sybil
Grandon, too, stood back in wonder that a simple country
girl should win and wear the laurels she had so long

claimed as her own; but as there was no help for it she contented herself as best she could with the admiration she did receive, and whenever opportunity occurred, said bitter things of Mrs. Wilford, whose parentage and low estate were through her pretty generally known. But it did not matter there what Katy *had been;* the people took her for what she *was now,* and Sybil's glory faded like the early dawn in the coming of the full day.

As it had been at Saratoga, so it was at Newport. Urged on by Mrs. Cameron and Bell, who enjoyed her notoriety, Katy plunged into the mad excitement of dancing and driving and coqueting, until Wilford himself became uneasy, locking her once in her room, where she was sleeping after dinner, and conveniently forgetting to release her until after the departure at evening of some young men from Cambridge, whose attentions to the Ocean House belle had been more strongly marked than was altogether agreeable to him. Of course it was a mistake—the locking of the door—and a great oversight in him not to have remembered it sooner, he said to Katy, by way of apology; and Katy, with no suspicion of the truth, laughed merrily at the joke, repeating it downstairs to the old dowagers, who shrugged their shoulders meaningly and whispered to each other that it might be well if more young wives were locked into their rooms and thus kept out of mischief.

Though flattered, caressed, and admired, Katy was not doing herself much credit at Newport; but save Wilford, there was no one to raise a warning voice, until Mark Ray came down for a few days' respite from the heated city, where he had spent the entire summer, taking charge of the business which belonged as much to Wilford as to himself. But Wilford had a wife; it was more necessary that he should leave, Mark had argued; his time would come by and by. And so he had remained at home until the last of August, when he appeared suddenly at the Ocean House one night when Katy, in her airy robes and child-like simplicity, was breaking hearts by the score. Like others, Mark was charmed, and not a little proud for Katy's sake, to see her thus appreciated; but when one day's experience had shown him more, and given him a look behind the scenes, he trembled for her, knowing how hard it would be for her to come out of that sea of dissipation as pure and spotless as she went in.

"If I were her brother I would warn her that her present career is not one upon which she will look back with pleasure when the excitement is over," he said to himself; "but if Wilford is satisfied it is not for me to interfere. It is surely nothing to me what Katy Cameron does," he kept repeating to himself; but as often as he said it there came up before him a pale, anxious face, shaded with Helen Lennox's bands of hair, and Helen Lennox's voice whispered to him: "Save Katy, for my sake," and so next day, when Mark found himself alone with Katy, while most of the guests were at the beach, he questioned her of her life at Saratoga and Newport, and gradually, as he talked, there crept into Katy's heart a suspicion that he was not pleased with her account, or with what he had seen of her since his arrival.

For a moment Katy was indignant, but when he said to her kindly: "Would Helen be pleased?" her tears started at once, and she attempted an excuse for her weak folly, accusing Sybil Grandon as the first cause of the ambition for which she hated herself.

"She had been held up as my pattern," she said, half bitterly, and forgetting to whom she was talking—"she, the one whom I was to imitate; and when I found that I could go beyond her, I yielded to the temptation, and exulted to see how far she was left behind. Besides that," she continued, "is it no gratification, think you, to let Wilford's proud mother and sister see the poor country girl, whom ordinarily they would despise, stand where they cannot come, and even dictate to them if she chooses so to do? I know it is wrong—I know it is wicked—but I like the excitement, and so long as I am with these people I shall never be any better. Mark Ray, you don't know what it is to be surrounded by a set who care for nothing but fashion and display, and how they may outdo each other. I hate New York society. There is nothing there but husks."

Katy's tears had ceased, and on her white face there was a new look of womanhood, as if in that outburst she had changed, and would never again be just what she was before.

"Say," she continued, "do *you* like New York society?"

"Not always—not wholly," Mark answered; "and still you misjudge it greatly, for all are not like the people you describe. Your husband's family represent one extreme, while there are others equally high in the social scale who do not make fashion the rule of their lives— sensible, cultivated, intellectual people, of whose acquaintance one might be glad—people whom I fancy your sister Helen would enjoy. I have only met her twice, but my impression is that *she* would not find New York distasteful."

Mark did not know why he had dragged Helen into that conversation, unless it were that she seemed very near to him as he talked with Katy, who replied:

"Yes, Helen finds good in all. She sees differently from what I do, and I wish so much that she was here."

"Why not send for her?" Mark asked, casting about in his mind whether in case Helen came, he, too, could tarry for a week and leave that business in Southbridge, which he must attend to ere returning to the city.

It would be a study to watch Helen Lennox there at Newport, and in imagination Mark was already her sworn knight, shielding her from criticism, and commanding for her respect from those who respected him, when Katy tore his castle down by answering impulsively:

"I doubt if Wilford would let me send for her, nor does it matter, as I shall not remain much longer. I do not need her now, since you have shown me how foolish I have been. I was angry at first, but now I thank you for it, and so will Helen. I shall tell her when I am in Silverton. I am going there from here and oh, I so wish it was to-day."

The guests were beginning to return from the beach by this time, and as Mark had said all he had intended saying, he left Katy with Wilford, who had just come in and joined a merry party of Bostonians only that day arrived. That night at the Ocean House the guests missed something from their festivities; the dance was not so exhilarating or the small-talk between so lively, while more

than one white-kidded dandy swore mentally at the innocent Wilford, whose wife declined to join in the gayeties,
and in a plain white muslin, with only a pond lily in her
hair, kept by her husband's side, notwithstanding that he
bade her leave him and accept some of her numerous
invitations to join the giddy dance. This sober phase of
Katy did not on the whole please Wilford as much as
her gayer ones had done. All he had ever dreamed of the
sensation his bride would create was more than verified.
Katy had fulfilled his highest expectations, reaching a
point from which, as she had said to Mark, she could
dictate to his mother, if she chose, and he did not care
to see her relinquish it.

But Katy remained true to herself. Dropping her
girlish playfulness, she assumed a quiet, gentle dignity,
which became her even better than her gayer mood had
done, making her ten times more popular and more sought
after, until she begged to go away, persuading Wilford
at last to name the day for their departure, and then,
never doubting for a moment that her destination was
Silverton, she wrote to Helen that she should be home
on such a day, and as they would come by way of Providence and Worcester, they would probably reach West
Silverton at ten o'clock, A. M.

"Wilford," she added in a postscript, "has gone down
to bathe, and as the mail is just closing, I shall send this
letter without his seeing it. Of course it can make no
difference, for I have talked all summer of coming, and
he understands it."

CHAPTER XX.

MARK RAY AT SILVERTON.

THE last day of summer was dying out in a fierce storm
of rain which swept in sheets across the Silverton hills,
hiding the pond from view, and beating against the windows of the farm-house, whose inmates were nevertheless
unmindful of the storm save as they hoped the morrow
would prove bright and fair, such as the day should be
which brought them back their Katy. Nearly worn out
with constant reference was her letter, the mother watch-

ing it up from time to time to read the part referring
to herself, where Katy had told how blessed it would be
"to rest again on mother's bed," just as she had so often
wished to do, "and hear mother's voice;" the deacon spell-
ing out by his spluttering tallow candle, with its long,
smoky wick, what she had said of "darling old Uncle
Eph," and the rides into the fields; Aunt Betsy, too, reading mostly from memory the words: "Good old Aunt
Betsy, with her skirts so limp and short, tell her she will
look handsomer to me than the fairest belle at Newport;"
and as often as Aunt Betsy read it she would ejaculate:
"The land! what kind of company must the child have
kept?" wondering next if Helen had never written of
the *hoop,* for which she paid a dollar, and which was
carefully hung in her closet, waiting for the event of to-
morrow, while the hem of her pongee had been let down
and one breadth gored to accommodate the hoop. On the
whole, Aunt Betsy expected to make a stylish appearance
before the little lady of whom she stood in awe, always
speaking of her to the neighbors as "My niece, Miss Cammen, from New York," and taking good care to report what
she had heard of "Miss Cammen's" costly dress and the
grandeur of her house, where the furniture of the best
chamber cost over fifteen hundred dollars.

"What could it be?" Aunt Betsy had asked in her simplicity, feeling an increased respect for Katy, and con-
senting the more readily to the change in her pongee, as
suggested to her by Helen.

But that was for to-morrow when Katy came; to-night
she only wore a dotted brown, whose hem just reached the
top of her "bootees," as she went to strain the milk brought
in by Uncle Ephraim, while Helen took her position near
the window, looking drearily out upon the leaden clouds,
and hoping it would brighten before the morrow. Like
the others, Helen had read Katy's letter many times,
dwelling longest upon the part which said: "I have been
so bad, so frivolous and wicked here at Newport, that it
will be a relief to make you my confessor, depending, as
I do, upon your love to grant me absolution."

From a family in Silverton, who had spent a few days
at a private house in Newport, Helen had heard something

of her sister's life; the lady had seen her once driving a
tandem team down the avenue, with Wilford at her side
giving her instructions.   Since then there had been some
anxiety felt for her at the farm-house, and more than Dr.
Grant had prayed that she might be kept unspotted from the
world; but when her letter came, so full of love and self-
reproaches, the burden was lifted, and there was nothing
to mar the anticipations of the event for which they had
made so many preparations, Uncle Ephraim going to the
expense of buying at auction a half-worn covered buggy,
which he fancied would suit Katy better than the corn-
colored wagon in which she used to ride.   To pay for this
the deacon had parted with the money set aside for the
" *great coat* " he so much needed for the coming winter,
his old gray having done him service for fifteen years.
But his comfort was nothing compared with Katy's happiness, and so, with his wrinkled face beaming with delight,
he had brought home his buggy, putting it carefully in
the barn, and saying no one should ride in it till Katy
came.   With untiring patience the old man mended up his
harness, for what he had heard of Katy's driving had impressed him strongly with her powers of horsemanship,
and raised her somewhat in his respect.   Could he have
afforded it Uncle Ephraim in his younger days would
have been a horse jockey, and even now he liked nothing
better than to make Old Whitey run when alone in the
strip of woods between his house and the head of the
pond.

"Katy inherits her love of horses from me," he said
complacently; and with a view of improving Whitey's
style and mettle, he took to feeding him on oats, talking
to him at times, and telling him who was coming.

Dear, simple-hearted Uncle Ephraim! the days which
he must wait seemed long to him as they did to the other
members of his family.   But they were all gone now,—
Katy would be home on the morrow, and with the shutting
in of night the candles were lighted in the sitting-room,
and Helen sat down to her work, wishing it was to-night
that Katy was coming.   As if in answer to her wish there
was the sound of wheels, which stopped before the house,
and dropping her work Helen ran quickly to the door,

just as from under the dripping umbrella held by a driver boy, a tall young man sprang upon the step, nearly upsetting her, but passing an arm around her shoulders in time to keep her from falling.

"I beg pardon for this assault upon you," the stranger said; and then turning to the boy he continued: "It's all right, you need not wait."

With a chirrup and a blow the horse started forward, and the mud-bespattered vehicle was moving down the road ere Helen had recovered her surprise at recognizing Mark Ray, who shook the rain-drops from his hair, and offering her his hand said in reply to her involuntary exclamation: "I thought it was Katy," "Shall I infer then that I am the less welcome?" and his bright, saucy eyes looked laughingly into hers. Business had brought him to Southbridge, he said, and it was his intention to take the cars that afternoon for New York, but having been detained longer than he expected, and not liking the looks of the hotel arrangements, he had decided to presume upon his acquaintance with Dr. Grant, and spend the night at Linwood. "But," and again his eyes looked straight at Helen, "it rained so hard and the light from your window was so inviting that I ventured to stop, so here I am, claiming your hospitality until morning, if convenient; if not, I will find my way to Linwood."

There was something in this pleasant familiarity which won Uncle Ephraim at once, and he bade the young man stay, as did Aunt Hannah and Mrs. Lennox, who now for the first time was presented to Mark Ray. Always capable of adapting himself to the circumstances around him, Mark did so now with so much ease and courteousness as to astonish Helen, and partly thaw the reserve she had assumed when she found the visitor was from the hated city.

"Are you expecting Mrs. Cameron?" he asked, adding, as Helen explained that she was coming to-morrow, "That is strange. Wilford wrote decidedly that he should be in New York to-morrow. Possibly, though, he does not intend himself to stop."

"I presume not," Helen replied, a weight suddenly lifting from her heart at the prospect of not having to entertain the formidable brother-in-law who, if he stayed long, would spoil all her pleasure.

Thus at her ease on this point, she grew more talkative, half-wishing that her dress was not a shilling-calico, or her hair combed back quite so straight, giving her that severe look which Morris had said was unbecoming. It was very smooth and glossy, and Sybil Grandon would have given her best diamond to have had in her own natural right the heavy coil of hair bound so many times around the back of Helen's head, and ornamented with neither ribbon, comb, nor bow. Only a single geranium leaf, with a white and scarlet blossom, was fastened just below the ear, and on the side where Mark could see it best, admiring its effect and forgetting the arrangement of the hair in his admiration of the well-shaped head, bending so industriously over the work which Helen had resumed—not crocheting, nor yet embroidery, but the very homely work of darning Uncle Ephraim's socks, a task which Helen always did, and on that particular night. Helen knew it was not delicate employment, and there was a moment's hesitancy as she wondered what Mark would think—then, with a grim delight in letting him see that she did not care, she resumed her darning-needle, and as a kind of penance for the flash of pride in which she had indulged, selected from the basket the very coarsest, ugliest sock she could find, stretching out the huge fracture at the heel to its utmost extent, and attacking it with a right good will, while Mark, with a comical look on his face, sat watching her. She knew he was looking at her, and her cheeks were growing very red, while her hatred of him was increasing, when he said, abruptly: "You follow my mother's custom, I see. She used to mend my socks on Tuesday nights."

"Your mother mend socks!" and Helen started so suddenly as to run the point of her darning-needle a long way into her thumb, the wound bringing a stream of blood which she tried to wipe away with her handkerchief.

"Bind it tightly round. Let me show you, please," Mark said, and ere she was aware of what she was doing, Helen was quietly permitting the young man to wind her handkerchief around her thumb which he held in his hand, pressing it until the blood ceased flowing, and the sharp pain had abated.

Perhaps Mark Ray liked holding that small, warm hand, even though it were not as white and soft as Juno's; at all events he did hold it until Helen drew it from him with a quick, sudden motion, telling him it would do very well, and she would not trouble him. Mark did not look as if he had been troubled, but went back to his seat and took up the conversation just where the needle had stopped it.

"My mother did not always mend herself, but she caused it to be done, and sometimes helped. I remember she used to say a woman should know how to do everything pertaining to a household, and she carried out her theory in the education of my sister."

"Have you a sister?" Helen asked, now really interested, and listening intently while Mark told her of his only sister Julia, now Mrs. Ernst, whose home was in New Orleans, though she at present was in Paris, and his mother was there with her. "After Julia's marriage, nine years ago, mother went to live with her," he said, "but latterly, as the little Ernsts increase so fast, she wishes for a more quiet home, and this winter she is coming to New York to keep house for me."

Helen thought she might like Mark's mother, who, he told her, had been twice married, and was now Mrs. Banker, and a widow. She must be different from Mrs. Cameron; and Helen let herself down to another degree of toleration for the man whose mother taught her daughter to mend the family socks. Still there was about her a reserve, which Mark wondered at, for it was not thus that ladies were accustomed to receive his advances. He did not guess that Wilford Cameron stood between him and Helen's good opinion; but when, after the family came in, the conversation turned upon Katy and her life in New York, the secret came out in the sharp, caustic manner with which she spoke of New York and its people.

"It's Will and the Camerons," Mark thought, blaming Helen less than he would have done, if he, too, had not known something of the Cameron pride.

It was a novel position in which Mark found himself

that night, an inmate of a humble farm-house, where he
could almost touch the ceiling with his hand, and where
his surroundings were so different from what he had been
accustomed to; but, unlike Wilford Cameron, he did not
wish himself away, nor feel indignant at Aunt Betsy's
old-fashioned ways, or Uncle Ephraim's grammar. He
noticed Aunt Betsy's oddities, it is true, and noticed Uncle
Ephraim's grammar; but the sight of Helen sitting there,
with so much dignity and self-respect, made him look
beyond all else, straight into her open face and clear brown
eyes, where there was nothing obnoxious or distasteful.
Her language was correct, her manner, saving a little stiffness, lady-like and refined: and Mark enjoyed his situation as self-invited guest, making himself so agreeable that
Uncle Ephraim forgot his hour of retiring, nor discovered
his mistake until, with a loud yawn, Aunt Betsy told him
that it was half-past nine, and she was " desput sleepy."

Owing to Helen's influence there had been a change of
the olden custom, and instead of the long chapter, through
which Uncle Ephraim used to plod so wearily, there were
now read the Evening Psalms. Aunt Betsy herself joined
in the reading, which she mentally classed with the
" quirks," but confessed to herself that it " was most as
good as the Bible."

As there were only Prayer Books enough for the family,
Helen, in distributing them, purposely passed Mark by,
thinking he might not care to join them. But when the
verse came round to Helen he quickly drew his chair near
to hers, and taking one side of her book, performed his
part, while Helen's face grew red as the blossoms in
her hair, and her hand, so near to Mark's, trembled visibly.

" A right nice chap, and not an atom stuck up," was
Aunt Betsy's mental comment, and then, as he often will
do, Satan followed the saintly woman even to her knees,
making her wonder if " Mr. Ray hadn't some notion after
Helen." She hoped not, for she meant that Morris should
have Helen, " though if 'twas to be it was, and she should
not go agin it;" and while Aunt Betsy thus settled the
case, Uncle Ephraim's prayer ended, and the conscience-
smitten woman arose from her knees with the conviction
that " the evil one had got the better of her once," mentally

asking pardon for her wandering thoughts and promising to do better.

Mark was in no haste to retire, and when Uncle Ephraim offered to conduct him to his room, he frankly answered that he was not sleepy, adding, as he turned to Helen: "Please let me stay until Miss Lennox finishes her socks. There are several pairs yet undarned. I will not detain you, though," he continued, bowing to Uncle Ephraim, who, a little uncertain what to do, finally departed, as did Aunt Hannah and his sister, leaving Helen and her mother to entertain Mark Ray. It had been Mrs. Lennox's first intention to retire also, but a look from Helen kept her, and she sat down by that basket of socks, while Mark wished her away. Awhile they talked of Katy and New York, Mark laboring to convince Helen that its people were not all heartless and fickle, and at last citing his mother as an instance.

"You would like mother, Miss Lennox. I hope you will know her some time," he said, and then they talked of books, Helen forgetting that Mark was city-bred in the interest with which she listened to him, while Mark forgot that the girl who appreciated and understood his views almost before they were expressed, was country born, and clad in homely garb, with no ornaments save those of her fine mind and the sparkling face turned so fully towards him.

"Mark Ray is not like Wilford Cameron," Helen said to herself, when as the clock was striking eleven she bade him good-night and went up to her room, and opening her window she leaned her hot cheek against the wet casement, and looked out upon the night, now so beautiful and clear, for the rain was over, and up in the heavens the bright stars were shining, each one bearing some resemblance to Mark's eyes as they kindled and grew bright with his excitement, resting always kindly on her—on Helen, who leaning thus from the window, felt stealing over her that feeling which, once born, can never be quite forgotten.

Helen did not recognize the feeling, for it was a strange one to her. She was only conscious of a sensation half pleasurable, half sad, of which Mark Ray had been the cause, and which she tried in vain to put aside. And then

there swept over her a feeling of desolation such as she
had never experienced before, a shrinking from living all
her life in Silverton, as she fully expected to do, and laying
her head upon the little stand, she cried passionately.

"This is weak, this is folly," she suddenly exclaimed,
as she became conscious of acting as Helen Lennox was
not wont to act, and with a strong effort she dried her tears
and crept quietly to bed just as Mark was falling into his
first sleep and dreaming of smothering.

Helen would not have acknowledged it, and yet it was
a truth not to be denied, that she stayed next morning a
much longer time than usual before her glass, arranging
her hair, which was worn more becomingly than on the
previous night, and which softened the somewhat too intellectual expression of her face, and made her seem more
womanly and modest. Once she thought to wear the light
buff gown in which she looked so well, but the thought
was repudiated as soon as formed, and donning the same
dark calico she would have worn if Mark had not been
there, she finished her simple toilet and went down stairs,
just as Mark came in at the side door, his hands full of
water lilies, and his boots bearing marks of what he had
been through to get them.   •

"Early country air is healthful," he said, "and as I
do not often have a chance to try it, I thought I would
improve the present opportunity. So I have been down by
the pond, and spying these lilies I persevered until I
reached them, in spite of mud and mire. There is no
blossom I like so well. Were I a young girl I would always wear one in my hair, as your sister did one night at
Newport, and I never saw her look better. Just let me
try the effect on you;" and selecting a half-opened bud,
Mark placed it among Helen's braids as skillfully as if
hair-dressing were one of his accomplishments. "The effect is good," he continued, turning her blushing face to
the glass and asking if it were not.

"Yes," Helen stammered, seeing more the saucy eyes
looking over her head than the lily in her hair. "Yes,
good enough, but hardly in keeping with this old dress,"
and vanity whispered the wish that the *buff* had really
been worn.

"Your dress is suitable for morning, I am sure," Mark replied, turning a little more to the right the lily, and noticing as he did so how very white and pretty was the neck and throat seen above the collar.

Mark liked a pretty neck, and he was glad to know that Helen had one, though why he should care was a puzzle. He could hardly have analyzed his feelings then, or told what he did think of Helen. He only knew that by her efforts to repel him she attracted him the more, she was so different from any young ladies he had known—so different from Juno, into whose hair he had never twined a water lily. It would not become her as it did Helen, he thought, as he sat opposite her at the table, admiring his handiwork, which even Aunt Betsy observed, remarking that "Helen was mightily spruced up for morning," a compliment which Helen acknowledged with a painful blush, while Mark began a disquisition upon the nature of lilies generally, which lasted until breakfast was ended.

It was arranged that Mark should ride to the cars with Uncle Ephraim when he went for Katy, and as this gave him a good two hours of leisure, he spoke of Dr. Grant, asking Helen if she did not suppose he would call round. Helen thought it possible, and then remembering how many things were to be done that morning, she excused herself from the parlor, and repairing to the platform out by the back door, where it was shady and cool, she tied on a broad check apron, and rolling her sleeves above her elbows, was just bringing the churn-dasher to bear vigorously upon the thick cream she was turning into butter, when, having finished his cigar, Mark went out into the yard, and following the winding path came suddenly upon her. Helen's first impulse was to stop, but with a strong nerving of herself she kept on while Mark, coming as near as he dared, said to her: "Why do you do that? Is there no one else?"

"No," Helen answered; "that is, we keep no servant, and my young arms are stronger than the others."

"And *mine* are stronger still," Mark laughingly rejoined, as he put Helen aside and plied the dasher himself, in spite of her protestations that he would certainly ruin his clothes.

"Tie that apron round me, then," he said, with the utmost nonchalance, and Helen obeyed, tying her check apron around the young man's neck, who felt her hands as they touched his hair, and knew that they were brushing queer fancies into his brain—fancies which made him wonder what his mother would think of Helen, or what she would say if she knew just how he was occupied that morning, absolutely churning cream until it turned to butter, for Mark persisted until the task was done, standing by while Helen gathered up the golden lumps, and admiring her plump, round arms quite as much as he had her neck.

She would be a belle like her sister, though of a different stamp, he thought, as he again bent down his head while she removed the apron and disclosed more than one big spot upon his broadcloth. Mark assured her that it did not matter; his coat was nearly worn out, and any way he never should regret that he had *churned* once in his life, or forget it either; and then he asked if Helen would be in New York the coming winter, talking of the pleasure it would be to meet her there, until Helen began to feel what she never before had felt, a desire to visit Katy in her own home.

"Remember if you come that I am your debtor for numerous hospitalities," he said, when he at last bade her good-bye and sprang into the covered buggy, which Uncle Ephraim had brought out in honor of Katy's arrival.

———

Old Whitey was hitched at a safe distance from all possible harm. Uncle Ephraim had returned from the store near by, laden with the six pounds of crush sugar and the two pounds of real old Java he had been commissioned to purchase with a view to Katy's taste, and now upon the platform at West Silverton he stood, with Mark Ray, waiting for the arrival of the train just appearing in view across the level plain.

"It's fifteen months since she went away," he said, and Mark saw that the old man's form trembled with the excitement of meeting her again, while his eyes scanned eagerly every window and door of the cars now slowly stopping before him. " There, there ! " and he laid his hand nervously on Mark's shoulder, as a white, jaunty feather appeared in view; but that was not Katy, and the dim eyes ran again along the whole line of the cars, from which so many were alighting.

But Katy did not come, and with a long breath of wonder and disappointment the deacon said: " Can it be she is asleep? Young man, you are spryer than I. Go through the cars and find her."

Mark knew there was plenty of time, and so he made the tour of the cars, but found, alas, no Katy.

" She's not there," was the report carried to the poor old man, who tremblingly repeated the words: " Not there, not come ! " while over his aged face there broke a look of touching sadness, which Mark never forgot, remembering it always just as he remembered the big tear drops which from his seat by the window he saw the old man wipe away with his coat-sleeve, as whispering softly to Whitey of his disappointment he unhitched the horse and drove away alone.

" Maybe she's writ. I'll go and see," he said, and driving to their regular office he found a letter directed by Wilford Cameron, but written by Katy; but he could not read it then, and thrusting it into his pocket he went slowly back to the home where the tempting dinner was prepared and the family waiting so eagerly for him. Even before he reached them they knew of the disappointment, for from the garret window Helen had watched the road by which he would come, and when the buggy appeared in sight she saw he was alone.

There was a mistake; Katy had missed the train, she said to her mother and aunts, who hoped she might be right. But Katy had not missed the train, as was indicated by the letter which Uncle Ephraim without a word put into Helen's hand, leaning on old Whitey's neck while she read aloud the attempt at an explanation which Katy had hurriedly written, a stain on the paper where a tear had fallen, attesting her distress at the bitter disappointment.

" Wilford did not know of the other letter," she said,

"and had made arrangements for her to go back with him
to New York, inasmuch as the house was already opened
and the servants there wanting a *head;* besides that, Wilford had been absent so long that he could not possibly
stop at Silverton himself, and as he would not think of
living without her, even for a few days, there was no alternative but for her to go with him on the boat directly
to New York. I am sorry, oh, so sorry, but indeed I am
not to blame," she added in conclusion, and this was the
nearest approach there was to an admission that anybody
was to blame for this disappointment which cut so cruelly,
making Uncle Ephraim cry, as out in the barn he hung
away the mended harness and covered the new buggy,
which had been bought for naught.

"I might have had the overcoat, for Katy will never
come home again, never. God grant that it's the Cameron
pride, not hers that kept her from us," the old man said,
as on the hay he knelt down and prayed that Katy had not
learned to despise the home where she was so beloved.

"Katy will never come to us again," seemed the prevail-
ing opinion at Silverton, where more than Uncle Ephraim
felt a chilling doubt at times as to whether she really
wished to come or not. If she did, it seemed easy of ac-
complishment to those who knew not how perfect and com-
plete were the fetters thrown around her, and how unbend-
ing the will which governed hers. Could they have seen
the look in Katy's face when she first understood that she
was not going to Silverton, their hearts would have bled
for the thwarted creature who fled up the stairs to her own
room, where Esther found her twenty minutes later, cold
and fainting upon the bed, her face as white as ashes, and
her hands clenched so tightly that the nails left marks
upon the palms.

"It was not strange that the poor child should faint—
indeed, it was only natural that nature should give way
after so many weeks of gayety, and she very far from
being strong," Mrs. Cameron said to Wilford, who was
beginning to repent of his decision, and who but for that
remark perhaps might have revoked it.

Indeed, he made an attempt to do so when, as consciousness came back, Katy lay so pale and still before him;

but Katy did not understand him, or guess that he wished
her to meet him more than half the way, and so the verdict
was unchanged, and in a kind of bewilderment, Katy wrote
the hurried letter, feeling less actual pain than did its
readers, for the disappointment had stunned her for a
time, and all she could remember of the passage home on
that same night when Mark Ray sat with Helen in the
sitting-room at Silverton, was that there was a fearful
storm of rain mingled with lightning flashes and thunder
peals, which terrified the other ladies, but brought to her
no other sensation save that it would not be so very hard
to perish in the dark waters dashing so madly about the
vessel's side.

CHAPTER XXI.

A NEW LIFE.

New York, December 16, 18—.

"TO MISS HELEN LENNOX, Silverton, Mass:
  "Your sister is very ill. Come as soon as possible.
                                        W. Cameron."

This was the purport of a telegram received at the farm-
house toward the close of a chill December day, and
Helen's heart almost stopped its beating as she read it
aloud, and then looked in the white, scared faces of those
around her. Katy was very ill—dying, perhaps—or Wilford had never telegraphed. What could it be? What
was the matter? Had it been somewhat later, they would
have known; but now all was conjecture, and in a half-
distracted state, Helen made her hasty preparations for the
journey of the morrow, and then sent for Morris, hoping
he might offer some advice or suggestion, for her to carry
to that sick-room in New York.

"Perhaps you will go with me," Helen said. "You
know Katy's constitution. You might save her life."

But Morris shook his head. If he was needed they
might send and he would come, but not without; and so
next day he carried Helen to the cars, saying to her as they
were waiting for the train, "I hope for the best, but it
may be Katy will die. If you think so, tell her, oh, tell

her, of the better world, and ask if she is prepared? I cannot lose her in Heaven."

And this was all the message Morris sent, though his heart and prayers went after the rapid train which bore Helen safely onward, until Hartford was reached, where there was a long detention, so that the dark wintry night had closed over the city ere Helen reached it, timid, anxious, and wondering what she should do if Wilford was not there to meet her. "He will be, of course," she kept repeating to herself, looking around in dismay, as passenger after passenger left, seeking in stages and street cars a swifter passage to their homes.

"I shall soon be all alone," she said, feeling some relief as the car in which she was seated began at last to move, and she knew she was being taken whither the others had gone, wherever that might be.

"Is Miss Helen Lennox here?" sounded cheerily in her ears as she stopped before the depot, and Helen uttered a cry of joy, for she recognized the voice of Mark Ray, who was soon grasping her hand, and trying to reassure her, as he saw how she shrank from the noise and clamor of New York, heard now for the first time. "Our carriage is here," he said, and in a moment she found herself in a close-covered vehicle, with Mark sitting opposite, tucking the warm blanket around her, asking if she were cold, and paying those numberless little attentions so gratifying to one always accustomed to act and think for herself.

Helen could not see Mark's face distinctly; but full of fear for Katy, she fancied there was a sad tone in his voice, as if he were keeping back something he dreaded to tell her; and then, as it suddenly occurred to her that Wilford should have met her, not Mark, her great fear found utterance in words, and leaning forward so that her face almost touched Mark's she said, "Tell me, Mr. Ray, is Katy dead?"

"Not dead, oh no, nor very dangerous, my mother hopes; but she kept asking for you, and so my—that is, Mr. Cameron sent the telegram."

There was an ejaculatory prayer of thankfulness, and then Helen continued, "Is it long since she was taken sick?"

"Her little daughter will be a week old to-morrow," Mark replied; while Helen, with an exclamation of surprise she could not repress, sank back into the corner, faint and giddy with the excitement of this fact, which invested little Katy with a new dignity, and drew her so much nearer to the sister who could scarcely wait for the carriage to stop, so anxious was she to be where Katy was, to kiss her dear face once more, and whisper the words of love she knew she must have longed to hear.

Awe-struck, bewildered and half terrified, Helen looked up at the huge brown structure, which Mark designated as "the place." It was so lofty, so grand, so like the Camerons, and so unlike the farm-house far away, that Helen trembled as she followed Mark into the rooms flooded with light, and seeming to her like fairy land. They were so different from anything she had imagined, so much handsomer than even Katy's descriptions had implied, that for the moment the sight took her breath away, and she sank passively into the chair Mark brought for her, himself taking her muff and tippet, and noting, as he did so, that they were not mink, nor yet Russian sable, but well-worn, well-kept fitch, such as Juno would laugh at and criticise. But Helen's dress was a matter of small moment to Mark, and he thought more of the look in her dark eyes than of all the furs in Broadway, as she said to him, "You are very kind, Mr. Ray. I cannot thank you enough." This remark had been wrung from Helen by the feeling of homesickness which swept over her, as she thought how really alone she should be there, in her sister's house, on this first night of her arrival, if it were not for Mark, thus virtually taking the place of the brother-in-law, who should have been there to greet her.

"He was with Mrs. Cameron," the servant said, and taking out a card Mark wrote down a few words, and handing it to the servant who had been looking curiously at Helen, he continued standing until a step was heard on the stairs and Wilford came quietly in.

It was not a very loving meeting, but Helen was civil and Wilford was polite offering her his hand and asking some questions about her journey.

"I was intending to meet you myself," he said, "but

Mrs. Cameron does not like me to leave her, and Mark
kindly offered to take the trouble off my hands."

He was looking pale and anxious, while there was on
his face the light of a new joy, as if the little life begun
so short a time ago had brought an added good to him,
softening his haughty manner and making him even endurable to the prejudiced sister watching him so closely.

"Does Phillips know you are here?" he asked, answering his own query by ringing the bell and bidding Esther,
who appeared, tell Phillips that Miss Lennox had arrived,
and wished for supper, explaining to Helen that since
Katy's illness they had dined at three, as that accommo-
dated them the best.

This done and Helen's baggage ordered to her room, he
seemed to think he had discharged his duty as host, and
as Mark had left he began to grow fidgety, for a tête-à-
tête with Helen was not what he desired. He had said to
her all he could think to say, for it never once occurred
to him to inquire after the deacon's family. He had asked
for Dr. Grant, but his solicitude went no further, and the
inmates of the farm-house might have been dead and buried
for aught he knew to the contrary. The omission was not
made purposely, but because he really did not feel enough
of interest in people so widely different from himself even
to ask for them, much less to suspect how Helen's blood
boiled as she detected the omission and imputed it to intended slight, feeling glad when he excused himself, saying he must go back to Katy, but would send his mother
down to see her. *His mother.* Then *she* was there, the
one whom Helen dreaded most of all, whom she had invested with every possible terror, hoping now that she
would not be in haste to come down. She might have
spared herself anxiety on this point, as the lady in question was not anxious to meet a person who, could she have
had her way, would not have been there at all.

From the first moment of consciousness after the long
hours of suffering Katy had asked for Helen, rather than
her mother.

"Send for Helen; I am so tired, and she could always
rest me," was her reply, when asked by Wilford what he
could do for her. "Send for Helen; I want her so

much," she had said to Mrs. Cameron, when she came, repeating the wish until a consultation was held between
the mother and son, touching the propriety of sending
for Helen. "She would be of no use whatever, and might
excite our Katy. Quiet is highly important just now,"
Mrs. Cameron had said, thus veiling under pretended concern for Katy her aversion to the girl whose independence
in declining her dress-maker had never been forgiven, and
whom she had set down in her mind as rude and ignorant.

"If her coming would do Katy harm she ought not to
come," Wilford thought, while Katy in her darkened room
moaned on—

"Send for sister Helen; please send for sister Helen."

At last, on the fourth day, Mrs. Banker, Mark Ray's
mother, came to the house, and in consideration of the
strong liking she had evinced for Katy ever since her arrival in New York, and the great respect felt for her by
Mrs. Cameron, she was admitted to the chamber and heard
the plaintive pleadings, "Send for sister Helen." until
her motherly heart was touched, and as she sat with her
son at dinner she spoke of the young girl-mother moaning
so for Helen.

Whether it was Mark's great pity for Katy, or whether
he was prompted by some more selfish motive, we do not
profess to say, but that he was greatly excited was very
evident from his manner as he exclaimed:

"Why not send for Helen, then? She is a splendid
girl, and they idolize each other. Talk of *her* injuring
Katy, that's all a humbug. She is just fitted for a nurse.
Almost the sight of her would cure one of nervousness, she
is so calm and quiet."

This was what Mark said, and the next morning Mrs.
Banker's carriage stood at the door of No. — Madison
Square, while Mrs. Banker herself was talking to Wilford
in the library, and urging that Helen be sent for at once.

"It may save her life. She is more feverish to-day than
yesterday, and this constant asking for her sister will wear
her out so fast," she added, and that last argument prevailed.

Helen was sent for, and now sat waiting in the parlor
for the coming of Mrs. Cameron. Wilford did not mean

Katy to hear him as he whispered to his mother that Helen
was below; but she did, and her blue eyes flashed brightly
as she started from her pillow, exclaiming:

"I am so glad, so glad! Kiss me, Wilford, because I
am so glad. Does she know? Have you told her? Wasn't
she surprised, and will she come up quick?"

They could not quiet her at once, and only the assurance
that unless she were more composed, Helen should not
see her that night, had any effect upon her; but when they
told her that, she lay back upon her pillow submissively,
and Wilford saw the great tears dropping from her hot
cheeks, while the pallid lips kept softly whispering
"Helen." Then the sister love took another channel, and
she said:

"She has not been to supper, and Phillips is always
cross at extras. Will somebody see to it. Send Esther to
me, please. Esther knows and is good-natured."

"Mother will do all that is necessary She is going
down," Wilford said; but Katy had quite as much fear
of leaving Helen to "mother" as to Phillips, and insisted
upon Esther until the latter came, receiving numerous injunctions as to the jam, the sweetmeats, the peaches, and
the cold ham Helen must have, each one being remembered
as her favorite.

Wholly unselfish, Katy thought nothing of herself or
the effort it cost her to care for Helen; but when it was
over and Esther was gone, she seemed so utterly exhausted
that Mrs. Cameron did not leave her, but stayed at her bedside, until the extreme paleness was gone, and her eyes
were more natural. Meanwhile the supper, which as Katy
feared had made Phillips cross, had been arranged by
Esther, who conducted Helen to the dining-room, herself
standing by and waiting upon her because the one whose
duty it was had gone out for the evening, and Phillips
had declined the "honor," as she styled it.

There was a homesick feeling tugging at Helen's heart
while she tried to eat, and only the certainty that Katy
was not far away kept her tears back. To her the very
grandeur of the house made it desolate, and she was so
glad it was Katy who lived there and not herself as she
went up the soft carpeted stairway, which gave back no

sound, and through the marble hall to the parlor, where, by the table on which her cloak and furs were lying, a lady stood, as dignified and unconscious as if she had not been inspecting the self-same *fur* which Mark Ray had observed, but not, like him, thinking it did not matter, for it did matter very materially with her, and a smile of contempt had curled her lip as she turned over the tippet which Phillips would not have worn.

"I wonder how long she means to stay, and if Wilford will have to take her out," she was thinking, just as Helen appeared in the door and advanced into the room.

By herself, it was easy to slight Helen Lennox, but in her presence Mrs. Cameron found it very hard to appear as cold and distant as she had meant to do, for there was something about Helen which commanded her respect, and she went forward to meet her, offering her hand and saying cordially:

"Miss Lennox, I presume—my daughter Katy's sister?"

Helen had not expected this, and the warm flush which came to her cheeks made her very handsome, as she returned Mrs. Cameron's greeting, and then asked more particularly for Katy than she had yet done. For a while they talked together, Mrs. Cameron noting carefully every item of Helen's attire, as well as the purity of her language and her perfect repose of manner after the first stiffness had passed away.

"Naturally a lady as well as Katy; there must be good blood somewhere, probably on the Lennox side," was Mrs. Cameron's private opinion, while Helen, after a few moments, began to feel far more at ease with Mrs. Cameron than she had done in the dining-room with Esther waiting on her, and the cross Phillips stalking once through the room for no ostensible purpose except to get a sight of her.

Helen wondered at herself, and Mrs. Cameron wondered too, trying to decide whether it were ignorance, conceit, obtuseness, or what, which made her so self-possessed when she was expected to appear so different.

"Strong-minded," was her final decision, as she said at last, "We promised Katy she should see you to-night. Will you go now?"

Then the color left Helen's face and lips and her limbs shook perceptibly, for the knowing she was soon to meet her sister unnerved her; but by the time the door of Katy's room was reached she was herself again, and there was no need for Mrs. Cameron to whisper, " Pray do not excite her."

Katy heard her coming, and it required all Wilford's and the nurse's efforts to keep her quiet.

" Helen, Helen, darling, darling sister! " she cried, as she wound her arms around Helen's neck, and laid her golden head on Helen's bosom, sobbing in a low, mournful way which told Helen more how she had been longed for than did the weak voice which whispered, " I've wanted you so much, oh Helen; you don't know how much I've missed you all the years I've been away. You will not leave me now," and Katy clung closer to the dear sister who gently unclasped the clinging arms and put back upon the pillow the quivering face, which she kissed so tenderly, whispering in her own old half soothing, half commanding way, " Be quiet now, Katy. It's best that you should. No, I will not leave you."

Next to Dr. Grant Helen had more influence over Katy than any living being, and it was very apparent now, for, as if her presence had a power to soothe, Katy grew very quiet, and utterly wearied out, slept for a few moments with Helen's hand fast locked in hers. When she awoke the tired look was gone, and turning to her sister she said, " Have you seen my baby? " while the young mother love which broke so beautifully over her pale face, made it the face of an angel.

" It seems so funny that it is Katy's baby," Helen said, taking the puny little thing, which with its wrinkled face and red, clinched fists was not very attractive to her, save as she looked at it with Katy's eyes.

She did not even kiss it, but her tears dropped upon its head as she thought how short the time since up in the old garret at home she had dressed rag dolls for the Katy who was now a mother. And still in a measure she was the same, hugging Helen fondly when she said good-night, and welcoming her so joyfully in the morning when she came again, telling her how just the sight of her sitting there by baby's crib did her so much good.

"I shall get well so fast," she said; and she was right, for Helen was worth far more to her than all the physician's powders, and Wilford was glad that Helen came, even if she did sometimes shock him with her independent ways, upsetting all his plans and theories with regard to Katy, and meeting him on other grounds with an opposition as puzzling as it was new to him.

To Mrs. Cameron Helen was a study; she seemed to care so little for what others might think of her, evincing no hesitation, no timidity, when told the second day after her arrival that Mrs. Banker was in the parlor, and had asked to see Miss Lennox. Mrs. Cameron did not suspect how under that calm, unmoved exterior, Helen was hiding a heart which beat painfully as she went down to meet the mother of Mark Ray, going first to her own room to make some little change in her toilet, and wishing that her dress was more like the dress of those around her— like Mrs. Cameron's, or even *Esther's* and the fashionable nurse's. One glance she gave to the brown silk, Wilford's gift, but her good sense told her that the plain merino she wore was more suitable to the sick room where she spent her time, and so with a fresh collar and cuffs, and another brush of her hair, she went to Mrs. Banker, forgetting herself in her pleasure at finding in the stranger a lady so wholly congenial and familiar, whose mild, dark eyes rested so kindly on her, and whose pleasant voice had something motherly in its tone, putting her at her ease, and making her appear at her very best.

Mrs. Banker was pleased with Helen, and she felt a kind of pity for the young girl thrown so suddenly among strangers, without even her sister to assist her.

"Have you been out at all?" she asked, and upon Helen's replying that she had not, she answered, "That is not right. Accustomed to the fresh country air, you will suffer from too close confinement. Suppose you ride with me. My carriage is at the door, and I have a few hours' leisure. Tell your sister I insist," she continued, as Helen hesitated between inclination and what she fancied was her duty.

To see New York with Mrs. Banker was a treat indeed, and Helen's heart bounded high as she ran up to Katy's room with the request.

"Yes, go by all means," Katy said. "It is so kind in Mrs. Banker, and so like her, too. I meant that Wilford should have driven with you to-day, and spoke to him about it, but Mrs. Banker will do better. Tell her I thank her so much for her thoughtfulness," and with a kiss Katy sent Helen away, while Mrs. Cameron, after twisting her rings nervously for a moment, said to Katy:

"Perhaps your sister will do well to wear your furs. Hers are small, and common fitch."

"Yes, certainly. Take them to her," Katy answered, knowing intuitively the feeling which had prompted this suggestion from her mother-in-law, who hastened to Helen's room with the rich sable she was to wear in place of the old fitch.

Helen appreciated the difference at once between her furs and Katy's and felt a pang of mortification as she saw how old and poor and *dowdy* hers were beside the others. But they were her own—the best she could afford. She would not begin by borrowing, and so she declined the offer, and greatly to Mrs. Cameron's horror went down to Mrs. Banker clad in the despised furs, which Mrs. Cameron would on no account have had beside her on Broadway in an open carriage. Mrs. Banker noticed them, too, but the eager, happy face, which grew each moment brighter as they drove down the street, more than made amends; and in watching that and pointing out the places which they passed, Mrs. Banker forgot the furs and the coarse straw hat whose strings of black had undeniably been dyed. Never in her life had Helen enjoyed a ride as she did that pleasant winter day, when her kind friend took her wherever she wished to go, showing her Broadway in its glory from Union Square to Wall Street, where they encountered Mark in the bustling crowd. He saw them, and beckoned to them, while Helen's face grew red, as, lifting his hat to her, he came up to the carriage, and at his mother's suggestion took a seat just opposite, asking where they had been, and jocosely laughing at his mother's taste in selecting such localities as the Five Points, the

Tombs and Barnum's Museum, when there were so many finer places to be seen.

Helen felt the hot blood pricking the roots of her hair for the Five Points, the Tombs and Barnum's Museum had been her choice as the points of which she had heard the most. So when Mark continued:

"You shall ride with me, Miss Lennox, and I will show you something worth your seeing," she frankly answered:

"Your mother is not in fault, Mr. Ray. She asked me where I wished to go, and I mentioned these places; so please attribute it wholly to my country breeding, and not to your mother's lack of taste."

There was something in the frank speech which won Mrs. Banker's heart, while she felt an increased respect for the young girl, who, she saw, was keenly sensitive, even with all her strength of character.

"You were right to commence as you have," she said, "for now you have a still greater treat in store, and Mark shall drive you to the Park some day. I know you will like that."

Helen could like anything with that friendly voice to reassure her, and leaning back she was thinking how pleasant it was to be in New York, how different from what she had expected, when a bow from Mark made her look up in time to see that they were meeting a carriage, in which sat Wilford, with two gayly dressed ladies, both of whom gave her a supercilious stare as they passed by, while the younger of the two half turned her head, as if for a more prolonged gaze.

"Mrs. Grandon and Juno Cameron," Mrs. Banker said, making some further remark to her son, while Helen felt that the brightness of the day had changed, for she could not be unconscious of the look with which she had been regarded by these two fashionable ladies, and again her *furs* came up before her, bringing a felling of which she was ashamed, especially as she had fancied herself above all weakness of the kind.

That night at the dinner, from which Mrs. Cameron was absent, Wilford was unusually gracious, asking "if she had enjoyed her ride, and if she did not find Mrs. Banker a very pleasant acquaintance."

Wilford felt a little uncomfortable at having suffered a stranger to do for Katy's sister what should have been done by himself. Katy had asked him to drive with Helen, but he had found it very convenient to forget it, and take a seat instead with Juno and Mrs. Grandon, the latter of whom complimented "Miss Lennox's fine intellectual face," after they had passed, and complimented it the more as she saw how it vexed Juno, who could see nothing "in those bold eyes and that masculine forehead," just because their *vis-à-vis* chanced to be Mark Ray. Juno was not pleased with Helen's first appearance in the street, but nevertheless she called upon her next day, with Sybil Grandon and her sister Bell. To this she was urged by Sybil, who, having a somewhat larger experience of human nature, foresaw that Helen would be popular just because Mrs. Banker had taken her up, and who, besides, had conceived a capricious fancy to patronize Miss Lennox. But in this she was foiled, for Helen was not to *be* patronized, and she received her visitors with that calm, assured manner so much a part of herself.

"Diamond cut diamond," Belle thought, as she saw how frigidly polite both Juno and Helen were, each recognizing in the other something antagonistic, which could not harmonize.

Had Juno never cared for Dr. Grant, or suspected Helen of standing between herself and him, and had Mark Ray never stopped at Silverton, or been seen on Broadway with her, she might have judged her differently, for there was something attractive in Helen's face and appearance as she sat talking to her guests, with as much quiet dignity as if she had never mended Uncle Ephraim's socks or made a pound of butter among the huckleberry hills. Bell was delighted, detecting at once traces of the rare mind which Helen Lennox possessed, and wondering to find it so.

"I hope we shall see each other often," she said, at parting. "I do not go out a great deal myself—that is, not so much as Juno—but I shall be always glad to welcome you to my *den*. You may find something there to interest you."

This was Bell's leave-taking, while Sybil's was, if possible, more friendly, for she took a perverse kind of pleasure in annoying Juno, who wondered "what she or Bell could see to like in that awkward country girl, who she knew had on one of Katy's cast-off collars, and whose wardrobe was the most ordinary she ever saw; *fitch furs,* think of that!" and Juno gave a little pull at the fastenings of her rich ermine collar, showing so well over her velvet basquine.

"Fitch furs or not, they rode with Mark Ray on Broadway," Bell retorted, with a wicked look in her eye, which roused Juno to a still higher pitch of anger, so that by the time the carriage stopped at No. —, the young lady was in a most unamiable frame of mind as regarded both Helen Lennox and the offending Mark.

That evening there was at Mrs. Reynolds's a little company of thirty or more, and as Mark was present, Juno seized the opportunity of ascertaining, if possible, his real opinion of Helen Lennox, joking him first about his having taken her to ride so soon, and insinuating that he must have a *penchant* for every new and pretty face.

"Then you think her pretty? You have called on her?" Mark replied, his manner evincing so much pleasure that Juno bit her lip to keep down her wrath, and flashing upon him her scornful eyes, replied: "Yes, Sybil and Belle insisted that I should. Of myself I would never have done it, for I have now more acquaintances than I can attend to, and do not care to increase the list. Besides that, I do not imagine that Miss Lennox can in any way add to my happiness, brought up as she has been among the woods and hills, you know."

"Yes, I have been there—to her home, I mean," Mark rejoined, and Juno continued:

"Only for a moment, though. You should have stayed, like Will, to appreciate it fully. I wish you could hear him describe the feather beds on which he slept—that is, describe them before he decided to take Katy; for after that he was chary of his remarks, and the feathers by some marvelous process were changed into hair, for what he knew or cared."

Mark hesitated a moment, and then said, quietly:

"I have stayed there all night, and have tested that feather bed, but found nothing disparaging to Helen, who was as much a lady in the farm-house as here in the city."

There was a look of withering scorn on Juno's face as she replied,

"Pray, how long since you took to visiting Silverton so frequently—becoming so familiar as to spend the night?"

There was no mistaking the jealousy which betrayed itself in every tone of Juno's voice as she stood before Mark, a fit picture of the enraged goddess whose name she bore. Soon recollecting herself, however, she changed her mode of attack, and said, laughingly,

"Seriously, though, this Miss Lennox seems a very nice girl, and is admirably fitted, I think, for the position she is to fill—that of a *country physician's wife*," and in the black eyes there was a wicked sparkle as Juno saw that her meaning was readily understood, Mark looking quickly at her, and asking if she referred to Dr. Grant.

"Certainly; I imagine that was settled as long ago as we met him in Paris. Once I thought it might have been our Katy, but was mistaken. I think the doctor and Miss Lennox well adapted to each other."

There was for a moment a dull, heavy pain at Mark's heart, caused by that little item of information which made him so uncomfortable. On the whole he did not doubt it, for everything he could recall of Morris had a tendency to strengthen the belief. Nothing could be more probable, thrown together as they had been, without other congenial society, and nothing could be more suitable.

"They *are* well matched," Mark thought, as he walked listlessly through Mrs. Reynolds's parlors, seeing only one face, and *that* the face of Helen Lennox, with the lily in her hair, just as it looked when she tied the apron about his neck and laughed at his appearance.

Helen was not the ideal which in his boyhood Mark had cherished of the one who was to be his wife, for that was of a woman more like Juno, with whom he had always been on the best of terms, giving her some reason for believing herself the favored one; but ideals change as years go on, and Helen Lennox had more attractions for him now than the most dashing belle of his acquaintance.

"I do not believe I am in love with her," he said to himself when, after his return from Mrs. Reynolds's he sat for a long time before the fire in his dressing-room, cogitating upon what he had heard, and wondering why it should affect him so much. "Of course I am not," he continued, feeling the necessity of reiterating the assertion by way of making himself believe it. "She is not at all what I used to imagine the future Mrs. Mark Ray to be. Half my friends would say she had no style, no beauty, and perhaps she has not. Certainly she does not look just like the ladies at Mrs. Reynolds's to-night, but give her the same advantages and she would surpass them all."

And then Mark Ray went off into a reverie, in which he saw Helen Lennox his wife, and with the aids by which he would surround her, rapidly developing into as splendid a woman as little Katy Cameron, who did not need to be developed, but took all hearts at once by that natural, witching grace so much a part of herself. It was a very pleasant picture which Mark painted upon the mental canvas; but there came a great blur blotting out its brightness as he remembered Dr. Grant.

"But it shall not interfere with my being just as kind to her as before. She will need some attendant here, and Wilford will be glad to shove her off his hands. He is so infernal proud," Mark said, and taking a fresh cigar he finished his reverie with the magnanimous resolve that were Helen a hundred times engaged she should be his especial care during her sojourn in New York.

CHAPTER XXII.

HELEN IN SOCIETY.

IT was three days before Christmas, and Katy was talking confidentially to Mrs. Banker, whom she had asked to see the next time she called.

"I want so much to surprise her," she said, speaking in a whisper, "and you have been so kind to us both that I thought it might not trouble you very much if I asked you to make the selection for me, and see to the engra .

ing. Wilford gave me fifty dollars, all I needed, as I had fifty more of my own, and now that I have a baby, I am sure I shall never again care to go out."

"Yes," Mrs. Banker said, thoughtfully, as she rolled up the bills, "you wish me to get as heavy bracelets as I can find—for the hundred dollars."

"Yes," Katy replied, "1 think that will please her, don't you?"

Mrs. Banker did not reply at once, for she felt certain that the hundred dollars could be spent in a manner more satisfactory to Helen. Still she hardly liked to interfere, until Katy, observing her hesitancy, asked again if she did not think Helen would be pleased.

"Yes, pleased with anything you choose to give her, but—excuse me, dear Mrs. Cameron, if I speak as openly as if I were the mother of you both. Bracelets are suitable for you who have everything else, but is there not something your sister needs more? Now, allowing me to suggest, I should say, buy her some *furs,* and let the bracelets go. In Silverton her furs were well enough, but here, as the sister of Mrs. Wilford Cameron, she is deserving of better."

Katy understood Mrs. Banker at once, her·cheeks reddening as there flashed upon her the reason *why* Wilford had never yet been in the street with Helen, notwithstanding that she had more than once requested it.

"You are right," she said. "It was thoughtless in me not to think of this myself. Helen shall have the furs, and whatever else is necessary. I am so glad you reminded me of it. You are as kind as my own mother," and Katy kissed her friend fondly as she bade her good-bye, charging her a dozen times not to let Helen know the surprise in store for her.

There was little need of this caution, for Mrs. Banker understood human nature too well to divulge a matter which might wound one as sensitive as Helen. Between the latter and herself there was a strong bond of friendship, and to the kind patronage of this lady Helen owed most of the attentions she had as yet received from her sister's friends, while Mark Ray did much toward lifting her to the place she held in spite of the common country dress, which Juno unsparingly criticised, and which, in fact, kept Wilford from taking her out as his wife so often asked him to do. And Helen, too, keenly felt the difference between herself and those with whom she came in contact, crying over it more than once, but never dreaming of the surprise in store for her, when on Christmas morning she went as usual to Katy's room, finding her alone, her face all aglow with excitement, and her bed a perfect show-case of dry goods, which she bade Helen examine and say how she liked them.

Wilford was no niggard with his money, and when Katy had asked for more it had been given unsparingly, even though he knew the purpose to which it was to be applied.

"Oh, Katy, Katy, why did you do it?" Helen cried, her tears falling like rain through the fingers she clasped over her eyes.

"You are not angry?" Katy said, in some dismay, as Helen continued to sob without looking at the handsome furs, the stylish hat, the pretty cloak, and rich patterns of blue and black silk, which Mrs. Banker had selected.

"No, oh no!" Helen replied. "I know it was all meant well; but there is something in me which rebels against taking this from Wilford, and placing myself under so great obligation to him."

"It was a pleasure for him to do it," Katy said, trying to reassure her sister, until she grew calm enough to examine and admire the Christmas gifts upon which no expense had been spared. Much as we may ignore dress, and sinful as is an inordinate love for it, there is yet about it an influence for good, when the heart of the wearer is right, holding it subservient to all higher, holier affections. At least Helen Lennox found it so, when clad in her new garments, she drove with Mrs. Banker, or returned Sybil Grandon's call, feeling that there was about her nothing for which Katy need to blush, or even Wilford, who was not afraid to be seen with her now, and Helen, while knowing the reason of the change, did not feel like quarreling with him for it, but accepted with a good-natured grace all that made her life in New York so happy. With Bell Cameron she was on the best of terms; while Sybil Grandon, always going with the tide, professed for her an admiration, which, whether fancied or real, did much toward making her popular; and when, as the mistress of her brother's house, she issued cards of invitation for a large party, she took especial pains to insist upon Helen's attending, even if Katy was not able. But from this Helen shrank. She could not meet so many strangers alone, she said, and so the matter was dropped, until Mrs. Banker offered to chaperone her, when Helen began to waver, changing her mind at last and promising to go.

Never since the days of *her* first party had Katy been so wild with excitement as she was in helping to dress Helen, who scarcely knew herself when, before the mirror, with the blaze of the chandelier falling upon her, she saw the picture of a young girl arrayed in rich pink silk, with an overskirt of lace, and the light pretty cloak, just thrown upon her uncovered neck, where Katy's pearls were shining.

"What would they say at home if they could only see you?" Katy exclaimed, throwing back the handsome cloak so as to show more of the well-shaped neck, gleaming so white beneath it.

"Aunt Betsy would say I had forgotten half my dress," Helen replied, blushing as she glanced at the arms, which never since her childhood had been thus exposed to view, except at such times as her household duties had required it.

Even this exception would not apply to the low neck, at which Helen had long demurred, yielding finally to Katy's entreaties, but often wondering what Mark Ray would think, and if he would not be shocked Mark Ray had been strangely blended with all Helen's thoughts as she submitted herself to Esther's practiced hands, and when the hair-dresser, summoned to her aid, asked what flowers she would wear, it was a thought of him which led her to select a single water-lily, which looked as natural as if its bed had really been the bosom of Fairy Pond.

"Nothing else? Surely mademoiselle will have these few green leaves?" Celine had said, but Helen would have nothing save the lily, which was twined tastefully amid the heavy braids of the brown hair, whose length and luxuriance had thrown the hair-dresser into ecstasies of delight, and made Esther lament that in these days of false tresses no one would give Miss Lennox credit for what was wholly her own.

"You will be the belle of the evening," Katy said as she kissed her sister good night and then ran back to her baby, while Wilford, yielding to her importunities that he should not remain with her, followed Mrs. Banker's carriage in his own private conveyance, and was soon set down at Sybil Grandon's door.

Meanwhile, at the elder Cameron's there had been a discussion touching the propriety of their taking Helen under their protection, instead of leaving her for Mrs. Banker to chaperone, Bell insisting that it ought to be done, while the father swore roundly at Juno, who would not "be bothered with that country girl."

"You would rather leave her wholly to Mark Ray and his mother, I suppose," Bell said, adding, as she saw the flush on Juno's face, "You know you are dying of jealousy, and nothing annoys you so much as to hear people talk of Mark's attentions to *Miss Lennox*."

"Do they talk?" Mrs. Cameron asked quickly, while in her gray eyes there gleamed a light far more dangerous and threatening to Helen than Juno's open scorn.

Mrs. Cameron had long intended Mark Ray for her daughter, and accustomed to have everything bend to her wishes, she had come to consider the matter as certain, even though he had never proposed in words. He had done everything else, she thought, attending Juno constantly, and frequenting their house so much that it was a standing joke for his friends to seek him there when he was not at home or at his office. Latterly, however, there had been a change, and the ambitious mother could not deny that since Helen's arrival in New York Mark had visted them less frequently and stayed a shorter time, while she had more than once heard of him at her son's in company with Helen. Very rapidly a train of thought passed through her mind; but it did not manifest itself upon her face, which was composed and quiet as she decided with Juno that Helen should not trouble them. With the utmost care Juno arrayed herself for the party, thinking with a great deal of complacency how impossible it was for Helen Lennox to compete with her in point of dress.

"She is such a prude, I dare say she will go in that blue silk, with the long sleeves and high neck, looking like a Dutch doll," she said to Bell, as she shook back the folds of her rich crimson, and turned her head to see the effect of her wide braids of hair.

"I am not certain that a high dress is worse than bones," Bell retorted, playfully touching Juno's neck, which, though white and gracefully formed, was shockingly guiltless of flesh.

There was an angry reply, and then, wrapping her cloak about her, Juno went out to their carriage, and was ere long one of the gay crowd thronging Sybil Grandon's parlors. Helen had not yet arrived, and Juno was hoping she would not come, when there was a stir at the door and Mrs. Banker appeared, and with her Helen Lennox, but so transformed that Juno hardly knew her, looking twice ere sure that the beautiful young lady, so wholly self-possessed, was the country girl she affected to despise.

"Who is she?" was asked by many, who at once acknowledged her claims to their attention, and as soon as practicable sought her acquaintance, so that Helen suddenly found herself the centre of a little court of which she was the queen and Mark her sworn knight.

Presuming upon his mother's chaperonage, he claimed the right of attending her, and Juno's glory waned as effectually as it had done when Katy was the leading star to which New York paid homage.

Juno had been annoyed then, but now fierce jealousy took possession of her heart as she watched the girl whom all seemed to admire, even Wilford feeling a thrill of pride that the possession of so attractive a sister-in-law reflected credit upon himself.

He was not ashamed of her now, nor did he retain a single thought of the farm-house or Uncle Ephraim as he made his way to her side, standing protectingly at her left, just as Mark was standing at her right, and at last asking her to dance.

With a heightened color Helen declined, saying frankly, " I have never learned."

" You miss a great deal," Wilford rejoined, appealing to Mark for a confirmation of his words.

But Mark did not heartily respond. He, too, had solicited Helen as a partner when the dancing first commenced, and her quiet refusal had disappointed him a little, for Mark was fond of dancing, and though as a general thing he disapproved of waltzes and polkas when he was the looker-on, he felt that there would be something vastly agreeable and exhilarating in clasping Helen in his arms and whirling her about the room just as Juno was being whirled by a young cadet, a friend of Lieutenant Bob's. But when he reflected that not his arm alone would encircle her waist, or his breath touch her neck, he was glad she did not dance, and professing a weariness he did not feel, he declined to join the dancers on the floor, but kept with Helen, enjoying what she enjoyed, and putting her so perfectly at her ease that no one would ever have dreamed of the curdy cheeses she had made, or the pounds of butter she had churned. But Mark thought of it as he secretly admired the neck and arms, seen once before, on that memorable day when he assisted Helen in the labors of the dairy. If nothing else had done so, the lily in her hair would have brought that morning to his mind, and once as they walked up and down the hall he spoke of the ornament she had chosen, and how well it became her.

" Pond lilies are my pets," he said, " and I have kept one of those I gathered when at Silverton. Do you remember them? " and his eyes rested upon Helen with a look which made her blush as she answered yes; but she did not tell him of a little box at home, made of cones and acorns, where was hidden a withered water lily, which she could not throw away, even after its beauty and fragrance had departed.

Had she told him this, it might have put to flight the doubts troubling Mark so much, and making him wonder if Dr. Grant had really a claim upon the girl stealing his heart so fast.

" I mean to sound her," he thought, and as Lieutenant

Bob passed by, making some jocose remark about his offending all the fair ones by the course he was taking, Mark said to Helen, who suggested returning to the parlor,

"As you like, though it cannot matter; a person known to be engaged is above Bob Reynolds's jokes."

Quick as thought the blood stained Helen's face and neck, for Mark had made a most egregious blunder giving her the impression that *he* was the engaged one referred to, not herself, and for a moment she forgot the gay scene around her in the sharpness of the pang with which she recognized all that Mark Ray was to her.

"It was kind in him to warn me. I wish it had been sooner," she thought, and then with a bitter feeling of shame she wondered how much he had guessed of her real feelings, and who the betrothed one was. "Not Juno Cameron," she hoped, as after a few moments Mrs. Cameron came up and, adroitly detaching Mark from her side, took his place while he sauntered to a group of ladies and was ere long dancing merrily with Juno.

"They are a well-matched pair," Mrs. Cameron said, assuming a very confidential manner towards Helen, who assented to the remark, while the lady continued, "There is but one thing wrong about Mark Ray: He is a most unscrupulous flirt, pleased with every new face, and this of course annoys *Juno*."

"Are they engaged?" came involuntarily from Helen's lips, while Mrs. Cameron's foot beat the carpet with a very becoming hesitancy, as she replied, "That was settled in our family a long time ago. Wilford and Mark have always been like brothers."

Mrs. Cameron could not quite bring herself to a deliberate falsehood, which, if detected, would reflect upon her character as a lady, but she could mislead Helen, and she continued, "It is not like us to bruit our affairs abroad, and were my daughters ten times engaged the world would be none the wiser. I doubt if even Katy suspects what I have admitted; but knowing how fascinating Mark can be, and that just at present he seems to be pleased with you, I have acted as I should wish a friend to act toward my own child. I have warned you

in time. Were it not that you are one of *our family*, I
might not have interfered, and I trust you not to repeat
even to Katy what I have said."

Helen nodded assent, while in her heart was a wild
tumult of feelings—flattered pride, disappointment, indignation, and mortification all struggling for the mastery—mortification to feel that she who had quietly ignored
such a passion as love when connected with herself, had,
nevertheless, been pleased with the attentions of one who
was only amusing himself with her, as a child amuses
itself with some new toy soon to be thrown aside—
indignation at him for vexing Juno at her expense—
disappointment that he should care for such as Juno, and
flattered pride that Mrs. Cameron should include her in
"our family." Helen had as few weak points as most
young ladies, but she was not free from them all, and the
fact that Mrs. Cameron had taken her into a confidence
which even Katy did not share, was soothing to her ruffled
spirits, particularly as after that confidence, Mrs. Cameron
was excessively gracious to her, introducing her to many
whom she did not know before, and paying her numberless
little attentions, which made Juno stare, while the clear-
seeing Bell arched her eye-brows, and wondered for what
Helen was to be made a *cat's paw* by her clever mother.
Whatever it was it did not appear, save as it showed itself
in Helen's slightly changed demeanor when Mark again
sought her society, and tried to bring back to her face the
look he had left there. But something had come between
them, and the young man racked his brain to find the
cause of this sudden indifference in one who had been
pleased with him only a short half hour before.

"It's that confounded waltzing which disgusted her,"
he said, "and no wonder, for if ever a man looks like an
idiot, it is when he is kicking up his heels to the sound
of a fiddle, and whirling some woman whose skirts sweep
everything within the circle of a rod, and whose face
wears that die-away expression I have so often noticed.
I've half a mind to swear I'll never dance again."

But Mark was too fond of dancing to quit it at once,
and finding Helen still indifferent, he yielded to circumstances, and the last she saw of him, as at a comparative

early hour she left the gay scene, he was dancing again
with Juno. It was a heavy blow to Helen, for she had
become greatly interested in Mark Ray, whose attentions had made her stay in New York so pleasant. But
these were over now;—at least the excitement they brought
was over, and Helen, as she sat in her dressing-room at
home, and thought of the future as well as the past, felt
stealing over her a sense of desolation and loneliness such
as she had experienced but once before, and that on the
night when leaning from her window at the farm-house
where Mark Ray was stopping she had shuddered and
shrank from living all her days among the rugged hills
of Silverton. New York had opened an entirely new
world to her, showing her much that was vain and
frivolous, with much too that was desirable and good; and
if there had crept into her heart the thought that a life
with such people as Mrs. Banker and those who frequented
her house would be preferable to a life in Silverton, where
only Morris understood her, it was but the natural result
of daily intercourse with one who had studied to please
and interest as Mark Ray had done. But Helen had too
much good sense and strength of will, long to indulge in
what she would have called "love-sick regrets" in others,
and she began to devise the best course for her to adopt
hereafter, concluding finally to treat him much as she
had done, lest he should suspect how deeply she had been
wounded. Now that she knew of his engagement, it would
be an easy matter so to demean herself as neither to annoy
Juno nor vex him. Thoroughly now she understood why
Juno Cameron had seemed to dislike her so much.

"It is natural," she said, "and yet I honestly believe
I like her better for knowing what I do. There must be
some good beneath that proud exterior, or Mark would
never seek her."

Still, look at it from any point she chose, it seemed a
strange, unsuitable match, and Helen's heart ached sadly
as she finally retired to rest, thinking what *might have
been* had Juno Cameron found some other lover more
like herself than Mark could ever be.

CHAPTER XXIII.

BABY'S NAME.

WILFORD had wished for a son, and in the first moment of disappointment he had almost been conscious of a resentful feeling toward Katy, who had given him only a daughter. A boy, a Cameron heir, was something of which to be proud; but a little girl, scarcely larger than the last doll with which Katy had played, was a different thing, and it required all Wilford's philosophy and common sense to keep him from showing his chagrin to the girlish creature, whose love had fastened with an idolatrous grasp upon her child, clinging to it with a devotion which made Helen tremble as she thought what if God should take it from her.

"He won't, oh, he won't," Katy said, when once she suggested the possibility, and in the eyes usually so soft and gentle there was a fierce gleam, as Katy hugged her baby closer to her and said,

"God does not willfully torment us. He will not take my baby, when my whole life would die with it. I had almost forgotten to pray, there was so much else to do, till baby came, but now I never go to sleep at night or waken in the morning, that there does not come a prayer of thanks for baby given to me. I could hardly love God if he took her away."

There was a chill feeling at Helen's heart as she listened to her sister and then glanced at the baby so passionately loved. In time it would be pretty, for it had Katy's perfect features, and the hair just beginning to grow was a soft, golden brown; but it was too small now, too puny to be handsome, while in its eyes there was a scared, hunted kind of look, which chafed Wilford more than aught else could have done, for that was the look which had crept into Katy's eyes at Newport when she found she was not going home.

Many discussions had been held at the elder Cameron's concerning its name, Mrs. Cameron deciding finally that

it should bear her own, *Margaret Augusta*, while Juno ad-
vocated that of *Rose Marie*, inasmuch as their new clergyman would Frenchify the pronunciation so perfectly,
rolling the *r*, and placing so much accent on the last syllable. At this the father Cameron swore as *"cussed nonsense."* "Better call it *Jemima*, a grand sight, than
saddle it with such a silly name as Rose Mah-*ree*, with a
roll to the *r*," and with another oath the disgusted old man
departed, while Bell suggested that *Katy* might wish to
have a voice in naming her own child.

This was a possibility that had formed no part of Mrs.
Cameron's thoughts, or Juno's. Of course Katy would
acquiesce in whatever Wilford said was best, and he
always thought as they did. Consequently there would
be no trouble whatever. It was time the child had a
name,—time it wore the elegant christening robe, Mrs.
Cameron's gift, which cost more money than would have
fed a hungry family for weeks. The matter must be
decided, and with a view of deciding it, a family dinner
party was held at No.—, Fifth Avenue, the day succeeding Sybil Grandon's party.

Very pure and beautiful Katy looked as she took her
old place in the chair they called hers at father Cameron's,
because it was the one she had always preferred to any
other,—a large, motherly easy-chair, which took in nearly
the whole of her petite figure, and against whose soft
cushioned back she leaned her curly head with a pretty
air of importance, as, after dinner was over, she came back
to the parlor with the other ladies, and waited for the
gentlemen to join them, when they were to talk up baby's
name.

Katy knew exactly what it would be called, but as Wilford had never asked her, she was keeping it a secret, not
doubting that the others would be quite as much delighted as herself with the novel name. Not long before
her illness she had read an English story, which had in
it a *Genevra,* and she had at once seized upon it as the
most delightful cognomen a person could well possess.
"Genevra Cameron!" She had repeated it to herself
many a time as she sat with her baby in her lap. She
had written it on sundry slips of paper, which had after-

wards found their way into the grate; and once she had
scratched with her diamond ring upon the window pane
in her dressing-room, where it now stood in legible char-
acters, "*Genevra Cameron!*" There should be no middle
name to take from the sweetness of the first—only Genevra
—that was sufficient; and the little lady tapped her foot
impatiently upon the carpet, wishing Wilford and his
father would hurry and come in.

Never for an instant had it entered her mind that she,
as the mother, would not be permitted to call her baby
what she chose; so when she heard Mrs. Cameron speaking to Helen of *Margaret Augusta,* she smiled complacently, tossing her curls of golden brown, and thinking
to herself, "Maggie Cameron—pretty enough, but not
like Genevra. Indeed, I shall not have any Margarets
now; next time perhaps I may."

The gentlemen came at last, and father Cameron drew
his chair close to Katy's side, laying his hand on her
little soft warm one, and giving it a squeeze as the bright
face glanced lovingly into his. Father Cameron had
grown a milder, gentler man since Katy came. He now
went much oftener into society, and did not so frequently
shock his wife with expressions and opinions which she
held as heterodox. Katy had a softening influence over
him, and he loved her as well perhaps as he had ever
loved his own children.

"Better," Juno said; and now she touched Bell's arm,
to have her see "how father was petting Katy."

But Bell did not care, while Wilford was pleased, and
himself drew nearer the chair, standing just behind it,
so that Katy could not see him as he smoothed her curly
head, and said, half indifferently, "Now for the all-important name. What shall we call our daughter?"

"Let your mother speak first," Katy said, and thus
appealed to, Mrs. Cameron came up to Wilford and expressed her preference for *Margaret,* as being a good
name, an aristocratic name, and her own.

"Yes, but not half so pretty and striking as Rose
Marie," Juno chimed in.

"Rose Mary! Thunder!" father Cameron exclaimed.
" Call her a *marygold,* or a *sunflower,* just as much. Don't

go to being fools by giving a child a heathenish name. Give us your opinion, Katy."

"*I* have known from the first," Katy replied, "and I am sure you will agree with me. 'Tis a beautiful name of a sweet young girl, and there was a great secret about her, too—GENEVRA, baby will be called," and Katy looked straight into the fire, wholly unconscious of the effect that name had produced upon Wilford and his mother.

Wilford's face was white as marble, and his eyes turned quickly to his mother, who, in her first shock, started so violently as to throw down from the stand a costly vase, which was broken in many pieces. This occasioned a little diversion, and by the time the flowers and fragments were gathered up, Wilford's lips were not quite so livid, but he dared not trust his voice yet, and listened while his sisters gave their opinion of the name, Bell deciding for it at once, and Juno hesitating until she had heard from a higher power than Katy.

"What put that fanciful name into your head?" Mrs. Cameron asked.

Katy explained, and with the removal of the fear, which for a few moments had chilled his blood, Wilford grew calm again; while into his heart there crept the thought that by giving that name to his child, some slight atonement might be made to her above whose head the English daisies had blossomed and faded many a year. But not so with his mother;—the child should not be called Genevra if she could prevent it; and she opposed it with all her powers, offering at last, as a great concession on her part, to let it bear the name of either of Katy's family—Hannah and Betsy excepted, of course Lucy Lennox, Helen Lennox, Katy Lennox, anything but Genevra. As usual, Wilford, when he learned her mind, joined with her, notwithstanding his secret preference, and the discussion became quite warm, especially as Katy evinced a willfulness for which Helen had never given her credit Hitherto she had been as yielding as wax, but on this point she was firm, gathering strength from the fact that Wilford did not oppose her as he usually did. She could not, perhaps, have resisted him, but his manner was not very decided, and so she quietly persisted, "Genevra or nothing," until the others gave up the contest, hoping she would feel differently after a few days' reflection. But Katy knew she shouldn't, and Helen could not overcome the exultation with which she saw her little sister put the Camerons to rout and remain master of the field.

"After all it does not matter," Mrs. Cameron said to her daughters, when, after Mrs. Wilford was gone, she sat talking of Katy's queer fancy and her obstinacy in adhering to it. "It does not matter, and on the whole I had as soon the christening would be postponed until the child is more presentable than now. It will be prettier by and by, and the dress will become it better. We can afford to wait."

This heartless view of the case was readily adopted by Juno, while Bell professed to be terribly shocked at hearing them talk thus of a baptism, as if it were a mere show and nothing more, wondering if the Saviour thought of dress or personal appearance when the Hebrew mothers brought their children to him. But little did Mrs. Cameron or Juno care for the baptism except as a display, and as both would be much prouder of a fine-looking child, they were well content to wait until such time as Katy should incline more favorably to their Margaret or Rose Marie. To Helen is seemed highly probable that after a private interview with Wilford Katy would change her mind, and she felt a wickedly agreeable degree of disappointment when, on the day following the dinner party, she found her sister even more resolved than ever upon having her own way. Like the Camerons, she did not feel the necessity of haste,—time enough by and by, when she would not have so much opposition to encounter, she said; and as Wilford did not care, it was finally arranged that they would wait awhile ere they gave a cognomen to the little nameless child, only known as Baby Cameron.

CHAPTER XXIV.

TROUBLE IN THE HOUSEHOLD.

As soon as it was understood that Mrs. Wilford Cameron was able to go out, there were scores of pressing invitations from the gay world which had missed her so much, but Katy declined them all on the plea that baby needed her care. She was happier at home, and as a mother it was her place to stay there. At first Wilford listened quietly, but when he found it was her fixed determination to abjure society entirely, he interfered in his cool, decisive way, which always carried its point.

"It was foolish to take that stand," he said. "Other mothers went and why should not she? She had already stayed in too much. She was injuring herself, and "—what was infinitely worse to Wilford—" she was losing her good looks."

As proof of this he led her to the glass, showing her the pale, thin face and unnaturally large eyes, so distasteful to him. Wilford Cameron was very proud of his handsome house,—proud to know that everything there was in keeping with his position and wealth, but when Katy was immured in the nursery, the bright picture was obscured, for it needed her presence to make it perfect, and he began to grow dissatisfied with his surroundings, while abroad he missed her quite as much, finding the opera, the party or the reception, insipid where she was not, and feeling fully conscious that Wilford Cameron, without a wife, and that wife Katy, was not a man of half the consequence he had thought himself to be. Even Sybil Grandon did not think it worth her while to court his attention, if Katy were not present, for unless some one saw and felt her triumph it ceased directly to be one. On the whole Wilford was not well pleased with society as he found it this winter, and knowing where the trouble lay, he resolved that Katy should no longer remain at home, growing pale and faded and losing her good looks. Wilford would not have confessed it, and perhaps was

not himself aware of the fact, that Katy's beauty was
quite as dear to him as Katy herself. If she lost it her
value was decreased accordingly, and so, as a prudent husband, it behooved him to see that what was so very precious
was not unnecessarily thrown away. It did not take long
for Katy to understand that her days of quiet were at
an end,—that neither crib nor cradle could avail her longer.
Mrs. Kirby, selected from a host of applicants, was wholly
competent for Baby Cameron, and Katy must throw aside
the mother, which sat so prettily upon her, and become
again the belle. It was a sad trial, but Katy knew that
submission was the only alternative, and so when Mrs.
Banker's invitation came, she accepted it at once, but
there was a sad look upon her face as she kissed her baby
for the twentieth time ere going to her dressing maid.

Never until this night had Helen realized how beautiful Katy was when in full evening dress, and her excla-
mations of delight brought a soft flush to Katy's cheek,
while she felt a thrill of the olden vanity as she saw herself once more arrayed in all her costly apparel. Helen
did not wonder at Wilford's desire to have Katy with
him, and very proudly she watched her young sister as
Esther twined the flowers in her hair and then brought
out the ermine cloak she was to wear as a protection
against the cold.

Wilford was standing by her, making a few suggestions, and expressing his approbation in a way which
reminded Helen of that night before the marriage, when
Katy's dress had been condemned, and of that sadder, bitterer time, when she had poured her tears like rain into
that trunk returned. All she had thought of Wilford
then was now more than confirmed, but he was kind to
her and very proud of Katy, so she forced back her feelings of disquiet, which, however, were roused again when
she saw the dark look on his face, as Katy, at the very
last, ran to the nursery to kiss baby good-bye, succeeding
this time in waking it, as was proven by the cry which
made Wilford scowl angrily and brought to his lips a
word of rebuke for Katy's childishness.

The party was not so large as that at Sybil Grandon's,
but it was more select, and Helen enjoyed it better, meet-

ing people who readily appreciated the peculiarities of
her mind, and who would have made her forget all else
around her if she had not been a guest at Mark Ray's
house. It was the first time she had met him away from
home since the night at Mrs. Grandon's, and as if forgetful of her reserve, he paid her numberless attentions,
which, coming from the master of the house, were the
more to be valued.

With a quiet dignity Helen received them all, the
thought once creeping into her heart that *she* was preferred, notwithstanding that engagement. But she soon
repudiated this idea as unworthy of her. She could not
be wholly happy with one who, to win her hand, had
trampled upon the affections of another, even if that other
were Juno Cameron.

And so she kept out of his way as much as possible,
watching her sister admiringly as she moved about with
an easy, assured grace, or floated like a snowflake through
the dance in which Wilford persuaded her to join, looking after her with a proud, all-absorbing feeling, which
left no room for Sybil Grandon's coquettish advances.

As if the reappearance of Katy had awakened all that
was weak and silly in Sybil's nature, she again put forth
her powers of attraction, but met only with defeat. Katy,
and even Helen, was preferred before her,—both belles
of a different type; but both winning golden laurels from
those who hardly knew which to admire more—Katy, with
her pure, delicate beauty and charming simplicity, or
Helen, with her attractive face, and sober, quiet manner.
But Katy grew tired early. She could not endure what
she once did; and when she came to Wilford with a weary
look upon her face, and asked him to go home, he did
not refuse, though Mark, who was near, protested against
their leaving so soon.

"Surely Miss Lennox might remain; the carriage could
be sent back for her; and he had hardly seen her at all."
But Miss Lennox chose to go; and after her white cloak
and hood had passed through the door into the street,
there was nothing attractive for Mark in his crowded parlors, and he was glad when the last guest had departed,
and he was left alone with his mother.

Operas, parties, receptions, dinners, matinees, morning calls, drives, visits, and shopping; how fast one crowded upon the other, leaving scarcely an hour of leisure to the devotee of fashion who attended to them all. How astonished Helen was to find what *high life* in New York implied, and she ceased to wonder that so many of the young girls grew haggard and old before their time, or that the dowagers grew selfish and hard and scheming. She should die outright, she thought, and she pitied poor little Katy, who, having once returned to the world, seemed destined to remain there, in spite of her entreaties and the excuses she made for declining the invitations which poured in so fast.

"Baby was not well—Baby needed her," was the plea with which she met Wilford's arguments, until the mention of his child was sure to bring a scowl upon his face, and it became a question in Helen's mind, whether he would not be happier if Baby had never come between him and his ambition.

To hear Katy's charms extolled, and know that he was envied the possession of so rare a gem, feeling all the while sure of her faith, was Wilford's great delight, and it is not strange that, without any very strong fatherly feeling or principle of right in that respect, he should be irritated by the little life so constantly interfering with his pleasure and so surely undermining Katy's health. For Katy did not improve, as Wilford hoped she might; and with his two hands he could span her slender waist, while the beautiful neck and shoulders were no longer worn uncovered, for Katy would not display her *bones,* whatever the fashion might be. In this dilemma Wilford sought his mother, and the result of that consultation brought a more satisfied look to his face than it had worn for many a day.

"Strange he had never thought of it, when it was what so many people did," he said to himself, as he hurried home. "It was the very best thing both for Katy and the child, and would obviate every difficulty."

Next morning, as she sometimes did when more than usually fatigued, Katy breakfasted in bed; while Wilford's face, as he sat opposite Helen at the table, had on it a

look of quiet determination, such as she had rarely seen
there before. In a measure, accustomed to his moods,
she felt that something was wrong, and never dreaming
that he intended honoring her with his confidence, she
was wishing he would finish his coffee and leave, when,
motioning the servant from the room, he said abruptly,
and in a tone which roused Helen's antagonistic powers
at once, it was so cool, so decided, "I believe you have
more influence over your sister than I have; at least, she
has latterly shown a willfulness in disregarding me and
a willingness to listen to you, which confirms me in this
conclusion——"

"Well," and Helen twisted her napkin ring nervously,
waiting for him to say more; but her manner discon-
certed him, making him a little uncertain as to what might
be hidden behind that rigid face, and a little doubtful as
to the expression it would put on when he had said all
he meant to say.

He did not expect it to wear a look as frightened and
hopeless as Katy's did when he last saw it upon the pillow, for he knew how different the two sisters were, and
much as he had affected to despise Helen Lennox, he
was afraid of her now. It had never occurred to him
before that he was somewhat uncomfortable in her presence—that her searching brown eyes often held him in
check; but it came to him now, that his wife's sister had
a *will* almost as firm as his own, and she was sure to
take Katy's part. He saw it in her face, even though
she had no idea of what he meant to say.

He must explain sometime, and so at last he continued.
"You must have seen how opposed Katy is to complying
with my wishes, setting them at naught, when she knows
how much pleasure she would give me by yielding as she
used to do."

"I don't know what you mean," Helen replied, "unless it is her aversion to going out, as that, I think, is the
only point where her obedience has not been absolute."

"Wilford did not like the words *obedience* and *absolute;*
that is, he did not like the *sound*. Their definition suited
him, but Helen's enunciation was at fault, and he answered quickly, "I do not require absolute obedience from

Katy. I never did; but in this matter to which you refer, I think she might consult my wishes as well as her own. There is no reason for her secluding herself in the nursery as she does. Do you think there is?"

He put the question direct, and Helen answered it.

"I do not believe Katy means to displease you, but she has conceived a strong aversion for festive scenes, and besides, baby is not healthy, you know, and like all young mothers, she may be over-anxious, while I fancy she has not the fullest confidence in the nurse, and this may account for her unwillingness to leave the child with her."

"Kirby was all that was desirable," Wilford replied. "His mother had taken her from a genteel, respectable house in Bond street, and he paid her an enormous price, consequently she must be right;" and then came the story that his mother had decided that neither Katy nor baby would improve so long as they remained together; that for both a separation was desirable; that she had recommended sending the child into the country, where it would be better cared for than it could be at home, with Katy constantly undoing all Mrs. Kirby had done, waking it from sleep whenever the fancy took her, and in short, treating it much as she probably did her doll when she was a little girl. With the child away, there would be nothing to prevent Katy's going out again and getting back her good looks, which were somewhat impaired.

"Why, she looks older than you do," Wilford said, thinking thus to conciliate Helen, who quietly replied,

"There is not two years difference between us, and I have always been well, and kept regular hours until I came here."

Wilford's compliment had failed, and more annoyed than before, he asked, not what Helen thought of the arrangement, but if she would influence Katy to act and think rationally upon it; "at least, you will not make it worse," he said, and this time there was something deferential and pleading in his manner.

Helen knew the matter was fixed,—that neither Katy's tears nor entreaties would avail to revoke the decision, and so, though her whole soul rose in indignation against a man who would deliberately send his nursing baby from his roof because it was in his way, and was robbing his bride's cheek of its girlish bloom, she answered composedly,

"I will do what I can, but I must confess it seems to me an unnatural thing. I had supposed parents less selfish than that."

"Wilford did not care what Helen had supposed, and her opposition only made him more resolved. Still he did not say so, and he tried to smile as he quitted the table and remarked to her,

"I hope to find Katy reconciled when I come home. I think I had better not go up to her again, so tell her I send a good-bye kiss by you. I leave her case in your hands."

It was a far more difficult case than either he or Helen imagined, and the latter started back in alarm from the white face which greeted her view as she entered Katy's room, and then with a moan hid itself in the pillow.

"Wilford thought he would not come up, but he sent a kiss by me," Helen said, softly touching the bright, disordered hair, all she could see of her sister.

"It does not matter," Katy gasped. "Kisses cannot help me if they take baby away. Did he tell you?" and she turned now partly towards Helen, who nodded affirmatively, while Katy continued, "Had he taken a knife and cut a cruel gash it would not have hurt me half so badly. I could bear that, but my baby—oh, Helen, do you think they will take her away?"

She was looking straight at Helen, who shivered as she met an expression so unlike Katy, and so like to that a hunted deer might wear if its offspring were in danger.

"Say, do you think they will?" she continued, shedding back with her t! in hand the mass of tangled curls which had fallen about her eyes.

"Whom do you mean by *they?*" Helen asked, coming near to her, and sitting down upon the bed.

There was a resentful gleam in the blue eyes usually so gentle, as Katy answered,

"*Whom* do I mean? *His folks,* of course! They have been the instigators of every sorrow I have known since

I left Silverton. Oh, Helen! never, never marry anybody who has *folks,* if you wish to be happy."

Helen could not repress a smile, though she pitied her
sister, who continued,

"I don't mean father Cameron, nor Bell, for I believe
they love me. Father does, I know, and Bell has helped
me so often; but Mrs. Cameron and Juno, oh, Helen, you
will never know what *they* have been to me."

Since Helen came to New York there had been so much
else to talk about that Katy had said comparatively little
of the Camerons. Now, however there was no holding
back on Katy's part, and beginning with the first night
of her arrival in New York, she told what is already
known to the reader, exonerating Wilford in word, but
dealing out full justice to his mother and Juno, the former of whom controlled him so completely.

"I tried so hard to love her," Katy said, "and if she
had given me ever so little in return I would have been
satisfied; but she never did—that is, when I hungered
for it most, missing you at home, and the loving care
which sheltered me in childhood. After the world took
me into favor she began to caress me, but I was wicked
enough to think it all came of selfishness. I know I am
hard and bad, for when I was sick, Mrs. Cameron was
really very kind, and I began to like her; but if she takes
baby away I shall surely die."

"Where is baby to be sent?" Helen asked, and Katy
answered,

"Up the river, to a house which Father Cameron owns,
and which is kept by a farmer's family. I can't trust
Kirby. I do not like her. She keeps baby asleep too long,
and acts so cross if I try to wake her, or hint that she
looks unnatural. I cannot give baby to her care, with no
one to look after her, though Wilford says I must."

Katy had never offered so violent opposition to any plan
as she did now to that of sending her child away.

"I can't, I can't," she repeated constantly, and Mrs.
Cameron's call, made that afternoon, with a view to reconcile the matter, only made it worse, so that Wilford,
on his return at night, felt a pang of self-reproach as he
saw the drooping figure holding his child upon its lap

and singing its lullaby in a plaintive voice, which told how sore was its heart.

Wilford did not mean to be either a savage or a brute. On the contrary, he had made himself believe that he was acting only for the good of both mother and child; but the sight of Katy touched him, and he might have given up the contest had not Helen, unfortunately, ,aken up the cudgels in Katy's defence, neglecting to conceal the weapons, and so defeating her purpose. It was at the dinner, from which Katy was absent, that she ventured to speak, not *asking* that the plan be given up, but speaking of it as an unnatrual one, which seemed to her not only useless, but cruel.

Wilford did not tell her that her opinion was not desired, but his manner implied as much, and Helen felt the angry blood prickling through her veins, as she listened to his reply, that it was neither unnatural nor cruel; that many people did it, and his would not be an isolated case.

"Then, if it must be," Helen said, "pray let it go to Silverton, and I will be its nurse. Katy will not object to that."

In a very ironical tone Wilford thanked her for her offer, which he begged leave to decline, intimating a preference for settling his own matters according to his own ideas. Helen knew that further argument was useless, and wished herself at home, where there were no *wills* like this, which, ignoring Katy's tears and Katy's pleading face, would not retract one iota, or even stoop to reason with the suffering mother, except to reiterate, "It is only for your good, and every one with common sense will say so."

Next morning Helen was surprised at Katy's proposition to drive round to Fourth street, and call on Marian.

"I have a strong presentiment that she can do me good," Katy said.

"Shall you tell *her?*" Helen asked, in some surprise; and Katy replied, "Perhaps I may, I'll see."

An hour later, and Katy, up in Marian's room, sat listening intently, while Marian spoke of a letter received a few days since from an old friend who had worked with her at Madam ——'s, and to whom she had been strongly attached, keeping up a correspondence with her after her marriage and removal to New London, in Connecticut, and whose little child had borne Marian's name. That child, born two months before Katy's, *was dead*, and the mother, finding her home so desolate, had written, beseeching Marian to come to her for the remainder of the winter.

There was an eager look in Katy's face, and her eyes danced with the new idea which had suddenly taken possession of her. She could *not* trust baby with Kirby up the river, but she could trust her in New London with Mrs. Hubbell, if Marian was there, and grasping the latter's arm, she exclaimed, "Is Mrs. Hubbell poor? Would she do something for money, a great deal of money, I mean?"

In a few moments Marian had heard Katy's trouble, and Katy's wish that Mrs. Hubbell should take her child in place of the little one dead. "Perhaps she would not harbor the thought for a moment, but she misses her own so much, it made me think she might take mine. Write to her, Marian,—write to-day,—now, before I go," Katy continued, clasping Marian's hand, with an expression which, more than aught else, won Marian Hazelton's consent to a plan which seemed so strange.

"Yes, I will write," she answered; "I will tell Amelia what you desire."

"But, Marian, you too must go, if baby does—I'll trust baby with you. Say, Marian, will you go with my darling?"

It was hard to refuse, with those great, wistful, pleading eyes, looking so earnestly into hers; but Marian must have time to consider. She had thought of going to New London to open a shop, and if she did, she should board with Mrs. Hubbell, and so be with the child. She would decide when the answer came to the letter.

This was all the encouragement she would give; but it was enough to change the whole nature of Katy's feelings, and her face looked bright and cheerful as she tripped down the stairway, talking to Helen of what seemed to both like a direct interposition of Providence, and what she was sure would please Wilford quite as well as the farm-house up the river.

"Surely he will yield to me in this," she said. Nor was she wrong; for, glad of an opportunity to make some concessions, and still in the main have his own way, Wilford raised no objection to the plan as communicated to him by Katy, when, at an earlier hour than usual, he came home to dinner, and with the harmony of his household once more restored, felt himself a model husband, as he listened to Katy's plan of sending baby to New London. On the whole, it might be better even than the farm-house up the river, he thought, for it was further away, and Katy could not be tiring herself with driving out every few days, and keeping herself constantly uneasy and excited. The distance between New York and New London was the best feature of the whole; and he wondered Katy had not thought of it as an objection. But she had not, and but for the pain when she remembered the coming separation, she would have been very happy that evening, listening with Wilford and Helen to a new opera brought out for the first time in New York.

Very differently from this was Marian's evening passed, and on her face there was a look such as Katy's had never worn, as she asked for guidance to choose the right, to lay all self aside, and if it were her duty, to care for the child she had never seen, but whose birth had stirred the pulsations of her heart and made the old wound bleed and throb with bitter anguish. And as she prayed there crept into her face a look which told that self was sacrificed at last, and Katy Cameron was safe with her.

    *   *   *   *   *   *   *   *

Mrs. Hubbell was willing—aye, more than that—was glad to take the child, and the generous remuneration offered would make them so comfortable in their little cottage, she wrote to Marian, who hastened to confer by note with Katy, adding in a postscript, "Is it still your wish that I should go? If so, I am at your disposal."

It *was* Katy's wish, and she replied at once, going next to the nursery to talk with Mrs. Kirby. Dark were the frowns and dire the displeasure of that lady when told that, instead of going up the river, as she had hoped, she was free to return to the "genteel and highly respectable home on Bond street," where Mrs. Cameron had found her.

"Wait till the *Madam* comes, and then we'll see," she thought, referring to Mrs. Cameron, and feeling delighted when, that very day, she heard that lady's voice in the parlor.

But Mrs. Cameron, though a little anxious with regard to both Mrs. Hubbell's and Marian's antecedents, saw that Wilford was in favor of New London, and so voted accordingly, only asking that she might write to New London with regard to Mrs. Hubbell and her fitness to take charge of a child in whose veins Cameron blood was flowing. To this Katy assented, and as the answer returned to Mrs. Cameron's letter was altogether favorable, it was decided that Mrs. Hubbell should come to the city at once for her little charge.

In a week's time she arrived, seeming everything Katy could ask for, and as Mrs. Cameron, too, approved her heartily as a modest, well-spoken young woman, who knew her place, it was arranged that she should return home with her little charge on Saturday, thus giving Katy the benefit of Sunday in which "to get over it and recover her usual spirits," Mrs. Cameron said. The fact that Marian was going to New London within a week after baby went, reconciled Katy to the plan, making her even cheerful during the last day of baby's stay at home. But as the daylight waned and the night came on, a shadow began to steal across her face, and her step was slower as she went up the stairs to the nursery, while only herself that night could disrobe the little creature and hush it into sleep.

" 'Tis the last time, you know," she said to Kirby, who went out, leaving the young mother and child alone.

Mournfully sad and sweet was the lullaby Katy sang, and Helen, who, in the hall, was listening to the low, sad moaning,—half prayer, half benediction,—likened it to a farewell between the living and dead. Half an hour later, when she glanced into the room, lighted only by the moonbeams, baby was sleeping in her crib, whilst Katy knelt beside, her face buried in her hands, and her form quiv-

ering with the sobs she tried to smother as she softly
prayed that her darling might come back again; that
God would keep the little child and forgive the erring
mother, who had sinned so deeply since the time she used
to pray in her home among the hills of Massachusetts.
She was very white next morning, and to Helen she seemed
to be expanding into something more womanly, more mature, as she disciplined herself to bear the pain welling
up so constantly from her heart, and at last overflowing
in a flood of tears, when Mrs. Hubbell was announced
as in the parlor below, waiting for her charge.

It was Katy who made her baby ready, trusting her to
no one else, and repelling with a kind of fierce decision
all offers of assistance made either by Helen, Mrs. Cameron, Bell, or the nurse, who were present, while Katy's
hands drew on the little bright, soft socks of wool, tied
the hood of satin and lace, and fastened the scarlet cloak,
her tears falling fast as she met the loving, knowing look
the baby was just learning to give her, half smiling, half
cooing, as she bent her face down to it.

"Please all of you go out," she said, when baby was
ready—"Wilford and all. I would rather be alone."

They granted her request, but Wilford stood beside the
open door, listening while the mother bade farewell to
her baby.

"Darling," she murmured, "what will poor Katy do
when you are gone, or what will comfort her as you have
done? Precious baby, my heart is breaking to give you
up; but will the Father in Heaven, who knows how much
you are to me, keep you from harm and bring you back
again? I'd give the world to keep you, but I cannot do
it, for Wilford says that you must go, and Wilford is your
father."

At that moment Wilford Cameron would have given
half his fortune to have kept his child for Katy's sake,
but it was now too late; the carriage was at the door,
and Mrs. Hubbell was waiting in the hall for the little
procession filing down the stairs. Mrs. Cameron and Bell,
Wilford and Katy, who carried the baby herself, her face
bent over it and her tears still dropping like rain. But it
was Wilford who took the baby to the carriage, going

with it to the train and seeing Mrs. Hubbell off; then, on his way back, he drove round to his own house, which even to him seemed lonely, with all the paraphernalia of babyhood removed. Still, now that the worst was over, he rather enjoyed it, for Katy was free from care; there was nothing to hinder her gratifying his every wish, and with his spirits greatly enlivened as he reflected how satisfactory everything had been managed at the last, h proposed taking both Helen and Katy to the theatre that night. But Katy answered, "No, Wilford, not to-night; it seems too much like baby's funeral. I'll go next week, but not to-night."

So Katy had her way, and among the worshipers who next day knelt in Grace Church, with words of prayer upon their lips, there was not one more in earnest than she, whose only theme was, "My child, my darling child."

She did not get over it by Monday, as Mrs. Cameron had predicted. She did not get over it at all, though she went without a word where Wilford willed that she should go, and was ere long a belle again, but nothing had power to draw one look from her blue eyes, the look which many observed, and which Helen knew sprang from the mother-love, hungering for its child. Only once before had Helen seen a look like this, and that had come to Morris's face on the sad night when she said to him, "It might have been." It had been there ever since, and Helen felt that by the pangs with which that look was born he was a better man, just as Katy was growing better for that hunger in her heart. God was taking His own way to purify them both, and Helen watched intently, wondering what the end would be.

CHAPTER XXV.

AUNT BETSY GOES ON A JOURNEY.

JUST through the woods, where Uncle Ephraim was wont to exercise old Whitey, was a narrow strip of land, extending from the highway to the pond, and fertile in nothing except the huckleberry bushes, and the rocky ledges over which a few sheep roamed, seeking for the short grass and stunted herbs, which gave them a meagre sustenance. As a whole, it was comparatively valueless, but to Aunt Betsy Barlow it was of gre..t importance, as it was—*her property*—the land on which she paid taxes willingly— the real estate, the deed of which was lying undisturbed in her hair trunk, where it had lain for years. Several dispositions the good old lady had mentally made of this property, sometimes dividing it equally between Helen and Katy, sometimes willing it all to the former, and again, when she thought of Mark Ray, leaving the *interest* of it to some missionary society in which she was interested.

How, then, was the poor woman amazed and confounded when suddenly there appeared a claimant to her property; not the whole, but a part, and that part taking in the big sweet apple-tree and the very best of the berry bushes, leaving her nothing but rocks and bogs, a pucker cherry-tree, a patch of tansy, and one small tree, whose gnarly apples were not fit, she said, to feed the pigs.

Of course she was indignant, and all the more so because the claimant was prepared to prove that the line fence was not where it should be, but ran into his own dominions for the width of two or three rods, a fact he had just discovered by looking over a bundle of deeds, in which the boundaries of his own farm were clearly defined.

In her distress, Aunt Betsy's first thoughts were turned to *Wilford* as the man who could redress her wrongs, if any one, and a long letter was written to him, in which her grievances were told in detail and his advice solicited. Commencing with " My dear Wilford," closing with " Your respected ant," sealed with a wafer, stamped with her thimble, and directed bottom side up, it nevertheless found its way to No. —— Broadway, and into Wilford's hands. But with a frown and pish of contempt he tossed it into the grate, and vain were all Aunt Betsy's inquiries as to whether there was any letter for her when Uncle Ephraim came home from the office. Letters there were from Helen, and sometimes one from Katy, but none from Wilford, and her days were passed in great perplexity and distress, until another idea took possession of her mind. She would go to New York herself! She had never traveled over half a dozen miles in the cars, it was true, but it was time she had, and now that she had a new bonnet and shawl, she could go to *York* as well as not!

Wholly useless were the expostulations of the family, for she would not listen to them, nor believe that she would not be welcome at that house on Madison Square, to which Mrs. Lennox had never been invited since Katy was fairly settled in it. Much at first had been said of her coming, and of the room she was to occupy; but all that had ceased, and in the mother's heart there had been a painful doubt as to the reason of the silence, until Helen's letters enlightened her, telling her it was Wilford who had built so high a wall between Katy and her friends.

Far better than she used, did Mrs. Lennox understand her son-in-law, and she shrank in horror from suffering her aunt to go where she would be so serious an annoyance, frankly telling her the reason for her objections, and asking if she wished to mortify the girls

At this Aunt Betsy took umbrage at once.

"She'd like to know what there was about her to mortify anybody? Wasn't her black silk dress made long and full, and the old pongee fixed into a Balmoral, and hadn't she a bran new cap with purple ribbon, and couldn't she travel in her delaine, and didn't she wear hoops always now, except at cleanin' house times? Didn't she *nuss* both the girls, especially Cather*ine,* carrying her in her arms one whole night when she had the canker-rash, and everybody thought she'd die? And when she swallered that tin whistle, didn't she spat her on the back and swing her in the air till she came to and blew the whistle clear across the room? Tell her that Cather*ine* would be ashamed! She knew better!"

Then, as a doubt began to cross her own mind as to Wilford's readiness to entertain her at his house, she continued,

"At any rate, the *Tubbses,* who moved from Silverton last fall, and who are living in such style on the Bowery, wouldn't be ashamed, and I can stop with them at first, till I see how the land lies. They have invited me to come, both Miss Tubbs and 'Tilda, and they are nice folks, who belong to the Orthodox Church. Tom is in town now, and if I see him I shall talk with him about it, even if I never go."

Most devoutly did Mrs. Lennox and Aunt Hannah hope that Tom would return to New York without honoring the farm-house with a call; but, unfortunately for them, he came that very afternoon, and instead of throwing obstacles in Aunt Betsy's way, urged her warmly to make the proposed visit.

"Mother would be so glad to see an old neighbor," the honest youth said, "for she did not know many folks in the city. '*Till* had made some flashy acquaintances, of whom he did not think much, and they kept a few boarders, but nobody had called, and mother was lonesome. He wished Miss Barlow would come; she would have no difficulty in finding them," and on a bit of paper he marked out the route of the Fourth Avenue cars, which passed their door, and which Aunt Betsy would take after arriving at the New Haven depot. "If he knew when she was coming, he would meet her," he said, but Aunt Betsy could not tell; she was not quite certain whether she should go at all, she was so violently opposed.

Still she did not give it up entirely, and when, a few days after Tom's return to New York, there came a pressing invitation from the daughter Matilda, or Mattie, as she signed herself, the fever again ran high, and this time with but little hope of its abating.

"We shall be delighted, both mother and me," Mattie wrote. "I will show you all the lions of the city, and when you get tired of us you can go up to Mrs. Cameron's. I know exactly where they live, and have seen her at the opera in full dress, looking like a queen."

Over the last part of this letter Aunt Betsy pondered for some time. "That as good an Orthodox as Miss Tubbs should let her girl go to the opera, passed her. She had wondered at Helen's going, but then, she was a 'Piscopal, and them 'Piscopals had queer notions about usin' the world and abusin' it." Still, as Helen did *not* attend the theatre, and *did* attend the opera, there must be a difference between the two places, and into the old lady's heart there slowly crept the thought that possibly *she* might try the opera, too, if 'Tilda Tubbs would go, and promise never to tell the folks at Silverton.

This settled, Aunt Betsy began to devise the best means of getting off with the least opposition. Both Morris and her brother would be absent from town during the next week, and she finally resolved to take that opportunity for starting on her visit to New York, wisely concluding to keep her own counsel until she was quite ready. Accordingly, on the very day Morris and the deacon left Silverton, she announced her intention so quietly and decidedly that further opposition was useless, and Mrs. Lennox did what she could to make her aunt presentable. And Aunt Betsy did look very respectable, in her dark delaine, with her hat and shawl, both Morris's gift, and both in very good taste. As for the black silk and the new cap, they were carefully folded away, one in a box and the other in a satchel she carried on her arm, and in one compartment of which were sundry papers of fennel, caraway, and catnip, intended for Katy's baby, and which could be sent to it from New York. There was also a package of dried plums and peaches for Katy herself, and a few cakes of yeast of her own make, better than any they had in the city! Thus equipped, she one morning took her seat in the Boston and New York train, which carried her swiftly on towards Springfield.

"If anybody can find their way in New York, it is Betsy," Aunt Hannah said to Mrs. Lennox, as the day wore on and their thoughts went after the lone woman, who, with satchel, umbrella and cap-box, was felicitating in the luxury of a whole seat, and the near neighborhood of a very nice young man, who listened with well-bred interest while she told of her troubles concerning the sheep-pasture, and how she was going to New York to consult a first-rate lawyer.

Once she thought to tell who the lawyer was, and perhaps enhance her own merits in the eyes of her auditor by announcing herself as aunt to Mrs. Wilford Cameron, of whom she had no doubt he had heard—nay, more, whom he possibly knew, inasmuch as his home was in New York, though he spent much of his time at West Point, where he had been educated. But certain disagreeable remembrances of Aunt Hannah's parting injunction, " not to tell everybody in the cars that she was Katy's aunt," kept her silent on that point, and so Lieutenant Bob Reynolds failed to be enlightened with regard to the relationship existing between the fastidious Wilford Cameron of Madison Square, and the quaint old lady whose very first act on entering the car had amused him vastly. At a glance he saw that she was unused to traveling, and as the car was crowded, he had kindly offered his seat near the door, taking the side one under the window, and so close to her that she gave him her cap-box to hold while she adjusted her other bundles. This done, and herself comfortably settled, she was just remaking that she liked being close to the door, in case of a fire, when the conductor appeared, extending his hand officially towards her as the first one convenient. For an instant Aunt Betsy scanned him closely, thinking she surely had never seen him before, but as he seemed to claim acquaintance, she could not find it in her kind heart to ignore him altogether, and so she grasped the offered hand, which she tried to shake, saying apologetically,

" Pretty well, thank you, but you've got the better of me, as I don't justly recall your name."

Instantly the eyes of the young man under the window met those of the conductor with a look which changed the frown gathering in the face of the latter into a comical smile, as he withdrew his hand and shouted,

" Ticket, madam, your ticket ! "

" For the land's sake, have I got to give that up so quick, when it's at the bottom of my satchel," Aunt Betsy replied, somewhat crest-fallen at her mistake, and fumbling in her pocket for the key, which was finally produced, and one by one the paper parcels of fennel, caraway, and catnip, dried plums, peaches and yeast cakes, were taken out, until at the very bottom, as she had said, the ticket was found, the conductor waiting patiently, and advising her, by way of avoiding future trouble, to pin the card to her shawl, where it could be seen.

" A right nice man," was Aunt Betsy's mental comment, but for a long time there was a red spot on her checks as she felt that she had made herself ridiculous, and hoped the *girls* would never hear of it.

The young man helped to reassure her, and in telling him her troubles she forgot her chagrin, feeling very sorry that he was going on to Albany, and so down the river to West Point. West Point was associated in Aunt Betsy's mind with that handful of noble men who within the walls of Sumter were then the centre of so much interest, and at parting with her companion she said to him.

"Young man, you are a soldier, I take it, from your havin' been to school at West Point. Maybe you'll never have to use your learning, but if you do, stick to the old flag. Don't you go against that, and if an old woman's prayers for your safety can do any good, be sure you'll have mine."

She raised her hand reverently, and Lieutenant Bob felt a kind of awe steal over him as if he might one day need that benediction, the first perhaps given in the cause then so terribly agitating all hearts both North and South.

"I'll remember what you say," he answered, and then as a new idea was presented he took out a card, and writing a few lines upon it, bade her hand it to the conductor just as she was getting into the city.

Without her glasses Aunt Betsy could not read, and thinking it did not matter now, she thrust the card into her pocket, and bidding her companion good-by, took her seat in the other train. Lonely and a very little home-sick she began to feel; for her new neighbors were not as willing to talk as Bob had been, and she finally relapsed into silence, which resulted in a quiet sleep, from which she awoke just as they were entering the long, dark tunnel, which she would have likened to Purgatory, had she believed in such a place.

"I didn't know we ran into cellars," she said faintly; but nobody heeded her, or cared for the anxious timid-looking woman, who grew more and more anxious, until suddenly remembering the card, she drew it from her pocket, and the next time the conductor appeared handed it to him, watching him while he read that "Lieut.

Robert Reynolds would consider it as a personal favor if he would see the bearer safely into the Fourth Avenue cars."

Surely there is a Providence which watches over all; and Lieutenant Reynolds's thoughtfulness was not a mere chance, but the answer to the simple trust Aunt Betsy had that God would take her safely to New York. The conductor knew Lieutenant Bob, and attended as faithfully to his wishes as if it had been a born princess instead of Aunt Betsy Barlow whom he led to a street car, ascertaining the number on the Bowery where she wished to stop, and reporting to the conductor, who bowed in acquiescence, after glancing at the woman, and knowing intuitively that she was from the country. Could she have divested herself wholly of the fear that the conductor would forget to put her off at the right place, Aunt Betsy would have enjoyed that ride very much; and as it was, she looked around with interest, thinking New York a mightily cluttered-up place, and wondering if all the folks were in the streets; then, as a lady in flaunting robes took a seat beside her, crowding her into a narrow space, the good old dame thought to show that she did not resent it, by an attempt at sociability, asking if she knew "Miss Peter Tubbs, whose husband kept a store on the Bowery?"

"I have not that honor," was the haughty reply, the lady drawing up her costly shawl and moving a little away from her interlocutor, who continued, "I thought like enough you might have seen 'Tilda, or Mattie as she calls herself now. She is a right nice girl, and Tom is a very forrard boy."

To this there was no reply; and as the lady soon left the car, Aunt Betsy did not make another attempt at conversation, except to ask once how far they were from the Bowery, adding, as she received a civil answer, "You don't know Mr. Peter Tubbs?"

That worthy man was evidently a stranger to the occupants of that car, which stopped at last upon a crossing, the conductor pointing back a few doors to the right, and telling her that was her number.

"I should s'pose he might have driv right up, instead

of leaving me here," she said, looking wistfully after the retreating car. " Coats, and trowsers, and jackets! I wonder if there is nothing else to be seen here," she continued, as her eye caught the long line of clothing so conspicuously displayed in that part of the Bowery. " 'Taint no great shakes," was the feeling struggling into Aunt Betsy's mind, as with Tom's outline map in hand she peered at the numbers of the doors, finding the right one, and ringing the bell with a force which brought Mattie at once to the rescue.

If Mattie was not glad to see her guest, she seemed to be, which answered every purpose for the tired woman, who followed her into the dark, narrow hall, and up the narrow stairs, through a still darker hall, and into the front parlor, which looked out upon the Bowery.

Mrs. Tubbs was glad to see Aunt Betsy. She did not take kindly to city life, and the sight of a familiar face, which brought the country with it, was very welcome to her. Mattie, on the contrary, liked New York, and there was scarcely a street where she had not been, with Tom for a protector; while she was perfectly conversant with all the respectable places of amusement—with their different prices and different grades of patrons. She knew where Wilford Cameron's office was, and also his house, for she had walked by the latter many a time, admiring the elegant curtains, and feasting her eyes upon the glimpses of inside grandeur, which she occasionally obtained as some one came out or went in. Once she had seen Helen and Katy enter their carriage, which the colored coachman drove away, but she had never ventured to accost them. Katy would not have known her if she had, for the family had come to Silverton while she was at Canandaigua, and as, after her return to Silverton, until her marriage, Mattie had been in one of the Lawrence factories, they had never met. With Helen, however, she had a speaking acquaintance; but she had never presumed upon it in New York, though to some of her young friends she had told how she once sat in the same pew with Mrs. Wilford Cameron's sister when she went to the " Episcopal meeting," and the consideration which this fact procured for her from those who had heard of Mrs. Wilford Cameron, of

Madison Square, awoke in her the ambition to know more of that lady, and, if possible, gain an entrance to her dwelling. To this end she favored Aunt Betsy's visit, hoping thus to accomplish her object, for, of course, when Miss Barlow went to Mrs. Cameron's, she was the proper person to go with her and point the way. This was the secret of Mattie's letter to Aunt Betsy, and the warmth with which she welcomed her to that tenement on the Bowery, over a clothing store, and so small that it is not strange Aunt Betsy wondered where they all slept, never dreaming of the many devices known to city house-keepers, who can change a handsome parlor into a kitchen or sleeping room, and *vice versa,* with little or no trouble. But she found it out at last, lifting her hands in speechless amazement, when, as the hour for retiring came, what she had imagined the parlor bookcase was converted in-to a comfortable bed, on which her first night in New York was passed in comfort if not in perfect quiet.

The next day had been set apart by Mattie for show-ing their guest the city, and possibly calling on Mrs. Wilford; but the poor old lady, unused to travel and ex-citement, was too tired to go out, and stayed at home the entire day, watching the crowds of people in the street, and occasionally wishing herself back in the clean, bright kitchen, where the windows looked out upon woods and fields instead of that never-ceasing rush which made her dizzy and faint. On the whole she was as nearly home-sick as she well could be, and so when Mattie asked if she would like to go out that evening, she caught eagerly at the idea, as it involved a change, and again the opera came before her mind, in spite of her attempts to thrust it away.

"Did 'Tilda know if Katy went to the opera now? Did she s'pose she would be there to-night? Was it far to the show? What was the price?—and was it a very wicked place?"

To all these queries Mattie answered readily. She presumed Katy would be there, as it was a new opera. It was not so very far. Distance in the city was noth-ing, and it was not a wicked place; but over the price Mattie faltered. Tickets for Aunt Betsy, herself and Tom, who of course must go with them, would cost more than her father had to give. The theatre was preferable, as that came within their means, and she suggested Wallack's, but from that Aunt Betsy recoiled as from Pandemonium itself.

"Catch *her* at a theatre—a deacon's sister, looked up to for a sample, and who run once for Vice-President of the Sewing Society in Silverton! It was too terrible to think of." But the opera seemed different. Helen went there; it could not be very wrong, particularly as the tickets were so high, and taking out her purse, Aunt Betsy counted its contents carefully, holding the bills thoughtfully for a moment, while she seemed to be balancing between what she knew was safe and what she feared might be wrong, at least in the eyes of Silverton.

"But Silverton will never know it," the tempter whispered, "and it is worth something to see the girls in full dress."

This last decided it, and Aunt Betsy generously offered "to pay the fiddler, provided 'Tilda would never let it get to Silverton, that Betsy Barlow was seen inside a play-house!" To Mrs. Tubbs it seemed impossible that Aunt Betsy could be in earnest, but when she found she was, she put no impediments in her way; and so, conspicuous among the crowd of transient visitors who that night entered the Academy of Music was Aunt Betsy Barlow, chaperoned by Miss Mattie Tubbs, and protected by Tom, a shrewd, well-grown youth of seventeen, who passed for some years older, and consequently was a sufficient escort for the ladies under his charge. It was not his first visit there, and he managed to procure a seat which commanded a good view of several private boxes, and among them that of Wilford Cameron. This Mattie pointed out to the excited woman gazing about her in a maze of bewilderment, and half doubting her own identity with the Betsy Barlow who, six weeks before, if charged with such a sin as she was now committing, would have exclaimed, "Is thy servant a dog, to do this thing?" Yet here she was, a deacon's sister, a candidate for the Vice-Presidency of the Silverton Sewing Society, a woman who, for sixty-three years and-a-half, had led a blameless life, frowning upon all worldly amusements and setting herself for a burning light to others—here she was in her black dress, her best shawl pinned across her chest, and her bonnet tied in a square bow which reached nearly to her ears. Here she was, in that huge building, where the lights were so blinding, and the crowd so great that she shut her eyes involuntarily, while she tried to realize what she could be doing.

"I'm in for it now, anyhow, and if it is wrong may the good Father forgive me," she said softly to herself, just as the orchestra struck up, thrilling her with its ravishing strains, and making her forget all else in her rapturous delight.

She was very fond of music, and listened eagerly, beating time with both her feet, and making her bonnet go up and down until the play commenced and she saw stage dress and stage effect for the first time in her life. This part she did not like; "they mumbled their words so nobody could understand more than if they spoke a heathenish tongue," she thought, and she was beginning to yawn when a nudge from Mattie and a whisper, "There they come," roused her from her stupor, and looking up she saw both Helen and Katy entering their box, and with them Mark Ray and Wilford Cameron.

Very rapidly Katy's eyes swept the house, running over the sea of heads below, but failing to see the figure which, half rising from its seat, stood gazing upon her, the tears running like rain over the upturned face, and the lips murmuring, "Darling Katy! blessed child! She's thinner than when I see her last, but oh! so beautiful and grand! Precious lambkin! It isn't wicked now for me to be coming here, where I can see her face again."

It was all in vain that Mattie pulled her dress, bidding her sit down as people were staring at her. Aunt Betsy did not hear, and if she had she would scarcely have cared for those who, following her eyes, saw the beautiful young ladies, behind whom Wilford and Mark were standing, but never dreamed of associating them with the "crazy thing" who sank back at last into her seat, keeping her eyes still upon the box where Helen and Katy sat, their heads uncovered, and their cloaks falling off just enough to show the astonished woman that their necks were uncovered too, while Helen's arms, raised to adjust her glass, were discovered to be in the same condition.

"Ain't they splendid in full dress!" Mattie whispered, while Aunt Betsy replied,

"Call that full dress? I'd sooner say it was no dress at all! They'll catch their death of cold. What would their mother say?"

Then, as the enormity of the act grew upon her, she continued more to herself than to Mattie,

"I mistrusted Catherine, but that *Helen* should come to this passes me."

Still, as she became more accustomed to it, and glanced at other full-dressed ladies, the first shock passed away, and she could calmly contemplate Katy's dress, wondering what it cost, and then letting her eyes pass on to Helen, to whom Mark Ray seemed so lover-like that Aunt Betsy remembered her impressions when he stopped at Silverton, her heart swelling with pride as she thought of both the girls making out so well.

"Who is that young man talking to Helen?" Mattie asked, between the acts, and when told it "was Mr. Ray, Wilford's partner," she drew her breath eagerly, and turned again to watch him, envying the young girl who did not seem as much gratified with the attentions as Mattie fancied she should be were she in Helen's place.

How could she, with Juno Cameron just opposite, watching her jealously, while Madam Cameron fanned herself indignantly, refusing to look upon what she so greatly disapproved.

But Mark continued his attentions until Helen wished herself away, and though a good deal surprised, was not sorry when Wilford abruptly declared the opera a *bore*, and suggested going home.

They would order an ice, he said, and have a much pleasanter time in their own private parlor.

"Please not go; I like the play to-night," Katy said; but on Wilford's face there was that look which never consulted Katy's wishes, and so the two ladies tied on their cloaks, and just as the curtain rose in the last act, left their box, while Aunt Betsy looked wistfully after them, but did not suspect *she* was the cause of their exit, and of Wilford's perturbation.

Running his eyes over the house below, they had fallen upon the trio, Aunt Betsy, Mattie, and Tom, the first of whom was at that moment partly standing, while she adjusted her heavy shawl, which the heat of the building had compelled her to unfasten.

There was a start, a rush of blood to the head and face, and then he reflected how impossible it was that *she* should be *there,* in New York, and at the opera, too.

The shawl arranged, Aunt Betsy took her seat and turned her face fully toward him, while Wilford seized Katy's glass and leveled it at her. He was not mistaken. It was Aunt Betsy Barlow, and Wilford felt the perspiration oozing out beneath his hair and about his lips, as he remembered *the letter* he had burned, wishing now that he had answered it, and so, perhaps, have kept her from his door. For she *was* coming there, nay, possibly had come, since his departure from home, and learning his whereabouts had followed on to the Academy of Music, leaving her baggage where he should stumble over it on entering the hall.

Such was the fearful picture conjured up by Wilford's imagination, as he stood watching poor Aunt Betsy, a dark cloud on his brow and fierce anger at his heart, that she should thus presume to worry and annoy him.

" If she spies us she will be finding her way up here; there's no piece of effrontery of which that class is not capable," he thought, wondering next who the vulgar-looking girl and *gauche* youth were who were with her.

" Country cousins, of whom I have never heard, no doubt," and he ground his teeth together as with his next breath he suggested going home, carrying out his suggestion and hurrying both Helen and Katy to the carriage as if some horrible dragon had been on their track.

There was *no* baggage in the hall; there had been no woman there, and Wilford's fears for a time subsided, but grew strong again about the time he knew the opera was out, while the sound of wheels coming towards his door was sufficient to make his heart stop beating, and every hair prickle at its roots.

But Aunt Betsy did not come except in Wilford's dreams, which she haunted the entire night, so that the morning found him tired, moody and cross. That day they entertained a select dinner party, and as this was something in which Katy excelled, while Helen's presence, instead of detracting from, would add greatly to the éclat of the affair, Wilford had anticipated it with no small degree of complacency. But now, alas, there was a phantom at his side,—a skeleton of horror, wearing Aunt Betsy's guise; and if it had been possible he would have given the dinner up. But it was too late for that; the guests were bidden, the arrangements made, and there was nothing now for him but to abide the consequences.

"She shall at least stay in her room, if I have to lock her in," he thought, as he went down to his office without kissing Katy or bidding her good-by.

Business that day had no interest for him, and in a listless, absent way he sat watching the passers-by and glancing at his door as if he expected the first assault to be made there. Then, as the day wore on, and he felt sure that what he so much dreaded had really come to pass, that the baggage expected last night had certainly arrived by this time and spread itself over his house, he could endure the suspense no longer, and startled Mark with the announcement that he was going home, and should not return again that day.

"Going home, when Leavit is to call at three!" Mark said, in much surprise, and feeling that it would be a relief to unburden himself to some one, the story came out that Wilford had seen Aunt Betsy at the opera, and expected to find her at Madison Square.

"I wish I had answered her letter about that confounded sheep pasture," he said, "for I would rather give a thousand dollars—yes, ten thousand—than have her with us to-day. I did *not* marry my wife's relations," he continued, excitedly, adding, as Mark looked quickly up, "Of course I don't mean Helen. Neither do I mean that doctor, for he is a gentleman. But this Barlow woman—oh! Mark, I am all of a dripping sweat just to think of it."

He did not say what he intended doing, but with Mark Ray's ringing laugh in his ears, passed into the street, and hailing a stage was driven towards home, just as a down town stage deposited on the walk in front of his office " that Barlow woman " and Mattie Tubbs!

CHAPTER XXVI.

AUNT BETSY CONSULTS A LAWYER.

AUNT Betsy did not rest well after her return from the opera. Novelty and excitement always kept her awake, and her mind was not wholly at ease with regard to what she had done. Not that she really felt she had committed a sin, except so far as the example might be bad, but she feared the result, should it ever reach the Orthodox church at Silverton.

"There's no telling what Deacon Bannister would do —send a *subpœna* after me, for what I know," she thought, as she laid her tired head upon her pillow and went off into a weary state, half way between sleep and wakefulness, in which operas, play-actors, Katy in full dress, Helen and Mark Ray, choruses, music by the orchestra, to which she had been guilty of beating her foot, Deacon Bannister, and the whole offended brotherhood, with constable and subpœnas, were pretty equally blended together.

But with the daylight her fears subsided, and at the breakfast table she was hardly less enthusiastic over the opera than Mattie herself, averring, however, that " once would do her, and she had no wish to go again."

The sight of Katy had awakened all the olden intense love she had felt for her darling, and she could not wait much longer without seeing her.

"Hannah and Lucy, and amongst 'em, advised me not to come," she said to Mrs. Tubbs, " and they hinted that I might not be wanted up there; but now I'm here I shall go, if I don't stay more than an hour."

" Of course I should," Mattie answered, herself anxious to stand beneath Wilford Cameron's roof, and see Mrs. Wilford at home. " She don't look as proud as Helen, and you are her aunt, her blood kin; why shouldn't you go there if you like?"

"I shall—I am going," Aunt Betsy replied, feeling that to take Mattie with her was not quite the thing, and not exactly knowing how to manage, for the girl must of course pilot the way. "I'll risk it and trust to Providence," was her final decision, and so after an early lunch she started out with Mattie as her escort, suggesting that they visit Wilford's office first, and get that affair off her mind.

At this point Aunt Betsy began to look upon herself as a most hardened wretch, wondering at the depths of iniquity to which she had fallen. The opera was the least of her offences, for was she not harboring pride and contriving how to be rid of 'Tilda Tubbs, as clever a girl as ever lived, hoping that if she found Wilford he would see her home, and so save 'Tilda the trouble? Play-houses, pride, vanity, subterfuges and deceit—it was a long catalogue she would have to confess to Deacon Bannister, if confess she did, and with a groan the conscience-smitten woman followed her conductor along the streets, and at last into the stage which took them to Wilford's office.

Broadway was literally jammed that day, and the aid of two policemen was required to extricate the bewildered countrywoman from the mass of vehicles and horses' heads, which took all her sense away. Trembling like a leaf when Mattie explained that the "two nice men" who had dragged her to the walk were police officers, and thinking again of the subpœna, the frightened woman who had escaped such peril, followed up the two flights of stairs and into Wilford's office, where she sank breathless into a chair, while Mark, not in the least surprised, greeted her cordially, and very soon succeeded in getting her quiet, bowing so graciously to Mattie when introduced that the poor girl dreamed of him for many a night, and by day built castles of what might have been had she been rich, instead of only 'Tilda Tubbs, whose home was on the Bowery. Why need Aunt Betsy in her introduction have mentioned that fact? Mattie thought, her cheeks burning scarlet; or why need she afterwards speak of her as *'Tilda,* who was kind enough to come with her to the office where she hoped to find Wilford? Poor Mattie, she knew some things very well, but she had never yet conceived of the immeasurable distance between herself and Mark Ray, who cared but little whether her home were on the Bowery or on Murray Hill, after the first sight which told him what she was.

"Mr. Cameron has just left the office and will not return to-day," he said to Aunt Betsy, asking if *he* could assist her in any way, and assuring her of his willingness to do so.

Aunt Betsy could talk with him better than with Wilford, and was about to give him the story of the sheep-pasture, in detail, when, motioning to a side door, he said, "Walk in here, please. You will not be liable to so many interruptions."

"Come, 'Tilda, it's no privacy," Aunt Betsy said; but *'Tilda* felt intuitively that she was not wanted, and rather haughtily declined, amusing herself by the window, while Aunt Betsy in the private office told her troubles to Mark Ray; and received in return the advice to let the claimant go to law if he chose; he probably would make nothing by it; even if he did, she would not sustain a heavy loss, according to her own statement of the value of the land.

"If I could keep the sweet apple-try, I wouldn't care," Aunt Betsy said, "for the rest ain't worth a law-suit; though it's my property, and I have thought of *willing* it to Helen, if she ever marries."

Here was a temptation which Mark Ray could not resist. Ever since Mrs. General Reynolds's party Helen's manner had puzzled him; but her shyness only made him more in love than ever, while the rumor of her engagement with Dr. Morris tormented him continually. Sometimes he believed it, and sometimes he did not, wishing always that he knew for certain. Here then was a chance for confirming his fears or for putting them at rest, and blessing 'Tilda Tubbs for declining to enter his back office, he said in reply to Aunt Betsy's "If she ever marries"— "And of course she will. She is engaged, I believe?"

"Engaged! *Who to?* When? Strange she never writ, nor Katy neither," Aunt Betsy exclaimed, while Mark, raised to an ecstatic state, replied, "I refer to Dr. Grant. Haven't they been engaged for a long time past?"

"Why—no—indeed," was the response, and Mark could have hugged the good old lady, who continued in a confidential tone, "I used to think they'd make a good match; but I've gin that up, and I sometimes mistrust 'twas Katy Morris wanted. Anyhow; he's mighty changed since she was married, and he never speaks her name. I never heard anybody say so, and maybe it's all a fancy, so you won't mention it."

"Certainly not," Mark replied, drawing nearer to her, and continuing in a low tone, "Isn't it possible that after all Helen is engaged to her cousin, and you do not know it?"

"No," and Aunt Betsy grew very positive. "I am sure she ain't, for only t'other day I said to Morris that I wouldn't wonder if Helen and *another chap* had a hankerin' for one another; and he said he wished it might be so, for *you*—no, that *other chap*, I mean—would make a splendid husband," and Aunt Betsy turned very red at the blunder, which made Mark Ray feel as if he walked on air, with no obstacle whatever in his way.

Still he could not be satisfied without probing her a little deeper, and so he said, "And that *other chap?* Does he live in Silverton?"

Aunt Betsy's look was a sufficient answer; for the old lady knew he was quizzing her, just as she felt that in some way she had removed a stumbling-block from his path. She had,—a very large stumbling-block, and in the first flush of his joy and gratitude he could do most anything. So when she spoke of going up to Katy's he set himself industriously at work to prevent it for that day at least. "They were to have a large dinner party," he said, "and both Mrs. Cameron and Miss Lennox would be wholly occupied. Would it not be better to wait until to-morrow? Did she contemplate a long stay in New York?"

"No, she might go back to-morrow,—certainly the day after," Aunt Betsy replied, her voice trembling at this fresh impediment thrown in the way of her seeing Katy.

The quaver in her voice touched Mark's sympathy. "She was old and simple-hearted. She was Helen's aunt," and this, more than aught else, helped him to a decision. " She must be homesick in the Bowery; he would take her to his mother's and keep her until the morrow, and perhaps until she left for home; telling Helen, of course, and then suffering her to act accordingly."

This he proposed to his client; assuring her of his mother's entire willingness to receive her, and urging so many reasons why she should go there, instead of " up to Katy's," where they were in such confusion, that Aunt Betsy was at last persuaded, and was soon riding up town in a Twenty-third Street stage, with Mark Ray her *vis-à-vis*, and Mattie at her right. Why Mattie was there Mark could not conjecture; and perhaps she did not know herself, unless it were that, disappointed in her call on Mrs. Cameron, she vaguely hoped for some redress by calling on Mrs. Banker. How then was she chagrined, when, as the stage left them at a handsome brownstone front, near Fifth Avenue Hotel, Mark said to her, as if she were not of course expected to go in, " Please tell your mother that Miss Barlow is stopping with Mrs. Banker to-day. Has she baggage at your house? If so, we will send round for it at once. Your number, please? "

His manner was so off hand and yet so polite that Mattie could neither resist him, nor be angry, though there was a pang of disappointment at her heart as she gave the required number, and then shook Aunt Betsy's hand, whispering in a choked voice,

" You'll come to us again before you go home? "

With a good-bye to Mark, whose bow atoned for a great deal, Mattie walked slowly away, leaving Mark greatly relieved. Aunt Betsy was as much as he cared to have on his hands at once, and as he led her up the steps, he began to wonder more and more what his mother would say to his bringing that stranger into her house, unbidden and unsought.

" I'll tell her the truth," was his rapid decision, and assuming a manner which warned the servant who answered his ring neither to be curious nor impertinent, he conducted his charge into the parlor, and bringing her a chair before the grate, went in quest of his mother, who he found was out.

"Kindle a fire then in the front guest-chamber," he said, "and see that it is made comfortable as soon as possible."

The servant bowed in acquiescence, wondering *who* had come, and feeling not a little surprised at the description given by John of the woman he had let into the house, and who now in the parlor was looking around her in astonishment and delight, condemning herself for the feeling of homesickness with which she remembered the Bowery, and contrasting her "cluttered quarters" there with the elegance around her. "Was Katy's house as fine as this?" she asked herself, feeling intuitively that such as she might be out of place in it, just as she began to fear she was out of her place here, bemoaning the fact that she had forgotten her *cap-box,* with its contents, and so could not remove her bonnet, as she had nothing with which to cover her gray head.

"What shall I do?" she was asking herself, when Mark appeared, explaining that his mother was absent, but would be at home in a short time.

"Your room will soon be ready," he continued, "and meantime you might lay aside your wrappings here if you find them too warm."

There was something about Mark Ray which inspired confidence, and in her extremity Aunt Betsy gasped, "I can't take off my bunnet till I get my caps, down to Mr. Tubbses. Oh, what a trouble I be."

Not exactly comprehending the nature of the difficulty, Mark suggested that she go without a cap until he could send for them; but Aunt Betsy's assertion that "she was grayer than a rat," enlightened him with regard to her dilemma, and full permission was given for her "to sit in her bonnet" until such time as a messenger could go to the Bowery and back. In this condition she was better in her own room, and as it was in readiness, Mark conducted her to it, the stern gravity of his face putting down the laugh which sprang to the waiting maid's eyes at the old lady's ejaculations of surprise that anything could be so fine as the house where she so unexpectedly found herself a guest.

"She is unaccustomed to the city, but a particular friend

of mine; so see that you treat her with respect," was all the explanation he vouchsafed to the curious girl.

But that was enough. A friend of Mr. Ray's must be somebody, even if she sat with two bonnets on instead of one, and appeared ten times more rustic than Aunt Betsy, who breathed freer when she found herself alone up stairs, and knew her baggage would soon be there.

In some little trepidation Mark paced up and down the parlor waiting for his mother, who came ere long, expressing her surprise to find him there, and asking if anything had happened that he seemed so agitated.

"Yes, I'm in a deuced scrape," he answered, coming up to her with the saucy, winning smile she could never resist, and continuing, "To begin at the foundation, you know how much I am in love with Helen Lennox?"

"No, I don't," was the reply, as Mrs. Banker removed her fur with the most provoking coolness. "How should I know when you have never told me?"

"Haven't you eyes? Can't you see? Don't you like her yourself?"

"Yes, very much."

"And are you willing she should be your daughter?"

Mark had his arm around his mother's neck, and bending his face to hers, kissed her playfully as he asked her the last question.

"Say, mother, are you willing I should marry Helen Lennox?"

There was a struggle in Mrs. Banker's heart, and for a moment she felt jealous of the girl who she had guessed was dearer to her son than ever his mother could be again; but she was a sensible woman. She knew that it was natural for another and a stronger love to come between her and her boy. She liked Helen Lennox. She was willing to take her as a daughter, and she said so at last, and listened half amazed and half amused to the story which had in it so much of Aunt Betsy Barlow, at that very moment an occupant of their best guest-chamber, waiting for her cap from the Bowery.

"Perhaps it was wrong to bring her home," he added, "but I did it to spare Helen. I knew what a savage Wilford would be if he found her there. Say, mother, was I wrong?"

He was not often wrong in his mother's estimation, and certainly he was not now, when he kissed her so often, begging her to say he had done right.

"Certainly he had. Mrs. Banker was very glad to find him so thoughtful; few young men would do as much," she said, and from feeling a little doubtful, Mark came to look upon himself as a very nice young man, who had done a most unselfish act, for of course he had not been influenced by any desire to keep Aunt Betsy from the people who would be present at the dinner, neither had Helen been at all mixed up in the affair.

It was all himself, and he began to whistle "Annie Laurie" very complacently, thinking the while what a clever fellow he was, and meditating other generous acts towards the old lady overhead, who was standing by the window, and wondering what the huge building could be gleaming so white in the fading sunlight.

"Looks as if it was made of stone cheena," she thought, just as Mrs. Banker appeared, her kind, friendly manner making Aunt Betsy feel wholly at ease, as she answered the lady's questions or volunteered remarks of her own.

Mrs. Banker had lived in the country, and had seen just such women as Aunt Betsy Barlow, understanding her intrinsic worth, and knowing how Helen Lennox, though her niece, could still be refined and cultivated. She could also understand how one educated as Wilford Cameron had been, would shrink from coming in contact with her, and possibly be rude if she thrust herself upon him. Mark did well to bring her here, she thought, as she left the room to order the tea which the tired woman so much needed. The satchel, umbrella, and cap-box, with a note from Mattie, had by this time arrived, and in her Sunday cap, with the purple bows, Aunt Betsy felt better, and enjoyed the tempting little supper, served on silver and Sèvres china, the attendant waiting in the hall instead of in her room, where her presence might embarrass one unaccustomed to such usages. They were very kind, and had Mark been her own son he could not have been more deferential than he appeared when just before starting for the dinner he went up to see her, asking what message he should take to Helen. Mrs. Banker, too, came in, her dress eliciting many compliments from her guest, who ventured to ask the price of the diamond pin which fastened the point lace collar. Five hundred dollars seemed an enormous sum, but Aunt Betsy was learning not to say all she thought, and merely remarked that Katy had some diamonds too, which she presumed cost full as much as that.

"She should do very well alone," she said; "she could read her Bible, and if she got too tired, go to bed," and with a good-bye she sent them away, after saying to Mrs. Banker, "Maybe you ain't the kissin' kind, but if you be, I wish you would kiss Katy once for me."

There was a merry twinkle in Mark's eyes as he asked, "And Helen too?"

"I meant your marm, not you," Aunt Betsy answered; while Mrs. Banker raised her hand to her mischievous son, who ran lightly down the stairs, carrying a happier heart than he had known since Helen Lennox first came to New York, and he met her at the depot.

CHAPTER XXVII.

THE DINNER PARTY.

It was a very select party which Wilford Cameron entertained that evening; and as the carriages rolled to his door and deposited the guests, the cloud which had been lifting ever since he came home and found "no Barlow woman" there, disappeared, leaving him the blandest, most urbane of hosts, pleased with everybody—himself, his guests, his sister-in-law, and his wife, who had never looked better than she did to-night, in pearls and light blue silk, which harmonized so perfectly with her wax-like complexion. Aunt Betsy's proximity was wholly unsuspected, both by her and Helen, who was very handsome, in crimson and black, with lilies in her hair. Nothing could please Mark better than his seat at table, where he could look into her eyes, which dropped so shyly whenever they met his gaze. Helen was beginning to doubt the story of his engagement with Juno. Certainly she could not mistake the nature of the attentions he paid to her, especially to-night, when he hovered continually near her, totally ignoring Juno's presence, and conscious apparently of only one form, one face, and that the face and form of Helen Lennox.

There was another, too, who felt the influence of Helen's beauty, and that was Lieutenant Bob, who, after dinner, attached himself to her side, while around them gathered quite a group, all listening with peals of laughter as Bob related his adventure of two days before, with "the most rustic and charming old lady it was ever his fortune to meet." Told by Bob the story lost nothing of its freshness; for every particular, except indeed the kindness he had shown her, was related, even to the *sheep-pasture,* about which she was going to New York to consult a lawyer.

"I thought once of referring her to you, Mr. Cameron," Bob said; "but couldn't find it in my heart to quiz her, she was so wholly unsuspicious. You have not seen her, have you?"

"No," came faintly from the lips which tried to smile; but Wilford knew who was the heroine of that story; wondering more and more where she was, and feeling a sensation of uneasiness, as he thought, "Can any accident have befallen her?"

It was hardly probable; but Wilford felt very uncomfortable after hearing the story, which had brought a pang of doubt and fear to another mind than his. From the very first Helen feared that Aunt Betsy was the "odd woman" who had gotten upon the train at some station which Bob could not remember; while, as the story progressed, she was sure of it, for she had heard of the sheep-pasture trouble, and of Aunt Betsy's projected visit to New York, privately writing to her mother not to suffer it, as Wilford would be greatly vexed. "Yes, it must be Aunt Betsy," she thought, and she turned so white that Mark, who was watching both her and Wilford, came as soon as possible to her side, and adroitly separating her from the group around, said softly, "You look tired, Miss Lennox. Come with me a moment. I have something to tell you."

Alone with her in the hall, he continued, "I have the sequel of Bob Reynolds's story. That woman——"

"Was Aunt Betsy," Helen gasped. "But where is she

now? That was two days ago. Tell me if you know. Mr. Ray, you *do* know," and in an agony of fear lest something dreadful had happened, she laid her hand on Mark's, beseeching him to tell her if he knew where Aunt Betsy was.

It was worth torturing her for a moment to see the pleading look in her eyes, and feel the soft touch of the hand which he took between both his own, holding it there while he answered her: "Aunt Betsy is at my house; kidnapped by me for safe keeping, until I could consult with you. Was that right?" he asked, as a flush came to Helen's cheek, and an expression to her eye which told that his meaning was understood.

"Is she there willingly? How did it happen?" was Helen's reply, her hand still in those of Mark, who, thus circumstanced, grew very warm and eloquent with the sequel to Bob's story, making it as long as possible, telling what he knew, and also what he had done.

He had not implicated Wilford in any way; but Helen read it all, saying more to herself than him, "And *she* was at the opera. Wilford must have seen her, and that is why he left so suddenly, and why he has appeared so absent and nervous to-day, as if expecting something. Excuse me," she suddenly added, drawing her hand away and stepping back a little, "I forgot that I was talking as if *you* knew."

"I do know more than you suppose—that is, I know human nature—and I know Will better than I did that morning when I first met you," Mark said, glancing at the freed hand he wished so much to take again.

But Helen kept her hands to herself, and answered him, "You did right under the circumstances. It would have been unpleasant for us all had she happened here to-night. I thank you, Mr. Ray—you and your mother, too—more than I can express. I will see her early to-morrow morning. Tell her so, please, and again I thank you."

There were tears in Helen's soft brown eyes, and they glittered like diamonds as she looked even more than spoke her thanks to the young man, who, for another look like that, would have driven Aunt Betsy amid the gayest crowd that ever frequented the Park, and sworn she was his blood relation! A few words from Mrs. Banker confirmed what Mark had said, and it was not strange if that night Miss Lennox, usually so entertaining, was a little absent, for her thoughts were up in that chamber on Twenty-third Street, where Aunt Betsy sat alone, but not lonely, for her mind was very busy with all she had been through since leaving Silverton, while something kept suggesting to her that it would have been wiser and better to have stayed at home than to have ventured where she was so sadly out of place. This last came gradually to Aunt Betsy as she thought the matter over, and remembered Wilford as he had appeared each time he came to Silverton.

"I ain't like him; I ain't like this Miss Banker; I ain't like anybody," she whispered. "I'm nothin' but a homely, old-fashioned woman, without larnin', without nothin'. I might know I wasn't wanted," and a rain of tears fell over the wrinkled face as she uttered this tirade against herself, standing before the long mirror, and inspecting the image it gave back of a plain, unpolished countrywoman, not much resembling Mrs. Banker, it must be confessed, nor much resembling the gay young ladies she had seen at the opera the previous night. "I won't go near Katy," she continued; "it would only mortify her, and I don't want to make her trouble. The poor thing's face looked as if she had it now, and I won't add to it. I'll start for home to-morrow. There's Miss Smith, in Springfield, will keep me over night, and Katy shan't be bothered."

When this decision was reached, Aunt Betsy felt a great deal better, and taking the Bible from the table, she sat down again before the fire, opening, as by a special Providence, to the chapter where the hewers of wood and drawers of water are mentioned as being necessary to mankind, each filling his appointed place.

"That's me—that's Betsy Barlow," she whispered, taking off her glasses to wipe away the moisture gathering so fast upon them. Then resuming them, she continued, "I'm a hewer of wood—a drawer of water. God made me so, and shall the clay find fault with the potter, for making it into a homely jug? No, indeed; and I was a very foolish old jug to think of sticking myself in with the china-ware. But I've larnt a lesson," and the philosophic old woman read on, feeling comforted to know that though a vessel of the rudest make, a paltry *jug*, as she called herself, the promises were still for her as much as for the finer wares—aye, that there was more hope of her entering at last where " the walls are all of precious stones and the streets are paved with gold," than of those whose good things are given so abundantly during their lifetime.

Assured, comforted, and encouraged, she fell asleep at last, and when Mrs. Banker returned she found her slumbering quietly in her chair, the Bible open on her lap, and her finger upon the passage referring to the hewers of wood and drawers of water, as if that was the last thing read.

Next morning, at a comparatively early hour, Helen stood ringing the bell of Mrs. Banker's house. She had said to Katy that she was going out, and could not tell just when she might return, and as Katy never questioned her acts, while Wilford was too intent upon his own miserable thoughts as to " where Aunt Betsy could be, or what had befallen her," to heed any one else, no inquiries were made, and no obstacles put in the way of her going direct to Mrs. Banker's, where Mark met her himself, holding her cold hand until he led her to the fire and placed her in a chair. He knew she would rather meet her aunt alone, and so when he heard her step in the hall he left the room, holding the door for Aunt Betsy, who wept like a little child at the sight of Helen, accusing herself of being a fool, who ought to be shut up in an insane asylum, but persisting in saying she was going home that very day without seeing Katy at all. " If she was here I'd like it, but I shan't go there, for I know Wilford don't want me." Then she told Helen all she did not already know of her trip to New York, her visit to the opera, her staying with the Tubbses and her meeting with Mark, the best young chap she ever saw, not even excepting Morris. " If he was my own son he couldn't be kinder," she added, " and I mistrust he hopes to be my nephew. You can't do better; and, if he offers, take him."

Helen's cheeks were crimson as she waived this part of the conversation, and wished aloud that she had come around in the carriage, as she could thus have taken Aunt Betsy over the city before the train would leave.

"Mark spoke of that when he heard I was going to-day," Aunt Betsy said; "I'll warrant you he'll attend to it."

Aunt Betsy was right, for when Mark and his mother joined their guests, and learned that Aunt Betsy's intention was unchanged, he suggested the ride, and offered the use of their carriage. Helen did not decline the offer, and ere a half hour had passed, Aunt Betsy, with her satchel, umbrella, and cap-box, was comfortably adjusted in Mrs. Banker's carriage with Helen beside her, while Mark bade his coachman drive wherever Miss Lennox wished to go, taking care to reach the train in time.

They were tearful thanks which Aunt Betsy gave to her kind friends as she was driven away to the Bowery to say good-bye, lest the Tubbses should "think her suddenly stuck up."

"Would you mind taking 'Tilda in? It would please her mightily," Aunt Betsy whispered, as they were alighting in front of Mr. Peter Tubbs's; and as the result of this suggestion, the carriage, when again it emerged into Broadway, held Mattie Tubbs, prouder than she had been in all her life before, while the gratified mother at home felt amply repaid for all the trouble her visitor had made her.

And Helen enjoyed it, too, finding Mattie a little insipid and tiresome, but feeling happy in the consciousness that she was making others happy. It was a long drive they took, and Aunt Betsy saw so much that her brain grew giddy, and she was glad when they started for the depot, taking Madison Square on the way, and passing Katy's house.

"I dare say it's all grand and smart," Aunt Betsy said, as she leaned out to look at it, "but I feel best at *hum,* where they are used to me."

And her face did wear a brighter look, when finally seated in the cars, than it had before since she left Silverton.

"You'll be home in April, and maybe Katy'll come too," she whispered as she kissed Helen good-bye, and shook hands with Mattie Tubbs, charging her again never to let the folks in Silverton know that "Betsy Barlow had been seen at a play-house."

Slowly the cars moved away, and Helen was driven home, leaving Mattie alone in her glory as she rolled down the Bowery, enjoying the éclat of her position, but feeling a little chagrined at not meeting a single acquaintance by whom to be envied and admired.

Katy did not ask where Helen had been, for she was wholly absorbed in Marian Hazelton's letter, telling how fast the baby improved, how pretty it was growing, and how fond both she and Mrs. Hubbell were of it, loving it almost as well as if it were their own.

"I know now it was best for it to go, but it was hard at first," Katy said, putting the letter away, and sighing wearily as she missed the clasp of the little arms and touch of the baby lips.

Several times Helen was tempted to tell her of Aunt Betsy's visit, but decided finally not to do so, and Katy never knew what it was which for many days made Wilford so nervous and uneasy, starting at every sudden ring, going often to the window, and looking out into the street as if expecting some one, while he grew strangely anxious for news from Silverton, asking when Katy had heard from home, and why she did not write. One there was, however, who knew, and who enjoyed watching Wilford, and guessing just how his anxiety grew as day after day went by; and she neither came nor was heard from in any way, for Helen did not show the letter apprising her of Aunt Betsy's safe arrival home, and so all in Wilford's mind was vague conjecture.

She *had* been in New York, as was proven by Bob Reynolds, but where was she now, and who were those people with her? Had they entrapped her into some snare, and possibly murdered her? Such things were not of rare occurrence, and Wilford actually grew thin with the uncertainty which hung over the fate of one whom in his present state of mind he would have warmly welcomed to his fireside, had there been a dozen dinner parties in progress. At last, as he sat one day in his office, with the same worried look on his face, Mark, who had been watching him, said,

"By the way, Will, how did that sheep pasture come out, or didn't the client appear?"

"Mark," and Wilford's voice was husky with emotion;

" you've stumbled upon the very thing which is tormenting my life out of me. Aunt Betsy has never turned up or been heard from since that night. For aught I know she was murdered, or spirited away, and I am half distracted. I'd give a thousand dollars to know what has become of her."

" Put down half that pile and I'll tell you," was Mark's *nonchalant* reply, while Wilford, seizing his shoulder, and compelling him to look up, exclaimed,

" You know, then? Tell me—you do know. Where is she?"

" Safe in Silverton, I presume," was the reply, and then Mark told his story, to which Wilford listened, half incredulous, half indignant, and a good deal relieved.

" You are a splendid fellow, Mark, though I must say you *meddled*, but I know you did not do it unselfishly. Perhaps with Katy not won I might do the same. Yes, on the whole, I thank you and Helen for saving me that mortification. I feel like a new man, knowing the old lady is safe at home, where I trust she will remain. And that Tom, who called here yesterday, asking to be our clerk, is the youth I saw at the opera. I thought his face was familiar. Let him come, of course. In my gratitude I feel like patronizing the entire Tubbs family."

And so it was this flash of gratitude for a peril escaped which procured for young *Tom Tubbs* the situation of clerk in the office of Cameron & Ray, the application for such situation having been urged by the ambitious Mattie, who felt her dignity considerably increased when she could speak of brother Tom in company with Messrs. Cameron and Ray.

CHAPTER XXVIII.

THE SEVENTH REGIMENT.

DOES the reader remember the pleasant spring days when the thunder of Fort Sumter's bombardment came echoing up the Northern hills and across the Western prairies, stopping for a moment the pulses of the nation, but quickening them again with a mighty power as from Maine to

California man after man arose to meet the misguided foe trailing our honored flag in the dust? Nowhere, perhaps, was the excitement so great or the feeling so strong as in New York, when the Seventh Regiment was ordered to Washington, its members never faltering or holding back, but with a nerving of the will and a putting aside of self, preparing to do their duty. Conspicuous among them was Mark Ray, who, laughing at his mother's fears, kissed her livid cheek, and then with a pang remembered Helen— wondering how she would feel, and thinking the path to danger would be so much easier if he knew that her prayers would go with him, shielding him from harm and bringing him back again to the sunshine of her presence.

And before he went Mark must know this for certain, and he chided himself for having put it off so long. True she had been sick and confined to her room for a long while after Aunt Betsy's memorable visit; and when she was able to go out, *Lent* had put a stop to her mingling in festive scenes, so that he had seen but little of her, and had never met her alone. But he would write that very day. She knew, of course, that he was going. She would say that he did well to go; and she would answer *yes* to the question he would ask her. Mark felt sure of that; but still the letter he wrote was eloquent with his pleadings for her love, while he confessed his own, and asked that she would give him the right to think of her as his affianced bride—to know she waited for his return, and would crown it at last with the full fruition of her priceless love.

"I meet a few of my particular friends at Mrs. Grandon's to-night," he added, in conclusion. " Can I hope to see you there, taking your presence as a token that I may speak and tell you in words what I have so poorly written?"

This note he would not trust to the post, but deliver himself, and thus avoid the possibility of a mistake, he said; and half an hour later he rang the bell at No. —, asking " if *Miss Lennox* was at home." She was; and handing the girl the note, Mark ran down the steps, while the servant carried the missive to the library, where upon the table lay other letters received that morning, and as yet unopened; for Katy was very busy, and Helen was dressing to go out with Juno Cameron, who had graciously asked her to drive with her and look at a picture she had set her heart on having.

Juno had not yet appeared; but Mark was scarcely out of sight when she came in with the familiarity of a sister, and entered the library to wait. Carelessly turning the books upon the table, she stumbled upon Mark's letter, which, through some defect in the envelope, had become unsealed, and lay with its edge lifted so that to peer at its contents was a very easy matter had she been so disposed. But Juno, who knew the handwriting—could not at first bring herself even to touch what was intended for her rival. But as she gazed the longing grew, until at last she took it in her hand, turning it to the light, and tracing distinctly the words, " My dear Helen," while a storm of pain and passion swept over her, mingled with a feeling of shame that she had let herself down so far.

" It does not matter now," the tempter whispered. " You may as well read it and know the worst. Nobody will suspect it," and she was about to take the folded letter from the envelope, intending to replace it after it was read, when a rapid step warned her some one was coming, and hastily thrusting the letter in her pocket, she dropped her veil to cover her confusion, and then confronted *Helen Lennox,* ready for the drive, and unconscious of the wrong which could not then be righted.

Juno did not mean to keep the letter, and all that morning she was devising measures for making restitution, thinking once to confess the whole, but shrinking from that as more than she could do. As they were driving home, they met Mark Ray; but Helen, who chanced to be looking in an opposite direction, did not see the earnest look of scrutiny he gave her, scarcely heeding Juno, whose voice trembled as she spoke of him to Helen and his intended departure. Helen observed the tremor in her voice, and pitied the girl whose agitation she fancied arose from the fact that her lover was so soon to go where danger and possibly death was waiting. In Helen's heart, too, there was a pang whenever she remembered Mark, and what had

so recently passed between them, raising hopes, which now
were wholly blasted. For he *was* Juno's, she believed, and
the grief at his projected departure was the cause of that
young lady's softened and even humble demeanor, as she
insisted on Helen's stopping at her house for lunch before
going home.

To this Helen consented—Juno still revolving in her
mind how to return the letter, which grew more and more
a horror to her. It was in her pocket, she knew, for she
had felt it there when, after lunch, she went to her room
for a fresh handkerchief. She would accompany Helen
home,—would manage to slip into the library alone, and
put it partly under a book, so that it would appear to be
hidden, and thus account for its not having been seen
before. This seemed a very clever plan, and with her
spirits quite elated, Juno drove round with Helen, finding
no one in the parlor below, and felicitating herself upon
the fact that Helen left her alone while she ran up to Katy.

"Now is my time," she thought, stealing noiselessly into
the library and feeling for the letter.

But *it was not there,* and no amount of search, no shaking of handkerchiefs, or turning of pocket inside out could
avail to find it. The letter was lost; and in the utmost
consternation Juno returned to the parlor, appearing so
abstracted as scarcely to be civil when Katy came down to
see her; asking if she was going that night to Sybil Grandon's, and talking of the dreadful war, which she hoped
would not be a war after all. Juno was too wretched to
talk, and after a few moments she started for home, hunting in her own room and through the halls, but failing in
her search, and finally giving it up, with the consoling
reflection that were it found in the street, no suspicion
could fasten on her; and as fear of detection, rather than
contrition for the sin, had been the cause of her distress,
she grew comparatively calm, save when her conscience
made itself heard and admonished confession as the only
reparation which was now in her power. But Juno could
not confess, and all that day she was absent-minded and
silent, while her mother watched her closely, wondering
what connection, if any, there was between her burning
cheeks and the letter she had found upon the floor in her

daughter's room just after she had left it; the letter, at whose contents she had glanced, shutting her lips firmly together, as he saw that her plans had failed, and finally putting the document away, where there was less hope of its ever finding its rightful owner, than if it had remained with Juno. Had Mrs. Cameron supposed that Helen had already seen it, she would have returned it at once; but of this she had her doubts, after learning that " Miss Lennox did not go up stairs at all." Juno, then, must have been the delinquent; and the mother resolved to keep the letter till some inquiry was made for it at least.

And so Helen did not guess how anxiously the young man was anticipating the interview at Sybil Grandon's, scarcely doubting that she would be there, and fancying just the expression of her eyes when they first met his. Alas for Mark, alas for Helen, that both should be so cruelly deceived. Had the latter known of the loving words sent from the true heart which longed for some word of hers to lighten the long march and beguile the tedious days of absence, she would not have said to Katy, when asked if she was going to Mrs. Grandon's, " Oh, no; please don't urge me. I would so much rather stay at home."

Katy would not insist, and so went alone with Wilford to the entertainment, given to a few young men who seemed as heroes then, when the full meaning of that word had not been exemplified, as it has been since in the life so cheerfully laid down, and the heart's blood poured so freely, by the tens of thousands who have won a martyr's and a hero's name. With a feeling of chill despair, Mark listened while Katy explained to Mrs. Grandon, that her sister had fully intended coming in the morning, but had suddenly changed her mind and begged to be excused.

" I am sorry, and so I am sure is Mr. Ray." Sybil said, turning lightly to Mark, whose white face froze the gay laugh on her lips and made her try to shield him from observation until he had time to recover himself and appear as usual.

How Mark blessed Sybil Grandon for that thoughtful kindness, and how wildly the blood throbbed through his veins as he thought " She would not come. She does not care. I have deceived myself in hoping that she did, and

now welcome *war,* welcome anything which shall help me
to forget."

Mark was very wretched, and his wretchedness showed
itself upon his face, making more than one rally him for
what they termed *fear,* while they tried to reassure him
by saying that to the Seventh there could be no danger
after Baltimore was safely passed. This was more than
Mark could bear, and at an early hour he left the house,
bidding Katy good-bye in the hall, and telling her he
probably should not see her again, as he would not have
time to call.

" Not call to say good-bye to Helen," Katy exclaimed.

" Helen will not care," was Mark's reply, as he hurried
away into the darkness of the night, more welcome in
his present state of mind than the gay scene he had
left.

And this was *all* Katy had to carry Helen, who had expected to see Mark once more, to bless him as a sister might
bless a brother, speaking to him words of cheer and bidding
him go on to where duty led. But he was not coming, and
she only saw him from the carriage window, as with proud
step and head erect, he passed with his regiment through
the densely crowded streets, where the loud hurrahs of the
multitude, which no man could number, told how terribly
in earnest the great city was, and how its heart was with
that gallant band, their pet, and pride, sent forth on a
mission such as it had never had before. But Mark did
not see Helen, and only his mother's face as it looked
when it said, " God bless my boy," was clear before his
eyes as he moved on through Broadway, and down Cort-
landt street, until the ferry-boat received him, and the
crowd began to disperse.

Now that Mark was gone, Mrs. Banker turned intuitively
to Helen, finding greater comfort in her quiet sympathy
than in the more wordy condolence offered her by Juno,
who, as she heard nothing from *the letter,* began to lose her
fears of detection, and even suffer her friends to rally her
upon the absence of Mark Ray, and the anxiety she must
feel on his account. Moments there were, however, when
thoughts of the stolen letter brought a pang, while Helen's
face was a continual reproach, and she was glad when, to-

wards the first of May, her rival left New York for Silverton, where, as the spring and summer work came on, her services were needed.

———

CHAPTER XXIX.

KATY GOES TO SILVERTON.

A SUMMER day in Silverton—a soft, bright August day, when the early rare-ripes by the well were turning their red cheeks to the sun, and the flowers in the garden were lifting their heads proudly, and nodding to each other as if they knew the secret which made that day so bright above all others. Old Whitey, by the hitching-post, was munching at his oats and glancing occasionally at the covered buggy standing on the green sward, fresh and clean as water from the pond could make it; the harness, lying upon a rock, where Katy used to feed the sheep with salt, and the whip standing upright in its socket, were waiting for the deacon, who was donning his best suit of clothes, even to a stiff shirt collar which almost cut his ears, his face shining with anticipations which he knew would be realized. Katy was really coming home, and in proof thereof there were behind the house and barn piles of rubbish, lath and plaster, mouldy paper and broken bricks, the tokens and remains of the repairing process, which for so long a time had made the farm-house a scene of dire confusion, driving its inmates nearly distracted, except when they remembered for whose sake they endured so much, inhaling clouds of lime, stepping over heaps of mortar, tearing their dress skirts on sundry nails projecting from every conceivable quarter, and wondering the while if the masons ever would finish or the carpenters be gone.

As a condition on which Katy might be permitted to come home, Wilford had stipulated an improvement in the interior arrangement of the house, offering to bear the expense even to the furnishing of the rooms. To this the family demurred at first, not liking Wilford's dictatorial manner, nor his insinuation that their home was not good enough for his wife. But Helen turned the tide, appreciating Wilford's feelings better than the others could do, and urging a compliance with his request.

"Anything to get Katy home," she said, and so the chimney was torn away, a window was cut here and an addition made there, until the house was really improved with its pleasant, modern parlor and the large airy bed-room, with bathing-room attached, the whole the idea of Wilford, who graciously deigned to come out once or twice from New London, where he was spending a few weeks, to superintend the work and suggest how it should be done.

The furniture, too, which he sent on from New York, was perfect in its kind, and suitable in every respect and Helen enjoyed the settling very much, and when it was finished it was hard telling which was the more pleased, she or good Aunt Betsy, who, having confessed in a general kind of way at a sewing society, that she did go to a play-house, and was not so very sorry either, except as the ex-ample might do harm, had nothing to fear from New York, and was proportionably happy. At least she would have been if Morris had not seemed so *off*, as she expressed it, taking but little interest in the preparations and evinc-ing no pleasure at Katy's expected visit. He had been polite to Wilford, had kept him at Linwood, taking him to and from the depot, but even Wilford had thought him changed, telling Katy how very sober and grave he had become, rarely smiling, and not seeming to care to talk unless it were about his profession or on some religious topic. And Morris *was* greatly changed. The wound which in most hearts would have healed by this time, had grown deeper with each succeeding year, while from all he heard he felt sure that Katy's marriage was a sad mistake, wishing sometimes that he had spoken, and so perhaps have saved her from the life in which she could not be wholly free. "She would be happier with me," he had said, with a sad smile to Helen, when she told him of some things which she had not mentioned else-where, and there were great tears in Morris's eyes, when Helen spoke of Katy's distress, and the look which came into her face when baby was taken away. Times there were when the silent Doctor, living alone at Linwood, felt that his grief was too great to bear. But the deep waters were always forded safely, and Morris's faith in God prevailed, so that only a dull heavy pain remained, with the consciousness that it was no sin to remember Katy as she was remembered now. Oh how he longed to see her, and yet how he dreaded it, lest poor weak human flesh should prove inadequate to the sight. But she was coming home; Providence had ordered that and he accepted it, looking eagerly for the time, but repressing his eagerness, so that not even Helen suspected how impatient he was for the day of her return. Four weeks she had been at the Pequot House in New London, occupying a little cottage and luxuriating in the joy of having her child with her almost every day. Country air and country nursing had wrought wonders in the baby, which had grown so beautiful and bright that it was no longer in Wilford's way save as it took too much of Katy's time, and made her care less for the gay crowd at the hotel.

Marian was working at her trade, and never came to the hotel except one day when Wilford was in New York, but that day sufficed for Katy to know that after herself it was Marian whom baby loved the best—Marian, who cared for it even more than Mrs. Hubbell. And Katy was glad to have it so, especially after Wilford and his mother decided that she must leave the child in New London while she made the visit to Silverton.

Wilford did not like her taking so much care of it as she was inclined to do. It had grown too heavy for her to lift; it was better with Mrs. Hubbell, he said, and so to the inmates of the farm-house Katy wrote that baby was not coming.

They were bitterly disappointed, for Katy's baby had been anticipated quite as much as Katy herself, and Aunt Betsy had brought from the wood-shed chamber a cradle which nearly forty years before had rocked the deacon's only child, the little boy, who died just as he had learned to lisp his mother's name. As a memento of those days the cradle had been kept, Katy using it sometimes for her kittens and her dolls, until she grew too old for that, when it was put away beneath the eaves whence Aunt Betsy dragged it, scouring it with soap and sand, until it was white as snow. But it would not be needed, and with a sigh the old lady carried it back, thinking "things had come to a pretty pass when a woman who could dance and carouse till twelve o'clock at night was too weakly to take care of her child," and feeling a very little awe of Katy who must have grown so fine a lady.

But all this passed away as the time drew near when Katy was to come, and no one seemed happier than Aunt Betsy on the morning when Uncle Ephraim drove from the door, setting old Whitey into a canter, which, by the time the "race" was reached, had become a rapid trot, the old man holding up his reins and looking proudly at the oat-fed animal, speeding along so fast.

He did not have long to wait this time, for the train soon came rolling across the meadow, and while his head was turned towards the car where he fancied she might be, a pair of arms was thrown impetuously round his neck, and a little figure, standing on tiptoe, almost pulled him down in its attempts to kiss him.

"Uncle Eph! oh, Uncle Eph, I've come! I'm here!" a young voice cried; but the words the deacon would have spoken were smothered by the kisses pressed upon his lips, kisses which only came to an end when a voice said rather reprovingly, "There, Katy, that will do. You have almost strangled him."

Wilford had not been expected, and the expression of the deacon's face was not a very cordial greeting to the young man who hastened to explain that he was going directly on to Boston. In his presence the deacon was not quite natural, but he lifted in his arms his "little Katy-did," and looked straight into her face, where there were as yet no real lines of care, only shadows, which told that in some respects she was not the same Katy he had parted with two years before. There was a good deal of the *city* about her dress and style; and the deacon felt a little overawed at first; but this wore off as, on their way to the farm-house, she talked to him in her old, loving manner, and asked questions about the people he supposed she had forgotten, nodding to everybody she met, whether she knew them or not, and at last, as the old house came in sight, hiding her face in a gush of happy tears upon his neck. Scarcely waiting for old Whitey to stop, but with one leap clearing the wheel, she threw herself into the midst of the women waiting on the door step to meet her. It was a joyful meeting, and when the first excitement was over, Katy inspected the improvements, praising them all and congratulating herself upon the nice time she was to have.

"You don't know what a luxury it is to feel that I can rest," she said to Helen.

"Didn't you rest at New London?" Helen asked.

"Yes, some," Katy replied; "but there were dances every night, or sails upon the bay, and I had to go, for many of our friends were there, and Wilford was not willing for me to be quiet."

This, then, was the reason why Katy came home so weary and pale, and craving so much the rest she had not had in more than two years. But she would get it now, and before the first dinner was eaten some of her old color came stealing back to her cheeks, and her eyes began to dance just as they used to do, while her merry voice rang out in silvery peals at Aunt Betsy's quaint remarks, which struck her so forcibly from not having heard them for so long a time. Freed from the restraint of her husband's presence, she came back at once to what she was when a young, careless girl she sat upon the door-steps and curled the dandelion stalks. She did not do this now, for there were none to curl; but she strung upon a thread the delicate petals of the phlox growing by the door, and then bound it as a crown about the head of her mother, who could not quite recognize her Katy in the elegant Mrs. Wilford Cameron, with rustling silk, and diamonds flashing on her hands every time they moved. But when she saw her racing with the old brown goat and its little kid out in the apple orchard, her head uncovered, and her bright curls blowing about her face, the feeling disappeared, and she felt that Katy had indeed come back again.

Katy had inquired for Morris immediately after her arrival, but in her excitement she had forgotten him again, until tea was over, when, just as she had done on the day of her return from Canandaigua, she took her hat and started on the well-worn path toward Linwood. Airily she tripped along, her light plaid silk gleaming through the

deep green of the trees and revealing her coming to the
tired man sitting upon a little rustic seat, beneath a chestnut tree, where he once had sat with Katy, and extracted a
cruel sliver from her hand, kissing the place to make it
well as she told him to.   She was a child then, a little
girl of twelve, and he was twenty, but the sight of her
pure face lifted confidingly to his had stirred his heart as
no other face had stirred it since, making him look forward to a time when the hand he kissed would be his own,
and his the fairy form he watched so carefully as it ex-
panded day by day into the perfect woman.   He was thinking of that time now, and how differently it had all turned
out, when he heard the bounding step and saw her coming
toward him, swinging her hat in childish abandon, and
warbling a song she had learned from him.

"Morris, oh, Morris!" she cried, as he ran eagerly forward; "I am so glad to see you.   It seems so nice to be
with you once more here in the dear old woods.   Don't
get up—please don't get up," she continued, as he started
to rise.

She was standing before him, a hand on either side of
his face, into which she was looking quite as wistfully as
he was regarding her.   Something she missed in his manner, which troubled her; and thinking she knew what it
was she said to him, "Why don't you kiss me, Morris?
You used to.   Ain't you glad to see me?"

"Yes, very glad," he answered, and drawing her down
beside him, he kissed her twice, but so gravely, that Katy
was not satisfied at all, and tears gathered in her eyes as
she tried to think what ailed Morris.

He was very thin, and there were a few white hairs
about his temples, so that, though four years younger than
her husband, he seemed to her much older, quite grand-
fatherly in fact, and this accounted for the liberties she
took, asking what was the matter, and trying to make him
like her again, by assuring him that she was not as vain
and foolish as he might suppose from what Helen had
probably told him of her life since leaving Silverton.   "I
do not like it at all," she said.   "I am in it, and must
conform; but, oh Morris! you don't know how much happier I should be if Wilford were just like you, and lived

at Linwood instead of New York. I should be so happy here with baby all the time."

It was well she spoke that name, for Morris could not have borne much more; but the mention of her child quieted him at once, so that he could calmly tell her she *was* the same to him she always had been, while with his next breath he asked, "Where is your baby, Katy?" adding with a smile, "I can remember when you were a baby, and I held you in my arms."

"Can you really?" Katy said: and as if that remembrance made him older than the hills, she nestled her curly head against his shoulder, while she told him of her bright-eyed darling, and as she talked, the mother-love which spread itself over her girlish face made it more beautiful than anything Morris had ever seen.

"Surely an angel's countenance cannot be fairer, purer than hers," he thought, as she talked of the only thing which had a power to separate her from him, making her seem as a friend, or at most as a beloved sister.

A long time they talked together, and the sun was setting ere Morris rose, suggesting that she go home, as the night dew would soon be falling.

"And you are not as strong as you once were," he added, pulling her shawl around her shoulders with careful solicitude, and thinking how slender she had become.

From the back parlor Helen saw them coming up the path, detecting the changed expression of Morris's face, and feeling a pang of fear when, as he left them after nine o'clock, she heard her mother say that he had not appeared so natural since Katy went away as he had done that night. Knowing what she did, Helen trembled for Morris, with this terrible temptation before him, and Morris trembled for himself as he went back the lonely path, and stopped again beneath the chestnut tree where he had so lately sat with Katy. There was a great fear at his heart, and it found utterance in words as kneeling by the rustic bench with only the lonely night around him and the green boughs over head, he asked that he might be kept from sin, both in thought and deed, and be to Katy Cameron just what she took him for, her friend and elder brother. And God, who knew the sincerity of the heart thus pleading before him, heard and answered the prayer, so that after that first night of trial Morris could look on Katy without a wish that she were otherwise than Wilford Cameron's wife and the mother of his child. He was happier because of her being at the farm-house, though he did not go there one-half as often as she came to him.

Those September days were happy ones to Katy, who became a child again—a petted, spoiled child, whom every one caressed and suffered to have her way. To Uncle Ephraim it was as if some bright angel had suddenly dropped into his path, and flooded it with sunshine. He was so glad to have again his "Katy-did," who went with him to the fields, waiting patiently till his work was done, and telling him of all the wondrous things she saw abroad, but speaking little of her city life. That was something she did not care to talk about, and but for Wilford's letters, and the frequent mention of baby, the deacon could easily have imagined that Katy had never left him. But these were barriers between the old life and the present; these were the insignia of *Mrs. Wilford Cameron*, who was watched and envied by the curious Silvertonians, and pronounced charming by them all. Still there was one drawback to Katy's happiness. She missed her child, mourning for it so much that her family, quite as anxious as herself to see it, suggested her sending for it. It would surely take no harm with them, and Marian would come with it, if Mrs. Hubbell could not. To this plan Katy listened more willingly from the fact that Wilford had gone West, and the greater the distance between them the more she dared to do. And so Marian Hazelton was one day startled at the sudden appearance at the cottage of Katy, who had come to take her and baby to Silverton.

There was no resisting the vehemence of Katy's arguments, and before the next day's sunsetting, the farm-house, usually so quiet and orderly, had been turned into one general nursery, where Baby Cameron reigned supreme, screaming with delight at the *tin* ware which Aunt Betsy brought out, from the cake-cutter to the dipper, the little creature beating a noisy tattoo upon the latter with an iron spoon, and then for diversion burying its fat dimpled hands in Uncle Ephraim's long white hair, for the old man went down upon all fours to do his great-grand-niece homage.

That night Morris came up, stopping suddenly as a loud baby laugh reached him, even across the orchard, and leaning for a moment against the wall, while he tried to prepare himself for the shock it would be to see Katy's child, and hold it in his arms, as he knew he must, or the mother be aggrieved.

He had supposed it was pretty, but he was not prepared for the beautiful little cherub which in its short white dress, with its soft curls of golden brown clustering about its head, stood holding to a chair, pushing it occasionally, and venturing now and then to take a step, while its infantile laugh mingled with the screams of its delighted auditors, watching it with so much interest.

There was one great, bitter, burning pang, and then, folding his arms composedly upon the window sill, Dr. Grant stood looking in upon the occupants of the room, whistling at last to baby, as he was accustomed to whistle to the children of his patients.

"Oh, Morris," Katy cried, "Baby can almost walk, Marian has taken so much pains, and she can say 'papa.' Isn't she a beauty?"

Baby had turned her head by this time, her ear caught by the whistle and her eye arrested by something in Morris which fascinated her gaze. Perhaps she thought of Wilford, of whom she had been very fond, for she pushed her chair towards him and then held up her fat arms for him to take her.

Never was mother prouder than Katy during the first few days succeeding baby's arrival, while the family seemed to tread on air, so swiftly the time went by with that active little life in their midst, stirring them up so constantly, putting to rout all their rules of order and keeping their house in a state of delightful confusion. It was wonderful how rapidly the child improved with so many teachers, learning to lisp its mother's name and taught by her, attempting to say "Doctor." From the very first the child took to Morris, crying after him whenever he went away, and hailing his arrival with a crow of joy and an eager attempt to reach him.

"It was altogether too forward for this world," Aunt
Betsy often said, shaking her head ominously, but not
really meaning what she predicted, even when for a few
days it did not seem as bright as usual, but lay quietly
in Katy's lap, a blue look about the mouth and a
flush upon its cheeks, which neither Morris nor Marian
liked.

More accustomed to children than the other members of
the family, they both watched it closely, Morris coming
over twice one day, and the last time he came regarding Katy with a look as if he would fain ward off
from her some evil which he feared.

"What is it, Morris?" she asked. "Is baby going to
be very sick?" and a great crushing fear came upon her
as she waited for his answer.

"I hope not," he said; "I cannot tell as yet; the symptoms are like cholera infantum, of which I have several
cases, but if taken in time I apprehend no danger."

There was a low shriek and baby opened its heavy lids
and moaned, while Helen came at once to Katy, who was
holding her hand upon her heart as if the pain had entered
there. To Marian it was no news, for ever since the early
morning she had suspected the nature of the disease stealing over the little child. All night the light burned in
the farm-house, where there were anxious, troubled faces,
Katy bending constantly over her darling, and even amid
her terrible anxiety, dreading Wilford's displeasure when
he should hear what she had done and its possible result.
She did not believe as yet that her child would die; but
she suffered acutely, watching for the early dawn when
Morris had said he would be there, and when at last he
came, begging of him to leave his other patients and care
only for baby.

"Would that be right?" Morris asked, and Katy blushed
for her selfishness when she heard how many were sick and
dying around them. "I will spend every leisure moment
here," he said, leaving his directions with Marian and then
hurrying away without a word of hope for the child, which
grew worse so fast that when the night shut down again it
lay upon the pillow, its blue eyes closed and its head thrown
back, while its sad moanings could only be hushed by

carrying it in one's arms about the room, a task which Katy could not do.

She had tried it at first, refusing all their offers with the reply, " Baby is mine, and shall I not carry her ? "

But the feeble strength gave out, the limbs began to totter, and staggering backward she cried, " Somebody must take her."

It was Marian who went forward, Marian, whose face was a puzzle as she took the infant in her stronger arms, her stony eyes, which had not wept as yet, fastening themselves upon the face of Wilford Cameron's child with a look which seemed to say, " Retribution, retribution."

But only when she remembered the father, now so proud of his daughter, was that word in her heart. She could not harbor it when she glanced at the mother, and her lips moved in earnest prayer that, if possible, God would not leave her so desolate. An hour later and Morris came, relieving Marian of her burden, which he carried in his own arms, while he strove to comfort Katy, who, crouching by the empty crib, was sitting motionless in a kind of dumb despair, all hope crushed out by his answer to her entreaties that he would tell her the truth, and keep nothing back.

" I think your baby will die," he said to her very gently, pausing a moment in awe of the white face, whose expression terrified him, it was so full of agony.

Bowing her head upon her hands, poor Katy whispered sadly, " God must not take my baby. Oh, Morris, pray that he will not. He will hear and answer you; I have been so bad I cannot pray, but I am not going to be bad again. If he will let me keep my darling I will begin a new life. I *will* try to serve him. Dear Lord, hear and answer, and not let baby die."

She was praying herself now, and Morris's broad chest heaved as he glanced at her kneeling figure, and then at the death-like face upon the pillow, with the pinched look about the nose and lips, which to his practiced eye was a harbinger of death.

" It's father should be here," he thought, and when Katy lifted up her head again he asked if she was sure her husband had not yet returned from Minnesota.

"Yes, sure—that is, I think he has not," was Katy's answer, a chill creeping over her at the thought of meeting Wilford, and giving him his daughter dead.

"I shall telegraph in the morning at all events," Morris continued, "and if he is not in New York, it will be forwarded."

"Yes, that will be best," was the reply, spoken so mournfully that Morris stopped in front of Katy, and tried to reason with her.

But Katy would not listen, and only answered that *he* did not know, he could not feel, he never had been tried.

"Perhaps not," Morris said; "but Heaven is my witness, Katy, that if I could save you this pain by giving up my life for baby's I would do it willingly; but God does not give us our choice. He knoweth what is best, and baby is better with Him than us."

For a moment Katy was silent; then, as a new idea took possession of her mind, she sprang to Morris's side and seizing his arm, demanded, "Can an unbaptized child be saved?"

"We nowhere read that baptism is a saving ordinance," was Morris's answer; while Katy continued, "but *do* you believe they will be saved?"

"Yes, I do," was the decided response, which, however, did not ease Katy's mind, and she moaned on, "A child of heathen parents may, but *I* knew better. I knew it was my duty to give the child to God, and for a foolish fancy withheld the gift until it is too late, and God will take it without the mark upon its forehead, the water on its brow. Oh, baby, baby, if she should be lost—*no name, no mark, no baptismal sign.*"

"Not water, but the blood of Jesus cleanseth from all sin," Morris said, "and as sure as he died so sure this little one is safe. Besides, there may be time for the baptism yet—that is, to-morrow. Baby will not die to-night, and if you like, it still shall have a name."

Eagerly Katy seized upon that idea, thinking more of the sign, the water, than the *name,* which scarcely occupied her thoughts at all. It did not matter what the child was called, so that it became one of the little ones in glory, and with a calmer, quieter demeanor than she had shown that day, she saw Morris depart at a late hour; and then turning to the child which Uncle Ephraim was holding, kissed it lovingly, whispering as she did so, " Baby shall be baptized—baby shall have the sign."

CHAPTER XXX.

LITTLE GENEVRA.

MORRIS had telegraphed to New York, receiving in reply that Wilford was hourly expected home, and would at once hasten on to Silverton. The clergyman, Mr. Kelly, had also been seen, but owing to a funeral which would take him out of town, he could not be at the farm-house until five in the afternoon, when, if the child still lived, he would be glad to officiate as requested. All this Morris had communicated to Katy, who listened in a kind of stupor, gasping for breath, when she heard that Wilford would soon be there, and moaning "that will be too late," when told that the baptism could not take place till night. Then kneeling by the crib where the child was lying, she fastened her great, sad blue eyes upon the pallid face with an earnestness as if thus she would hold till nightfall the life flickering so faintly and seeming so nearly finished. The wailings had ceased, and they no longer carried it in their arms, but had placed it in its crib, where it lay perfectly still, save as its eyes occasionally unclosed and turned wistfully towards the cups, where it knew was something which quenched its raging thirst. Once indeed, as the hours crept on to noon and Katy bent over it so that her curls swept its face, it seemed to know her, and the little wasted hand was uplifted and rested on her cheek with the same caressing motion it had been wont to use in health. Then hope whispered that it might live, and with a great cry of joy Katy sobbed, " She knows me, Morris— mother, see; she knows me. Maybe she will live! "

But the dull stupor which succeeded swept all hope away, and again Katy resumed her post, watching first her dying child, and then the long hands of the clock which crept on so slowly, pointing to only two when she thought it must be five. Would that hour never come, or coming, would it find baby there? None could answer that last question—they could only wait and pray; and as they waited the warm September sun neared the western sky till its yellow beams came stealing through the window and across the floor to where Katy sat watching its onward progress, and looking sometimes out upon the hills where the purplish autumnal haze was lying just as she once loved to see it. But she did not heed it now, nor care how bright the day with the flitting shadows dancing on the grass, the tall flowers growing by the door, and old Whitey standing by the gate, his head stretched towards the house in a kind of dreamy, listening attitude, as if he, too, knew of the great sorrow hastening on so fast. The others saw all this, and it made their hearts ache more as they thought of the beautiful little child going from their midst when they wished so much to keep her. Katy had only one idea, and that was of the child, growing very restless now, and throwing up its arms as if in pain. It was striking five, and with each stroke the dying baby moaned, while Katy strained her ear to catch the sound of horses' hoofs hurrying up the road. The clergyman had come and the inmates of the house gathered round in silence, while he made ready to receive the child into Christ's flock.

Mrs. Lennox had questioned Helen about the name, and Helen had answered, " Katy knows, I presume. It does not matter," but no one had spoken directly to Katy, who had scarcely given it a thought, caring more for the rite she had deferred so long.

"He must hasten," she said to Morris, her eyes fixed upon the panting child she had lifted to her own lap, and thus adjured the clergyman failed to make the usual inquiry concerning the name he was to give.

Calm and white as a marble statue, Marian Hazelton glided to the back of Katy's chair, and pressing both her hands upon it, leaned over Katy so that her eyes, too, were fixed upon the little face, from which they never turned but once, and that when the clergyman's voice was heard asking for a *name*. There was an instant's silence, and Katy's lips began to move, when one of Marian's hands was laid upon her head, while the other took in

its own the limp, white baby fingers, and Marian's voice
was very steady in its tone as it said, GENEVRA."

"Yes, Genevra," Katy whispered, and the solemn
words were heard, " *Genevra*, I baptize thee in the name
of the Father, the Son, and the Holy Ghost."

Softly the baptismal waters fell upon the pale forehead,
and at their touch the little Genevra's eyes unclosed, the
waxen fingers withdrew themselves from Marian's grasp,
and again sought the mother's cheek, resting there for an
instant; while a smile broke around the baby's lips, which
tried to say " Mam-ma." Then the hand fell back, down
upon Marian's, the soft eyes closed, the limbs grew rigid,
the shadow of death grew deeper, and while the prayer
was said, and Marian's tears fell with Katy's upon the
brow where the baptismal waters were not dried, the
angel came, and when the prayer was ended, Morris,
who knew what the rest did not, took the lifeless form
from Katy's lap, and whispered to her gently, " Katy,
your baby is dead ! "

An hour later, and the sweet little creature, which had
been a sunbeam in that house for a few happy days, lay
upon the bed where Katy said it must be laid; its form
shrouded in the christening robe which grandma Cameron
had bought, flowers upon its pillow, flowers upon its
bosom, flowers in its hands, which Marian had put there;
for Marian's was the mind which thought of everything
concerning the dead child; and Helen, as she watched
her, wondered at the mighty love which showed itself in
every lineament of her face, the blue veins swelling in
her forehead, her eyes bloodshot, and her lips shut firmly
together, as if it were by mere strength of will that she
kept back the scalding tears as she dressed the little
Genevra. They spoke of that name in the kitchen when
the first great shock was over, and Helen explained why
it had been Katy's choice.

It was Morris's task to comfort poor, stricken Katy,
telling her of the blessed Saviour who loved the little
children while here on the earth, and to whom her darling
had surely gone.

" Safe in His arms, it would not come back if it could,"
he said, " and neither would you have it."

But Katy was the mother, the human love could not so soon submit, but went out after the lost one with a piteous, agonizing wail.

"Oh, I want my baby back. I know she is safe, but I want her back. She was my life—all I had to love," Katy moaned, rocking to and fro in this her first hour of bereavement, "and Wilford will blame me so much for bringing my baby here to die. He will say it was my fault; and that I can't bear. I know I killed my baby; but I did not mean to. I would give my life for hers, if like her I was ready," and into Katy's face there came a look of fear which Morris failed to understand, not knowing Wilford as well as Katy knew him.

At nine o'clock next day there came a telegram. Wilford had reached New York and would be in Silverton that afternoon, accompanied by Bell. At this last Marian Hazelton caught as an excuse for what she intended doing. She could not remain there after Wilford came, nor was it necessary. Her task was done, or would be when she had finished the wreath and cross of flowers she was making for the coffin. Laying them on baby's pillow, Marian went in quest of Helen, to whom she explained that as Bell Cameron was coming, and the house would be full, she had decided upon going to West Silverton, as she wished to see the old lady with whom she once boarded, and who had been so kind to her.

"I might stay," she added, as Helen began to protest, "but you do not need me. I have done all I can, and would rather go where I can be quiet for a little."

To this last argument there could be no demur, and so the same carriage which at ten o'clock went for Wilford Cameron carried Marian Hazleton to the village where she preferred being left.

*   *   *   *   *   *   *   *

In much anxiety and distress Wilford Cameron read the telegram announcing baby's illness.

"At Silverton!" he said. "How can that be when the child was at New London?" and he glanced again at the words:

"Your child · is dying at Silverton. Come at once.
M. Grant"

There could be no mistake, and Wilford's face grew
dark, for he guessed the truth, censuring Katy much,
but censuring her family more. They of course had
encouraged her in the plan of taking her child from New
London, where it was doing so well, and this was the
result. Wilford was proud of his daughter now, and
during the few weeks he had been with it, the little thing
had found a strong place in his love. Many times he
had thought of it during his journey West, indulging
in bright anticipations of the coming winter, when he
would have it home again. It would not be in his way
now. On the contrary, it would add much to his luxurious home, and the young father's heart bounded with
thoughts of the beautiful baby as he had last seen it,
crowing its good-bye to him and trying to lisp his name,
its sweet voice haunting him for weeks, and making him
a softer, better man, who did not frown impatiently upon
the little children in the cars, but who took notice of them
all, even laying his hand once on a little curly head which
reminded him of baby's.

Alas for him! he little dreamed of the great shock in
store for him. The child was undoubtedly very sick,
he said, but that it could die was not possible; and so,
though he made ready to hasten to it, he did not withhold his opinion of the rashness which had brought it
to such peril.

"Had Katy obeyed *me* it would not have happened,"
he said, pacing up and down the parlor and preparing
to say more, when Bell came to Katy's aid, and lighting
upon him, asked what he meant by blaming his wife so
much.

"For my part," she said, "I think there has been too
much fault-finding and dictation from the very day of
the child's birth till now, and if God takes it, I shall
think it a judgment upon you. First you were vexed
with Katy because it was not a boy, as if she were to
blame; then you did not like it because it was not more
promising and fair; next it was in your way, and so you

sent it off, never considering Katy any more than if she were a mere automaton. Then you must needs forbid her taking it home to her own family, as if they had no interest in it. I tell you, Will, it is not *all* Cameron—there is some Barlow blood in its veins—Aunt Betsy Barlow's, too, and you cannot wash it out. Katy had a right to take her own child where she pleased, and you are not a man if you censure her for it, as I see in your eyes you mean to do. Suppose it had stayed in New London and been struck with lightning—*you* would have been to blame, of course, according to your own view of things."

There was too much truth in Bell's remarks for Wilford to retort, even had he been disposed, and he contented himself with a haughty toss of his head as she left the room to get herself in readiness for the journey she insisted upon taking. Wilford was glad she was going, as her presence at Silverton would relieve him of the awkward embarrassment he always felt when there; and magnanimously forgiving her for the plainness of her speech, he was the most attentive of brothers until Silverton was reached and he found Dr. Grant awaiting for him. Something in his face, as he came forward to meet them, startled bith Wilford and Bell, the latter of whom asked quickly,

"Is the baby better?"

"Baby is dead," was the brief reply, and Wilford staggered back against the door-post, where he leaned a moment for support in that first great shock for which he was not prepared.

Upon the door-step Bell sat down, crying quietly, for she had loved the child, and she listened anxiously while Morris repeated the particulars of its illness and then spoke of Katy's reproaching herself so bitterly for having brought it from New London. "She seems entirely crushed," he continued, when they were driving towards the farm-house. "For a few hours I trembled for her reason, while the fear that you might reproach her added much to the poignancy of her grief."

Morris said this very calmly, as if it were not what he had all the while intended saying, and his eye turned towards Wilford, whose lips were compressed with the emotion he was trying to control. It was Bell who spoke first, Bell who said impulsively, " Poor Katy, I knew she would feel so, but it is unnecessary, for none but a *savage* would reproach her now, even if she were in fault."

Morris blessed Bell Cameron in his heart, knowing how much influence her words would have upon her brother, who brushed away the first tear he had shed, and tried to say that " of course she was not to blame."

They were in sight of the farm-house now, and Bell, with her city ideas, was looking curiously at it, mentally pronouncing it a nicer, pleasanter place than she had supposed. It was very quiet about the house, and old Whitey's neigh as Morris's span of bays came up was the only sound which greeted them. In the wood-shed door Uncle Ephraim sat smoking his clay pipe and likening the feathery waves which curled above his head to the little soul so recently gone upward; while by his side, upon a log of wood, holding a pan of the luscious peaches she was slicing up for tea, sat a woman whom Bell knew at once for Aunt Betsy Barlow, and who, pan in hand, came forward to meet her, curtsying very low when introduced by Morris, and asking to be excused from shaking hands, inasmuch as hers were not fit to be touched. Bell's quick eye took her in at a glance, from her clean spotted gown to her plain muslin cap tied with a black ribbon, put on that day with a view to mourning, and then darted off to Uncle Ephraim, who won her heart at once when she heard how his voice trembled as he took Wilford's hand and said so pityingly, so father-like, " Young man, this is a sad day for you, and you have my sympathy, for I remember well how my heart ached when, on just such a day as this, my only child lay dead as yours is lying."

Every muscle of Wilford's face quivered, but he was too proud to show all that he felt, and he was glad when Helen appeared in the door, as that diverted his mind, and he greeted her cordially, stooping down and kissing her forehead, a thing he had never done before. But sorrow is a great softener, and Wilford was very sorry, feeling his loss more here, where everything was so quiet, so suggestive of death.

" Where is Katy? " he asked.

" She is sleeping for the first time since the baby died. She is in here with the child. She will stay nowhere else," Helen said, opening the door of the bedroom and motioning Wilford in.

With hushed breath and a beating heart, Wilford stepped across the threshold, and Helen closed the door, leaving him alone with the living and the dead. Pure and beautiful as some fair blossom, the dead child lay upon the bed, the curls of golden hair clustering about its head, and on its lips the smile which settled there when it tried to say " mamma." Its dimpled hands were folded upon its breast, where lay the cross of flowers which Marian Hazelton had made. There were flowers upon its pillow, flowers around its head, flowers upon its shroud, flowers everywhere, and itself the fairest flower of all, Wilford thought, as he stood gazing at it and then let his eye move on to where poor, tired, worn-out Katy had crept up so close beside it that her breath touched the marble cheek and her own disordered hair rested upon the pillow of her child. Even in her sleep her tears kept dropping and the pale lips quivered in a grieved, touching way. Hard indeed would Wilford have been had he cherished one bitter thought against the wife so wounded. He could not when he saw her, but no one ever knew just what passed through his mind during the half hour he sat there beside her, scarcely stirring and not daring to kiss his child lest he should awaken her. He could hear the ticking of his watch and the beating of his heart as he waited for the first sound which should herald's Katy's waking.

Suddenly there was a low, gasping moan, and Katy's eyes unclosed and rested on her husband. He was bending over her in an instant, and her arms were round his neck, while she said to him so sadly,

" Our baby is dead—you've nobody left but me; and oh! Wilford, you will not blame me for bringing baby here? I did not think she'd die. I'd give my life for hers if that would bring her back. Would you rather it was me lying as baby lies, and she here in your arms? "

" No, Katy," Wilford answered, and by his voice Katy

knew that she was wholly forgiven, crying on his neck in a plaintive, piteous way, while Wilford soothed and pitied and caressed, feeling subdued and humbled, and we must confess it, feeling too how very good and generous he was to be thus forbearing, when but for Katy's act of disobedience they might not now be childless!

With a great gush of tears Bell Cameron bent over the little form, and then enfolded Katy in a more loving embrace than she had ever given her before; but whatever she might have said was prevented by the arrival of the coffin, and the confusion which followed.

Much Wilford regretted that New York was so far away, for a city coffin was more suitable, he thought, for a child of his, than the one which Dr. Grant had ordered. But that was really of less consequence than the question where the child should be buried. A costly monument at Greenwood was in accordance with his ideas, but all things indicated a contemplated burial there in the country churchyard, and sorely perplexed, he called on Bell as the only Cameron at hand, to know what he should do.

"Do just as Katy prefers," was Bell's reply, as she led him to the coffin and pointed to the name: "Little Genevra Cameron, aged nine months and twenty days."

"What is it, Wilford—what is the matter?" she asked, as her brother turned whiter than his child.

Had "Genevra Lambert, aged 22," met his eye, he could not have been more startled than he was; but soon rallying, he said to Morris,

"The child was baptized, then?"

"Yes, baptized Genevra. That was Katy's choice, I understand," Morris replied, and Wilford bowed his head, wishing the *Genevra* across the sea might know that his child bore her name.

"Perhaps she does," he thought, and his heart grew warm with the fancy that possibly in that other world, whose existence he never really doubted, the Genevra he had wronged would care for his child, if children there need care. "She will know it is mine at least," he said, and with a thoughtful face he went in quest of Katy, whom he found sobbing by the side of the mourning garments just sent in for her inspection.

Wilford was averse to black. It would not become Katy, he feared, and it would be an unanswerable reason for her remaining closely home for the entire winter.

"What's this?" he asked, lifting the crape veil and dropping it again with an impatient gesture as Helen replied, "It is Katy's mourning veil."

Contrary to his expectations, black was becoming to Katy, who looked like a pure white lily, as, leaning on Wilford's arm next day, she stood by the grave where they were burying her child.

Wilford had spoken to her of Greenwood, but she had begged so hard that he had given up that idea, suggesting next, as more in accordance with city custom, that she remain at home while *he* only followed to the grave; but from this Katy recoiled in such distress that he gave that up too, and bore, magnanimously as he thought, the sight of all the Barlows standing around that grave, alike mourners with himself, and all a right to be there. Wilford felt his loss deeply, and his heart ached to its very core as he heard the gravel rattling down upon the coffin-lid which covered the beautiful child he had loved so much. But amid it all he never for a moment forgot that he was *Wilford Cameron,* and infinitely superior to the crowd around him—except, indeed, his wife, his sister, Dr. Grant, and Helen. He could bear to see them sorry, and feel that by their sorrow they honored the memory of his child. But for the rest—the village herd, with the Barlows in their train—he had no affinity, and his manner was as haughty and distant as ever as he passed through their midst back to the carriage, which took him again to the farm-house.

CHAPTER XXXI.

AFTER THE FUNERAL.

Had there been a train back to New York that afternoon Wilford would most certainly have suggested going; but as there was none he passed the time as well as he could, finding Bell a great help to him, but wondering that she could assimilate so readily with such people, declaring herself in love with the farm-house, and saying she should like to remain there for weeks, if the days were all as sunny as this, the dahlias as gorgeously bright, and the peaches by the well as delicious and ripe. To these the city girl took readily, visiting them the last thing before retiring, while Wilford found her there when he arose next morning, her dress and slippers nearly spoiled with the heavy dew, and her hands full of the fresh fruit which Aunt Betsy knocked from the tree with a quilting rod; *her* dress pinned around her waist, and disclosing a petticoat scrupulously clean, but patched and mended with so many different patterns and colors that the original ground was lost, and none could tell whether it had been red or black, buff or blue. Between Aunt Betsy and Bell the most amicable feeling had existed ever since the older lady had told the younger how all the summer long she had been drying fruit, "thimble-berries, blue-bries, and huckle-berries" for the soldiers, and how she was now drying peaches for Willard Buxton—once their hired man. These she should tie up in a *salt bag,* and put in the next box sent by the society of which she seemed to be head and front, "kind of fust directress" she said, and Bell was interested at once, for among the soldiers down by the Potomac was one who carried with him the whole of Bell Cameron's heart; and who for a few days had tarried at just such a dwelling as the farm-house, writing back to her so pleasant descriptions of it, with its fresh grass and shadowy trees, that she had longed to be there too. So it was through this halo of romance and love that Bell looked at the farm-house and its occupants, preferring good Aunt Betsy because she seemed the most interested in the soldiers, working as soon as breakfast was over upon the peaches, and kindly furnishing her best check apron, together with pan and knife for Bell, who offered her assistance, notwithstanding Wilford's warning that the fruit would stain her hands, and his advice that she had better be putting up her things for going home.

" She was not going that day," she said, point blank, and as Katy too had asked to stay a little longer, Wilford was compelled to yield, and taking his hat sauntered off toward Linwood; while Katy went listlessly into the kitchen, where Bell Cameron sat, her tongue moving much faster than her hands, which pared so slowly and cut away so much of the juicy pulp, besides making so frequent journeys to her mouth, that Aunt Betsy looked in alarm at the rapidly disappearing fruit, wishing to herself that " Miss Camern had not 'listed."

But *Miss Camern* had enlisted, and so had Bob, or rather he had gone to his duty, and as she worked, she repeated to Helen the particulars of his going, telling how, when the war first broke out, and Sumter was bombarded, Bob, who, from long association with Southern men at West Point, had imbibed many of their ideas, was very sympathetic with the rebelling States, gaining the cognomen of a secessionist, and once actually thinking of casting in his lot with that side rather than the other. But a little incident saved him, she said. The remembrance of a queer old lady whom he met in the cars, and who, at parting held her wrinkled hand above his head in benediction, charging him not to go against the flag, and promising her prayers for his safety if found on the side of the Union.

" I wish you could hear Bob tell the story, the funny part I mean," she continued, narrating as well as she could the particulars of Lieutenant Bob's meeting with Aunt Betsy, who, as the story progressed and she recognized herself in the queer old Yankee woman, who shook hands with the conductor and was going to law about a sheep pasture, dropped her head lower and lower over her pan of peaches, while a scarlet flush spread itself all over her thin face, but changed to a grayish white as Bell concluded with "Bob says the memory of that hand lifted above his head haunted him day and night, during the period of his uncertainty, and was at last the means of saving him from treachery to his country."

"Thank God!" came involuntarily from Aunt Betsy's quivering lips, and, looking up, Bell saw the great tears running down her cheeks, tears which she wiped away with her arm, while she said faintly, "That old woman, who made a fool of herself in the cars, was *me!*"

"You, Miss Barlow, you!" Bell exclaimed, forgetting in her astonishment to carry to her mouth the luscious half peach she had intended for that purpose, and dropping it untasted into the pan, while Katy, who had been listening with considerable interest, came quickly forward saying, "You, Aunt Betsy! when were you in New York, and why did I never know it?"

It could not be kept back and, unmindful of Bell, Helen explained to Katy as well as she could the circumstances of Aunt Betsy's visit to New York the previous winter.

"And she never let me know it, or come to see me, be-cause—because—" Katy hesitated, and looked at Bell, who said, pertly, "Because Will is so abominably proud, and would have made such a fuss. Don't spoil a story for relation's sake, I beg," and the young lady laughed good humoredly, restoring peace to all save Katy, whose face wore a troubled look, and who soon stole away to her mother, whom she questioned further with regard to a circumstance which seemed so mysterious to her.

"Miss Barlow," Bell said, when Katy was gone, "you will forgive me for repeating that story as I did. Of course I had no idea it was you of whom I was talking."

Bell was very earnest, and her eyes looked pleadingly upon Aunt Betsy, who answered her back, "There's nothing to forgive. You only told the truth. I did make an old fool of myself, but if I helped that boy to a right decision, my journey did some good, and I ain't sorry now if I did go to the play-house. I confessed that to the sewing circle, and Mrs. Deacon Bannister hain't seemed the same towards me since, but I don't care. I beat her on the election to first directress of the Soldier's Aid. She didn't run half as well as me. That chap—you call Bob—is he anything to you. Is he your beau?"

"It was Bell's turn now to blush and then grow white, while Helen, lightly touching the superb diamond on her first finger, said, "That indicates as much. When did it happen, Bell?"

Mrs. Cameron had said they were not a family to bruit their affairs abroad, and if so, Bell was not like her family, for she answered frankly, "Just before he went away. It's a splendid diamond, isn't it?" and she held it up for Helen to inspect.

The basket was empty by this time, and as Aunt Betsy went to fill it from the trees, Bell and Helen were left alone, and the former continued in a low, sad tone, "I've been so sorry sometimes that I did not tell Bob I *loved* him, when he wished me to so much."

"Not tell him you loved him! How then could you tell him yes, as it appears you did?" Helen asked, and Bell answered, "I could not well help that; it came so sudden and he begged so hard, saying my promise would make him a better man, a better soldier and all that. It was the very night before he went, and so I said that out of *pity* and *patriotism* I would give the promise, and I did, but it seemed too much for a woman to tell a man all at once that she loved him, and I wouldn't do it, but I've been sorry since; oh, so sorry, during the two days when we heard nothing from him after that dreadful battle at Bull Run. We knew he was in it, and I thought I should die until his telegram came saying he was safe. I did sit down then and commence a letter, confessing all, but I tore it up, and he don't know now just how I feel."

"And do you really love him?" Helen asked, puzzled by this strange girl, who laughingly held up her soft, white hand, stained and blackened with the juice of the fruit she had been paring, and said, "Do you suppose I would spoil my hands like that, and incur *ma chère mamma's* displeasure, if Bob were not in the army and I did not care for him? And now allow me to catechise you. Did Mark Ray ever propose and you refuse him?"

"Never!" and Helen's face grew crimson, while Bell

continued: "That is funny. Half our circle think so, though how the impression was first given I do not know. Mother told me, but would not tell where she received her information. I heard of it again in a few days, and have reason to believe that Mrs. Banker knows it too, and feels a little uncomfortable that her son should be refused when she considers him worthy of the Empress herself."

Helen was very white, as she asked, "And how with Mark and Juno?"

"Oh, there is nothing between them," Bell replied. "Mark has scarcely called on us since he returned from Washington with his regiment. You are certain you never cared for him?"

This was so abrupt, and Bell's eyes were so searching that Helen grew giddy for a moment, and grasped the back of the chair, as she replied: "I did not say I never cared for him. I said he never proposed; and that is true; he never did."

"And if he had?" Bell continued, never taking her eyes from Helen, who, had she been less agitated, would have denied Bell's right to question her so closely. Now, however, she answered blindly, "I do not know. I cannot tell. I thought him engaged to Juno."

"Well, if that is not the rarest case of cross-purposes that I ever knew," Bell said, wiping her hands upon Aunt Betsy's apron, and preparing to attack the piled up basket just brought in.

Farther conversation was impossible, and, with her mind in a perfect tempest of thought, Helen went away, trying to decide what it was best for her to do. Some one had spread the report that *she* had refused Mark Ray, telling of the refusal of course, or how else could it have been known? and this accounted for Mrs. Banker's long continued silence. Since Helen's return to Silverton Mrs. Banker had written two or three kind, friendly letters, which did her so much good; but these had suddenly ceased, and Helen's last remained unanswered. She saw the reason now, every nerve quivering with pain as she imagined what Mrs. Banker must think of one who could make a refusal public, or what was tenfold worse, pretend to an offer she never received. "She must despise

me, and Mark Ray, too, if he has heard of it," she
said, resolving one moment to ask Bell to explain to Mrs.
Banker, and then changing her mind and concluding to
let matters take their course, inasmuch as interference
from her might be construed by the mother into undue
interest in the son. "Perhaps Bell will do it without
my asking," she thought, and this hope did much toward
keeping her spirits up on that last day of Katy's stay at
home, for she was going back in the morning.

They did not see Marian Hazelton again, and Katy
wondered at it, deciding that in some things Marian was
very peculiar, while Wilford and Bell were disappointed,
as both had a desire to meet and converse with one who
had been so like a second mother to the little dead Genevra. Wilford spoke of his child now as Genevra, but to
Katy it was Baby still; and, with choking sobs and passionate tears, she bade good-bye to the little mound
underneath which it was lying, and then went back to
New York.

CHAPTER XXXII.

THE FIRST WIFE.

KATY was very unhappy in her city home, and the
world, as she looked upon it, seemed utterly cheerless.
For much of this unhappiness Wilford was himself to
blame. After the first few days, during which he was all
kindness and devotion, he did not try to comfort her,
but seemed irritated that she should mourn so deeply for
the child which, but for her indiscretion, might have
been living still. He did not like staying at home, and
their evenings, when they were alone, passed in gloomy
silence. At last Mrs. Cameron brought her influence to
bear upon her daughter-in-law, trying to rouse her to
something like her olden interest in the world; but all
to no effect, and matters grew constantly worse, as Wilford thought Katy unreasonable and selfish, while Katy
tried hard not to think him harsh in his judgment of
her, and exacting in his requirements. "Perhaps she
was the one most in fault; it could not be pleasant for

him to see her so entirely changed from what she used to be," she thought, one morning late in November, when her husband had just left her with an angry frown upon his face and reproachful words upon his lips.

Father Cameron and his daughters were out of town, and Mrs. Cameron had asked Wilford and Katy to dine with her. But Katy did not wish to go, and Wilford had left her in anger, saying "she could suit herself, but he should go at all events."

Left alone, Katy began to feel that she had done wrong in declining the invitation. Surely she could go there, and the echo of the *bang* with which Wilford had closed the street door was still vibrating in her ear, when her resolution began to give way, and while Wilford was riding moodily down town, thinking harsh things against her, she was meditating what she thought might be an agreeable surprise. She would go round and meet him at dinner, trying to appear as much like her old self as she could, and so atone for anything which had hitherto been wrong in her demeanor.

Later in the day Esther was sent for to arrange her mistress's hair, as she had not arranged it since baby died. Wilford had been annoyed by the smooth bands combed so plainly back, and at the blackness of the dress, but now there was a change, and graceful curls fell about the face, giving it the girlish expression which Wilford liked. The soberness of the dark dress was relieved by simple folds of white crape at the throat and wrists, while the handsome jet ornaments, the gift of Wilford's father, added to the style and beauty of the childish figure, which had seldom looked lovelier than when ready and waiting for the carriage. At the door there was a ring, and Esther brought a note to Katy, who read as follows:

DEAR KATY:—I have been suddenly called to leave the city on business, which will probably detain me for three days or more, and as I must go on the night train, I wish Esther to have my portmanteau ready with whatever I may need for the journey. As I proposed this morning, I shall dine with mother, but come home immediately after dinner.

W. CAMERON.

Katy was glad now that she had decided to meet him at his mother's, as the knowing she had pleased him would make the time of his absence more endurable, and after seeing that everything was ready for him she stepped with a comparatively light heart into her carriage, and was driven to No.—Fifth Avenue.

Mrs. Cameron was out, the servant said, but was expected every minute with Mr. Wilford.

"Never mind," Katy answered; "I want to surprise them, so please don't tell them I am here when you let them in," and going into the library she sat down before the grate, waiting rather impatiently until the door-bell rang and she heard both Wilford's and Mrs. Cameron's voices in the hall.

Contrary to her expectations, they did not come into the library, but went into the parlor, the door of which was partially ajar, so that every word they said could be distinctly heard where Katy sat. It would seem that they were continuing a conversation which had been interrupted by their arriving home, for Mrs. Cameron said, with the tone she always assumed when sympathizing with her son. "Is she never more cheerful than when I have seen her?"

"Never," and Katy could feel just how Wilford's lips shut over his teeth as he said it; "never more cheerful, but worse if anything. Why, positively the house seems so like a funeral that I hate to leave the office and go back to it at night, knowing how mopish and gloomy Katy will be."

"My poor boy, it is worse than I feared," Mrs. Cameron said, with a little sigh, while Katy, with a great gasping sob, tried to rise and go to them, to tell them she was there—the mopish Katy, who made her home so like a funeral to her husband.

But her limbs refused to move, and she sank back powerless in her chair, compelled to listen to things which no true husband would ever say to a mother of his wife, especially when that wife's error consisted principally in mourning for the child "which but for her imprudence might have been living then." These were Wilford's very words, and though Katy had once expected him to say them, they came upon her now with a dreadful shock, making her view herself as the murderer of her child, and thus blunting the pain she might otherwise have felt as he went on to speak of Silverton and its inhabitants just as he would not have spoken had he known she was so near. Then, encouraged by his mother, he talked again of her in a way which made her poor aching heart throb as she whispered, sadly, "He is disappointed in me. I do not come up to all that he expected. I do very well, considering my low origin, but I am not what his wife should be."

Wilford had not said all this, but Katy inferred it, and every nerve quivered with anguish as the wild wish came over her that she had died on that day when she sat in the summer grass at home waiting for Wilford Cameron. Poor Katy! she thought her cup of sorrow full, when, alas! only a drop had as yet been poured into it. But it was filling fast, and Mrs. Cameron's words, "It might have been better with Genevra," was the first outpouring of the overwhelming torrent which for a moment bore her life and sense away. She thought they meant her baby—the little Genevra sleeping under the snow in Silverton—and her white lips answered, "Yes, it would be better," before Wilford's voice was heard, saying, as he always said, "No, I have never wished Genevra in Katy's place; though I have sometimes wondered what the result would have been had I learned in season how much I wronged her."

Was heaven and earth coming together, or what made Katy's brain so dizzy and the room so dark, as, with head bent forward and lips apart, she strained her ear to catch every word of the conversation which followed, and in which she saw glimpses of that *leaf* offered her once to read, and from which she had promised not to shrink should it ever be thrust upon her? But she did shrink, oh! so shudderingly, holding up her hands and striking them through the empty air as if she would thrust aside the terrible spectre risen so suddenly before her. She had heard all that she cared to hear then. Another word and she should surely die where she was, within hearing of the voices still talking of *Genevra*.

Stopping her ears to shut out the dreadful sound, she tried to think what she should do. To gain the door and reach the street was her desire, and throwing on her wrappings she went noiselessly into the hall, and carefully turning the lock and closing the door behind her, she found herself alone in the street in the dusk of a November night. But Katy was not afraid, and drawing her hood closely over her face she sped on until her own house was reached, alarming Esther with her frightened face, but explaining that she had been taken suddenly ill and returned before dinner

"Mr. Cameron will be here soon," she said. "I do not need anything to-night, so you can leave me alone and go where you like—to the theatre, if you choose. I heard you say you wished to go. Here is the money for you and Phillips," and handing a bill to the puzzled Esther, she dismissed her from the room.

Meanwhile, at the elder Cameron's, no one had a suspicion of Katy's recent presence, for the girl who had admitted her had gone to visit a sick sister, with whom she was to spend the night. Thus Katy's secret was safe, and Wilford, when at last he bade his mother good-bye and started for home, was not prepared for the livid face, the bloodshot eyes, and the strange, unnatural look which met him at the threshold.

Katy answered his ring herself, her hands grasping his fiercely, dragging him up the stairs to her own room, where, more like a maniac than Katy Cameron, she confronted him with the startling question,

"Who is *Genevra Lambert?* It is time I knew before committing greater sin. Tell me, Wilford, who *is* she?"

She was standing before him, her slight figure seeming to expand into a greater height, the features glowing with strong excitement, and her hot breath coming hurriedly through her dilated nostrils, but never opening the pale lips set so firmly together. There was something terrible in her look and attitude, and it startled Wilford, who recoiled a moment from her, scarcely able to recognize the Katy hitherto so gentle and quiet. She had learned his secret, but the facts must have been distorted, he knew, or she had never been so agitated.

From beneath his hair the great sweat-drops came pouring, as he tried to approach her and take the uplifted hands, motioning him aside with the words, " Not touch me; no, not touch me till you have told me *who* is *Genevra Lambert.*"

She repeated the question twice, and rallying all his strength Wilford answered her at last, " *Genevra Lambert was my wife!*"

"I thought so," and the next moment Katy lay in Wilford's arms, dead, as he feared, for there was no motion about the eyelids, no motion that he could perceive about the pulse or heart, as he laid the rigid form upon the bed and then bent every energy to restore her, even though he feared that it was hopeless.

If possible he would prefer that no one should intrude upon them now, and he chafed her icy hands and bathed her face until the eyes unclosed again, but with a shudder turned away as they met his. Then, as she grew stronger and remembered the past, she started up, exclaiming, "If Genevra Lambert is your wife, what then *am I?* Oh, Wilford, how could you make me *not* a wife, when I trusted and loved you so much?"

He knew she was laboring under a mistake, and he did not wonder at the violence of her emotions if she believed he had wronged her so cruelly, and coming nearer to her he said, " Genevra Lambert *was* my wife once, but is not now, for she is dead. Do you hear me, Katy? Genevra died years ago, when you were a little girl playing in the fields at home."

By mentioning Silverton, he hoped to bring back something of her olden look, in place of the expression which troubled and frightened him. The experiment was successful, and great tears gathered in Katy's eyes, washing out the wild, unnatural gleam, while the lips whispered, " And it was her picture Juno saw. She told me the night I came, and I tried to question you. You remember?"

Wilford did remember it, and he replied, " Yes, but I did not suppose you knew I had a picture. You have been a good wife, Katy, never to mention it since then;" and he tried to kiss her forehead, but she covered it

with her hands, saying sadly, " Not yet, Wilford, I cannot bear it now. I must know the whole about Genevra.
Why didn't you tell me before? Why have you deceived
me so?"

" Katy," and Wilford grew very earnest in his attempts
to defend himself, " do you remember that day we sat
under the buttonwood tree, and you promised to be mine?
Try and recall the incidents of that hour and see if I
did not hint at some things in the past which I wished
had been otherwise, and did not offer to show you the
blackest page of my whole life, but you would not see
it. Was that so, Katy?"

" Yes," she answered, and he continued: " You said
you were satisfied to take me as I was. You would
not hear evil against me, and so I acquiesced, bidding
you not shrink back if ever the time should come when
you must read that page. I was to blame, I know, but
there were many extenuating circumstances, much to
excuse me for withholding what you would not hear."

Wilford did not like to be censured, neither did he
like to censure himself, and now that Katy was out of
danger and comparatively calm, he began to build about
himself a fortress of excuses for having kept from her
the secret of his life.

" When did you hear of Genevra?" he asked.

Katy told him when and how she heard the story, and
then added, " Oh, Wilford, why did you keep it from me?
What was there about it wrong, and where is she
buried?"

" In Alnwick, at St. Mary's," Wilford answered, deter-
mining now to hold nothing back, and by his abruptness
wounding Katy afresh.

" In Alnwick, at St. Mary's," Katy cried. " Then I
have seen her grave, and that is why you were so anxious
to get there—so unwilling to go away. Oh, if I were lying
there instead of Genevra, it would be so much better, so
much better."

Katy was sobbing now, in a moaning, plaintive way,
which touched Wilford tenderly, and smoothing her tangled
hair, he said, " I would not exchange my Katy for all
the Genevras in the world. She was never as dear to me

as you. I was but a boy, and did not know my mind, when I met her. Shall I tell you about her now? Can you bear to hear the story of Genevra?"

There was a nod of assent, and Katy turned her face to the wall, clasping her hands tightly together, while Wilford drew his chair to her side and began to read the page he should have read to her long before.

CHAPTER XXXIII.

WHAT THE PAGE DISCLOSED.

I WAS little more than nineteen years of age when I left Harvard College and went abroad with my only brother, the John or Jack of whom you have so often heard. Both himself and wife were in delicate health, and it was hoped a voyage across the sea would do them good. For nearly a year we were in various parts of England, stopping for two months at Brighton, where, among the visitors, was a widow from the vicinity of Alnwick, and with her an orphan niece, whose dazzling beauty attracted my youthful fancy. She was not happy with her aunt, upon whom she was wholly dependent, and my sympathies were all enlisted, when, with the tears shining in her lustrous eyes, she one day accidentally stumbled upon her trouble and told me how wretched she was, asking if in America there was not something for her to do.

"It was at this time that Jamie was born, and Mary, the girl who went out with us, was married to an Englishman, making it necessary for Hatty to find some one to take her place. Hearing of this, Genevra came one day, and offered herself as half companion, half waiting-maid to Hatty. Anything was preferable to the life she led, she said, pleading so hard that Hatty, after an interview with the old aunt—a purse-proud, vulgar woman, who seemed glad to be rid of her charge—consented to receive her, and Genevra became one of our family, an equal rather than a menial, whom Hatty treated with as much consideration as if she had been a sister. I wish I could tell you how beautiful Genevra Lambert was at that period of her life, with her brilliant English complexion, her eyes so full of poetry and passion, her perfect features, and, more than all, the wondrous smile, which would have made a plain face handsome.

"Of course I came to love her, and loved her all the more for the opposition I knew my family would throw in the way of my marrying the daughter of an English apothecary, and one who was voluntarily filling a servant's place. But with my mother across the sea, I could do anything; and when Genevra told me of a base fellow, who, since she was a child, had sought her for his wife, and still pursued her with his letters, my passions were roused, and I offered myself at once. Her answer was a decided refusal. She knew *her* position, she said, and she knew mine, just as she knew the nature of the feeling which prompted me to act thus toward her. Although just my age, she was older in judgment and experience, and she seemed to understand the difference between our relative positions. I was not indifferent to her, she said, and were she my equal her answer might be otherwise than the decided no.

"Madly in love, and fancying I could not live without her, I besieged her with letters, some of which she returned unopened, while on others she wrote a few hurried lines, calling me a boy, who did not know my own mind, and asking what my friends would say.

"I cared little for friends, and urged my suit the more vehemently, as we were about going into Scotland, where our marriage could be celebrated in private at any time. I did not contemplate making the affair public at once. That would take from the interest and romance, while, unknown to myself, there was at heart a fear of my family.

"But not to dwell too long upon those days, which seem to me now like a dream, we went to Scotland and were married privately, for I won her to this at last.

"My brother's failing health, as well as Hatty's, prevented them from suspecting what was going on, and when at last we went to Italy they had no idea that Genevra was my wife. At Rome her beautiful face attracted much attention from tourists and residents, among whom were a few young men, who, looking upon her as Jamie's nurse, or at most a companion for his mother, made no attempt to disguise their admiration. For this I had no redress except in an open avowal of the relation in which I stood to her, and this I could not then do, for the longer it was deferred the harder I found it to acknowledge her my wife. I loved her devotedly, and that perhaps was one great cause of the jealousy which began to spring up and embitter my life.

"I do not now believe that Genevra was at heart a coquette. She was very fond of admiration, but when she saw how much I was disturbed she made an effort to avoid those who flattered her, but her manner was unfortunate, while her voice—the sweetest I ever heard—was calculated to invite rather than repel attention. As the empress of the world, she would have won and kept the homage of mankind, from the humblest beggar in the street to the king upon the throne, and had I been older I should have been proud of what then was my greatest annoyance. But I was a mere boy—and I watched her jealously, until a new element of disquiet was presented to me in the shape of a ruffianly looking fellow, who was frequently seen about the premises, and with whom I once found Genevra in close converse, starting and blushing guiltily when I came upon her, while her companion went swiftly from my sight.

"It was an old English acquaintance, who was poor and asking charity," she said, when questioned, but her manner led me to think there was something wrong, particularly as I saw her with him again, and thought she held his hand.

"It was evident that my brother would never see America again, and at his request my mother came to us, in company with a family from Boston, reaching us two weeks before he died. From the first she disliked Genevra, and suspected the liking between us, but never dreaming of the truth until a week after Jack's death, when in a fit of anger at Genevra for listening to an English artist, who had asked to paint her picture, the story of the marriage came out, and like a child dependent on its mother for advice, I asked, ' What shall I do ? '

" You know mother, and can in part understand how she would scorn a girl who, though born to better things, was still found in the capacity of a waiting-maid. I never saw her so moved as she was for a time, after learning that her only living son, from whom she expected so much, had thrown himself away, as she expressed it. Sister Hatty, who loved Genevra, did all she could to heal the growing difference between us, but I trusted mother most. I believed that what she said was right, and so matters grew worse, until one night, the last we spent in Rome, I missed Genevra from our rooms, and starting in quest of her, found her, in a little flower garden back of our dwelling. There, under the deep shadow of a tree, and partly concealed from view, she stood with her arm around the neck of the same rough-looking man who had been there before. She did not see me as I watched her while she parted with him, suffering him to kiss her hand and forehead as he said, " Good-bye, my darling."

" In a tremor of anger and excitement I quitted the spot, my mind wholly made up with regard to my future. That there was something wrong about Genevra I did not doubt, and I would not give her a chance to explain by telling her what I had seen, but sent her back to England, giving her ample means for defraying the expenses of her journey and for living in comfort after her arrival there. From Rome we went to Naples, and then to Switzerland, where Hatty died, leaving us alone with little Jamie. It was at Berne that I received an anonymous letter from England, the writer stating that Genevra was with her aunt, that the whole had ended as he thought it would, that he could readily guess at the nature of the trouble, and hinting that if a *divorce* was desirable on my return to England, all necessary proof could be obtained by applying to such a number in London, the writer announcing himself a brother of the man who had once sought Genevra, and saying he had always opposed the match, knowing Genevra's family.

" This was the first time the idea of a *divorce* had

entered my mind, and I shrank from a final separation. But mother felt differently. It was not a new thought to her, knowing as she did that the validity of a Scotch marriage, such as ours, was frequently contested in the English Courts. Once free from Genevra the world this side the water would never know of that mistake, and she set herself steadily to accomplish her purpose. To tell you all that followed our return to England, and the steps by which I was brought to sue for a divorce, would make my story too long, and so I will only state that, chiefly by the testimony of the anonymous letter-writer, whose acquaintance we made, a divorce was obtained, Genevra putting in no defence, but, as I heard afterwards, settling down into an apathy from which nothing had power to rouse her until the news of her freedom from me was carried to her, when, amid a paroxysm of tears and sobs, she wrote me a few lines, assuring me of her innocence, refusing to send back her wedding ring, and saying God would not forgive me for the great wrong I had done her. I saw her once after that by appointment, and her face haunted me for years, for, Katy, *Genevra was innocent,* as I found after the time was past when reparation could be made."

Wilford's voice trembled, and for a moment there was silence in the room, while he composed himself to go on with the story:

" She would not live with me again if she could, she said, denouncing bitterly the Cameron pride, and saying she was happier to be free; and there we parted, but not until she told me that her traducer was the old discarded suitor who had sworn to have revenge, and who. since the divorce, had dared seek her again. A vague suspicion of this had crossed my mind once before, but the die was cast, and even if the man were false, what I saw myself in Rome still stood against her, and so my conscience was quieted, while mother was more than glad to be rid of a daughter-in-law of whose family I knew nothing. Rumors I did hear of a cousin whose character was not the best, and of the father who for some crime had fled the country, and died in a foreign land, but as that was nothing to me now, I passed it by, feeling it was best to be released from one of so doubtful antecedents.

"In the spring of 185– we came back to New York, where no one had ever heard of the affair, so quietly had it been managed. I was still an unmarried man to the world, as no one but my mother knew my secret. With her I often talked of Genevra, wishing sometimes that I could hear from her, a wish which was finally gratified. One day I received a note requesting an interview at a down town hotel, the writer signing himself as Thomas Lambert, and adding that I need have no fears, as he came to perform an act of justice, not of retribution. Three hours later I was locked in a room with Genevra's father, the same man whom I had seen in Rome. Detected in forgery years before, he had fled from England and had hidden himself in Rome, where he accidentally met his daughter, and so that stain was removed. He had heard of the divorce by a letter which Genevra managed to send him, and braving all difficulties and dangers he had come back to England and found his child, hearing from her the story of her wrongs, and as well as he was able setting himself to discover the author of the calumny. He was not long in tracing it to *Le Roy*, Genevra's former suitor, whom he found in a dying condition; and who with his last breath confessed the falsehood which was imposed upon me, he said, partly from motives of revenge, and partly, with a hope that free from me, Genevra would at the last turn to him. As proof that Mr. Lambert told me truth, he brought the dying man's confession, written in a cramped, trembling hand, which I recognized at once. The confession ended with the solemn assertion, 'For aught I know or believe, Genevra Lambert is as pure and true as any woman living.'

"I cannot describe the effect this had upon me. I did not love Genevra then. I had out-lived that affection, but I felt remorse and pity for having wronged her, and asked how I could make amends.

"'You cannot,' the old man said, 'except in one way, and that she does not desire. I did not come here with any wish for you to take her for your wife again. It was an unequal match which never should have been;

but if you believe her innocent, she will be satisfied. She wanted you to know it—I wanted you to know it, and so I crossed the sea to find you."

The next I heard of her was in the columns of an English newspaper, which told me she was dead, while in another place a pencil mark was lightly traced around a paragraph, which said that 'a forger, Thomas Lambert, who escaped years ago and was supposed to be dead, had recently reappeared in England, where he was recognized, but not arrested, for the illness which proved fatal. He was attended," the paper said, 'by his daughter, a beautiful young girl, whose modest mien and gentle manner had done much towards keeping the officers of justice from her dying father, no one being able to withstand her pleadings that her father might die in peace.'

"I was grateful for this tribute to Genevra, for I felt that it was deserved; and I turned again to the notice of her death, which must have occurred within a short time of her father's, and was probably induced by past troubles and recent anxiety for him.

"Genevra Lambert died at Alnwick, aged 22. There could be no mistake, and with a tear to the memory of the dead whom I had loved and injured, I burned the paper, feeling that now there was no clue to the secret I was as anxious to preserve as was my mother.

"And so the years wore on till I met and married you, withholding from you that yours was not the first love which had stirred my heart. I meant to tell you, Katy, but I could not for the great fear of losing you if you knew all. And then an error concealed so long is hard to be confessed. I took you across the sea to Brighton, where I first met Genevra, and then to Alnwick, seeking out the grave which made assurance doubly sure. It was natural that I should make some inquiries concerning her last days; I questioned the old sexton who was at work near by. Calling his attention to the name, I said it was an uncommon one and asked if he knew the girl.

"'Not by sight, no,' he said. 'She was only here a few days before she died. I've heard she was very win-

some and that there was a scandal of some kind mixed
up with her.'

"I would not ask him any more; and without any
wrong to you, I confess that my tears dropped upon the
turf under which I knew Genevra lay."

"I am glad they did; I should hate you if you had not
cried," Katy exclaimed, her voice more natural than it
had been since the great shock came.

"Do you forgive me, Katy? Do you love me as well
as ever?" Wilford asked, stooping down to kiss her, but
Katy drew her face away and would not answer then.

She did not know herself how she felt towards him.
He did not seem just like the husband she had trusted in
so blindly. It would take a long time to forget that another head than hers had lain upon his bosom, and it would
take longer yet to blot out the memory of complaining
words uttered to his mother. She had never thought he
could do that, never dreamed of such a thing, knowing
that she would sooner have parted with her right hand
than complained of him. Her idol had fallen in more respects than one, and the heart it had bruised in the fall
refused at once to gather the shattered pieces up and call
them as good as new. She was not so obstinate as Wilford began to fancy. She was only stunned and could not
rally at his bidding. He confessed the whole, keeping
nothing back, and he felt that Katy was unjust not to
acknowledge his magnanimity and restore him to her
favor. Again he asked forgiveness, and bent down to kiss
her, but Katy answered, "Not yet, Wilford, not till I
feel all right towards you. A wife's kiss should be
sincere."

"As you like," trembled on Wilford's lips, but he beat
back the words and walked up and down the room,
knowing now that his journey must be deferred till
morning, and wondering if Katy would hold out till
then.

It was long past midnight, but to retire was impossible,
and so for one whole hour he paced through the room,
while Katy lay with her eyes closed and her lips moving
occasionally in words of prayer she tried to say, asking
God to help her, and praying that she might in future

lay her treasures up where they could not so suddenly be swept away. Wearily the hours passed, and the gray dawn was stealing into the room when Wilford again approached his wife and said, "You know I was to have left home last night on business. As I did not go then it is necessary that I leave this morning. Are you able to stay alone for three days more? Are you willing?"

"Yes—oh yes," Katy replied, feeling that to have him gone while she battled with the pain lying so heavy at her heart, would be a great relief.

Perhaps he suspected this feeling in part, for he bit his lip impatiently, and without another word called up the servant whose duty it was to prepare his breakfast. Cold and cheerless seemed the dining-room, to which an hour later he repaired, and tasteless was the breakfast without Katy there to share it. She had been absent many times before, but never just as now, with this wide gulf between them, and as he broke his egg and tried to drink his coffee, Wilford felt like one from whom every support had been swept away. He did not like the look on Katy's face or the sound of her voice, and as he thought upon them, self began to whisper again that she had no right to stand out so long when he had confessed everything, and by the time his breakfast was finished, Wilford Cameron was, in his own estimation, an abused and injured man, so that it was with an air of defiance rather than humility that he went again to Katy. She, too, had been thinking, and as the result of her thoughts she lifted up her head as he came in and said, "I can kiss you now, Wilford."

It was human nature, we suppose—at least it was Wilford's nature—which for an instant tempted him to decline the kiss proffered so lovingly; but Katy's face was more than he could withstand, and when again he left that room the kiss of pardon was upon his lips and comparative quiet was in his heart.

"The picture, Wilford,—please bring me the picture, I want to see it," Katy called after him, as he was running down the stairs.

Wilford would not refuse, and hastily unlocking his private drawer he carried the case to Katy's room, saying

to her, " I would not mind it now.　Try and sleep awhile.
You need the rest so much."

Katy knew she had the whole day before her, and so she
nestled down among her pillows and soon fell into a
quiet sleep, from which Esther at last awakened her, asking if she should bring her breakfast to her room.

" Yes, do," Katy replied, adjusting her dress and trying
to arrange the matted curls, which were finally confined
in a net until Esther's more practiced hands were ready
to attack them, then sending Esther from the room Katy
took the picture of Genevra from the table where Wilford had laid it.

CHAPTER XXXIV.

THE EFFECT.

VERY cautiously the lid was opened, and a lock of soft
brown hair fell out, clinging to Katy's hand and making
her shudder as she shook off the silken tress and
remembered that the head it once adorned was lying
in St. Mary's churchyard, where the English daisies
grew.

" She had pretty hair," she thought; " darker, richer
than mine," and into Katy's heart there crept a feeling
akin to jealousy, lest Genevra had been fairer than herself, as well as better loved.　" I won't be foolish any
longer," she said, and turning resolutely to the light, she
opened the lid again and saw Genevra Lambert, starting
quickly, then looking again more closely—then, with a
gasp, panting for breath; while like lightning flashes the
past came rushing over her, as, with her eyes fixed upon
that picture, she tried to whisper, " *It is—it is!* "

She could not then say whom, for if she were right in
her belief, Genevra was not dead.　There were no daisies
growing on her grave, for she still walked the earth a
living woman, whom Katy knew so well—*Marian Hazelton.*　That was the name Katy could not speak, as, with
the blood curdling in her veins and freezing about her

heart, she sat comparing the face she remembered so
well with the one before her. In some points they were
unlike, for thirteen years had slightly marred the youthful contour of the face she knew once—had sharpened the
features and thinned the abundant hair; but still there
could be no mistake. The eyes, the brow, the smile, the
nose, all were the same, and with a pang bitterer than
she yet had felt, poor Katy fell upon her face and asked
that she might die. In her utter ignorance of law, she
fancied that if Genevra were alive, she had no right to
Wilford's name—no right to be his wife—especially as
the sin for which Genevra was divorced had by her never
been committed, and burning tears of bitter shame ran
down her cheeks as she whispered, "'What God has
joined together let no man put asunder.' Those are
God's words, and how dare the world act otherwise?
she *is* his wife, and I—oh! I don't know what I am!"
and on the carpet where she was kneeling Katy writhed
in agony as she tried to think what she must do. Not
stay there—she could not do that now—not, at least,
until she knew for sure that she was Wilford's wife, in
spite of Genevra's living. "Oh, if there was only some
one to advise me—some one who knew and would tell me
what was right," Katy moaned, feeling herself inadequate
to meet the dark hour alone.

But to whom should she go? To Father Cameron?
No, nor to his mother. They might counsel wrong for
the sake of secrecy. Would Mark Ray or Mrs. Banker
know? Perhaps; but they were strangers;—her trouble
must not be told to them, and then with a great bound
her heart turned at last to *Morris*. He knew everything. He would not sanction a wrong. He would tell
her just what was right, and she could trust him fully in
everything. There was no other person whom she could
believe just as she could him. Uncle Ephraim was equally
as good and conscientious, but he did not know as much
as Morris—he did not understand everything. Morris
was her refuge, and to him she would go that very day,
leaving a note for Wilford in case she never came back,
as possibly she might not. Had Marian been in the city
she would have gone to her at once, but Marian was where

long rows of cots were ranged against the hospital walls, each holding a maimed and suffering soldier, to whom she ministered so tenderly, the brightness of her smile and the beauty of her face deluding the delirious ones into the belief that the journey of life for them was ended and heaven reached at last, where an angel in woman's garb attended upon them. Marian was impossible, and Dr. Grant was the only alternative left.

But when she attempted to prepare for the journey to Silverton, she found herself wholly inadequate to the exertion. The terrible excitement through which she had passed had exhausted her strength, and every nerve was quivering, while spasms of pain darted through her head, warning her that Silverton was impossible. "I can telegraph and Morris will come," she whispered, and without pausing to think what the act might involve, she wrote upon a slip of paper, "Cousin Morris, come to me in the next train. I am in great trouble, Katy."

She would not add the Cameron. She had no right to that name, she feared, and folding the paper, she rang for Esther, bidding her give the telegram to the boy Phil, with instructions to take it at once to the office and see that it went immediately.

* ———— .·

CHAPTER XXXV.

THE INTERVIEW.

DR. MORRIS was very tired, for his labors that day had been unusually severe, and it was with a feeling of comfort and relief that at an earlier hour than usual, he had turned his steps homeward, finding a bright fire waiting him in the library, where his late dinner was soon brought by the housekeeper. It was very pleasant in that cosy library of oak and green, with the bright fire on the hearth, and the smoking dinner set so temptingly before him. And Morris felt the comfort of his home, thanking the God who had given him all this, and chiding his wayward heart that it had ever dared to repine. He was not repining to-night, as with his hands crossed upon his head he sat looking into the fire and watching the bits of glowing anthracite dropping into the pan. He was thinking of the sick-bed which he had visited last, and how a faith in Jesus can make the humblest room like the gate of Heaven; thinking how the woman's eyes had sparkled when she told him of the other world, where she would never know pain or hunger or cold again, and how quickly their lustre was dimmed when she spoke of her absent husband, the soldier to whom the news of her death, with the child he had never seen, would be a crushing blow.

"They who have neither wife nor child are the happier perhaps," he said; and then he thought of Katy and her great sorrow when baby died, wondering if to spare herself that pain she would rather baby had never been. "No—oh, no," he answered to his own inquiry. "She would not lose the memory which comes from that little grave for all the world contains. It is better once to love and lose than not to love at all. In Heaven we shall see and know why these things were permitted, and marvel at the poor human nature which rebelled against them."

Just at this point of his soliloquy, the telegram was brought to him. "Come in the next train. I am in great trouble."

He read it many times, growing more and more perplexed with each reading, and then trying to decide what his better course would be. There were no patients needing him that night, that he knew of; he might perhaps go if there was yet time for the train which passed at four o'clock. There was time, he found, and telling Mrs. Hull that he had been suddenly called to New York, he bade his boy bring out his horse and take him at once to the depot. It was better to leave no message for the deacon's family, as he did not wish to alarm them unnecessarily. "I shall undoubtedly be back to-morrow," he thought, as he took his seat in the car, wondering what could be the trouble which had prompted that strange despatch.

It was nearly midnight when he reached the city, but

a light was shining from the windows of that house in Madison Square, and Katy, who had never for a moment doubted his coming, was waiting for him. But not in the parlor; she was too sick now to go down there, and when she heard his ring and his voice in the hall asking for her, she bade Esther show him to her room. More and more perplexed, Morris ran up to the room where Katy lay, or rather crouched, upon the sofa, her eyes so wild and her face so white that, in great alarm, Morris took the cold hands she stretched feebly towards him, and bending over her said, "What is it, Katy? Has anything dreadful happened? and where is your husband?"

At the mention of her husband Katy shivered, and rising from her crouching position, she pushed her hair back from her forehead and replied, "Oh, Morris! I am so wretched,—so full of pain! I have heard of something which took my life away. I am *not* Wilford's wife, for he had another before me,—a wife in Italy,—who is not dead! And *I*, oh Morris! what *am* I? I knew you would know just what I was, and I sent for you to tell me and take me away from here, back to Silverton. Help me, Morris! I am choking! I am—yes—I am—going to faint!"

It was the first time Katy had put the great horror in words addressed to another, and the act of doing so made it more appalling, and with a moan she sank back among the pillows of the couch, while Morris tried to comprehend the strange words he had heard, "I am not Wilford's wife, for he had another before me,—a wife in Italy, —who is not dead."

Dr. Morris was thoroughly a man, and though much of his sinful nature had been subdued, there was enough left to make his heart rise and fall with great throbs of joy as he thought of Katy *free,* even though that freedom were bought at the expense of dire disgrace to others, and of misery to her. But only for a moment did he feel thus— only till he knelt beside the pallid face with the dark rings beneath the eyes, and saw the faint, quivering motion around the lips, which told that she was not wholly unconscious.

"My poor little wounded bird," he said, as pityingly as

if he had been her father, while much as a father might kiss his suffering child, he kissed the forehead and the eyelids where the tears began to gather.

Katy was not insensible, and the name by which he called her, with the kisses that he gave, thawed the ice around her heart and brought a flood of tears, which Morris wiped away, lifting her gently up and pillowing her hot head upon his arm, while she moaned like a weary child.

"It rests me so just to see you, Morris. May I go back with you, as your housekeeper, instead of Mrs. Hull;—that is, if I am not his wife? The world might despise me, but you would know I was not to blame. I should go nowhere but to the farm-house, to church, and baby's grave. Poor baby! I am glad God gave her to me, even if I am not Wilford's wife; and I am glad now that she died."

She was talking to herself rather than to Morris, who, smoothing back her hair and chafing her cold hands, said,

"My poor child, you have passed through some agitating scene. Are you able now to tell me all about it, and what you mean by another wife?"

There was a shiver, and the white lips grew still whiter as Katy began her story, going back to St. Mary's churchyard and then coming to her first night in New York, when Juno had told her of a picture and asked her whose it was. Then she told of Wilford's admission of an earlier love, who, he said, was dead; of the trouble about the baby's name, and his aversion to Genevra; but when she approached the dinner at the elder Cameron's, her lip quivered in a grieved kind of way as she remembered what Wilford had said of *her* to his mother, but she would not tell this to Morris,—it was not necessary to her story,—and so she said, "They were talking of what I ought never to have heard, and it seemed as if the walls were closing me in so I could not move to let them know I was there. I said to myself, 'I shall go mad after this,' and I thought of you all coming to see me in the mad-house, your kind face, Morris, coming up distinctly before me, just as it would look at me if I were really crazed. But all this was swept away like a hurricane when I heard the rest, the part about *Genevra*, Wilford's other wife."

Katy was panting for breath, but she went on with the story, which made Morris clench his hands as he comprehended the deceit which had been practiced so long. Of course he did not look at it as Katy did, for he knew that according to all civil law she was as really Wilford's wife as if no other had existed, and he told her so, but Katy shook her head. " He can't have two wives living. And I tell you I knew the picture—*Genevra is not dead*, I have seen her; I have talked with her,—Genevra is not dead."

" Granted that she is not," Morris answered, " the divorce remains the same."

" I do not believe in divorces. Whom God hath joined together let not man put asunder," Katy said with an air which implied that from this argument there could be no appeal.

" That is the Scripture, I know," Morris replied, " but you must know that for one sin our Saviour permitted a man to put away his wife, thus making it perfectly right."

" But in Genevra's case the sin did not exist. She was as innocent as I am, and that must make a difference."

She was very earnest in her attempts to prove that Genevra was still a lawful wife, so earnest that a dark suspicion entered Morris's mind, finding vent in the question, " Katy, don't you love your husband, that you try so hard to prove he is not yours?"

There were red spots all over Katy's face and neck as she saw the meaning put upon her actions, and, covering her face with her hands, she sobbed violently as she replied, " I do, oh, yes, I do! I never loved any one else. I would have died for him once. Maybe I would die for him now; but, Morris, he is disappointed in me. Our tastes are not alike, and we made a great mistake, or Wilford did when he took me for his wife. I was better suited to most anybody else, and I have been so wicked since, forgetting all the good I ever knew, forgetting prayer save as I went through the form from old habit's sake; forgetting God, who has punished me so sorely that every nerve smarts with the stinging blows."

Oh, how lovingly, how earnestly Morris talked to Katy then, telling her of Him who smites but to heal, who chastens not in anger, and would lead the lost one back into the quiet fold where there was perfect peace.

And Katy, listening eagerly, with her great blue eyes fixed upon his face, felt that to experience that of which he talked, was worth more than all the world beside. Gradually, too, there stole over her the *rest* she always felt with him—the indescribable feeling which prompted her to care for nothing except to do just what he bade her do, knowing it was right; so when he said to her, "You cannot go home with me, Katy; your duty is to remain here in your husband's house," she offered no remonstrance. Indeed, Morris doubted if she fully understood him, she looked so sick and appeared so strange.

"It is not safe for you to be alone. Esther must stay with you," he continued, feeling her rapid pulse and noticing the alternate flushing and paling of her cheek.

A fever was coming on, he feared, and summoning Esther to the room, he said,

"Your mistress is very sick. You must stay with her till morning, and if she grows worse, let me know. I shall be in the library."

Then, with a few directions with regard to the medicine he fortunately had with him, he left the chamber, and repaired to the library below, where he spent the few remaining hours of the night, pondering on the strange story he had heard, and praying for poor Katy whose heart had been so sorely wounded.

The quick-witted Esther saw that something was wrong, and traced it readily to Wilford, whose exacting nature she thoroughly understood. She had not been blind during the two years and a half she had been Katy's maid, and no impatient word of Wilford's, or frown upon his face, had escaped her when occurring in her presence, while Katy's uniform sweetness and entire submission to his will had been noted as well, so that in Esther's opinion Wilford was a domestic tyrant, and Katy was an angel. Numerous were her conjectures as to the cause of the present trouble, which must be something serious, or Katy had never telegraphed for Dr. Grant, as she felt certain she had.

"Whatever it is, I'll stand her friend," she said, as she bent over her young mistress, who was talking of Genevra and the grave at St. Mary's, which was no grave at all.

She was growing worse very rapidly, and frightened at last at the wildness of her eyes, and her constant ravings, Esther went down to Morris, and bade him come quickly to Mrs. Cameron.

"She is taken out of her head, and talks so queer and raving."

Morris had expected this, but he was not prepared to find the fever so high, or the symptoms so alarming.

"Shall I send for Mrs. Cameron and another doctor, please?" Esther asked.

Morris had faith in himself, and he would rather no other hand should minister to Katy; but he knew he could not stay there long, for there were those at home who needed his services. Added to this, her family physician might know her constitution, now, better than he knew it, and so he answered that it would be well to send for both the doctor and Mrs. Cameron.

It was just daylight when Mrs. Cameron arrived, questioning Esther closely, and appearing much surprised when she heard of Dr. Grant's presence in the house. That he came by chance, she never doubted, and as Esther merely answered the questions put directly to her, Mrs. Cameron had no suspicion of the telegram.

"I am glad he happened here at this time," she said. "I have the utmost confidence in his skill. Still it may be well for Dr. Craig to see her. I think that is his ring."

The city and country physicians agreed exactly with regard to Katy's illness, or rather the city physician bowed in acquiescence when Morris said to him that the fever raging so high had, perhaps, been induced by natural causes, but was greatly aggravated by some sudden shock to the nervous system. This was before Mrs. Cameron came up, but it was repeated in her presence by Dr. Craig, who thus left the impression that the idea had originated with himself, rather than with Dr. Grant, as perhaps he thought it had. He was at first inclined to patronize the country doctor, but soon found that he had reckoned without his host. Morris knew more of Katy, and quite as much of medicine as he did himself, and when Mrs. Cameron begged him to stay longer, he answered that her son's wife was as safe in his brother physician's hands as she could be in his.

Mrs. Cameron was very glad that Dr. Grant was there, she said. It was surely Providence who sent him to New York on that particular day, and Morris shivered as he wondered if it were wrong not to explain the whole to her.

"Perhaps it is best she should not know of the telegram," he thought, and merely bowing to her remarks, he turned to Katy, who was growing very restless and moaning as if in pain.

"It hurts," he said, turning her head from side to side; "I am lying on Genevra."

With a sudden start, Mrs. Cameron drew nearer, but when she remembered the little grave at Silverton, she said, "It's the baby she's talking about."

Morris knew better, and as Katy still continued to move her head as if something were really hurting her, he passed his hand under her pillow and drew out the picture she must have kept near her as long as her consciousness remained. He knew it was Genevra's picture, and was about to lay it away, when the cover dropped into his hand, and his eye fell upon a face which was not new to him, while an involuntary exclamation of surprise escaped him, as Katy's assertion that Genevra was living was thus fully confirmed. Marian had not changed past recognition since her early girlhood, and Morris knew the likeness at once, pitying Katy more than he had pitied her yet, as he remembered how closely Marian Hazelton had been interwoven with her married life, and the life of the little child which had borne her name.

"What is that?" Mrs. Cameron asked, and Morris passed the case to her, saying, "A picture which was under Katy's pillow."

Morris did not look at Mrs. Cameron, but tried to busy himself with the medicines upon the stand, while she too recognized Genevra Lambert, wondering how it came in Katy's possession and how much she knew of Wilford's secret.

"She must have been rummaging," she thought, and then as she remembered what Esther had said about her mistress appearing sick and unhappy, when her husband left home, she repaired to the parlor and summoning Esther to her presence, asked her again, "When she first observed traces of indisposition in Mrs. Cameron."

"When she came home from that dinner at your house. She was just as pale as death, and her teeth fairly chattered as I took off her things."

"Dinner? What dinner?" Mrs. Cameron asked, and Esther replied, "Why, the night Mr. Wilford went away or was to go. She changed her mind about meeting him at your house, and said she meant to surprise him. But she came home before Mr. Cameron, looking like a ghost, and saying she was sick. It's my opinion something she ate at dinner hurt her."

"Very likely, yes. You can go now," Mrs. Cameron said, and Esther departed, never dreaming how much light she had inadvertently thrown upon the mystery.

"She must have been in the library and heard all we said," Mrs. Cameron thought, as she nervously twisted the fringe of her breakfast shawl. "I remember we talked of Genevra, and that we both heard a strange sound from some quarter, but thought it came from the kitchen. That was Katy. She was there all the time and let herself quietly out of the house. I wonder does Wilford know," and then there came over her an intense desire for Wilford to come home—a desire which was not lessened when she returned to Katy's room and heard her talking of Genevra and the grave at St. Mary's "where nobody was buried."

In a tremor of distress, lest she should betray something which Morris must not know Mrs. Cameron tried to hush her, talking as if it was the baby she meant, but Katy answered promptly, "It's Genevra Lambert I mean, Wilford's other wife; the one across the sea. She was innocent, too—as innocent as I, whom you both deceived."

Here was a phase of affairs for which Mrs. Cameron was not prepared, and excessively mortified that Morris should hear Katy's ravings, she tried again to quiet her, consoling herself with the reflection that as Morris was Katy's cousin, he would not repeat what he heard, and feeling gratified now that Dr. Craig was absent, as she could not be so sure of him. If Katy's delirium continued, no one must be admitted to the room except those who could be trusted, and as there had been already several rings, she said to Esther that as the fever was probably malignant and contagious, no one must be admitted to the house with the expectation of seeing the patient, while the servants were advised to stay in their own quarters, except as their services might be needed elsewhere. And so it was that by the morrow the news had spread of some infectious disease at No. — on Madison Square, which was shunned as carefully as if small-pox itself had been raging there instead of the brain fever, which increased so fast that Morris suggested to Mrs. Cameron that she telegraph for Wilford.

"They might find him, and they might not, Mother Cameron said. "They could try, at all events," and in a few moments the telegraphic wires were carrying the news of Katy's illness, both to the west, where Wilford had gone, and to the east, where Helen read with a blanched cheek that Katy perhaps was dying, and she must hasten to New York.

This was Mrs. Cameron's suggestion, wrung out by the knowing that some woman besides herself was needed in the sick-room, and by feeling that Helen could be trusted with the story of the first marriage, which Katy talked of constantly, telling it so accurately that only a fool would fail of being convinced that there was much of truth in those delirious ravings.

CHAPTER XXXVI.

THE FEVER AND ITS RESULTS.

WILFORD could not forget Katy's face, so full of reproach. It followed him continually, and was the magnet which turned his steps homeward before his business was quite done, and before the telegram had found him. Thus it was with no knowledge of existing circumstances that he reached New York just at the close of the day, and ordering a carriage, was driven rapidly towards home. All the shutters in the front part of the house were closed, and not a ray of light was to be seen in the parlors as he entered the hall, where the gas was burning dimly.

"Katy is at home," he said, as he went into the library, where a shawl was thrown across a chair, as if some one had lately been there.

It was his mother's shawl, and Wilford was wondering if she was there, when down the stairs came a man's rapid step, and the next moment Dr. Grant came into the room, starting when he saw Wilford, who felt intuitively that something was wrong.

"Is Katy sick?" was his first question, which Morris answered in the affirmative, holding him back as he was starting for her room, and saying to him, "Let me send your mother to you first."

What passed between Wilford and his mother was never known exactly, but at the close of the interview Mrs. Cameron was very pale, while Wilford's face looked dark and anxious as he said, "You think he understands it then?"

"Yes, in part, but the world will be none the wiser for his knowledge. I knew Dr. Grant before you did, and there are few men living whom I respect as much, and no one whom I would trust as soon."

Mrs. Cameron had paid a high compliment to Morris

Grant, and Wilford bowed in assent, asking next how she managed Dr. Craig.

"That was easy, inasmuch as he believed it an insane freak of Katy's to have no other physician than her cousin. It was quite natural, he said, adding that she was as safe with Dr. Grant as any one. And I was glad, for I could not have a stranger know of that affair. You will go up now," Mrs. Cameron continued, and a moment after Wilford stood in the dimly-lighted room, where Katy was talking of Genevra and St. Mary's, and was only kept upon her pillow by the strong arm of Morris, who stood over her when Wilford entered, trying in vain to quiet her.

She knew him, and writhing herself away from Morris's arms, she said to him, "Genevra is not in that grave at St. Mary's; she is living, and you are not my husband. So you can leave the house at once. Morris will settle the estate, and no bill shall be sent in for your board and lodging.

In some moods Wilford would have smiled at being thus summarily dismissed from his own house; but he was too sore now, too sensitive to smile, and his voice was rather severe as he laid his hand on Katy's and said,

"Don't be foolish, Katy. Don't you know me? I am Wilford, your husband."

"That *was,* you mean," Katy rejoined, drawing her hand quickly away. "Go find your first love, where bullets fall like hail, and where there is pain, and blood, and carnage. Genevra is there."

She would not let him come near her, and grew so excited with his presence that he was forced either to leave the room or sit where she could not see him. He chose the latter, and from his seat by the door watched with a half jealous, angry heart, Morris Grant doing for his wife what he should have done.

With Morris Katy was gentle as a little child, talking still of Genevra, but talking quietly, and in a way which did not wear her out as fast as her excitement did.

"What God hath joined together let not man put asunder," was the text from which she preached several short sermons as the night wore on, but just as the morning dawned she fell into the first quiet sleep she had had during the last twenty-four hours. And while she slept Wilford ventured near enough to see the sunken cheeks and hollow eyes which wrung a groan from him as he turned to Morris, and asked what he supposed was the immediate cause of her sudden illness?

"A terrible shock, the nature of which I understand, but you have nothing to fear from me," Morris replied. "I accuse you to no man, but leave you to settle it with your conscience whether you did right to receive her so long."

Morris spoke as one having authority, and Wilford simply bowed his head, feeling no resentment towards one who had ventured to reprove him. Afterwards he might remember it differently, but now he was too anxious to keep Morris there to quarrel with him, and so he made no reply, but sat watching Katy as she slept, wondering if she would die, and feeling how terrible life would be without her. Suddenly Genevra's warning words rang in his ear.

"God will not forgive you for the wrong you have done me."

Was Genevra right? Had God remembered all this time, and overtaken him at last? It might be, and with a groan Wilford hid his face in his hands, believing that he repented of his sin, and not knowing that his fancied repentance arose merely from the fact that he had been detected. Could the last few days be blotted out, and Katy stand just where she did, with no suspicion of him, he would have cast his remorse to the winds, and as it is not such repentance God accepts, Wilford had only begun to sip the cup of retribution presented to his lips.

Worn out with watching and waiting, Mrs. Cameron, who would suffer neither Juno nor Bell to come near the house, waited uneasily for the arrival of the New Haven train, which she hoped would bring Helen to her aid. Under ordinary circumstances she would rather not have met her, for her presence would keep the letter so constantly in mind; but now anybody who could be trusted was welcome, and when at last there came a cautious ring, she went herself to the hall, starting back with undisguised vexation when she saw the timid-looking woman following close behind Helen, and whom the latter presented as " My mother, Mrs. Lennox."

Convinced that Morris's sudden journey to New York had something to do with Katy's illness, and almost distracted with fears for her daughter's life, Mrs. Lennox could not remain at home and wait for the tardy mail or careless telegraph. She must go to her child, and casting off her dread of Wilford's displeasure, she had come with Helen, and was bowing meekly to Mrs. Cameron, who neither offered her hand nor gave any token of greeting except a distant bow and a simple " Good morning, madam."

But Mrs. Lennox was too anxious to notice the lady's haughty manner as she led them to the library and then went for her son. Wilford was not glad to see his mother-in-law, but he tried to be polite, answering her questions civilly, and when she asked if it were true that he had sent for Morris, assuring her that it was not. " Dr. Grant happened here very providentially, and I hope to keep him until the crisis is past, although he has just told me he must go back to-morrow." It hurt Wilford's pride that *she,* whom he considered greatly his inferior, should learn his secret; but it could not now be helped, and within an hour after her arrival she was looking curiously at him for an explanation of the strange things she heard from Katy's lips.

" *Was* you a widower when you married my daughter?" she said to him, when at last Helen left the room and she was alone with him.

" Yes, madam," he replied, " some would call me so, though I was divorced from my wife. As this was a matter which did not in any way concern your daughter, I deemed it best not to tell her. Latterly she has found it out, and it is having a very extraordinary effect upon her."

And this was all Mrs. Lennox knew until alone with Helen, who told her the story as she had heard it from Morris. His sudden journey to New York was thus accounted for, and Helen explained it to her mother, advising her to say nothing of it, as it might be better for

Wilford not to know that Katy had telegraphed for Morris. It seemed very necessary that Dr. Grant should return to Silverton, and the day following Helen's arrival in New York, he made arrangements to do so.

"You have other physicians here," he said to Wilford, who objected to his leaving. "Dr. Craig will do as well as I."

Wilford admitted that he might, but it was with a sinking heart that he saw Morris depart, and then went to Katy, who began to grow very restless and uneasy, bidding him go away and send Dr. Morris back. It was in vain that they administered the medicine just as Morris directed. Katy grew constantly worse, until Mrs. Lennox asked that another doctor be called. But to this Wilford would not listen. Fear of exposure and censure was stronger than his fears for Katy's life, which seemed balancing upon a thread as that long night and the next day went by. Three times Wilford telegraphed for Morris, and it was with unfeigned joy that he welcomed him back at last, and heard that he had so arranged his business as to stay with Katy while the danger lasted.

With a monotonous sameness the days now came and went, people still shunning the house as if the plague was there. Once, Bell Cameron came round to call on Helen, holding her breath as she passed through the hall, and never asking to go near Katy's room. Two or three times, too, Mrs. Banker's carriage stood at the door, and Mrs. Banker herself came in, appearing so cool and distant that Helen could scarcely keep back her tears as she guessed the cause. Mark, too, was in the city, having returned with the Seventh Regiment; but from Esther, Helen learned that he was about joining the army as captain of a company, composed of the finest men in the city. The next she heard was from Mrs. Banker, who, incidentally, remarked, "I shall be very lonely now that Mark is gone. He left me to-day for Washington."

There were tears on the mother's face, and her lip quivered as she tried to keep them back, by looking from the window into the street, instead of at her companion, who, overcome with the rush of feeling which swept over her, laid her face on the sofa arm and sobbed aloud.

"Why, Helen! Miss Lennox, I am surprised! I had supposed—I was not aware—I did not think you would care," Mrs. Banker exclaimed, coming closer to Helen, who stammered out, "I beg you will excuse me, I cannot help it. I care for *all* our soldiers. It seems so terrible."

At the words "I care for *all* the soldiers," a shadow of disappointment flitted over Mrs. Banker's face. She knew her son had offered himself and been refused, as she supposed; and she believed too that Helen had given publicity to the affair, feeling justly indignant at this breach of confidence and lack of delicacy in one whom she had liked so much, and whom she still liked, in spite of the wounded pride which had prompted her to appear so cold and distant.

"Perhaps it is all a mistake," she thought, as she continued standing by Helen, "or it may be she has relented," and for a moment she felt tempted to ask why her boy had been refused.

But Mark would not be pleased with her interference, she knew, and so the golden moment fled, and when she left the house, the misunderstanding between herself and Helen was just as wide as ever. Wearily after that the days passed with Helen until all thoughts of herself were forgotten in the terrible fear that death was really brooding over the pillow where Katy lay, insensible to all that was passing around her. The lips were silent now, and Wilford had nothing to fear from the tongue hitherto so busy. Juno, Bell, and father Cameron all came to see her, dropping tears upon the face looking so old and worn with suffering. Mrs. Cameron, too, was very sorry, very sad, but managed to find some consolation in mentally arranging a grand funeral, which would do honor to her son, and wondering if "those Barlows in Silverton would think they must attend." And while she thus arranged, the mother who had given birth to Katy wrestled in earnest prayer that God would spare her child, or at least grant some space in which she might be told of the world to which she was hastening. What Wilford suffered none could guess. His face was very white, and its expression almost stern, as he sat by the young wife who had been his for little more than two brief years, and who, but for his sin, might not have been lying there, unconscious of the love and grief around her. With lip compressed, and brows firmly knit together, Morris, too, sat watching Katy, feeling for the pulse, and bending his ear to catch the faintest breath which came from her parted lips, while in his heart there was an earnest prayer for the safety of the soul, hovering so evenly between this world and the next. He did not ask that she might live, for if all were well hereafter he knew it was better for her to die in her young womanhood, than to live till the heart, now so sad and bleeding, had grown callosed with sorrow. And yet it was terrible to think of Katy dead; terrible to think of that face and form laid away beneath the turf of Greenwood, where those who loved her best could seldom go to weep.

And as they sat there thus, the night shadows stole into the room, and the hours crept on till from a city tower a clock struck *ten,* and Morris, motioning Helen to his side, bade her go with her mother to rest. "We do not need you here," he said; "your presence can do no good. Should a change occur, you shall be told at once."

Thus importuned, Helen and her mother withdrew, and only Morris and Wilford remained to watch that heavy slumber, so nearly resembling death.

CHAPTER XXXVII.

THE CONFESSION.

GRADUALLY, the noise in the streets died away; the tread of feet, the rumbling wheels, and the tinkle of car bells ceased, and not a sound was heard, save as the distant fire bells pealed forth their warning voices, or some watchman went hurrying by. The great city was asleep, and to Morris the silence brooding over the countless throng was deeper, more solemn, than the silence of the country, where nature gives out her own mysterious notes and lullabies for her sleeping children. Slowly the minutes went by, and Morris became at last aware that Wilford's eyes, instead of resting on the pallid face, which seemed to grow each moment more pallid and ghastly, were fixed on *him* with an expression which made him drop the pale hand he was holding between his own, *pooring* it occasionally, as a mother might *poor* and pity the hand of her dying baby.

Before his marriage, a jealous thought of Morris Grant had found a lodgment in Wilford's breast; but he had tried to drive it out, and fancied that he had succeeded, experiencing a sudden shock when he felt it lifting its green head, and poisoning his mind against the man who was doing for Katy only what a brother might do. He forgot that it was his own entreaties which kept Morris there, away from his Silverton patients, who were missing him so much, and complaining of his absence. Jealous men never reason clearly, and in this case, Wilford did not reason at all, but jumped readily at his conclusion, calling to his aid as proof all that he had ever seen pass between Katy and her cousin. That Morris Grant loved Katy was, after a few moments' reflection, as fixed a fact in his mind, as that she lay there between them, moaning feebly, as if about to speak. Years before, jealousy had made Wilford almost a madman, and it now held him again in its powerful grasp, whispering suggestions he would have spurned in a calm frame of mind. There was a clenching of his fist, a knitting of his brows, and a gathering blackness in his eyes as he listened while Katy, rousing partially from her lethargy, talked of the days when she was a little girl, and Morris had built the play-house for her by the brook, where the thorn-apples grew and the waters fell over the smooth, white rocks.

"Take me back there," she said, "and let me lie on the grass again. It is so long since I was there, and I've suffered so much since then. Wilford meant to be kind, but he did not understand or know how I loved the country with its birds and flowers and the grass by the well, where the shadows come and go. I used to wonder where they were going, and one day when I watched them I was waiting for Wilford and wondering if he would ever come again. Would it have been better if he never had?"

Wilford's body shook as he bent forward to listen, while Katy continued:

"Were there no Genevra, I should not think so, but there is, and yet Morris said that made no difference when I telegraphed for him to come and take me away."

Morris felt keenly the awkwardness of his position, but he could offer no explanation then. He could not speak with those fiery eyes upon him, and he sat erect in his chair, while Katy talked of Silverton, until her voice grew very faint, ceasing at last as she fell into a second sleep, heavier, more deathlike, than the first. Something in her face alarmed Morris, and in spite of the eyes watching him he bent every energy to retain the feeble pulse, and the breath which grew shorter with each respiration.

"Do you think her dying?" Wilford asked, and Morris replied, "The look about the mouth and nose is like the look which so often precedes death."

And that was all they said until another hour went by, when Morris's hand was laid upon the forehead and moved up under the golden hair where there were drops of perspiration.

"She is saved! thank God, Katy is saved!" was his joyful exclamation, and burying his face in his hands, he wept for a moment like a child.

On Wilford's face there was no trace of tears. On the contrary, he seemed hardening into stone, and in his heart fierce passions were contending for the mastery. What did Katy mean by sending for Morris to take her away? Did she send for him, and was that the cause of his being there? If so, there was something between the cousins more than mere friendship. The thought was a maddening one. And, rising slowly at last, Wilford came round to Morris's side, and grasping his shoulder, said,

"Morris Grant, you love Katy Cameron."

Like the peal of a bell on the frosty air the words rang through the room, starting Morris from his bowed attitude, and for an instant curdling the blood in his veins, for he understood now the meaning of the look which had so puzzled him. In Morris's heart there was a moment's hesitancy to know just what to answer—an ejaculatory prayer for guidance—and then lifting up his head, his calm blue eyes met the eyes of black unflinchingly as he replied,

" I have loved her always."

A blaze like sheet lightning shot from beneath Wilford's eyelashes, and a taunting sneer curled his lip as he said,

" *You,* a *saint,* confess to this? "

It was in keeping with human nature for Wilford to thrust Morris's religion in his face, forgetting that never on this side the eternal world can man cease wholly to sin; that so long as flesh and blood remain, there will be temptation, error, and wrong, even among God's children. Morris felt the sneer keenly; but the consciousness of peace with his Maker sustained him in the shock, and with the same tone he had at first assumed, he said,

" Should my being what you call a saint prevent my confessing what I did? "

" No, not the confession, but the fact," Wilford answered, savagely. " How do you reconcile your acknowledged love for Katy with the injunctions of the Bible whose doctrines you indorse? "

" A man cannot always control his feelings, but he can strive to overcome them and put them aside. One does not sin in *being* tempted, but in listening *to* the temptation."

" Then according to your own reasoning you have sinned, for you not only have been tempted but have yielded to the temptation," Wilford retorted, with a sinister look of exultation in his black eyes.

For a moment Morris was silent, while a struggle of some kind seemed going on in his mind, and then he said,

" I never thought to lay open to you a secret which, after myself, is, I believe, known to only one living being."

" And that one—is—is Katy? " Wilford exclaimed, his voice hoarse with passion, and his eyes flashing with fire.

" No, not Katy. She has no suspicion of the pain

which, since I saw her made another's, has eaten into my heart, making me grow old so fast, and blighting my early manhood."

Something in Morris's tone and manner made Wilford relax his grasp upon the arm, and sent him back to his chair while Morris continued,

"Most men would shrink from talking to a husband of the love they bore his wife, and an hour ago I should have shrunk from it too, but you have forced me to it, and now you must listen while I tell you of my love for Katy. It began longer ago than she can remember—began when she was my baby sister, and I hushed her in my arms to sleep, kneeling by her cradle and watching her with a feeling I have never been able to define. She was in all my thoughts, her face upon the printed page of every book I studied, and her voice in every strain of music I ever heard. Then when she grew older, I used to watch the frolicsome child by the hour, building castles of the future, when she would be a woman, and I a man, with a man's right to win her. I know that she shielded me from many a snare into which young men are apt to fall, for when the temptation was greatest, and I was at its verge, a thought of her was sufficient to lead me back to virtue. I carried her in my heart across the sea, and said when I go back I will ask her to be mine. I went back, but at my first meeting with Katy after her return from Canandaigua, she told me of *you*, and I knew then that hope for me was gone. God grant that you may never experience what I experienced on that day which made her your wife, and I saw her go away. It seemed almost as if God had forgotten me as the night after the bridal I sat alone at home, and met that dark hour of sorrow. In the midst of it *Helen* came, discovering my secret, and sympathizing with me until the pain at my heart grew less, and I could pray that God would grant me a feeling for Katy which should not be sinful. And He did at last, so I could think of her without a wish that she was mine. Times there were when the old love would burst forth with fearful power, and then I wished that I might die. These were my moments of temptation which

I struggled to overcome. Sometimes a song, a strain of music, or a ray of moonlight on the floor would bring the past to me so vividly that I would stagger beneath the burden, and feel that it was greater than I could bear. But God was very merciful, and sent me work which took up all my time, and drove me away from my own pain to soothe the pain of others. When Katy came to us last summer there was an hour of trial, when faith in God grew weak, and I was tempted to question the justice of His dealing with me. But that too passed, and in my love for your child I forgot the mother in part, looking upon her as a sister rather than the Katy I had loved so well. I would have given my life to have saved that child for her, even though it was a bar between us, something which separated her from me more than the words she spoke at the altar. Though dead, that baby is still a bar, and Katy is not the same to me she was before that little life came into being. It is not wrong to love her as I do now. I feel no pang of conscience save when something unexpected carries me back to the old ground where I have fought so many battles."

Morris paused a moment, while Wilford said, " She spoke of telegraphing for you. Why was that, and when ? "

Thus interrogated, Morris told of the message which had brought him to New York, and narrated as cautiously as possible the particulars of the interview which followed.

Morris's manner was that of a man who spoke with perfect sincerity, and it carried conviction to Wilford's heart, disarming him for a time of the fierce anger and resentment he had felt while listening to Morris's story. Acting upon the good impulse of the moment, he arose, and offering his hand to Morris, said,

" Forgive me that I ever doubted you. It was natural that you should come, but foolish in Katy to send or think Genevra is living. I have seen her grave myself. I know that she is dead. Did Katy name any one whom she believed to be Genevra ? "

" No one. She merely said she had seen the original of the picture," Morris replied.

"A fancy,—a mere whim," Wilford muttered to himself, as, greatly disquieted and terribly humbled, he paced the room moodily, trying not to think hard thoughts either against his wife or Dr. Grant, who, feeling that it would be pleasanter for Wilford if he were gone, suggested returning to Silverton at once, inasmuch as the crisis was past and Katy out of danger. There was a struggle in Wilford's mind as to the answer he should make to this suggestion, but at last he signified his willingness for the doctor to leave when he thought best.

It was broad day when Katy woke, so weak as to be unable to turn her head upon the pillow, but in her eyes the light of reason was shining, and she glanced wonderingly, first at Helen, who had come in, and then at Wilford, as if trying to comprehend what had happened.

"Have I been sick?" she asked in a whisper, and Wilford, bending over her, replied, "Yes, very sick for nearly two whole weeks—ever since I left home that morning, you know?"

"Yes," and Katy shivered a little. "Yes, I know. But where is Morris? He was here the last I can remember."

Wilford's face grew dark at once, and stepping back as Morris came in, he said, "She asks for you." Then with a rising feeling of resentment he watched them, while Morris spoke to Katy, telling her she must not allow herself in any way to be excited.

"Have I been crazy? Have I talked much?" she asked; and when Morris replied in the affirmative, she said, "Of whom have I talked most?"

"Of *Genevra*," was the answer, and Katy continued, "Did I mention any one else?"

Morris guessed of whom she was thinking, and answered indifferently, "You spoke of Miss Hazelton in connection with baby, but that was all."

Katy was satisfied, and closing her eyes fell away to sleep again, while Morris made his preparations for leaving. It hardly seemed right for him to go just then, but the only one who could have kept him maintained a frigid silence with regard to a longer stay, and so the first train which left New York for Springfield carried Dr. Grant, and Katy was without a physician.

Wilford had hoped that Mrs. Lennox, too, would see the propriety of accompanying Morris, but she would not leave Katy, and Wilford was fain to submit to what he could not help. No explanation whatever had he given to Mrs. Lennox or Helen with regard to Genevra. He was too proud for that, but his mother had deemed it wise to smooth the matter over as much as possible, and enjoin upon them both the necessity of secrecy.

"When I tell you that neither my husband nor daughters know it, you will understand that I am greatly in earnest in wishing it kept," she said. "It was a most unfortunate affair, and though the divorce is, of course, to be lamented, it is better that she died. We never could have received her as our equal."

"Was anything the matter, except that she was poor?" Mrs. Lennox asked, with as much dignity as was in her nature to assume.

"Well, no. She had a good education, I believe, and was very pretty; but it makes trouble always where there is a great inequality between a husband's family and that of his wife."

Poor Mrs. Lennox understood this perfectly, but she was too much afraid of the great lady to venture a reply, and a tear rolled down her cheek as she wet the napkin for Katy's head, and wished she had back again the daughter whose family the Camerons despised. The atmosphere of Madison Square did not suit Mrs. Lennox, especially when, as the days went by and Katy began to amend, troops of gay ladies called, mistaking her for the nurse, and staring a little curiously when told she was Mrs. Cameron's mother. Of course Wilford chafed and fretted at what he could not help, making himself so generally disagreeable that Helen at last suggested returning home. There was a faint remonstrance on his part, but Helen did not waver in her decision, and the next day was fixed upon for her departure.

"You don't know how I dread your going, or how wretched I shall be without you," Katy said, when for a few moments they were alone. "Everything which once made me happy has been removed or changed. Baby is dead, and Wilford, oh! Helen, I sometimes wish I had not heard of Genevra, for I am afraid it can never be with us as it was once; I have n•t the same trust in him, and he seems so changed."

As well as she could, Helen comforted her sister, and commending her to One who would care for her far more than earthly friends could do, she bade her good-bye, and with her mother went back to Silverton.

CHAPTER XXXVIII.

DOMESTIC TROUBLES.

WILFORD was in a most unhappy frame of mind. He had been humbled to the very dust, and it was Katy who had done it—Katy, towards whom his heart kept hardening as he thought over all the past. What right had she to go to his mother's after having once declined; or, being there, what right had she to listen and thus learn the secret he would almost have died to keep; or, having learned it. why need she have been so much excited, and sent for *Dr. Grant* to tell her if she were really a wife, and if not to take her away? That was the point which hurt him most, for added to it was the galling fact that Morris Grant loved his wife, and was undoubtedly more worthy of her than himself. He had said that he forgave Morris, and at the time he said it he fancied he did, but as the days went by, and thought was all the busier from the moody silence he maintained, there gradually came to life a feeling of hatred for the man whose name he could not hear without a frown, while he watched Katy closely to detect, if possible, some sign by which he should know that Morris's love was reciprocated. But Katy was innocence itself, and tried so hard to do her duty as a wife, going often to the Friend of whom Helen had told her, and finding there the grace which helped her bear what otherwise she could not have borne and lived. The entire history of her life during that wretched winter was never told save as it was written on her face, which was a volume in itself of meek and patient suffering.

Wilford had never mentioned Genevra to her since the day of his return, and Katy sometimes felt it would be well to talk that matter over. It might lead to a better understanding than existed between them now, and dissipate the cloud which hung so darkly on their domestic horizon. But Wilford repulsed all her advances on that subject, and Genevra was a dead name in their household. Times there were when for an entire day he would appear like his former self, caressing her with unwonted tenderness, but never asked her forgiveness for all he had made her suffer. He was too proud to do that, and his tenderness always passed away when he remembered Morris Grant and Katy's remark to Helen which he accidentally overheard. "I am afraid it can never be with us as it was once. I have not the same trust in him."

"She had no right to complain of me," he thought, forgetting the time when he had been guilty of a similar offence in a more aggravated form. He could not reason upon anything naturally, and matters grew daily worse, while Katy's face grew whiter and her voice sadder in its tone.

When the Lenten days came on, oh how Katy longed to be in Silverton—to kneel again in its quiet church, and offer up her penitential prayers with the loved ones at home. At last she ventured to ask Wilford if she might go, her spirits rising when he did not refuse her request at once, but asked,

"Whom do you wish to see the most?"

His black eyes seemed reading her through, and something in their expression brought to her face the blush he construed according to his jealousy, and when she answered, "I wish to see them all," he retorted,

"Say, rather, you wish to see *that doctor,* who has loved you so long, and who but for me would have asked you to be his wife!"

"What doctor, Wilford? whom do you mean?" she asked, and Wilford replied,

"Dr. Grant, of course. Did you never suspect it?"

"Never," and Katy's face grew very white, while Wilford continued,

"I had it from his own lips; he sitting on one side of you and I upon the other. I so forgot myself as to charge him with loving you, and he did not deny it, but confessed as pretty a piece of romance as I ever read, except that, according to his story, it was a one-sided affair, confined wholly to himself. *You* never dreamed of it, he said."

"Never, no never," Katy said, panting for her breath, and remembering suddenly many things which confirmed what she had heard.

"Poor Morris, how my thoughtlessness must have wounded him," she murmured, and then all the pent up passion in Wilford's heart burst out in an impetuous storm.

He did not charge his wife directly with returning Morris's love; but he said she was sorry she had not known it earlier, asking her pointedly if it were not so, and pressing her for an answer, until the bewildered creature cried out,

"Oh, I don't know. I never thought of it before."

"But you can think of it now," Wilford continued, his cold, icy tone making Katy shiver, as, more to herself than to him, she whispered,

"A life at Linwood with him would be perfect rest, compared with *this*."

Wilford had goaded her on to say that which roused him to a pitch of frenzy.

"You can go to your *rest* at Linwood as soon as you like, and I will go my way," he whispered hoarsely, and believing himself the most injured man in existence, he left the house, and Katy heard his step, as it went furiously down the steps. For a time she sat stunned with what she had heard, and then there came stealing into her heart a glad feeling that Morris deemed her worthy of his love when she had so often feared the contrary. And in this she was not faithless to Wilford. She could pray with just as pure a heart as before, and she did pray, thanking God for the love of this good man, but asking that long ere this he might have learned to be content without her. Never once did the thought "It might have been," intrude itself upon her, nor did she send one regret after the life she had missed. She seemed to rise above all that, and Wilford, had he read her heart, would have found no evil there.

"Poor Morris," she kept repeating, while little throbs of pleasure went dancing through her veins, and the world was not one half so dreary for knowing he had loved her. Towards Wilford, too, her heart went out in a fresh gush of tenderness, for she knew how one of his jealous nature must have suffered.

And all that day she was thinking of him, and how pleasantly she would meet him when he came home at night, and how she would try to win him from the dark silent mood now so habitual to him. More than usual pains she took with her toilet, arranging her bright hair in the long, glossy curls, which she knew he used to admire, and making sundry little changes in her black dress. Excitement had brought a faint flush to her cheeks, and she was conscious of a feeling of gratification that for the first time in months she was looking like her former self. Slowly the minutes crept on, and the silver-toned clock in the dining-room said it was time for Wilford to come; then the night shadows gathered in the rooms, and the gas was lighted in the hall and in the parlor, where Katy's face was pressed against the window pane, and Katy's eyes peered anxiously out into the darkening streets, but saw no one alighting at their door. Wilford did not come. Neither six, nor seven, nor eight brought him home, and Katy sat down alone to her dinner, which, save the soup and coffee, was removed untasted. She could not eat with the terrible dread at her heart that this long protracted absence portended something more than common. Ten, eleven, and twelve struck from a distant tower. He *had* stayed out as late as that frequently, but rarely later, and Katy listened again for him, until the clock struck one, and she grew sick with fear and apprehension. It was a long, long, wretched night, but morning came at last, and at an early hour Katy drove down to Wilford's office, finding no one there besides Tom Tubbs and Mills, the other clerk. Katy could not conceal her agitation, and her face was very white as she asked what time Mr. Cameron left the office the previous day.

If Katy had one subject more loyal than another it was young Tom Tubbs, whose boyish blood had often boiled with rage at the cool manner with which Wilford treated his wife, when, as she sometimes did, she came into the office. Tom worshiped Katy Cameron, who, in his whispered confidences to Mattie, was an angel, while Wilford was accused of being an overbearing tyrant, whom Tom would like to thrash. He saw at once, that something unusual was troubling her, and hastening to bring her a chair, told her that Mr. Cameron left the office about four o'clock; that he had spent the most of the day in his private office writing and looking over papers; that he had given his clerks so many directions with regard to certain matters, that Mills had remarked upon it, saying, "It would seem as if he did not expect to be here to see to it himself;" and this was all Katy could learn, but it was enough to increase the growing terror at her heart, and dropping her veil, she went out to her carriage, followed by Tom, who adjusted the gay robe across her lap, and then looked wistfully after her as she drove up Broadway.

"To father Cameron's," she said to the driver, who turned his horses towards Fifth Avenue, where, just coming down the steps of his own house, they met the elder Cameron.

Katy would rather see him first alone, and motioning him to her side she whispered: "Oh, father, is Wilford here?"

"Wilford be——"; the old man did not say what, for the expression of Katy's face startled him.

That there was something wrong, and father Cameron knew it, was Katy's conviction, and she gasped out,

"Tell me the worst. Is Wilford dead?"

Father Cameron was in the carriage by this time, and riding towards Madison Square, for he did not care to introduce Katy into his household, which, just at present, presented a scene of dire confusion and dismay, occasioned by a note received from Wilford to the intent that he had left New York, and did not know when he should return.

"Katy can tell you why I go," he added, and father Cameron was going to Katy when she met him at his door.

To Katy's repeated question, "Is he dead?" he answered, "Worse than that, I fear. He has left the city, and no one knows for what, unless you do. From something he wrote, my wife is led to suppose there was trouble between you two. Was there?" and father Cameron's gray eyes rested earnestly on the white, frightened face which looked up so quickly as Katy gasped,

"*There has* been trouble—that is, he has not appeared quite the same since——"

She was interrupted by the carriage stopping before her door; but when they were in the parlor, father Cameron said,

"Go on now. Wilford has not been the same since when?"

Thus importuned, Katy continued,

"Since baby died. I think he blamed me as the cause of its death."

"Don't babies die every day?" father Cameron growled, while Katy, without considering that he had never heard of Genevra, continued,

"And then it was worse after I found out about Genevra, his first wife."

"Genevra! Genevra, Wilford's first wife! Thunder and lightning! what are you talking about?" and father Cameron bent down to look in Katy's face, thinking she was going mad.

But Katy was not mad, and knowing it was now too late to retract, she told the story of Genevra Lambert to the old man, who, utterly confounded, stalked up and down the room, kicking away chairs and footstools, and whatever came in his way, and swearing promiscuously at his wife and Wilford, whom he pronounced a precious pair of fools, with a dreadful adjective appended to the *fools,* and an emphasis in his voice which showed he meant what he said.

"It's all accounted for now," he said; "the piles of money that boy had abroad, his privacy with his mother, and all the other tomfoolery I could not understand. Katy," and pausing in his walk, Mr. Cameron came close to his daughter-in-law, who was lying with her face upon the sofa. "Katy, be glad your baby died. Had it lived it might have proved a curse, just as mine have done— not all, for Bell, though fiery as a pepper-pod, has some heart, some sense—and there was Jack, my *oldest* boy, a little fast it's true, but when he died over the sea, I forgave all that, and forgot the chair he broke over a tutor's head, and the scrapes for which I paid as high as a thousand at one time. He sowed his wild oats, and died before he could reap them—died a good man, I believe, and went to Heaven. Juno you know, and you can judge whether she is such as would delight a parent's heart; while Wilford, my only boy, to deceive me so; I knew he was a fool in some things, but I did trust Wilford."

The old man's voice shook now, and Katy felt his tears dropping on her hair as he stooped over her. Checking them, however, he said,

"And he was cross because you found him out. Was there no other reason?"

Katy thought of Dr. Morris, but she could not tell of that, and so she answered,

"There was—but please don't ask me now. I can't tell, only I was not to blame. Believe me, father, I was not to blame."

"I'll swear to that," was the reply, and father Cameron commenced his walking again, just as Esther came to the door with the morning letters.

There was one from Wilford for Katy, who nervously tore off the envelope and read as follows:

"Will you be sorry when you read this and find that I am gone, that you are free from the husband you do not love,—whom, perhaps, you never loved, though I thought you did. I trusted you once, and now I do not blame you as much as I ought, for you are young and easily influenced. You are very susceptible to flattery, as was proven by your career at Saratoga and Newport. I had no suspicion of you then, but now that I know you better, I see that it was not all childish simplicity which made you smile so graciously upon those who sought your favor. You are a coquette, Katy, and the greater one because of that semblance of artlessness which is the perfection of art. This, however, I might forgive, if I had not learned that another man loved you first and wished to make you his wife, while you, in your secret heart, wish you had known it sooner. Don't deny it, Katy; I saw it in your face when I first told you of Dr. Grant's confession, and I heard it in your voice as well as in your words when you said ' A life at Linwood would be perfect rest compared with this.' That hurt me cruelly, Katy. I did not deserve it from one for whom I have done and borne so much, and it was the final cause of my leaving you, for I am going to Washington to enroll myself in the service of my country. You will be happier without me for awhile, and perhaps when I return, Linwood will not look quite the little paradise it does now.

"I might reproach you with having telegraphed to Dr. Grant about that miserable Genevra affair which you had not discretion enough to keep to yourself. Few men would care to have their wives send for a former lover in their absence and ask that lover to take them away. Your saintly cousin, good as he is, cannot wonder at my vexation, or blame me greatly for going away. Perhaps he will offer you comfort, both religious and otherwise: but if you ever wish me to return, avoid him as you would shun a deadly poison. Until I countermand the order, I wish you to remain in the house which I bought for you. Helen and your mother both may live with you, while father will have a general oversight of your affairs; I shall send him a line to that effect. "YOUR DISAPPOINTED HUSBAND."

This was the letter, and there was perfect silence while Katy read it through, Mr. Cameron never taking his eyes from her face, which turned first white, then red, then spotted, and finally took a leaden hue as Katy ran over the lines, comprehending the truth as she read, and when the letter was finished, lifting her dry, tearless eyes to Father Cameron, and whispering to herself,

" Deserted ! "

She let him read the letter, and when he had finished, explained the parts he did not understand, telling him now what Morris had confessed—telling him too that in her first sorrow, when life and sense seemed reeling, she had sent for Dr. Grant, knowing she could trust him and be right in doing whatever he advised.

" *Why* did you say you sent for him—that is, *what* was the special reason? " Mr. Cameron asked, and Katy told him her belief that Genevra was living—that it was she who made the bridal trousseau for Wilford's second wife, she who nursed his child until it died, giving to it her own name, arraying it for the grave, and then leaving before the father came.

" I never told Wilford," Katy said. " I felt as if I would rather he should not know it yet. Perhaps I was wrong, but if so, I have been terribly punished."

Mr. Cameron could not look upon the woman who stood before him, so helpless and stricken in her desolation, and believe her wrong in anything. The guilt lay in another direction, and when, as the terrible reality that she was indeed a deserted wife came rushing over Katy, she tottered toward him for help; he stretched his arms out for her, and taking the sinking figure in them, laid it upon the sofa as gently, as kindly, as Wilford had ever touched it in his most loving days.

Katy did not faint nor weep. She was past all that; but her face was like a piece of marble, and her eyes were like those of the hunted fawn when the chase is at its height, and escape impossible.

" Wilford will come back, of course," the father said, " but that does not help us now. What the plague—who is ringing that bell enough to break the wire? " he added, as a sharp, rapid ring echoed through the house, and was answered by Esther. " It's my wife," he continued, as he caught the sound of her voice in the hall.

" You stay here while I meet her first alone. *I'll* give it to her for cheating me so long, and raising thunder generally ! "

Katy tried to protest, but he was half way down the stairs, and in a moment more was with his wife, who, impatient at his long delay, had come herself, armed and equipped, to censure Katy as the cause of Wilford's disappearance, and to demand of her what she had done. But the lady who came in so haughty and indignant was a very different personage from the lady who, after listening for fifteen minutes to a fearful storm of oaths and reproaches, mingling with startling truths and bitter denunciations against herself and her boy, sank into a chair, pale and trembling, and overwhelmed with the harvest she was reaping.

But her husband was not through with her yet. He had reserved the bitterest drop for the last, and coming close to her he said,

" And *who* think you the woman is—this Genevra, Wilford's and your divorced wife? You were too proud to acknowledge an apothecary's daughter! See if you like better a dressmaker, a nurse to Katy's baby, *Marian Hazelton!*"

He whispered the last name, and with a shriek the lady fainted. Mr. Cameron would not summon a servant; and as there was no water in the room, he walked to the window, and lifting the sash scraped from the sill a handful of the light spring snow which had been falling since morning. With this he brought his wife back to consciousness, and then marked out her future course.

" I know what is in your mind," he said; " people *will* talk about Wilford's going off so suddenly, and you would like to have all the blame rest on Katy; but, madam, hear me: Just so sure as through your means one breath of suspicion falls on her, I'll *bla-at* out the whole story of Genevra. Then see who is censured. On the other hand, if you hold your tongue, and make Juno hold hers, and stick to Katy through thick and thin, acting as if you would like to swallow her whole, I'll say nothing of this Genevra. Is it a bargain?"

" Yes," came faintly from the sofa cushions, where Mrs. Cameron had buried her face, sobbing in a confused, frightened way, and after a few moments asking to see Katy, whom she kissed and caressed with unwonted tenderness, telling her Wilford would come back, and adding, that in any event no one could or should blame her. "Wilford was wrong to deceive you about Genevra. I was wrong to let him; but we will have no more concealments. You think she is living still—that she is Marian Hazelton?" and Mrs. Cameron smoothed Katy's hair as she talked, trying to be motherly and kind, while her heart beat more painfully at thoughts of a Genevra living, than it ever had at thoughts of a Genevra dead.

She did not doubt the story, although it seemed so strange, and it made her faint as she wondered if the world would ever know, and what it would say if it did. That her husband would tell, if she failed in a single point, she was sure; but she would not fail. She would swear Katy was innocent of everything, if necessary, while Juno and Bell should swear too. Of course, they must know, and she should tell them that very night, she said to herself; and hence it was that in the gossip which followed Wilford's disappearance, not a word was breathed against Katy, whose cause the family espoused so warmly, —Bell and the father because they really loved and pitied her, and Mrs. Cameron and Juno because it saved them from the disgrace which would have fallen on Wilford, had the fashionable world known then of Genevra.

Wilford's leaving home so suddenly to join the army, could not fail, even in New York, to cause some excitement, especially in his own immediate circle of acquaintance, and for several days the matter was discussed in all its phases, and every possible opinion and conjecture offered, as to the cause of his strange freak. They could not believe in domestic troubles when they saw how his family clung to and defended Katy from the least approach of censure, Juno taking up her abode with her "afflicted sister," Mrs. Cameron driving round each day to see her; Bell always speaking of her with genuine affection, while the father clung to her like a hero, the quartette forming a barrier across which the shafts of scandal could not reach.

CHAPTER XXXIX.

WHAT FOLLOWED.

WHEN Wilford left Katy so abruptly he had no definite purpose in his mind. He was very sore with the remembrance of all that had passed since baby's death, and very angry at his wife, who he believed preferred another to himself, or who would have done so had she known in time what she did now. Like most angry people, he forgot wherein he had been in fault, but charged it all to Katy as he went down Broadway that spring morning, finding on his table a letter from an old classmate, who was then in Washington getting up a company, and who wrote urging his friend to join him at once, and offering him the rank of First Lieutenant. Here was a temptation,— here an opportunity to revenge himself on Katy, against whom he wrote a sad list of errors, making it sadder by brooding over and magnifying it until he reached a point from which he would not swerve.

"I shall do it," he said, and his lips were pressed firmly together, as in his private office he sat revolving the past, and then turning to the future, opening so darkly before him, and making him shudder as he thought of what it might bring. "I will spare Katy as much as possible," he said, "for hers is a different nature from Genevra's. She cannot bear as well," and a bitter groan broke the silence of the room as Katy came up before him just as she had looked that very morning standing by the window, with tears in her eyes, and a wistful, sorry look on her white face.

But Wilford was not one to retract when a decision was reached, and so he arranged his business matters as well as his limited time would allow; then, after the brief note to his father, wrote the letter to Katy, and then followed to the Jersey ferry a regiment of soldiers who were going on to Washington that night. Four days

more and Lieutenant Wilford Cameron, with no regret
as yet for the past, marched away to swell the ranks of
men who, led by General McClellan, were pressing on, as
they believed, to Richmond and victory. A week of terrible suspense went by, and then there came a letter to
Mr. Cameron from his son, requesting him to care for
Katy, but asking no forgiveness for himself. There were
no apologies, no explanations, no kind words for Katy,
whose eyes moved slowly over the short letter, and then
were lifted sadly to her father's face as she said,

"I will write to him myself, and on his answer will
depend my future course."

This she said referring to the question she had raised
as to whether she should remain in New York or go to
Silverton, where the family as yet knew nothing except
that Wilford had joined the army. And so the days went
by, while Katy's letter was sent to Wilford, together with
another from his father, who called his son a "confounded
fool," telling him to throw up his shoulder straps, which
only honest men had a right to wear, and come home
where he belonged.

To this there came an indignant answer, bidding the
father attend to his own business, and allow the son to
attend to his. To Katy, however, Wilford wrote in a
different strain, showing here and there marks of tenderness and relenting, but saying what he had done could
not now be helped,—he was in for a soldier's life for
two years, and should abide his choice.

This was the purport of Wilford's letter, and Katy,
when she finished reading it, said sorrowfully,

"Wilford never loved me, and I cannot stay in *his*
home, knowing that I am not trusted and respected as a
wife should be. I will go to Silverton. There is room
for me there.

Meanwhile at Silverton there was much anxiety for
Katy, and many doubts expressed lest something was
wrong. That Wilford should go away so suddenly, when
he had never been noted for any very great amount of
patriotism, seemed strange, and Uncle Ephraim at last
made up his mind to the herculean task of going to New
York to see what was the matter.

Presuming upon her experience as a traveler, Aunt Betsy had proffered sundry pieces of advice with reference to what it was best for him to do on the road, telling him which side of the car to sit, where to get out, and above all things not to shake hands with the conductor when asked for his ticket.

Uncle Ephraim heard her good-humoredly, and stuffing into his pocket the paper of ginger-snaps, fried cakes and cheese, which Aunt Hannah had prepared for his lunch, he started for the cars, and was soon on his way to New York.

In his case there was no Bob Reynolds to offer aid and comfort, and the old man was nearly torn in pieces by the hackmen, who, the moment he appeared to view, pounced upon him as lawful prey, each claiming the honor of taking him wherever he wished to go, and raising such a din about his ears that he turned away thoroughly disgusted, telling them—

"He had feet and legs, and common sense, and he guessed he could find his way without 'em. "Bleeged to you, gentlemen, but I don't need you," and with a profound bow the honest looking old deacon walked away, asking the first man he met the way to Madison Square, and succeeding in finding the number without difficulty.

With a scream of joy Katy threw herself into Uncle Ephraim's arms, and then led him to her own room, while the first tears she had shed since she knew she was deserted rained in torrents over her face.

"What is it, Katy-did? I mistrusted something was wrong. What has happened?" Uncle Ephraim asked; and with his arm around her, Katy told him what had happened, and asked what she should do.

"Do?" the old man repeated. "Go home with me to your own folks until he comes from the wars. He is your husband, and I shall say nothing agin him; but if it was to go over I would forbid the banns. That chap has misused you the wust way. You need not deny it, for it's writ all over your face," he continued, as Katy tried to stop him, for sore as was her heart with the great injustice done her, she would not have Wilford blamed, and she was glad when dinner was announced, as that would put an end to the painful conversation.

Leading Uncle Ephraim to the table, she presented him to Juno, whose cold nod and haughty stare were lost on the old man, bowing his white head so reverently as he asked the first blessing which had ever been asked at that table.

It had not been a house of prayer—no altar had been erected for the morning and evening sacrifice. God had almost been forgotten, and now He was pouring His wrath upon the handsome dwelling, making it so distasteful that Katy was anxious to leave it, and expressed her desire to accompany Uncle Ephraim to Silverton as soon as the necessary arrangements could be made.

"I don't take it she comes for good," Uncle Ephraim said that evening, when Mr. Cameron opposed her going. "When the two years are gone, and her man wants her back, she must come of course. But she grows poor here in the city. It don't agree with her like the scent of the clover and the breeze from the hills. So, shet up the house for a spell, and let the child come with me."

Mr. Cameron knew that Katy would be happier at Silverton, and he finally consented to her going, and placed at her disposal a sum which seemed to the deacon a little fortune in itself.

To Mrs. Cameron and Juno it was a relief to have Katy taken from their hands, and though they made a show of opposition, they were easily quieted, and helped her off with alacrity, the mother promising to see that the house was properly cared for, and Juno offering to send the latest fashions which might be suitable, as soon as they appeared. Bell was heartily sorry to part with the young sister, who seemed going from her forever.

"I know you will never come back. Something tells me so," she said, as she stood with her arms around Katy's waist, and her lips occasionally touching Katy's forehead. "But I shall see you," she continued; "I am coming to the farm-house in the summer, and you may say to Aunt Betsy that I like her ever so much, and "— Bell glanced behind her, to see that no one was listening, and then continued—"tell her a certain officer was sick a few days in a hospital last winter, and one of his men brought to him a dish of the most delicious dried peaches he ever ate. That man was from *Silverton,* and the fruit was sent to him, he said, in a salt bag, by a nice old lady, for whose brother he used to work. Just to think that the peaches I helped to pare, coloring my hands so that the stain did not come off in a month, should have gone so straight to *Bob!* " and Bell's fine features shone with a light which would have told Bob Reynolds he was beloved, if the lips did refuse to confess it.

"I'll tell her," Katy said, and then bidding them all good-bye, and putting her hand on Uncle Ephraim's arm, she went with him from the home where she had lived but two years, and those the saddest, most eventful ones of her short life.

CHAPTER XL.

MARK AND HELEN.

THERE was much talk in Silverton when it was known that Katy had come to stay until her husband returned from the war, and at first the people watched her curiously as she came among them again, so quiet, so subdued, so unlike the Katy of old that they would have hardly recognized her but for the beauty of her face and the sunny smile she gave to all, and which rested oftenest on the poor and suffering, who blessed her as the angel of their humble homes, praying that God would remember her for all she was to them. Wilford had censured her at first for going to Silverton, when he preferred she should stay in New York, hinting darkly at the reason of her choice, and saying to her once, when she told him how the Sunday before her twenty-first birthday she had knelt before the altar and taken upon herself the vows of confirmation, "Your saintly cousin is, of course, de-.

lighted, and that I suppose is sufficient, without my congratulations."

Perhaps he did not mean it, but he seemed to take delight in teasing her, and Katy sometimes felt she should be happier without his letters than with them. He never said he was sorry he had left her so suddenly—indeed he seldom referred to the past in any way; or if he did, it was in a manner which showed that he thought himself the injured party, if either.

Katy did not often go to Linwood, and seldom saw Morris alone. After what had passed she thought it better to avoid him as much as possible, and was glad when early in June he accepted a situation offered him as surgeon in a Georgetown hospital, and left Silverton for his new field of labor.

True to her promise, Bell came the last of July to Silverton, proving herself a dreadful romp, as she climbed over the rocks in Aunt Betsy's famous sheep-pasture, or raked the hay in the meadow, and proving herself, too, a genuine woman, as with blanched cheek and anxious heart she waited for tidings from the battles before Richmond, where the tide of success seemed to turn, and the North, hitherto so jubilant and hopeful, wore weeds of mourning from Maine to Oregon. Lieut. Bob was there, and Wilford, too; and so was Captain Ray, digging in the marshy swamps, where death floated·up in poisonous exhalations—plodding on the weary march, and fighting all through the seven days, where the sun poured down its burning heat and the night brought little rest. No wonder, then, that three faces at the farm-house grew white with anxiety, or that three pairs of eyes grew dim with watching the daily papers. But the names of neither Wilford, Mark, nor Bob were ever found among the wounded, dead, or missing, and with the fall of the first autumn leaf Bell returned to the city more puzzled, more perplexed than ever with regard to Helen Lennox's real feelings toward Captain Ray.

The week before Christmas, Mark came home for a few days, looking ruddy and bronzed from exposure and hardship, but wearing a disappointed, listless look which Bell was quick to detect, connecting it in some way with

Helen Lennox. Only once did he call at Mr. Cameron's and then as Juno was out Bell had him to herself, talking of Silverton, of Helen and Katy, in the latter of whom he seemed far more interested than her sister. Many questions he asked concerning Katy, expressing his regret that Wilford had left her, and saying he believed Wilford was sorry, too. He was in the hospital now, with a severe cold and a touch of the rheumatism, he said; but as Bell knew this already she did not dwell long upon that subject, choosing rather to talk of Helen, who, she said, was "as much interested in the soldiers, as if she had a brother or a lover in the army," and her bright eyes glanced meaningly at Mark, who answered carelessly,

"*Dr. Grant* is there, and that may account for her interest."

Mark knew he must say something to ward off Bell's attacks, and he continued talking of Dr. Grant and how much he was liked by the poor wretches who needed some one like him to keep them from dying of home-sickness if nothing else; then, after a few bantering words concerning Lieutenant Bob and the *picture* he carried into every battle, buttoned closely over his heart, Mark Ray took his leave, while Bell ran up to her mother's room as a seamstress was occupying her own. Mrs. Cameron was out that afternoon, and that she had dressed in a hurry was indicated by the unusual confusion of her room. Drawers were left open and various articles scattered about, while on the floor, just as it had fallen from a glove-box, lay a *letter* which Bell picked up, intending to replace it.

"*Miss Helen Lennox,*" she read in astonishment. "How came Helen Lennox's letter *here,* and from *Mark Ray* too," she continued, still more amazed as she took the neatly folded note from the envelope and glanced at the name. "Foul play somewhere. Can it be mother?" she asked, as she read enough to know that she held in her hand Mark's offer of marriage, which had in some mysterious manner found its way to her mother's room. "I don't understand it," she said, racking her brain for a solution of the mystery. "But I'll send it to Helen this very day, and to-morrow I'll tell Mark Ray."

Procrastination was not one of Bell Cameron's faults, and for full half an hour before her mother and Juno came home, the stolen letter had been lying in the mail box where Bell herself deposited it, together with a few hurriedly-written lines, telling how it came into her hands, but offering no explanation of any kind.

"Mark is home now on a leave of absence which expires day after to-morrow," she wrote, "I am going round to see him, and if you do not hear from him in person I am greatly mistaken."

The next day a series of hindrances kept Bell from making her call as early as she had intended, so that Mrs. Banker and Mark were just rising from dinner when told she was in the parlor.

"I meant to have come before," she said, seating herself by Mark, "but I could not get away. I have brought you some good news. I think,—that is,—yes, I know there has been some mistake, some wrong somewhere. Mark Ray, yesterday afternoon I found,—no matter where or how—a letter intended for Helen Lennox, which I am positive she never saw or heard of; at least her denial to me that a certain Mark Ray had ever offered himself is a proof that she never saw what *was* an offer made just before you went away. I read enough to know that, and then I took the letter and——"

She hesitated, while Mark's eyes turned dark with excitement, and even Mrs. Banker, scarcely less interested, leaned eagerly forward, saying,

"And what? Go on, Miss Cameron. What did you do with that letter?"

"I sent it to its rightful owner, Helen Lennox. I posted it myself. But why don't you thank me, Captain Ray?" she asked, as Mark's face was overshadowed with anxiety.

"I was wondering whether it were well to send it—wondering how it might be received," he said, and Bell replied.

"She will not answer no. As one woman knows another, I know Helen Lennox. I have sounded her on that point. I told her of the rumor there was afloat, and she denied it, seeming greatly distressed, but showing

plainly that had such offer been received she would not
have refused it. You should have seen her last summer,
Captain Ray, when we waited so anxiously for news from
the Potomac. Her face was a study as her eyes ran over
the list of casualties, searching *not* for her amiable
brother-in-law, nor yet for *Willard Braxton,* their hired
man. It was plain to me as daylight, and all you have
to do is to follow up that letter with another, or go yourself, if you have time," Bell said, as she rose to go,
leaving Mark in a state of bewilderment as to what he
had heard.

Who withheld that letter? and why? were questions
which troubled him greatly, nor did his mother's assurance
that it did not matter so long as it all came right at
last, tend wholly to reassure him. One thing, however,
was certain. He would see Helen before he returned to
his regiment. He would telegraph in the morning to
Washington, and then run the risk of being a day behind
the time appointed for his return to duty.

"Suppose you have three children when I return, instead of two, is there room in your heart for the third?"
he asked his mother when next morning he was about
starting for Silverton.

"Yes, always room for Helen," was the reply, as with
a kiss of benediction Mrs. Banker sent her boy away.

CHAPTER XLI.

CHRISTMAS EVE AT SILVERTON.

THERE was to be a Christmas tree at St. John's, and
all the week the church had been the scene of much confusion. But the work was over now; the church was swept
and dusted, the tree with its gay adornings was in its
place, the little ones, who had hindered so much, were
gone, as were their mothers, and Helen only tarried with
the organ boy to play the Christmas Carol, which Katy
was to sing alone, the children joining in the chorus as

they had been trained to do. It was very quiet there, and
pleasant, with the fading sunlight streaming through the
chancel window, lighting up the cross above it, and falling
softly on the wall where the evergreens were hung with
the sacred words, "Peace on earth and good will towards men." And Helen felt the peace stealing over her
as she sat down by the register for a moment ere going
to the organ loft where the boy was waiting for her. Not
even the remembrance of the dark war-cloud hanging over
the land disturbed her then, as her thoughts went backward eighteen hundred years to Bethlehem's manger and
the little Child whose birth the angels sang. And as she
thought, that Child seemed to be with her, a living presence to which she prayed, leaning her head upon the railing of the pew in front, and asking Him to keep her in
the perfect peace she felt around her now. For Mark
Ray, too, she prayed, asking God to keep him in safety
wherever he might be, whether in the lonely watch, or in
some house of God, where the Christmas carols would be
sung and the Christmas story told.

As she lifted up her head her hand struck against the
pocket of her dress, where lay the letter brought to her
an hour or so ago—Bell's letter—which she had put aside
to read at a more convenient season.

Taking it out, she tore open the envelope, starting suddenly as another letter, soiled and unsealed, met her eye.
She read Bell's first, and then, with a throbbing heart,
which as yet would not believe, she took up Mark's, understanding now much that was before mysterious to her.
Juno's call came to her mind, and though she was unwilling to charge so foul a wrong upon that young lady,
she could find no other solution to the mystery. There
was a glow of indignation—Helen had scarcely been
mortal without it;—but that passed away in pity for the
misguided girl and in joy at the happiness opening so
broadly before her. That Mark would *come* to Silverton
she had no hope, but he would write—his letter, perhaps,
was even then on the way; and kissing the one she held,
she hid it in her bosom and went up to where the organ-
boy had for several minutes been kicking at stools and
books, and whistling *Old John Brown* by way of attracting

attention. The boy was in a hurry, and asked in so forlorn
a tone, "*Is* we going to play?" that Helen answered good-
humoredly, "Just a few minutes, Billy. I want to try
the carol and the opening, which I've hardly played at
all."

With an air of submission Bill took his post and Helen
began to play, but she could only see before her, "I have
loved you ever since that morning when I put the lilies in
your hair," and played so out of time and tune that Billy
asked, "What makes 'em go so bad?"

"I can't play now; I'm not in the mood," she said.
"I shall feel better by and by. You can go home if you
like."

Bill needed no second bidding, but catching up his cap
ran down the stairs and out into the porch, just as up
the steps a young man came hurriedly.

"Hallo, boy," he cried, grasping the collar of Bill's
roundabout and holding him fast, "who's in the
church?"

"Darn yer, Jim Sykes, you let me be, or I'll——" the
boy began, but when he saw his captor was not *Jim Sykes,*
but a tall man, wearing a soldier's uniform, he changed
his tone, and answered civilly, "I thought you was Jim
Sykes, the biggest bully in town, who is allus hectorin'
us boys. Nobody is there but she——Miss Lennox——up
where the organ is," and having given the desired information, Bill ran off, wondering first if it wasn't Miss
Helen's *beau,* and wondering next, in case she should sometime get married in church, if he wouldn't fee the *organ-
boy* as well as the sexton. "He orto," Bill soliloquized,
"for I've about blowed my gizzard out sometimes, when
she and Mrs. Cameron sings the Te Deum."

Meanwhile Mark Ray, who had driven first to the farm-
house in quest of Helen, entered the church, and stole
noiselessly up the stairs to where Helen sat in the dim
light, reading again the precious letter withheld from her
so long. She had moved her stool nearer to the window,
and her back was towards the door, so that she neither
saw, nor heard, nor suspected anything, until Mark, bending over her so as to see what she had in her hand,

as well as the *tear* she had dropped upon it, clasped both
his arms about her neck, and drawing her face over back,
kissed her fondly, calling her his darling, and saying to
her, as she tried to struggle from him,

"I know I have a right to call you darling, by that tear
on my letter, and the look upon your face. Dear Helen,
we have found each other at last."

It was so unexpected that Helen could not speak, but
she let her head rest on his bosom, where he had laid it,
and her hand crept into his, so that he was answered,
and for a moment he only kissed and caressed the fair
girl he knew now was his own. They could not talk
together very long, for Helen must go home; but he
made good use of the time he had, telling her many
things, and then asking her a question which made her
start away from him as she replied. "No, no, oh! no, not
to-night—not so soon as that!"

"And why not, Helen?" he asked, with the manner
of one who was not to be denied. "Why not to-night, so
there need be no more misunderstanding? I'd rather
leave you as my wife than my betrothed. Mother will
like it better. I hinted it to her and she said there was
room for you in her love. It will make me a better man,
and a better soldier, if I can say 'my wife,' as other
soldiers do. You don't know what a charm there is in that
word, Helen. It keeps a man from sin, and if I should die
I would rather you should bear my name, and share in my
fortune. Will you, Helen, when the ceremonies are closed,
will you go up to that altar and pledge your vows to me.
I cannot wait till to-morrow; my leave of absence expires
to-day. I must go back to-night, but you must first be
mine."

Helen was shaking as with a chill, but she made him
no reply, and wrapping her cloak and furs about her,
Mark led her down to the sleigh, and taking his seat
beside her, drove back to the farm-house where the family
were waiting for her. Katy, to whom Mark first communicated his desire, warmly espoused his cause, and that
went far towards reassuring Helen, who for some time
past had been learning to look up to Katy as to an

older sister, so sober, so earnest, so womanly had Katy grown since Wilford went away.

"It is so sudden, and people will talk," Helen said, knowing, while she said it, how little she cared for people, and smiling at Katy's reply.

"They may as well talk about you awhile as me. It is not so bad when once you are used to it."

After Katy, Aunt Betsy was Mark's best advocate. It is true this was not just what she had expected when Helen was married. The *infair* which Wilford had declined was still in Aunt Betsy's mind; but that, she reflected, might be yet. If Mark went back on the next train there could be no proper wedding party until his return, when the loaves of frosted cake, and the baked fowls she had seen in imagination should be there in real, tangible form, and as she expressed it they would have a "high." Accordingly she threw herself into the scale beginning to balance in favor of Mark, and when at last old Whitey stood at the door, ready to take the family to the church, Helen sat upon the lounge listening half bewildered while Katy assured her that *she* could play the voluntary, even if she had not looked at it, that she could lead the children without the organ, and in short do everything Helen was expected to do except go to the altar *with Mark.*

"That I leave for you," and she playfully kissed Helen's forehead, as she tripped from the room, looking back when she reached the door, and charging the lovers not to forget to come, in their absorption of each other.

St. John's was crowded that night, the children occupying the front seat, with looks of expectancy upon their faces, as they studied the heavily laden tree, the boys wondering if that ball, or whistle, or wheelbarrow was for them, and the girls appropriating the tastefully-dressed dolls showing so conspicuously among the dark green foliage. The Barlows were rather late, for upon Uncle Ephraim devolved the duty of seeing to the license, and as he had no seat in that house, his arrival was only known by Aunt Betsy's elbowing her way to the front, and near to the Christmas tree which she had helped to dress, just as she had helped to trim the church. She did not believe in such "flummeries" it is true and she classed them with the "quirks," but rather than "see the gals slave themselves to death," she had this year lent a helping hand. Donning two shawls, a camlet cloak, a knit scarf for her head, and a hood to keep from catching cold, she had worked early and late, fashioning the most wonderfully shaped wreaths, tying up festoons, and even trying her hand at a triangle; she turned her back resolutely upon *crosses,* which were more than her Puritanism could endure. The cross was a "quirk," with which she'd have nothing to do, though once, when Katy seemed more than usually bothered and wished somebody would hand her *tacks,* Aunt Betsy relented so far as to bring the hoop she was winding close to Katy, holding the little nails in her mouth, and giving them out as they were wanted; but with each one given out, conscientiously turning her head away, lest her eyes should fall upon what she conceived the symbol of the Romish Church. But when the whole was done, none were louder in their praises than Aunt Betsy, who was guilty of asking Mrs. Deacon Bannister, when she came in to inspect, "why the Orthodox couldn't get up some such doin's for their Sunday school. It pleased the children mightily."

But Mrs. Deacon Bannister answered with some severity,

"We don't believe in shows and *plays,* you know," thus giving a double thrust, and showing that the opera had never been quite forgotten. "Here's a pair of skates, though, and a smellin' bottle I'd like to have put on for John and Sylvia," she added, handing her package to Aunt Betsy, who, while seeing the skates and smelling bottle suspended from a bough, was guilty of wondering if "the partaker wasn't most as bad as the thief."

This was in the afternoon, and was all forgotten now, when with her Sunday clothes she never would have worn in that jam but for the great occasion, Aunt Betsy elbowed her way up the middle aisle, her face wearing a very important and knowing look, especially when Uncle Ephraim's tall figure bent for a moment under the hemlock boughs, and then disappeared in the little vestry room where he held a private consultation with the rector. That she knew something her neighbors didn't was evident, but she kept it to herself, turning her head occasionally to look up at the organ where Katy was presiding. Others too, there were, who turned their heads as the soft music began to fill the church, and the heavy bass rolled up the aisles, making the floor tremble beneath their feet and sending a thrill through every vein. It was a skillful hand which swept the keys that night, for Katy played with her whole soul—not the voluntary there before her in printed form, nor any one thing she had ever heard, but taking parts of many things, and mingling them with strains of her own improvising she filled the house as it had never been filled before, playing a soft, sweet refrain when she thought of Helen, then bursting into louder, fuller tones, when she remembered Bethlehem's Child and the song the angels sang, and then as she recalled her own sad life since she knelt at the altar a happy bride, the organ notes seemed much like human sobs, now rising to a stormy pitch of passion, wild and uncontrolled, and then dying out as dies the summer wind after a fearful storm. Awed and wonderstruck the organ boy looked at Katy as she played, almost forgetting his part of the performance in his amazement, and saying to himself when she had finished,

"Guy, ain't she a brick?" and whispering to her, "Didn't we go that strong?"

The people had wondered where Helen was, as, without the aid of music, Katy led the children in their carols, and this wonder increased when it was whispered round that "Miss Lennox had come, and was standing with a *man* back by the register."

After this Aunt Betsy grew very calm, and could enjoy the distributing of the gifts, going up herself two or three times, and wondering why anybody should think of *her,* a good-for-nothing old woman. The skates and the smelling bottle both went safely to Sylvia and John, while Mrs. Deacon Bannister looked radiant when her name was called and she was made the recipient of a jar of butternut pickles, such as only Aunt Betsy Barlow could make.

"*Miss Helen Lennox.* A soldier in uniform, from one of her Sunday-school scholars,"

The words rang out loud and clear, as the Rector held up the sugar toy before the amused audience, who turned to look at Helen, blushing so painfully, and trying to hold back the man in a soldier's dress who went quietly up the aisle, receiving the gift with a bow and smile which turned the heads of half the ladies near him, and then went back to Helen, to whom he whispered something which made her cheeks grow brighter than they were before, while she dropped her eyes modestly.

"Who is he?" a woman asked, touching Aunt Betsy's shoulder.

"Captain Ray, from New York," was the answer, as Aunt Betsy gave to her dress a little broader sweep, and smoothed the bow she had tried to tie beneath her chin, just as Mattie Tubbs had tied it on the memorable opera night.

The tree, by this time, was nearly empty. Every child had been remembered, save one, and that the organ boy, who, separated from his companions, stood near Helen, watching the tree wistfully, while shadows of hope and disappointment passed alternately over his face, as one after another the presents were distributed and nothing came to him.

"There ain't a darned thing on it for me," he exclaimed at last, when boy nature could endure no longer; and Mark turned towards him just in time to see the gathering mist, which but for the most heroic efforts would have merged into tears.

"Poor Billy!" Helen said, as she too heard his comment, "I fear he *has* been forgotten. His teacher is absent, and he so faithful at the organ too."

Mark knew now who the boy was, and after a hurried consultation with Helen, who suggested that *money* would probably be more acceptable than even skates or jackknives, neither of which were possible now, folded something in a bit of paper, on which he wrote a name, and then sent it to the Rector.

"Billy Brown, our faithful organ boy," sounded through the church; and with a brightened face Billy went up the aisle and received the little package, ascertaining before he reached his standpoint near the door, that he was the owner of a five dollar bill, and mentally deciding to add both peanuts and molasses candy to the stock of apples he daily carried into the cars.

"*You* gin me this," he said, nodding to Mark, "and you," turning to Helen, "poked him up to it."

"Well then, if I did," Mark replied, laying his hand on the boy's coarse hair, "you must take good care of Miss Lennox when I am gone. I leave her in your charge. She is to be my wife."

"Gorry, I thought so;" and Bill's cap went towards the plastering, just as the last string of pop-corn was given from the tree, and the exercises were about to close.

It was not in Aunt Betsy's nature to keep her secret till this time; and simultaneously with Billy's going up for his gift, she whispered it to her neighbor, who whispered it to hers, who whispered it to hers, until nearly all the audience knew of it, and kept their seats after the benediction was pronounced.

At a sign from the rector, Katy went with her mother to the altar, followed by Uncle Ephraim, his wife, and Aunt Betsy, while Helen, throwing off the cloud she had worn upon her head, and giving it, with her cloak and fur, into Billy's charge, took Mark's arm, and with beating heart and burning cheeks passed between the sea of eyes fixed so curiously upon her, up to where Katy once stood on the June morning, when she had been the bride. Not now, as then, were aching hearts present at the bridal. No Marian Hazelton fainted by the door; no Morris felt the world grow dark and desolate as the marriage vows were spoken; and no sister doubted if it were all right and would end in happiness.

The ceremony lasted but a few moments, and then the astonished audience pressed around the bride, offering their kindly congratulations, and proving to Mark Ray that the bride he had won was dear to others as well as to himself. Lovingly he drew her hand beneath his arm, fondly he looked down upon her as he led her back to her chair by the register, making her sit down while he tied on her cloak, and adjusted the fur about her neck.

"Handy and gentle as a woman," was the verdict pronounced upon him by the female portion of the congregation, as they passed out into the street, talking of the ceremony, and contrasting Helen's husband with the haughty Wilford, who was not a favorite with them.

It was Billy Brown who brought Mark's cutter round, and held the reins, while Mark helped Helen in, and then he tucked the buffalo robes about her with the remark, "It's all-fired cold, Miss Ray. Shall you play in church to-morrow?"

Assured that she would, Billy walked away, and Mark was alone with his bride, and slowly following the deacon's sleigh, which reached the farm-house a long time before the little cutter, so that a fire was already kindled in the parlor when Helen arrived, and also in the kitchen stove, where the tea-kettle was boiling; for Aunt Betsy said "the chap should have some supper before he went back to York."

Four hours he had to stay, and they were spent in talking of himself, of Wilford, and of Morris, and in planning Helen's future. Of course she would spend a portion of her time at the farm-house, he said; but his mother had a claim upon her, and it was his wish that she should be in New York as much as possible.

Swiftly the last moments went by, and a "Merry Christmas" was said by one and another as they took their seats at the plentiful repast Aunt Betsy had provided, Mark feasting more on Helen's face than on the viands spread before him. It was hard for him to leave her, hard for her to let him go; but the duty was imperative, and so when at last the frosty air grew keener as the small hours of night crept on, he stood with his arms about her, nor thought it unworthy of a soldier that his own tears mingled with hers, as he bade her good-bye, kissing her again and again, and calling her his precious wife, whose memory would make his camp life brighter, and shorten the days of absence. There was no one with them, when at last Mark's horse dashed from the yard over the creaking snow, leaving Helen alone upon the doorstep, with the glittering stars shining above her head, and her husband's farewell kiss wet upon her lips.

"When shall we meet again?" she sobbed, gazing up at the clear blue sky, as if to find the answer there.

But only the December wind sweeping down from the steep hillside, and blowing across her forehead, made reply to that questioning, as she waited till the last faint sound of Mark Ray's bells died away in the distance, and then, shivering with cold, re-entered the farmhouse.

CHAPTER XLII.

AFTER CHRISTMAS EVE.

MERRILY rang the bells next day, but Helen's heart was very sad as she met the smiling faces of her friends, and Mark had never been prayed for more earnestly than on that Christmas morning, when Helen knelt at the altar rail, and received the sacred symbols of a Saviour's dying love, asking that God would keep the soldier husband, hastening on to New York, and from thence to Washington. Much the Silvertonians discussed the wedding, and had Helen been the queen, she could hardly have been stared at more curiously than she was that Christmas day, when late in the afternoon she drove through the town with Katy, the villagers looking admiringly after her, noting the tie of her bonnet, the arrangement of her face trimmings, and discovering in both style and fitness they had never discovered before. As the wife of Mark Ray, Helen became suddenly a heroine, in whose presence poor Katy subsided completely; nor was the interest at all diminished when, two days later, Mrs. Banker came to Silverton and was met at the depot by Helen, whom she hugged affectionately, calling her "my dear daughter," and holding her hand all the way to the covered sleigh waiting there for her.

Mrs. Banker was very fond of Helen; and not even the sight of the farm-house, with its unpolished inmates, awakened a feeling of regret that her only son had not looked higher for a wife. She was satisfied with her new daughter, and insisted upon taking her back to New York.

"I am very lonely now, lonelier than you can possibly be," she said to Mrs. Lennox, "and you will not refuse her to me for a few weeks at least. It will do us both good, and make the time of Mark's absence so much shorter."

"Yes, mother, let Helen go. I will try to fill her place," Katy said, though while she said it her heart throbbed with pain and dread as she thought how desolate she should be without her sister.

But it was right, and Katy urged Helen's going, bearing up bravely so long as Helen was in sight, but shedding bitter tears when at last she was gone, tears which were only stayed when kind old Uncle Ephraim offered to take her to the little grave, where, from experience, he knew she always found rest and peace. The winter snows were on it now, but Katy knew just where the daisies were, and the blue violets which with the spring would bloom again, feeling comforted as she thought of that eternal spring in the bright world above, where her child had gone. And so that night, when they gathered again around the fire in the pleasant little parlor, the mother and the old people did not miss Helen half so much as they had feared they might, for Katy sang her sweetest songs and wore her sunniest smile, while she told them of Helen's new home, and talked of whatever else she thought would interest and please them.

"Little Sunbeam," Uncle Ephraim called her now, instead of "Katy-did," and in his prayer that first night of Helen's absence he asked, in his touching way, "that God would bless his little Sunbeam, and not let her grow tired of living there alone with folks so odd and old."

*   *   *   *   *   *

"MARRIED—On Christmas Eve, at St. John's Church, Silverton, Mass., by the Rev. Mr. Kelly, Capt. MARK RAY, of the —th Regiment, N. Y. S. Vols., to MISS HELEN LENNOX, of Silverton."

The Cameron Pride. 347

Such was the announcement which appeared in several of the New York papers two days after Christmas, and such the announcement which Bell Cameron read at the breakfast table on the morning of the day when Mrs. Banker started for Silverton.

"Here is something which will perhaps interest *you*," she said, passing the paper to Juno, who had come down late, and was looking cross and jaded from the effects of last night's dissipation.

Taking the paper from her sister's hand, Juno glanced at the paragraph indicated by Bell; then, as she caught Mark's name, she glanced again with a startled, incredulous look, her cheeks and lips turning white as she read that Mark Ray was lost to her forever, and that in spite of the stolen letter Helen Lennox was his wife.

"What is it, Juno?" Mrs. Cameron asked, noticing her daughter's agitation.

Juno told her what it was, and then handing her the paper let her read it for herself.

"Impossible! there is some mistake! How was it brought about?" Mrs. Cameron said, darting a curious glance at Bell, whose face betrayed nothing as she leisurely sipped her coffee and remarked, "I always thought it would come to this, for I knew he liked her. It is a splendid match."

Whatever Juno thought she kept it to herself, just as she kept her room the entire day, complaining of a racking headache, and ordering the curtains to be dropped, as the light hurt her eyes, she said to Bell, who, really pitying her now, never suggested that the darkened room was more to hide her tears than to save her eyes, and who sent away all callers with the message that Juno was sick—all but Sybil Grandon, who insisted so hard upon seeing her *dear friend* that she was admitted to Juno's room, talking at once of the wedding, and making every one of Juno's nerves quiver with pain as she descanted upon the splendid match it was for Helen, or indeed for any girl.

"I had given you to him," she said, "but I see I was mistaken. It was Helen he preferred, unless you jilted him, as perhaps you did."

Here was a temptation Juno could not resist, and she replied, haughtily,

"I am not one to boast of conquests, but ask Captain Ray himself if you wish to know why I did not marry him."

Sybil Grandon was not deceived, but she good-naturedly suffered that young lady to hope she was, and answered, laughingly, "I can't say I honor your judgment in refusing him, but you know best. However, I trust that will not prevent your friendly advances towards his bride. Mrs. Banker has gone after her, I understand, and I want you to call with me as soon as convenient. *Mrs. Mark Ray* will be the belle of the season, depend upon it," and gathering up her furs Mrs. Grandon kissed Juno affectionately and then swept from the room.

That Mrs. Cameron had hunted for and failed to find the stolen letter, and that she associated its disappearance with Mark Ray's sudden marriage, Bell was very sure, from the dark, anxious look upon her face when she came from her room, whither she had repaired immediately after breakfast; but whatever her suspicions were, they did not find form in words. Mark was lost. It was too late to help that now, and as a politic woman of the world, Mrs. Cameron decided to let the matter rest, and by *patronizing* the young bride prove that she had never thought of Mark Ray for her son-in-law. Hence it was that the Cameron carriage and the Grandon carriage stood together before Mrs. Banker's door, while the ladies who had come in the carriages paid their respects to Mrs. Ray, rallying her upon the march she had stolen upon them, telling her how delighted they were to have her back again, and hoping they should see each other a great deal during the coming winter.

The Camerons and Sybil Grandon were not alone in calling upon the bride. Those who had liked Helen Lennox did not find her less desirable now that she was Helen Ray, and numberless were the attentions bestowed upon her and the invitations she received.

But with few exceptions Helen declined the latter, feeling that with her husband in so much danger, it was better not to mingle in gay society. She was very happy with Mrs. Banker, who petted and caressed and loved her almost as much as if she had been her own daughter. Mark's letters, too, which came nearly every day, were bright sun-spots in her existence, so full were they of tender love and kind thoughtfulness for her. He was very happy, he wrote, in knowing that at home there was a dear little brown-haired wife, waiting and praying for him, and but for the separation from her he was well content with a soldier's life. Once Helen thought seriously of going to him for a week or more, but the project was prevented by the sudden arrival in New York of Katy, who came one night to Mrs. Banker's, with her face as white as ashes, and a wild expression in her eyes as she said to Helen,

"I am going to Wilford. He is dying. He has sent for me. I ought to go on to-night, but cannot, my head aches so," and pressing both her hands upon her head Katy sank fainting into Helen's arms.

CHAPTER XLIII.

GEORGETOWN HOSPITAL.

GEORGETOWN, February—, 1862.

MRS. WILFORD CAMERON:

Your husband cannot live long. Come immediately.

M. HAZELTON."

So read the telegram received by Katy one winter morning, and which stunned her for a few minutes so that she could neither feel nor think. But the reaction came soon enough, bringing with it only the remembrance of Wilford's love. All the wrong, the harshness, was forgotten, and only the desire remained to fly at once to Wilford. Bravely she kept up until New York was reached, when the tension of her nerves gave way, and she fainted, as we have seen.

At Father Cameron's a telegram had been received, telling of Wilford's danger. But the mother could not go to him. A lung difficulty, to which she was subject, had confined her to the house for many days, and so it was the father and Bell who made their hasty preparations for the hurried journey to Georgetown. They heard of Katy's arrival, and Bell came at once to see her.

"She will not be able to join us to-morrow," was the report Bell carried home, for she saw more than mere exhaustion in the white face lying so motionless on Helen's pillow, with the dark rings about the eyes, and the quiver of the muscles about the mouth.

"It is very hard, but God knows best," poor Katy moaned, when the next day her father and Bell went without her.

"Yes, darling, God knows best," Helen answered, smoothing the bright hair, and thinking sadly of the young officer sitting by his camp-fire, and waiting so eagerly for the bride who could not go to him now. "God knows what is best, and does all for the best."

Katy said it many times that long, long week, during which she stayed with Helen, living from day to day upon the letters sent by Bell, who gave but little hope that Wilford would recover. Not a word did she say of Marian, and only twice did she mention Morris, who was one of the physicians in that hospital, so that when at last Katy was strong enough to venture on the journey, she had but little idea of what had transpired in Wilford's sick room.

Those were sad, weary days which Wilford first passed upon his hospital cot, and as he was not sick but crippled, he had ample time for reviewing the past, which came up before his mind as vividly as if he had been living again the scenes of bygone days. Of Katy he thought continually, repenting of his rashness, and wishing so much that the past could be undone. Disgusted with soldier life, he had wished himself at home a thousand times, but never by a word had he admitted such a wish to any living being, and when, on the dark, rainy afternoon which first saw him in the hospital, he turned his face to the wall and wept, he replied to one who said to him soothingly,

"Don't feel badly, my young friend. We will take as good care of you here as if you were at home."

"It's the pain which brings the tears. I'd as soon be here as at home."

Gradually, however, there came a change, and Wilford grew softer in his feelings, half resolving to send for Katy, who had offered to come, and to whom he had replied, "It is not necessary." But as often as he resolved, his evil genius whispered, "She does not care to come," and so the message was never sent, while the longing for home faces brought on a nervous fever, which made him so irritable that his attendants turned from him in disgust, thinking him the most unreasonable man they ever met with. Once he dreamed Genevra was there—that her fingers threaded his hair as they used to do in the happy days at Brighton—that her hand was on his brow, her breath upon his face, and with a start he awoke, just as the rustle of female garments died away in the hall.

"The nurse in the second ward has been in here," a comrade said. "She seemed specially interested in you, and if she had not been a stranger, I should have said she was crying over you."

With a quick, sudden movement, Wilford put his hand to his cheek, where there was a tear, either his own or that of the "nurse," who had recently bent over him. Retaining the same proud reserve which had characterized his whole life, he asked no questions, but listened to what his companions were saying of the beauty and tenderness of the "young girl," as they called her, who had glided for a few moments into their presence, winning their hearts in that short space of time, and making them wish she would come back again. Wilford wished so too, conjuring up all sorts of conjectures about the unknown nurse, and once going so far as to fancy it was Katy herself. But Katy would hardly venture there as nurse, and if she did she would not keep aloof from him. It was not Katy, and if not, who was it that twice when he was sleeping came and looked at him, his comrades said, rallying him upon the conquest he had made, and so exciting his imagination that the fever began to increase, and the blood throbbed hotly through his veins, while his brows were knit together with thoughts of the mysterious stranger. Then, with a great shock it occurred to him that Katy had affirmed, "*Genevra* is alive."

What if it were so, and this nurse were Genevra? The very idea fired Wilford's brain, and when next his physician came he looked with alarm upon the great change for the worse exhibited by his patient.

"Shall I send for your friends?" he asked, and Wilford answered, savagely,

"I have no friends—none at least, but what will be glad to know I'm dead."

And that was the last, except the wild words of a maniac, which came from Wilford's lips for many a day and night. When they said he was unconscious, Marian Hazelton obtained permission to attend him, and again the eyes of the other occupants of the room were turned wonderingly towards her as she bent over the sick man, parting his matted hair, smoothing his pillow, and holding the cooling draught to the parched lips which muttered strange things of Brighton, of Alnwick and Rome—of the heather on the Scottish moors, and the daisies on Genevra's grave, where Katy once sat down.

"She did not know Genevra was there," he said; "but I knew, and I felt as if the dead were wronged by that act of Katy's. Do *you* know Katy?" and his black eyes fastened upon Marian, who soothed him into quiet, while she talked to him of Katy, telling of her graceful beauty, her loving heart, and the sorrow she would feel when she heard how sick he was.

"Shall I send for her?" she asked, but Wilford answered,

"No, I am satisfied with you."

This was her first day with him, but there were other days when all her strength, and that of Morris, who, at her earnest solicitation, came to her aid, was required to keep him on his bed. He was going home, he said, going to Katy; and like a giant he writhed under a force superior to his own, and which held him down and controlled him, while his loud outcries filled the building, and sent a shudder to the hearts of those who heard them. As the two men, who at first had occupied the room with him, were well enough to leave for home, Marian and Morris both begged that, unless absolutely necessary, no other one should be sent to that small apartment, where all the air was needed for the patient in their charge. And thus the room was left alone for Wilford, who grew worse so fast that Marian telegraphed to Katy, bidding her come at once.

*   *   *   *   *   *

Slowly the wintry night was passing, the fifth since Marian's message was sent to Katy, and Morris sat by Wilford's cot, when suddenly he met Wilford's eyes fixed upon him with a look of recognition he could not mistake.

"Do you know me?" he asked so kindly, and with so much of genuine sympathy in his voice, that the heavy eyelids quivered for an instant, as Wilford nodded his head, and whispered,

"Dr. Grant."

There had been a momentary flash of resentment when he saw the watcher beside him, but Wilford was too weak, too helpless to cherish that feeling long, and besides there were floating through his still bewildered mind visions of some friendly hand, which had ministered to him daily— of a voice and form, distinct from the one he thought an angel's, and which was not there now with him. That voice, that form, he felt sure belonged to Morris Grant, and remembering his past harshness toward him, a chord of gratitude was touched, and when Morris took his hand he did not at once withdraw it, but let his long, white fingers cling around the warm, vigorous ones, which seemed to impart new life and strength.

"You have been very sick," Morris said, anticipating the question Wilford would ask. "You are very sick still, and at the request of your nurse I came to attend you."

A pressure of the hand was Wilford's reply, and then

there was silence between them, while Wilford mastered all his pride, and with quivering lips whispered,

"*Katy!*"

"We have sent for her. We expect her every train," Morris replied, and Wilford asked,

"Who has been with me—the nurse, I mean? Who is she?"

Morris hesitated a moment, and then said,

"Marian Hazelton."

"I know—yes," Wilford replied, having no suspicion as to *who* was standing outside his door, and listening, with a throbbing heart, to his rational questions.

In all their vigils held together no sign had ever passed from Dr. Grant to Marian that he knew her, but he had waited anxiously for this moment, knowing that Wilford must not be shocked, as a sight of Marian would shock him. He knew she was outside the door, and as Wilford turned his head upon the pillow, he went to her, and leading her to a safe distance, said softly,

"His reason has returned."

"And my services are ended," Marian rejoined, looking him steadily in the face, but not in the least prepared for his affirmative question.

"You are *Genevra Lambert?*"

There was a low, gasping sound of surprise, and Marian staggered forward a step or too, then steadying herself, she said.

"And if I am, it surely is not best for him to see me. You would not advise it?"

She looked wistfully at Morris, the great desire to be recognized, to be spoken to kindly by the man who once had been her husband overmastering for a moment all her prudence.

"It would not be best, both for his sake and *Katy's*," Morris said, and with a moan like the dying out of her last hope, Marian turned away, her eyes dim with tears and her heart heavy with a sense of something lost, as in the gray dawn of the morning she went back to her former patients, who hailed her coming with childish joy, one fair young boy from the Granite hills kissing the hand which bandaged his poor crushed arm so tenderly, and thanking her that she had returned to him again.

*   *   *   *   *   *

" Mr. J. Cameron, Miss Bell Cameron," were the names on the cards sent to Dr. Grant late that afternoon, and in a few moments he was with the father and sister who asked so anxiously for Wilford and explained why Katy was not with them.

Wilford was sleeping when they entered his room, his face looking so worn and thin, and his hands folded so helplessly upon his breast, that with a gush of tears Bell knelt beside him, and laying her warm cheek against his bony one, woke him with her sobs. For a moment he seemed bewildered, then recognizing her, he raised his feeble arm and winding it about her neck, kissed her more tenderly than he had ever done before. He had not been demonstrative of his affection for his sisters. But Bell was his favorite, and he held her close to him while his eyes moved past his father, whom he did not see, on to the door as if in quest of someone. It was Katy, and guessing his thoughts, Bell said,

" She is not here. She could not come now. She is sick in New York, but will join us in a few days."

There was a look of intense disappointment in Wilford's face, which even his father's warm greeting could not dissipate, and Morris saw the great tears as they dropped upon the pillow, the proud man trying hard to repress them, and asking no questions concerning any one at home. He was too weak to talk, but he held Bell's hand in his as if afraid that she would leave him, while his eyes rested alternately upon her face and that of his father, who, wholly unmanned at the fearful change in his son, laid his head upon the bed and cried aloud.

Next morning Bell was very white and her voice trembled as she came from a conference with Dr. Morris, who had told her that her brother would die.

" He may live a week, and he may not," he said, adding solemnly, " As his sister you will tell him of his danger, while there is time to seek the refuge without which death is terrible."

"Oh, if I could only pray with and for him!" Bell thought, as she went to her brother, mourning her mis-spent days, and feeling her courage giving way when at last she stood in his presence and met his kindly smile.

"I dreamed that you were not here after all," he said, "I am so glad to find it real. How long before I can go home, do you suppose?"

He had stumbled upon the very thing Bell was there to talk about, his question indicating that he had no sus-picion of the truth. Nor had he; and it came like a thunderbolt when Bell, forgetting all her prudence, said impetuously,

"Oh, Wilford, maybe you'll never go home. Maybe you'll——"

"*Not die*," Wilford exclaimed, clasping his hands with sudden emotion. "Not die—you don't mean that? Who told you so?"

"Dr. Grant," was Bell's reply, which brought a fierce frown to Wilford's face, and awoke all the angry passions of his heart.

"Dr. Grant," he repeated. "He would like me re-moved from his path; but it shall not be. I will not die. Tell him that. I will not die," and Wilford's voice was hoarse with passion as he raised his clenched fists in the air.

He was terribly excited, and in her fright Bell ran for Dr. Grant. But Wilford motioned him back, hurling after him words which kept him from the room the entire day, while the sick man rolled, and tossed, and raved in the delirium, which had returned, and which wore him out so fast. No one had the least influence over him, except Marian Hazelton, who, without a glance at Mr. Cameron or Bell, glided to his side, and with her presence and gentle words soothed him into comparative quiet, so that the bitter denunciations against the *saint*, who wanted him to die, ceased, and he fell into a troubled sleep.

With a strange feeling of interest Mr. Cameron and Bell watched her, wondering if she were indeed Genevra, as Katy had affirmed. They would not ask her; and

Both breathed more freely when, with a bow in acknowledgment of Mr. Cameron's compliment to her skill in quieting his son, she left the room.

That night they watched with Wilford, who slept off his delirium, and lay with his face turned from them, so that they could not guess by its expression what was passing in his mind.

All the next day he maintained the most frigid silence, answering only in monosyllables, while Bell kept wiping away the great drops of sweat constantly oozing out upon his forehead and about the pallid lips.

Just at nightfall he startled Bell by asking that Dr. Grant be sent for.

"Please leave me alone with him," he said, when Dr. Morris came; then turning to Morris, as the door closed upon his father and his sister, he said abruptly,

"Pray for me, if you can pray for one who yesterday hated you so for saying he must die."

Earnestly, fervently, Morris prayed, as for a dear brother; and when he finished, Wilford's faint "Amen" sounded through the room.

"I am not right yet," the pale lips whispered, as Morris sat down beside him. "Not right with God, I mean. I've sometimes said there was no God; but I did not believe it; and now I know there is. He has been moving upon me all the day, driving out my bitterness toward you, and causing me to send for you at last. Do you think there is hope for me? I have much to be forgiven."

"Though your sins be as scarlet, they shall be white as snow," Morris replied; and then he tried to point that erring man to the Lamb of God, who taketh away the sins of the world, convincing him that there *was* hope even for him, and leaving him with the conviction that God would surely finish the good work begun, nor suffer this soul to be lost which had turned to Him at the eleventh hour.

Wilford knew his days were numbered, and he talked freely of it to his father and sister the next morning when they came to him. He did not say that he was ready or willing to die, only that he must, and he asked them to forget, when he was gone, all that had ever been amiss in him as a son and brother.

"I was too proud, too selfish, to make others happy," he said, "I thought it all over yesterday, and the past came back again so vividly, especially the part connected with Katy. Oh, Katy, I did abuse her!" and a bitter sob attested the genuineness of Wilford's grief for his treatment of Katy. "I despised her family, I treated them with contempt. I broke Katy's heart, and now I must die without telling her I am sorry. But you'll tell her, Bell, how I tried to pray, but could not for thoughts of my sin to her. She will not be glad that I am dead. I know her better than to think that; and I believe she loves me. But, after I am gone, and the duties of the world have closed up the gap I shall leave, I see a brighter future for her than her past has been; and you may tell her I am——" He could not say, "I am willing." Few husbands could have done so then, and he was not an exception.

Wholly exhausted, he lay quiet for a moment, and when he spoke again, it was of *Genevra*. Even here he did not try to screen himself. He was the one to blame, he said, Genevra was true, was innocent, as he ascertained too late.

"Would you like to see her, if she was living?" came to Bell's lips; but the fear that it would be too great a shock, prevented their utterance.

He had no suspicion of her presence; and it was best he should not. Katy was the one uppermost in his mind; and in the letter Bell sent to her next day, he tried to write, "Good-bye, my darling;" but the words were scarcely legible, and his nerveless hand fell helpless at his side as he said,

"She will never know the effort it cost me, nor hear me say that I hope I am forgiven. It came to me last night; and now the way is not so dark, but Katy will not know."

CHAPTER · XLIV.

LAST HOURS.

KATY *would know;* for she was coming at last. A tele-gram had announced that she was on the road; and with nervous restlessness Wilford asked repeatedly what time it was, reducing the hours to minutes, and counting his own pulses to see if he could last so long.

"Save me, Doctor," he whispered to Morris, "keep me alive till Katy comes. I must see Katy again."

And Morris, tenderer than a brother, did all he could to keep the feeble breath from going out ere Katy came.

The train was due at five; but it was dark in the hos-pital, and from every window a light was shining, when Morris carried, rather than led, a quivering figure up the stairs and through the hall to the room where the Cam-erons were, the father standing at the foot of Wilford's bed, and Bell bending over his pillow, administering the stimulants which kept her brother alive. When Katy came in, she moved away, as did her father, while Morris too stepped back into the hall; and thus the husband and wife were left alone.

"Katy, precious Katy, you have forgiven me?" Wil-ford whispered, and the rain of tears and kisses on his face was Katy's answer as she hung over him.

She had forgiven him, and she told him so when she found voice to talk, wondering to find him so changed from the proud, exacting, self-worshiping man to the humble, repentant and self-accusing person, who took all blame of the past to himself, and exonerated her from every fault. But when he drew her close to him, and whispered something in her ear, she knew whence came the change, and a reverent "Thank the good Father," dropped from her lips.

"The way was dark and thorny," Wilford said, making her sit down where he could see her as he talked, "and only for God's goodness I should have lost the path. But he sent Morris Grant to point the road, and I trust I am in it now. I wanted to tell you with my own lips how sorry I am for what I have made you suffer; but sorriest of all for sending Baby away. Oh, Katy, you do not know how that rested upon my conscience. Forgive me, Katy, that I robbed you of your child."

He was growing very weak, and he looked so white and ghastly that Katy called for Bell, who came with her father, and the three stood together around the bedside of the dying.

"You will remember me, Katy," he said, "but you cannot mourn for me always, and sometime in the future you will cease to be my *widow,* and, Katy, I am willing. I wanted to tell you this, so that no thought of me should keep you from a life where you will be happier than I have made you."

Wholly bewildered, Katy made no reply, and Wilford was silent a few moments, in which he seemed partially asleep. Then rousing up, he said,

"You said once that Genevra was not dead. Did you mean it, Katy?"

Frightened and bewildered, Katy turned appealingly to her father-in-law, who answered for her, "She meant it—Genevra is not dead," while a blood-red flush stained Wilford's face, and his fingers beat the bedspread thoughtfully.

"I fancied once that she was here—that she was the nurse the boys praise so much. But that was a delusion," he said, and without a thought of the result, Katy asked impetuously, "if she were here would you care to see her?"

There was a startled look on Wilford's face, and he grasped Katy's hand nervously, his frame trembling with a dread of the great shock which he felt impending over him.

"Is she here? Was the nurse Genevra?" he asked. Then, as his mind went back to the past, he answered his own question by asserting "Marian Hazelton is Genevra."

They did not contradict him, nor did he ask to see her.

With Katy there he felt he had better not; but after a moment he continued, "It is all so strange. I thought her dead. I do not comprehend how it can be. She has been kind to me. Tell her I thank her for it. I was unjust to her. I have much to answer for."

Between each word he uttered there was a gasp for breath, and Father Cameron opened the window to admit the cool night air. But nothing had power to revive him. He was going very fast, Morris said, as he took his stand by the bedside and watched the approach of death. There were no convulsive struggles, only heavy breathings, which grew farther and farther apart, until at last Wilford drew Katy close to him, and winding his arm around her neck, whispered,

"I am almost home, my darling, and all is well. Be kind to Genevra for my sake. I loved her once, but not as I love you."

He never spoke again, and a few minutes later Morris led Katy from the room, and then went out to give orders for the embalming.

* * * * * * *

In the little room she called her own, Marian Hazelton sat, her beautiful hair disordered, and her eyes dim with the tears she had shed. She knew that Wilford was dead, and as if his dying had brought back all her olden love she wept bitterly for the man who had so darkened her life. She had not expected to see him with Katy present; but now that it was over she might go to him. There could be no harm in that. No one but Morris would know who she was, she thought, when there came a timid knock upon her door, and Katy entered, her face very pale, and her manner very calm, as she came to Marian, and kneeling down beside her, laid her head in her lap with the air of a weary child who has sought its mother for rest.

"Poor little Katy!" Marian said; "your husband, they tell me, is dead."

"Yes;" and Katy lifted up her head, and fixing her eyes earnestly upon Marian, continued, "Wilford is dead,

but before he died he left a message for *Genevra Lambert.*
Will she hear it now?"

With a sudden start Marian sprang to her feet, and demanded, "Who told *you* of Genevra Lambert?"

"Wilford told me months ago, showing me her picture,
which I readily recognized, and I have pitied you so
much, knowing you were innocent. Wilford thought you
were dead," Katy said, flinching a little before Marian's
burning gaze, which fascinated even while it startled her.

It is not often that two women meet bearing to each
other the relations these two bore, and it is not strange
that both felt constrained and embarrassed as they stood
looking at each other. As Marian's was the stronger
nature, so she was the first to rally, and with the tears
swimming in her eyes she drew Katy closely to her, and
said,

"Now that he is gone I am glad you know it. Mine
has been a sad life, but God has helped me to bear it.
You say he believed me dead. Sometime I will tell you
how that came about; but now, his message,—he left one,
you say?"

Carefully Katy repeated every word Wilford had said,
and with a gasping cry Marian wound her arms around
her neck, exclaiming,

"And you *will* love me, because I have suffered so
much. You will let me call you Katy when we are alone.
It brings you nearer to me."

Marian was now the weaker of the two, and it was
Katy's task to comfort her, as sinking back in her chair
she sobbed,

"He did love me once. He acknowledged it at the last,
before them all, his wife, his father and his sister. Do
they know?" she suddenly asked, and when assured that
they did, she relapsed into a silent mood, while Katy stole
quietly out and left her there alone.

Half an hour later and a female form passed hurriedly
through the hall and across the threshold into the chamber where the dead man lay. There was no one with him
now, and Marian was free to weep out the pent-up sorrow
of her life, which she did with choking sobs and passionate words poured into the ear, deaf to every human

sound. A step upon the floor startled her, and turning round she stood face to face with Wilford's father, who was regarding her with a look which she mistook for one of reproof and displeasure that she should be there.

"Forgive me," she said; "he was my husband once, and surely now that he is dead you will not begrudge me a few last moments with him for the sake of the days when he loved me."

There were many tender chords in the heart of Father Cameron, and offering Marian his hand, he said,

"Far be it from me to refuse you this privilege. I pity you, Genevra; I believe he dealt unjustly by you,—but I will not censure him now that he is gone. He was my only boy. Oh, Wilford, Wilford! you have left me very lonely."

He released her hand, and Marian fled away, meeting next with Bell, who felt that she must speak to her, but was puzzled what to say. Bell could not define her feelings towards Marian, or why she shrunk from approaching her. It was not pride, but rather a feeling of prejudice, as if Marian were in some way to blame for all the trouble which had come to them, while her peculiar position as the divorced wife of her brother made it the more embarrassing. But she could not resist the mute pleading of the eyes lifted so tearfully to her, as if asking for a nod of recognition, and stopping before her she said, softly,

"*Genevra.*"

That was all, but it made Genevra's tears flow in torrents, and she involuntarily held her hand out to Bell, who took it, and holding it between her own, said,

"You were very kind to my brother. I thank you for it, and will tell my mother, who will feel so grateful to you."

This was a good deal for Bell to say, and after it was said, she hastened away while Marian went on her daily round of duties, speaking softer if possible to her patients that day, and causing them to wonder what had come over that sweet face to make it so white and tear-stained. That night in Marian's room Katy sat and listened to what she did not before know of the strange story kept from her so long. Marian confirmed all Wilford had

told, breathing no word of blame against him now that
he was dead, only stating facts, and leaving Katy to
draw her own conclusions.

"I knew that I was handsome," she said, "and I
liked to test my power; but for that weakness I have been
sorely punished. I had not at first any intention of making him believe that I was dead, and when I sent the
paper containing the announcement of father's death, I
was not aware that it also contained the death of my
cousin, a beautiful girl just my age, who bore our grand-
mother's name of Genevra, and about whom and a young
English lord, who had hunted one season in her father's
neighborhood, there were some scandalous reports. Afterwards it occurred to me that Wilford would see that notice,
and naturally think it referred to me, inasmuch as he knew
nothing of my cousin Genevra.

"It was just as well, I said—I *was* dead to him, and I
took a strange satisfaction in wondering if he would care.
Incidentally I heard that the postmaster at Alnwick had
been written to by an American gentleman, who asked if
such a person as *Genevra Lambert* was buried at St.
Mary's; and then I knew he believed me dead, even though
the name appended to the letter was not Wilford Cameron, nor was the writing his; for, as the cousin of the
dead Genevra, I asked to see the letter, and my request was
granted. It was Mrs. Cameron who wrote it, I am sure,
signing a feigned name and bidding the postmaster answer to that address. He did so, assuring the inquirer
that Genevra Lambert was buried there, and wondering to
me if the young American who seemed interested in her
could have been a lover of the unfortunate girl.

"I was now alone in the world, for the aunt with
whom my childhood was passed died soon after my father,
and so I went at last to learn a trade on the Isle of
Wight, emigrating from thence to New York, with the
determination in my rebellious heart that sometime, when
it would cut the deepest, I would show myself to the
proud Camerons, whom I so cordially hated. This was
before God had found me, or rather before I had listened
to the still, small voice which took the hard, vindictive
feelings away, and made me feel kindly towards the

mother and sisters when I saw them, as I often used to do, driving gayly by. Wilford was sometimes with them, and the sight of him always sent the hot blood surging through my heart. But the greatest shock I ever had came to me when I heard from your sister of his approaching marriage with you. Those were terrible days that I passed at the farm-house, working on your bridal trousseau; and sometimes I thought it more than I could bear. Had you been other than the little, loving, confiding, trustful girl you were, I must have disclosed the whole, and told that you would not be the first who had stood at the altar with Wilford. But pity for you kept me silent, and you became his wife.

"I loved your baby almost as much as if it had been my own, and when it died there was nothing to bind me to the North, and so I came here, where I hope I have done some good; at least I was here to care for Wilford, and that is a sufficient reward for all the toil which falls to the lot of a hospital nurse. I shall stay until the war is ended, and then go I know not where. It will not be best for us to meet very often, for though we respect each other, neither can forget the past, nor that one was the lawful, the other the divorced wife of the same man. I have loved you, Katy Cameron, for your uniform kindness shown to the poor dressmaker. I shall always love you, but our paths lie widely apart. Your future I can predict, but mine God only knows."

Marian had said all she meant to say, and all Katy came to hear. The latter was to leave in the morning, and when they would meet again neither could tell. Few were the parting words they spoke, for the great common sorrow welling up from their hearts; but when at last they said good-bye, the bond of friendship between them was more strongly cemented than ever, and Katy long remembered Marian's parting words,

"God bless you, Katy Cameron! You have been a bright sun spot in my existence since I first knew you, even though you have stirred some of the worst impulses of my nature. I am a better woman for having known you. God bless you, Katy Cameron!"

CHAPTER XLV.

MOURNING.

THE grand funeral which Mrs. Cameron once had planned for Katy was a reality at last, but the breathless form lying so cold and still in the darkened room at No. — Fifth Avenue, was that of a soldier embalmed—an only son brought back to his father's house amid sadness and tears. They had taken him there rather than to his own house, because it was the wish of his mother, who, however hard and selfish she might be to others, had idolized her son, and mourned for him truly, forgetting in her grief to care how grand the funeral was, and feeling only a passing twinge when told that *Mrs. Lennox* had come from Silverton to pay the last tribute of respect to her late son-in-law. Some little comfort it was to have her boy lauded as a faithful soldier, and to hear the commendations lavished upon him during the time he lay in state, with his uniform around him; but when the whole was over, and in the gray of the wintry afternoon her husband returned from Greenwood, there came over her a feeling of such desolation as she had never known—a feeling which drove her at last to the little room upstairs, where sat a lonely man, his head bowed upon his hands, and his tears dropping silently upon the hearth-stone as he, too, thought of the vacant parlor below and the new grave at Greenwood.

"Oh, husband, comfort me!" fell from her lips as she tottered to her husband, who opened his arms to receive her, forgetting all the years which had made her the cold, proud woman, who needed no sympathy, and remembering only that bright green summer when she was first his bride, and came to him for comfort in every little grievance, just as now she came in this great, crushing sorrow.

He did not tell her she was reaping what she had

sown, that but for her pride and deception concerning Genevra, Wilford might never have gone to the war, or they been without a son. He did not reproach her at all, but soothed her tenderly, calling her by her maiden name, and awkwardly smoothing her hair, silvered now with gray, and feeling for a moment that Wilford had not died in vain, if by his dying he gave back to his father the wife so lost during the many years since fashion and folly had been the idols she worshiped. But the habits of years could not be lightly broken, and Mrs. Cameron's mind soon became absorbed in the richness of her mourning, and the strict etiquette of her mourning days. To Katy she was very kind, caressing her with unwonted affection, and scarcely suffering her to leave her sight, much less to stay for a day at Mrs. Banker's, where Katy secretly preferred to be. Of Genevra, too, she talked with Katy, and at her instigation wrote a friendly letter, thanking *Mrs. Lambert* for all her kindness to her son, expressing her sorrow that she had ever been so unjust to her, and sending her a handsome locket, containing on one side a lock of Wilford's hair, and on the other his picture, taken from a large sized photograph. Mrs. Cameron felt herself a very good woman after she had done all this, together with receiving Mrs. Lennox at her own house, and entertaining her for one whole day; but at heart there was no real change, and as time passed on she gradually fell back into her old ways of thinking, and went no more for comfort to her husband as she had on that first night after the burial.

With Mr. Cameron the blow struck deeper, and his Wall Street friends talked together of the old man he had grown since Wilford died, while Katy often found him bending over his long-neglected Bible, as he sat alone in his room at night. And when at last she ventured to speak to him upon the all important subject, he put his hand in hers, and bade her teach him the narrow way which she had found, and wherein Wilford too had walked at the very last, they hoped.

For many weeks Katy lingered in New York, and the June roses were blooming when she went back to Silverton, a widow and the rightful owner of all Wilford's ample fortune. They had found among his papers a will, drawn up and executed not long before his illness, and in which Katy was made his heir, without condition or stipulation All was hers to do with as she pleased, and Katy wept passionately when she heard how generous Wilford had been. Then, as she thought of Marian and the life of poverty before her, she crept to Father Cameron's side, and said to him, pleadingly,

"Let *Genevra* share it with me. She needs it quite as much."

Father Cameron would not permit Katy to divide equally with Marian. It was not just, he said; but he did not object to a few thousands going to her, and before Katy left New York for Silverton, she wrote a long, kind letter to Marian, presenting her with ten thousand dollars, which she begged her to accept, not so much as a gift, but as her rightful due. There was a moment's hesitancy on the part of Marian when she read the letter, a feeling that she could not take so much from Katy; but when she looked at the pale sufferers around her, and remembered how many wretched hearts that money would help to cheer, she said,

"I will keep it."

CHAPTER XLVI.

PRISONERS OF WAR.

THE heat, the smoke, the thunder of the battle were over, and the fields of Gettysburg were drenched with human blood and covered with the dead and dying. The contest had been fearful, and its results carried sorrow and anguish to many a heart waiting for tidings from the war, and looking so anxiously for the names of the loved ones who, on the anniversary of the day which saw our nation's Independence, lay upon the hills and plains of Gettysburg, their white faces upturned to the summer sky, and wet with the rain drops, which, like tears for the noble dead, the pitying clouds had shed upon them. And nowhere, perhaps, was there a whiter face or a more anxious heart than at the farm-house, where both Helen and her mother-in-law were spending the hot July days. Since the Christmas eve when Helen had watched her husband going from her across the wintry snow, he had not been back, though several times he had made arrangements to do so. Something, however, had always happened to prevent. Once it was sickness which kept him in bed for a week or more; again his regiment was ordered to advance, and the third time it was sent on with others to repel the invaders from Pennsylvanian soil. Bravely through each disappointment Helen bore herself, but her cheek always grew paler and her eye darker in its hue when the evening papers came, and she read what progress our soldiery had made, feeling that a battle was inevitable, and praying so earnestly that Mark Ray might be spared. Then, when the battle was over and up the northern hills came the dreadful story of thousands and thousands slain, there was a fearful look in her eye, and her features were rigid as marble, while the quivering lips could scarcely pray for the great fear tugging at her heart. Mark Ray was not with his men when they came from that terrific onslaught. A dozen had seen him fall, struck down by a rebel ball, and that was all she heard for more than a week, when there came another relay of news.

Captain Mark Ray was a prisoner of war, with several of his own company. An inmate of Libby Prison and a sharer from choice of the apartment where his men were confined. As an officer he was entitled to better quarters; but Mark Ray had a large, warm heart, and he would not desert those who had been so faithful to him, and so he took their fare, and by his genial humor and unwavering cheerfulness kept many a heart from fainting, and made the prison life more bearable than it could have been without him. To young Tom Tubbs, who had enlisted six months before, he was a ministering angel, and many times the poor homesick boy crept to the side of his captain, and laying his burning head in his lap, wept himself to sleep and dreamed he was at home again. The horrors of that prison life have never been told, but Mark bore up manfully, suffering less in mind, perhaps, than did the friends at home, who lived, as it were, a thousand years in that one brief summer while he remained in Richmond.

At last, as the frosty days of October came on, they began to hope he might be exchanged, and Helen's face grew bright again, until one day there came a soiled, half-worn letter, in Mark's own hand-writing. It was the first word received from *him* since his capture in July, and with a cry of joy Helen snatched it from Uncle Ephraim, for she was still at the farm-house, and sitting down upon the doorstep just where she had been standing, read the words which Mark had sent to her. He was very well, he said, and had been all the time, but he pined for home, longing for the dear girl-wife never so dear as now, when separated by so many miles, with prison walls on every side, and an enemy's line between them.

"But be of good cheer, darling," he wrote, "I shall come back to you some time, and life will be all the brighter for what you suffer now. I am so glad my darling consented to be my wife, even though I could stay with her but a moment. The knowing you are really mine makes me happy even here, for I think of you by day, and in my dreams I always hold you in my arms and press you to my heart."

A hint he gave of being sent further south, and then hope died out of Helen's heart.

"I shall never see him again," she said despairingly; and when the message came that Mark had been removed, and that too just at the time when an exchange was constantly expected, she gave him up as lost, feeling almost as much widowed as Katy in her weeds.

Slowly the winter passed away, and the country was rife with stories of our men, daily dying by hundreds, while those who survived were reduced to maniacs or imbeciles. And Helen, as she listened, grew nearly frantic with the sickening suspense. She did not know now where her husband was. He had made several attempts to escape, and with each failure had been removed to safer quarters, so that his chances for being exchanged seemed very far away. Week after week, month after month passed on, until came the memorable battle of the Wilderness, when Lieutenant Bob, as yet unharmed, stood bravely in the thickest of the fight, his tall figure towering above the rest, and his soldier's uniform buttoned over a dark tress of hair, and a face like Bell Cameron's. Lieutenant Bob had taken two or three furloughs; but the one which had left the sweetest, pleasantest memory in his heart, was that of the autumn before, when the crimson leaves of the maple, and the golden tints of the beech, were burning themselves out on the hills of Silverton, where his furlough was mostly passed, and where with Bell Cameron he scoured the length and breadth of Uncle Ephraim's farm, now stopping by the shore of Fairy Point and again sitting for hours on a ledge of rocks, far up the hill, where beneath the softly whispering pines, nodding above their heads, Bell gathered the light-brown cones, and said to him the words he had so thirsted to hear.

Much of Bell's time was passed with Katy, at the farmhouse, and here Lieutenant Reynolds found her, accepting readily of Uncle Ephraim's hearty invitation to remain, and spending his entire vacation there with the exception of three days, given to his family. Perfectly charmed with quaint Aunt Betsy, he flattered and courted her almost as much as he did Bell, but did not take her with him in his long rambles over the hills, or sit with her at night alone in the parlor until the clock struck twelve—a habit which Aunt Betsy greatly disapproved, but overlooked for this once, seeing, as she said, that

" The young leftenant was none of her *kin,* and *Isabel* only a little."

Those were halcyon days which Robert passed at Silverton; but one stood out prominently before him, whether sitting before his camp-fire or plunging into the battle; and that the one when, casting aside all pride and foolish theories, Bell Cameron freely acknowledged her love for the man to whom she had been so long engaged, and paid him back the kisses she had before refused to give.

" I shall be a better soldier for this," Robert had said, as he guided her down the steep ledge of rocks, and with her hand in his, walked slowly back to the farm-house, which, on the morrow, he left to take again his place in the army.

There were no more furloughs for him after that; and the winter passed away, bringing the spring again, when came that battle in the Wilderness, where, like a hero, he fought until, becoming separated from his comrades, he fell into the enemy's hands; and two days after, there sped along the telegraphic wires to New York,

"Lieutenant Robert Reynolds, captured the first day of the battle."

Afterwards came news that Andersonville was his destination, together with many others made prisoners that day.

"It is better than being shot, and a great deal better than being burned, as some of the poor wretches were," Juno said, trying to comfort Bell, who doubted a little her sister's word.

True there was now the shadow of a hope that he might return; but the probabilities were against it; and Bell's face grew almost as white as Helen's, while her eyes acquired that restless, watchful, anxious look which has crept into the eyes of so many sorrowing women, looking away to the southward, where the dear ones were dying.

CHAPTER XLVII.

DOCTOR GRANT.

MORRIS had served out his time as surgeon in the army, had added to it an extra six months; and by his humanity, his skill, and Christian kindness, made for himself a name which would be long remembered by the living to whom he had ministered so carefully; while many a dying soldier had blessed him for pointing out the way which leadeth to the life everlasting; and in many a mourning family his name was a household word, for the good he had done to a dying son and brother. But Morris's hospital work was over. He had gone a little too far, and incurred too much risk, until his own strength had failed; and now, in the month of June, when Linwood was bright with the early summer blossoms, he was coming back with health greatly impaired, and a dark cloud before his vision, so that he could not see how beautiful his home was looking, or gaze into the faces of those who waited so anxiously to welcome their beloved physician. *Blind* some said he was; but the few lines sent to Helen, announcing the day of his arrival, contradicted that report. His eyes were very much diseased, his amanuensis wrote; but he trusted that the pure air of his native hills, and the influence of old scenes and associations would soon effect a cure. "If not too much trouble," he added, "please see that the house is made comfortable, and have John meet me on Friday at the station."

Helen was glad Morris was coming home, for he always did her good; he could comfort her better than any one else, unless it were Katy, whose loving, gentle words of hope were very soothing to her.

"Poor Morris!" she sighed, as she finished his letter, and then took it to the family, who were sitting upon the pleasant piazza, which, at Katy's expense and her own, had been added to the house, and overlooked Fairy Pond and the pleasant hills beyond.

"Morris is coming home," she said. "He will be here on Friday, and he wishes us to see that all things are in order at Linwood for his reception. His eyes are badly diseased, but he hopes that coming back to us will cure him," she added, glancing at Katy, who sat upon a step of the piazza, her hands folded together upon her lap, and her blue eyes looking far off into the fading sunset.

When she heard Morris's name, she turned her head a little, so that the ripple of her golden hair was more distinctly visible beneath the silken net she wore; but she made no comment nor showed by any sign that she heard what they were saying. Katy was very lovely and consistent in her young widowhood, and not a whisper of gossip had the Silvertonians coupled with her name since she came to them, leaving her husband in Greenwood. There had been no parading of her grief before the public, or assumption of greater sorrow than many others had known; but the soberness of her demeanor, and the calm, subdued expression of her face, attested to what she had suffered. Sixteen months had passed since Wilford died, and she still wore her deep mourning weeds, except the widow's cap, which, at her mother's and Aunt Betsy's earnest solicitations, she had laid aside, substituting in its place a simple net, which confined her waving hair and kept it from breaking out in flowing curls, as it was disposed to do.

Katy had never been prettier than she was now, in her mature womanhood, and to the poor and sorrowful whose homes she cheered so often she was an angel of goodness.

Truly she had been purified by suffering; the dross had been burned out, and only the gold remained, shedding its brightness on all with which it came in contact.

They would miss her at the farm-house now more than they did when she first went away, for she made the sunshine of their home, filling Helen's place when she was in New York, and when she came back proving to her a stay and comforter. Indeed, but for Katy's presence Helen often felt that she could not endure the sickening suspense and doubt which hung so darkly over her husband's fate.

"He is alive; he *will* come back," Katy always said, and from her perfect faith Helen, too, caught a glimpse of hope.

Could they have forgotten Mark they would have been very happy at the farm-house now, for with the budding spring and blossoming summer Katy's spirits had returned, and her old musical laugh rang through the house just as it used to do in the happy days of girlhood, while the same silvery voice which led the choir in the brick church, and sang with the little children their Sunday hymns, often broke forth into snatches of songs, which made even the robins listen, as they built their nests in the trees.

If Katy thought of Morris, she never spoke of him when she could help it. It was a morbid fancy to which she clung, that duty to Wilford's memory required her to avoid the man who had so innocently come between them; and when she heard he was coming home she felt more pain than pleasure, though for an instant the blood throbbed through her veins as she thought of Morris at Linwood, just as he used to be.

The day of his return was balmy and beautiful, and at an early hour Helen went over to Linwood to see that everything was in order for his arrival, while Katy followed at a later hour, wondering if Wilford would object if he knew she was going to welcome Morris, who might misconstrue her motives if she stayed away.

There was very little for her to do, Helen and Mrs. Hull having done all that was necessary, but she went from room to room, lingering longest in Morris's own apartment, where she made some alterations in the arrangement of the furniture, putting one chair a little more to the right, and pushing a stand or table to the left, just as her artistic eye dictated. By some oversight no flowers had been put in there, but Katy gathered a bouquet and left it on the mantel, just where she remembered to have seen flowers when Morris was at home.

" He will be tired," she said. " He will lie down after dinner," and she laid a few sweet English violets upon his pillow, thinking their perfume might be grateful to him after the pent-up air of the hospital and cars. " He will think Helen put them there, or Mrs. Hull," she thought, as she stole softly out and shut the door behind her, glancing next at the clock, and feeling a little impatient that a whole hour must elapse before they could expect him.

Poor Morris ! he did not dream how anxiously he was waited for at home, nor of the crowd assembled at the depot to welcome back the loved physician, whose name they had so often heard coupled with praise as a true hero, even though his post was not in the front of the battle. Thousands had been cared for by him, their gaping wounds dressed skillfully, their aching heads soothed tenderly, and their last moments made happier by the words he spoke to them of the world to which they were going, where there is no more war or shedding of man's blood. In the churchyard at Silverton there were three soldiers' graves, whose pale occupants had died with Dr.

Grant's hand held tightly in theirs, as if afraid that he
would leave them before the dark river was crossed, while
in more than one Silverton home there was a wasted
soldier, who never tired of telling Dr. Morris's praise
and dwelling on his goodness. But Dr. Morris was not
thinking of this as, faint and sick, with the green shade
before his eyes, he leaned against the pile of shawls his
companion had placed for his back, and wondered if they
were almost there.

"I smell the pond lilies; we must be near Silverton,"
he said, and a sigh escaped him as he thought of coming
home and not being able to *see* it or the woods and fields
around it. "Thy will be done," he had said many times
since the fear first crept into his heart that for him the
light had faded.

But now, when home was almost reached, and he began to breathe the air from the New England hills and
the perfume of the New England lilies, the flesh rebelled
again, and he cried out within himself, "Oh, I cannot
be blind! God will not deal thus by me!" while keen as
the cut of a sharpened knife was the pang with which he
thought of Katy, and wondered would she care if he were
blind.

Just then the long train stopped at Silverton, and, led
by his attendant, he stepped feebly into the crowd, which
sent up deafening cheers for Dr. Grant come home again.
At the sight of his helplessness, however, a feeling of awe
fell upon them, and whispering to each other, "I did not
suppose he was so bad," they pressed around him, offering
their hands and inquiring anxiously how he was.

"I have been sick, but I shall get better now. The
very sound of your friendly voices does me good," he
said, as he went slowly to his carriage, led by Uncle
Ephraim, who could not keep back his tears when he
saw how weak Morris was, and how he panted for breath
as he leaned back among the cushions.

It was very pleasant that afternoon, and Morris enjoyed
the drive so much, assuring Uncle Ephraim, that he was
growing better every moment. He did seem stronger
when the carriage stopped at Linwood, and he went up the

steps where Helen, Katy, and Mrs. Hull were waiting
for him. He could not by sight distinguish one from the
other, but without the aid of her voice he would have
known when Katy's hand was put in his, it was so small,
so soft, and trembled so as he held it. She forgot Wilford in her excitement. Pity was the strongest feeling of
which she was conscious, and it manifested itself in various ways.

"Let *me* lead you, Cousin Morris," she said, as she saw
him groping his way to his room, and without waiting for
his reply, she held his hand again in hers and led him
to his room, where the English violets were.

"I used to lead *you*," Morris said, as he took his seat by
the window, "and I little thought then that you would
one day return the compliment. It is very hard to be
blind."

The tone of his voice was inexpressibly sad, but his
smile was as cheerful as ever as his face turned towards
Katy, who could not answer for her tears. It seemed so
terrible to see a strong man so stricken, and that strong
man Morris—terrible to watch him in his helplessness,
trying to appear as of old, so as to cast on others no part
of the shadow resting so darkly on himself. When dinner
was over and the sun began to decline, many of his former
friends came in; but he looked so pale and weary that
they did not tarry long, and when the last one was gone,
Morris was led back to his room, which he did not leave
again until the summer was over, and the luscious fruits
of September were ripening upon the trees.

Towards the middle of July, Helen, whose health was
suffering from her anxiety concerning Mark, was taken
by Mrs. Banker to Nahant, where Mark's sister, Mrs.
Ernst, was spending the summer, and thus on Katy fell
the duty of paying to Morris those acts of sisterly attention such as no other member of the family knew how to
pay. In the room where he lay so helpless Katy was not
afraid of him, nor did she deem herself faithless to Wilford's memory, because each day found her at Linwood,
sometimes bathing Morris's inflamed eyes, sometimes
bringing him the cooling drink, and again reading to him

by the hour, until, soothed by the music of her voice, he would fall away to sleep and dream he heard the angels sing.

"My eyes are getting better," he said to her one day toward the latter part of August, when she came as usual to his room. "I knew last night that Mrs. Hull's dress was blue, and I saw the sun shine through the shutters. Very soon, I hope to see you, Katy, and know if you have changed."

She was standing close by him, and as he talked he raised his hand to rest it on her head, but, with a sudden movement, Katy eluded the touch, and stepped a little further from him.

When next she went to Linwood there was in her manner a shade of dignity, which both amused and interested Morris. He did not know for certain that Wilford had told Katy of the confession made that memorable night when her recovery seemed so doubtful, but he more than half suspected it from the shyness of her manner, and from the various excuses she began to make for not coming to Linwood as often as she had heretofore done.

In his great pity for Katy when she was first a widow, Morris had scarcely remembered that she was free, or if it did flash upon his mind, he thrust the thought aside as injustice to the dead; but as the months and the year went by, and he heard constantly from Helen of Katy's increasing cheerfulness, it was not in his nature never to think of what might be, and more than once he had prayed, that if consistent with his Father's will, the woman he had loved so well, should yet be his. If not, he could go his way alone, just as he had always done, knowing that it was right.

Such was the state of Morris's mind when he returned from Washington, but now it was somewhat different. The weary weeks of sickness, during which Katy had ministered to him so kindly, had not been without their effect, and if Morris had loved the frolicsome, child-like Katy Lennox, he loved far more the gentle, beautiful woman, whose character had been so wonderfully developed by suffering, and who was more worthy of his love than in her early girlhood.

"I cannot lose her now," was the thought constantly in Morris's mind, as he experienced more and more how desolate were the days which did not bring her to him. "It is twenty months since Wilford died," he said to himself one wet October afternoon, when he sat listening dreamily to the patter of the rain falling upon the windows, and looking occasionally across the fields to the farm-house, in the hope of spying in the distance the little airy form, which, in its water-proof and cloud, had braved worse storms than this at the time he was so ill.

But no such figure appeared. He hardly expected it would; but he watched the pathway just the same, and the smoke-wreaths rising so high above the farm-house. The deacon burned out his chimney that day, and Morris, whose sight had greatly improved of late, knew it by the dense, black volume of smoke, mingled with rings of fire, which rose above the roof, remembering so well another rainy day, twenty years ago, when the deacon's chimney was cleaned, and a little toddling girl, in scarlet gown and white pinafore, had amused herself with throwing into the blazing fire upon the hearth a straw at a time, almost upsetting herself with standing so far back, and making such efforts to reach the flames. A great deal had passed since then. The little girl in the pinafore had been both wife and mother. She was a widow now, and Morris glanced across his hearth toward the empty chair he had never seen in imagination filled by any but herself.

"Surely, she would some day be his own," and leaning his head upon the cane he carried, he prayed earnestly for the good he coveted, keeping his head down so long that, until it had left the strip of woods and emerged into the open fields, he did not see the figure wrapped in water-proof and hood, with a huge umbrella over its head and a basket upon its arm, which came picking its way daintily toward the house, stopping occasionally, and lifting up the little high-heeled Balmoral, which the mud was ruining so completely. Katy was coming to Linwood. It had been baking-day at the farm-house, and remembering how much Morris used to love her custards, Aunt Betsy had prepared him some, and asked Katy to take them over, so he could have them for tea.

"The rain won't hurt you an atom," she said as Katy began to demur, and glance at the lowering sky. "You can wear your waterproof boots and my shaker, if you like, and I do so want Morris to have them to-night."

Thus importuned, Katy consented to go, but declined the loan of Aunt Betsy's shaker, which being large of the kind, and capeless, too, was not the most becoming head-gear a woman could wear. With the basket of custards, and cup of jelly, Katy finally started, Aunt Betsy saying to her, as she stopped to take up her dress, "It must be dretful lonesome for Morris to-day. S'posin' you stay to supper with him, and when it's growin' dark I'll come over for you. You'll find the custards fust rate."

Katy made no reply, and walked away, while Aunt Betsy went back to the coat she was patching for her brother, saying to herself,

"I'm bound to fetch that round. It's a shame for two young folks, just fitted to each other, to live apart when they might be so happy, with Hannah, and Lucy, and me, close by, to see to 'em, and allus make their soap, and see to the butcherin', besides savin' peneryle and catnip for the children, if there was any."

Aunt Betsy had turned match-maker in her old age, and day and night she planned how to bring about the match between Morris and Katy. That they were made for each other, she had no doubt. From something which Helen inadvertently let fall, she had guessed that Morris loved Katy prior to her marriage with Wilford. She had suspected as much before; she was sure of it now, and straightway put her wits to work "to make it go," as she expressed it. But Katy was too shy to suit her, and since Morris's convalescence, had stayed too much from Linwood. To-day, however, Aunt Betsy "felt it in her bones," that if properly managed something would happen, and the custards were but the means to the desired end. With no suspicion whatever of the good dame's intentions, Katy picked her way to Linwood, and leaving her damp garments in the hall, went at once into the library, where Morris was sitting near to a large chair kept sacred for her, his face looking unusually cheerful, and the room unusually pleasant, with the bright wood fire on the hearth.

"I have been so lonely, with no company but the rain," he said, pushing the chair a little towards her, and bidding her sit near the fire, where she could dry her feet.

Katy obeyed, and sat down so near to him that had he chosen he might have touched the golden hair, fastened in heavy coils low on her neck, and giving to her a very girlish appearance, as Morris thought, for he could see her now, and while she dried her feet he looked at her eagerly, wondering that the fierce storm she had encountered had left so few traces upon her face. Just about the mouth there was a deep cut line, but this was all; the remainder of the face was fair and smooth as in her early girlhood, and far more beautiful, just as her character was lovelier, and more to be admired.

Morris had done well to wait if he could win her now. Perhaps he thought so, too, and this was why his spirits became so gay as he kept talking to her, suggesting at last that she should stay to tea. The rain was falling in torrents when he made the proposition. She could not go then, even had she wished it, and though it was earlier than his usual time, Morris at once rang for Mrs. Hull, and ordered that tea be served as soon as possible.

"I ought not to stay. It is not proper," Katy kept thinking, as she fidgeted in her chair, and watched the girl setting the table for two, and occasionally deferring some debatable point to her as if she were mistress there.

"You can go now, Reekie," Morris said, when the boiling water was poured into the silver kettle, and tea was on the table. "If we need you we will ring."

With a vague wonder as to who would toast the doctor's bread, and butter it, Reekie departed, and the two were left together. It was Katy who toasted the bread, kneeling upon the hearth, burning her face and scorching the bread in her nervousness at the novel position in which she so unexpectedly found herself. It was Katy, too, who prepared Morris's tea, and tried to eat, but could not. She was not hungry, she said, and the custard was the only thing she tasted, besides the tea, which she sipped at

frequent intervals so as to make Morris think she was eating more than she was. But Morris was not deceived, nor
disheartened. Possibly she suspected his intention, and if
so, the sooner he reached the point the better. So when
the tea equipage was put away, and she began again to
speak of going home, he said,

"No, Katy, you can't go yet, till I have said what's in
my mind to say," and laying his hand upon her shoulder
he made her sit down beside him and listen while he. told
her of the love he had borne for her long before she knew
the meaning of that word as she knew it now—of the
struggle to keep that love in bounds after its indulgence
was a sin; of his temptations and victories, of his sincere
regret for Wilford, and of his deep respect for her grief,
which made her for a time as a sister to him. But that
time had passed. She was not his sister now, nor ever
could be again. She was Katy, dearer, more precious,
more desired even than before another called her wife,
and he asked her to be his, to come up there to Linwood
and live with him, making the rainy days brighter,
balmier, than the sunniest had ever been, and helping him
in his work of caring for the poor and sick around them.

"Will Katy come? Will she be the wife of Cousin
Morris?"

There was a world of pathos and pleading in the voice
which asked this question, just as there was a world of
tenderness in the manner with which Morris caressed and
fondled the bowed head resting on the chair arm. And
Katy felt it all, understanding what it was to be offered
such a love as Morris offered, but only comprehending in
part what it would be to refuse that love. For her blinded
judgment said she must refuse it. Had there been no sad
memories springing from that grave in Greenwood, no
bitter reminiscences connected with her married life—
had Wilford never heard of Morris's love and taunted her
with it, she might perhaps consent, for she craved the
rest there would be with Morris to lean upon. But the
happiness was too great for her to accept. It would seem
too much like faithlessness to Wilford, too much as if he
had been right, when he charged her with preferring
Morris to himself.

"It cannot be;—oh, Morris, it cannot be," she sobbed, when he pressed her for an answer. "Don't ask me why —don't ever mention it again, for I tell you it cannot be. My answer is final; it cannot be. I am sorry for you, so sorry! I wish you had never loved me, for it cannot be."

She writhed herself from the arms which tried to detain her, and rising to her feet left the room suddenly, and throwing on her wrappings quitted the house without another word, leaving basket and umbrella behind, and never knowing she had left them, or how the rain was pouring down upon her unsheltered person, until, as she entered the narrow strip of woodland, she was met by Aunt Betsy, who exclaimed at seeing her, and asked,

"What has become of your *umberell?* Your silk one too. It's hopeful you haven't lost it. What has happened you?" and coming closer to Katy, Aunt Betsy looked searchingly in her face. It was not so dark that she could not see the traces of recent tears, and instinctively suspecting their nature she continued, " Catherine, have you gin Morris the mitten?"

"Aunt Betsy, is it possible that you and Morris contrived this plan?" Katy asked, half indignantly, as she began in part to understand her aunt's great anxiety for her to visit Linwood that afternoon.

"Morris had nothing to do with it," Aunt Betsy replied. "It was my doin's wholly, and this is the thanks I git. You quarrel with him and git mad at me, who thought only of your good. Catherine, you know you like Morris Grant, and if he asked you to have him why don't you?"

"I can't, Aunt Betsy. I can't, after all that has passed. It would be unjust to Wilford."

"Unjust to Wilford—fiddlesticks!" was Aunt Betsy's expressive reply, as she started on toward Linwood, saying, "she was going after the umberell before it got lost, with nobody there to tend to things as they should be tended to. Have you any word to send?" she asked, hoping Katy had relented.

But Katy had not; and with a toss of her head, which shook the rain drops from her capeless shaker, Aunt Betsy went on her way, and was soon confronting Morris, sitting just where Katy had left him, and looking very pale and sad.

He was not glad to see Aunt Betsy. He would rather be alone until such time as he could control himself and still his throbbing heart. But with his usual affability, he bade Aunt Betsy sit down, shivering a little when he saw her in the chair where Katy had sat, her thin, angular body presenting a striking contrast to the graceful, girlish figure which had sat there an hour since, and the huge india rubbers she held up to the fire, as unlike as posible to the boot of fairy dimensions he had admired so much when it was drying on the hearth.

"I met Catherine," Aunt Betsy began, "and mistrusted at once that something was to pay, for a girl don't leave her umberell in such a rain and go cryin' home for nothin'."

Morris colored, resenting for an instant this interference by a third party; but Aunt Betsy was so honest and simple-hearted, that he could not be angry long, and he listened calmly, while she continued,

"I have not lived sixty odd years for nothing, and I know the signs pretty well. I've been through the mill myself."

Here Aunt Betsy's voice grew lower in its tone, and Morris looked up with real interest, while she went on,

"There's Joel Upham—you know Joel—keeps a tin-shop now, and seats the folks in meetin'. He asked me once for my company, and to be smart I told him *no,* when all the time I meant *yes,* thinkin' he would ask agin; but he didn't, and the next I knew he was keepin' company with Patty Adams, now his wife. I remembered I sniveled a little at being taken at my word, but it served me right, for saying one thing when I meant another. However, it don't matter now. Joel is as clever as the day is long, but he is a shiftless critter, never splits his kindlins till jest bedtime, and Patty is pestered to death for wood, while his snorin' nights she says is awful, and that I never could abide; so, on the whole, I'm better off than Patty."

Morris laughed a loud, hearty laugh, which emboldened his visitor to say more than she had intended saying.

"You just ask her agin. Once ain't nothing at all, and she'll come to. She likes you; 'taint that which made her say no. It's some foolish idea about faithfulness to Wilford, as if he deserved that she should be faithful. They never orto have had one another,—never; and now that he is well in Heaven, as I do suppose he is, it ain't I who hanker for him to come back. Neither does Katy, and all she needs is a little urging, to tell you yes. So ask her again, will you?"

"I think it very doubtful. Katy knew what she was doing, and meant what she said," Morris replied; and with the consoling remark that if young folks would be fools it was none of her business to bother with them, Aunt Betsy pinned her shawl across her chest, and hunting up both basket and umbrella, bade Morris good night, and went back across the fields to the farm-house, hearing from Mrs. Lennox that Katy had gone to bed with a racking headache.

CHAPTER XLVIII.

KATY.

"ARE you of the same mind still?" Helen asked, when three weeks later she returned from New York, and at the hour for retiring sat in her chamber watching Katy as she brushed her hair, occasionally curling a tress around her fingers and letting it fall upon her snowy night-dress.

They had been talking of Morris, whom Katy had seen but once since that rainy night, and that at church, where he had been the previous Sunday. Katy had written an account of the transaction to her sister, who had chosen to reply by word of mouth rather than by letter, and so the first moment they were alone she seized the opportunity to ask if Katy was of the same mind still as when she refused the doctor.

"Yes, why shouldn't I be?" Katy replied. "You, better than any one else, know what passed between Wilford——"

"Do you love Morris?" Helen asked, abruptly, without waiting for Katy to finish her sentence.

For an instant the hands stopped in their work, and Katy's eyes filled with tears, which dropped into her lap as she replied,

"More than I wish I did, seeing I must always tell him no. It's strange, too, how the love for him keeps coming, in spite of all I can do. I have not been there since, nor spoken with him until last Sunday, but I knew the moment he entered the church, and when in the first chant I heard his voice, my fingers trembled so that I could hardly play, while all the time my heart goes out after the rest I always find with him. But it cannot be. Oh, Helen! I wish Wilford had never known that Morris loved me."

She was sobbing now, with her head in Helen's lap, and Helen, smoothing her bright hair, said gently,

"You do not reason correctly. It is right for you to answer Morris yes, and Wilford would say so, too. When I received your letter I read it to Bell, who then told what Wilford said before he died. You must have forgotten it, darling. He referred to a time when you would cease to be his widow, and he said he was willing,—said so to her, and you. Do you remember it, Katy?"

"I do now, but I *had* forgotten. I was so stunned then, so bewildered, that it made no impression. I did not think he meant Morris, Helen; *do* you believe he meant Morris?" and lifting up her face Katy looked at her sister with a wistfulness which told how anxiously she waited for the answer.

"I *know* that he meant Morris," Helen replied. "Both Bell and her father think so, and they bade me tell you to marry Dr. Grant, with whom you will be so happy."

"I cannot. It is too late. I told him no, and Helen, I told him a falsehood, too, which I wish I might take back," she added. "I said I was sorry he ever loved me, when I was not, for the knowing that he *had* made me very happy. My conscience has smitten me cruelly for that falsehood, told not intentionally, for I did not consider what I said."

Here was an idea at which Helen caught at once, and the next morning she went to Linwood and brought Morris home with her. He had been there two or three times since his return from Washington, but not since Katy's refusal, and her cheeks were scarlet as she met him in the parlor and tried to be natural. He did not look unhappy. He was not taking his rejection very hard, after all, she thought, and the little lady felt a very little piqued to find him so cheerful, when she had scarcely known a moment's quiet since the day she carried him the custards and forgot to bring away her umbrella.

As it had rained that day, so it did now, a decided, energetic rain, which set in after Morris came, and precluded the possibility of his going home that night.

"He would catch his death of cold," Aunt Betsy said, while Helen, too, joined her entreaties, until Morris consented, and the carriage which came round for him at dark returned to Linwood with the message that the doctor would pass the night at Deacon Barlow's.

During the evening he did not often address Katy directly, but he knew each time she moved, and watched every expression of her face, feeling a kind of pity for her, when, without appearing to do so intentionally, the family, one by one, stole from the room,—Uncle Ephraim and Aunt Hannah without any excuse; Aunt Betsy to mix the cakes for breakfast; Mrs. Lennox to wind the clock, and Helen to find a book for which Morris had asked.

Katy might not have thought strange of their departure, were it not that neither one came back again, and after the lapse of ten minutes or more she felt convinced that she had purposely been left alone with Morris.

The weather and the family had conspired against her, but after one throb of fear she resolved to brave the difficulty, and meet whatever might happen as became a woman of twenty-three, and a widow. She knew Morris was regarding her intently as she fashioned into shape the coarse wool sock, intended for some soldier, and she could almost hear her heart beat in the silence which fell

between them ere Morris said to her, in a tone which re-
assured her,

"And so you told me a falsehood the other day, and
your conscience has troubled you ever since?"

"Yes, Morris, yes; that is, I told you I was sorry that
you ever loved me, which was not exactly true, for, after
I knew you did, I was happier than before."

Her words implied a knowledge of his love previous to
that night at Linwood when he had himself confessed it,
and he said to her inquiringly,

"You knew it, then, before I told you?"

"From Wilford,—yes," Katy faltered.

"I understand now why you have been so shy of me,"
Morris said; "but, Katy, must this shyness continue always? Think, now, and say if you did not tell more than
one falsehood the other night,—as you count falsehoods?"

Katy looked wonderingly at him, and he continued,

"You said you could not be my wife. Was that true?
Can't you take it back, and give me a different answer?"

Katy's cheeks were scarlet, and her hands had ceased to
flutter about the knitting which lay upon her lap.

"I meant what I said," she whispered; "for, knowing
how Wilford felt, it would not be right for me to be so
happy.

"Then it's nothing personal? If there were no harrowing memories of Wilford, you could be happy with me.
Is that it, Katy?" Morris asked, coming close to her now,
and imprisoning her hands, which she did not try to take
away, but let them lie in his as he continued, "Wilford
was willing at the last. Have you forgotten that?"

"I had, until Helen reminded me," Katy replied.
"But, Morris, the talking of this thing brings Wilford's
death back so vividly, making it seem but yesterday since
I held his dying head."

She was beginning to relent, Morris knew, and bending nearer to her he said,

"It was not yesterday. It will be two years in February; and this, you know, is November. I need you,
Katy. I want you so much. I have wanted you all your
life. Before it was wrong to do so, I used each day to
pray that God would give you to me, and now I feel just

as sure that he has opened the way for you to come to me as I am sure that Wilford is in heaven. He is happy there, and shall a morbid fancy keep you from being happy here? Tell me, then, Katy, will you be my wife?"

He was kissing her cold hands, and as he did so he felt her tears dropping on his hair.

"If I say yes, Morris, you will not think that I never loved Wilford, for I did, oh, yes! I did. Not exactly as I might have loved you, had you asked me first, but I loved him, and I was happy with him, for if there were little clouds, his dying swept them all away."

Katy was proving herself a true woman, who remembered only the good there was in Wilford, and Morris did not love her less for it. She was all the dearer to him, all the more desirable, and he told her so, winding his arms about her, and resting her head upon his shoulder, where it lay just as it had never lain before, for with the first kiss Morris gave her, calling her "My own little Katy," she felt stealing over her the same indescribable peace she had always felt with him, intensified now, and sweeter from the knowing that it would remain if she should will it so. And she did will it so, kissing Morris back when he asked her to, and thus sealing the compact of her second betrothal. It was not exactly like the first. There was no tumultuous emotions, or ecstatic joys, but Katy felt in her inmost heart that she was happier now than then; that between herself and Morris there was more affinity than there had been between herself and Wilford, and as she looked back over the road she had come, and remembered all Morris had been to her, she wondered at her blindness in not recognizing and responding to the love in which she had now found shelter.

It was very late that night when Katy went up to bed, and Helen, who was not asleep, knew by the face on which the lamp-light fell that Morris had not sued in vain. Aunt Betsy knew it, too, next morning, by the same look on Katy's face when she came down stairs, but this did not prevent her saying abruptly, as Katy stood by the sink,

"Be you two engaged?"

"We are," was Katy's frank reply, which brought back

all Aunt Betsy's visions of roasted fowls and frosted
cake, and maybe a dance in the kitchen, to say nothing
of the feather bed which she had not dared to offer Katy
Cameron, but which she thought would come in play for
" Miss Dr. Grant."

CHAPTER XLIX.

THE PRISONERS.

MANY of the captives were coming home, and all along
the Northern lines loving hearts were waiting, and
friendly hands outstretched to welcome them back to
" God's land," as the poor, suffering creatures termed the
soil over which waved the stars and stripes, for which
they had fought so bravely. Wistfully thousands of eyes
ran over the long columns of names of those returned,
each eye seeking for its own, and growing dim with tears
as it failed to find it, or lighting up with untold joy when
it was found.

" Lieut. Robert Reynolds," and " Thomas Tubbs," Helen
read among the list of those just arrived at Annapolis, but
" Captain Mark Ray " was not there, and, with a sickening feeling of disappointment, she passed the paper to
her mother-in-law, and hastened away, to weep and pray
that what she so greatly feared might not come upon her.

It was after Katy's betrothal, and Helen was in New
York, hoping to hear news from Mark, and perhaps to
see him ere long, for as nearly as she could trace him
from reports of others, he was last at Andersonville. But
there was no mention made of him, no sign by which she
could tell whether he still lived, or had long since been
relieved from suffering.

Early next day she heard that Mattie Tubbs had received a telegram from Tom, who would soon be at home,
while later in the day Bell Cameron came round to say that
Bob was living, but that he had lost his right arm, and
was otherwise badly crippled. It never occurred to Helen
to ask if this would make a difference. She only kissed

Bell fondly, rejoicing at her good fortune, and then sent her back to the home where there were hot discussions regarding the propriety of receiving into the family a maimed and crippled member.

"It was preposterous to suppose Bob would expect it," Juno said, while the mother admitted that it was a most unfortunate affair, as indeed the whole war had proved. For her part she sometimes wished the North had let the South go quietly, as they wanted to, and so saved thousands of lives, and prevented the country from being flooded with cripples and negroes, and calls for more men and money. On the whole, she doubted the propriety of prolonging the war; and she certainly doubted the propriety of giving her daughter to a cripple. There was Arthur Grey, who had lately been so attentive; he was a wealthier man than Lieutenant Bob, and if Bell had any discretion she would take him in preference to a disfigured soldier.

Such was the purport of Mrs. Cameron's remarks, to which her husband listened, his eyes blazing with passion, which, the moment she finished, burst forth in a storm of oaths and invectives against what, with his pet adjective, he called her "Copperhead principles," denouncing her as a traitor, reproaching her for the cruelty which would separate her daughter from Robert Reynolds, because he had lost an arm in the service of his country; and then turning fiercely to Bell with the words,

"But it isn't for you to say whether he shall or shall not have Bell. She is of age. Let her speak for herself."

And she did speak, the noble, heroic girl, who had listened, with bitter scorn, to what her mother and sister said, and who now, with quivering nostrils, and voice hoarse with emotion, answered slowly and impressively,

"I would marry Lieutenant Reynolds if he had only his *ears* left to hear me tell him how much I love and honor him! Arthur Grey! Don't talk to me of him! the craven coward, who swore he was fifty to avoid the draft."

After this, no more was said to Bell, who, the moment she heard Bob was at home, went to his father's house and asked to see him.

He was sleeping when she entered his room; and pushing back the heavy curtain, so that the light would fall more directly upon him, Mrs. Reynolds went out and left her there alone.

With a beating heart she stood looking at his hollow eyes, his sunken cheek, his short, dry hair, and thick gray skin, but did not think of his arm, until she glanced at the wall, where hung a large-sized photograph, taken in full uniform, the last time he was at home, and in which his well-developed figure showed to good advantage. Could it be that the wreck before her had ever been as full of life and vigor as the picture would indicate, and was that arm which held the sword severed from the body, and left a token of the murderous war?

"Poor Bob! how much he must have suffered," she whispered, and kneeling down beside him she hid her face in her hands, weeping bitter tears for her armless, hero.

The motion awakened Robert, who gazed for a moment in surprise at the kneeling, sobbing maiden; then when sure it was she, he raised himself in bed, and ere Bell could look up, *two arms,* one quite as strong as the other, were wound around her neck, and her head was pillowed upon the breast, which heaved with strong emotions as the soldier said,

"My darling Bell, you don't know how much good this meeting does me!"

He kissed her many times, and Bell did not prevent it, but gave him kiss after kiss, then, still doubting the evidence of her eyes, she unclasped his clinging arms, and holding both his poor hands in hers, gave vent to a second gush of tears as she said,

"I am so glad—oh, so glad!"

Then, as it occurred to her that he might perhaps misjudge her, and put a wrong construction upon her joy, she added,

"I did not care for myself, Robert. Don't think I cared for myself, or was ever sorry a bit on my own account."

Bob looked a little bewildered as he replied, "Never were sorry and never cared!—I can scarcely credit that, for surely your tears and present emotions belie your words."

Bell knew he had not understood her, and said,

"Your *arm*, Robert, your arm. We heard that it was cut off, and that you were otherwise mutilated."

"Oh, that's it, then!" and something like his old mischievous smile glimmered about Bob's mouth as he added, "They spared my *arms,* but, Bell," and he tried to look very solemn, "suppose I tell you that they hacked off both my legs, and if you marry me, you must walk all your life by the side of *wooden pins* and *crutches!*"

Bell knew by the curl of his lip that he was teasing her, and she answered laughingly,

"Wooden pins and crutches will be all the fashion when the war is over—badges of honor of which any woman might be proud."

"Well, Bell," he replied, "I am afraid there is no such honor in store for my wife, for if I ever get back my strength and the flesh upon my bones, she must take me with legs and arms included. Not even a scratch or wound of any kind with which to awaken sympathy."

He appeared very bright and cheerful; but when after a moment Bell asked for Mark Ray, there came a shadow over his face, and with quivering lips he told a tale which blanched Bell's cheeks, and made her shiver with pain and dread as she thought of Helen—for Mark *was dead*—shot down as he attempted to escape from the train which took them from one prison to another. He was always devising means of escape, succeeding several times, but was immediately captured and brought back, or sent to some closer quarter, Robert said; but his courage never deserted him, or his spirits either. He was the life of them all, and by his presence kept many a poor fellow from dying of homesickness and despair. But he was dead; there could be no mistake, for Robert saw him when he jumped, heard the ball which went whizzing after him, saw him as he fell on the open field, saw a man from a rude dwelling near by go hurriedly towards him, firing his own revolver, as if to make the death deed doubly sure. Then as the train slacked its speed, with a view, perhaps, to take the body on board, he heard the man who had reached Mark, and was bending over him, call out, " Go on, I'll tend to him, the bullet went right through here; " and he turned the dead man's face towards the train, so all could see the blood pouring from the temple which the finger of the ruffian touched.

" Oh, Helen! poor Helen! how can I tell her, when she loved him so much ! " Bell sobbed.

" You will do it better than any one else," Bob said. " You will be very tender with her; and, Bell, tell her, as some consolation, that he did not break with the treatment, as most of us wretches did; he kept up wonderfully—said he was perfectly well—and, indeed, he looked so. Tom Tubbs, who was his shadow, clinging to him with wonderful fidelity, will corroborate what I have said. He was with us; he saw him, and only animal force prevented him from leaping from the car and going to him where he fell. I shall never forget his shriek of agony at the sight of that blood-stained face, turned an instant towards us."

" Don't, don't! " Bell cried again; " I can't endure it! " and as Mrs. Reynolds came in she left her lover and started for Mrs. Banker's, meeting on the steps Tom Tubbs himself, who had come on an errand similar to her own.

" Sit here in the hall a moment," she said to him, as the servant admitted them both. " I must see Mrs. Ray first."

Helen was reading to her mother-in-law; but she laid down her book and came to welcome Bell, detecting at once the agitation in her manner, and asking if she had bad news from Robert.

" No, Robert is at home; I have just come from there, and he told me—oh! Helen, can you bear it?—*Mark is dead* —shot twice as he jumped from the train taking him to another prison. Robert saw it and knew that he was dead."

Bell could get no further, for Helen, who had never fainted in her life, did so now, lying senseless so long that the physician began to think it would be a mercy if she never came back to life, for her reason, he fancied, had fled. But Helen did come back to life, with reason unimpaired, and insisted upon hearing every detail of the dreadful story, both from Bell and Tom. The latter confirmed all Lieutenant Reynolds had said, besides adding many items of his own. Mark was dead, there could be no doubt of it; but with the tenacity of a strong, hopeful nature, the mother clung to the illusion that possibly the ball stunned, instead of killing—that he would yet come back; and many a time as the days went by, that mother started at the step upon the walk, or ring of the bell, which she fancied might be his, hearing him sometimes calling in the night storm for her to let him in, and hurrying down to the door only to be disappointed and go back to her lonely room to weep the dark night through.

With Helen there were no such illusions. After talking calmly and rationally with both Robert and Tom, she knew her husband was dead, and never watched and waited for him as his mother did. She had heard from Mark's companions in suffering all they had to tell, of his captivity and his love for her which manifested itself in so many different ways. Passionately she had wept over the tress of faded hair which Tom Tubbs brought to her, saying, " he cut it from his head just before we left the prison, and told me if he never got home and I did, to give the lock to you, and say that all was well between him and God—that your prayers had saved him. He wanted you to know that, because, he said, it would comfort you most of all."

And it did comfort her when she looked up at the clear wintry heavens and thought that her lost one was there. It was her first real trial, and it crushed her with its magnitude, so that she could not submit at once, and many a cry of desolate agony broke the silence of her room, where the whole night through she sat musing of the past, and raining kisses upon the little lock of hair which from the Southern prison had come to her, sole relic of the husband so dearly loved and truly mourned. How faded it was from the rich brown she remembered so well, and Helen gazing at it could realize in part the suffering and want which had worn so many precious lives away. It was strange she never dreamed of him. She often prayed that she might, so as to drive from her mind, if possible, the picture of the prostrate form upon the low, damp field, and the blood-stained face turned in its mortal agony towards the southern sky and the pitiless foe above it. So she always saw him, shuddering as she wondered if the foe had buried him decently or left his bones to bleach upon the open plain.

Poor Helen, she was widowed indeed, and it needed not the badge of mourning to tell how terribly she was bereaved. But the badge was there, too, for in spite of the hope which said, " he is not dead," Mrs. Banker yielded to Helen's importunities, and clothed herself and daughter-in-law in the habiliments of woe, still waiting, still watching, still listening for the step she should recognize so quickly, still looking down the street; but looking, alas! in vain. The winter passed away. Captive after captive came home, heart after heart was cheered by the returning loved one, but for the inmates of No.— the heavy cloud grew blacker, for the empty chair by the hearth remained unoccupied, and the aching hearts uncheered. *Mark Ray did not come back.*

CHAPTER L.

THE DAY OF THE WEDDING.

THOSE first warm days of March, 1865, when spring and summer seemed to kiss each other and join hands for a brief space of time, how balmy, how still, how pleasant they were, and how bright the farm-house looked, where preparations for Katy's second bridal were going rapidly forward. Aunt Betsy was in her element, for now had come the reality of the vision she had seen so long, of house turned upside down in one grand onslaught of suds and sand, then, righted again by magic power, and smelling very sweet and clean from its recent ablutions—of turkeys dying in the barn, of chickens in the shed, of loaves of frosted cake, with cards and cards of snowy biscuit piled upon the pantry shelf—of jellies, tarts, and chicken salad —of home-made wine, and home-brewed beer, with tea and coffee portioned out and ready for the evening.

In the dining-room the table was set with the new China ware and silver, a joint Christmas gift from Helen and Katy to their good Aunt Hannah, as real mistress of the house.

"Not plated ware, but the gen-oo-ine article," Aunt Betsy had explained at least twenty times to those who came to see the silver, and she handled it proudly now as she took it from the flannel bags in which Mrs. Deacon Bannister said it must be kept, and placed it on a side-table.

The coffee-urn was Katy's, so was the tea-kettle and the massive pitcher, but the rest was " ours," Aunt Betsy complacently reflected as she contemplated the glittering array, and then hurried off to see what was burning on the stove, stumbling over Morris as she went, and telling him " he had come too soon—it was not fittin' for him to be there under foot until he was wanted."

Without replying directly to Aunt Betsy, Morris knocked with a vast amount of assurance at a side-door, which opened directly, and Katy's glowing face looked out, and Katy's voice was heard, saying joyfully,

"Oh, Morris, it's you. I'm so glad you've come, for I wanted "——

But what she wanted was lost to Aunt Betsy by the closing of the door, and Morris and Katy were alone in the little sewing room where latterly they had passed so many quiet hours together, and where lay the bridal dress with its chaste and simple decorations. Katy had clung tenaciously to her mourning robe, asking if she *might* wear black, as ladies sometimes did. But Morris had promptly answered no. His bride, if she came to him willingly, must not come clad in widow's weeds, for when she became his wife she would cease to be a widow.

And so black was laid aside, and Katy, in soft tinted colors, with her bright hair curling on her neck, looked as girlish and beautiful as if in Greenwood there were no pretentious monument, with Wilford's name upon it, nor any little grave in Silverton where Baby Cameron slept. She had been both wife and mother, but she was quite as dear to Morris as if she had never borne other name than Katy Lennox, and as he held her for a moment to his

heart he thanked God who had at last given to him the
idol of his boyhood and the love of his later years. Across
their pathway no shadow was lying, except when they remembered Helen, on whom the mantle of widowhood had
fallen just as Katy was throwing it off.

Poor Helen! the tears always crept to Katy's eyes when
she thought of her, and now, as she saw her steal across
the road and strike into the winding path which led to the
pasture where the pines and hemlock grew, she nestled
closer to Morris, and whispered,

"Sometimes I think it wrong to be so happy when
Helen is so sad. I pity her so much to-day."

And Helen was to be pitied, for her heart was aching
to its very core. She had tried to keep up through the
preparations for Katy's bridal, tried to seem interested
and even cheerful, while all the time a hidden agony was
tugging at her heart, and life seemed a heavier burden
than she could bear.

All her portion of the work was finished now, and in
the balmy brightness of that warm April afternoon she
went into the fields where she could be alone beneath the
soft summer-like sky, and pour out her pent-up anguish
into the ear of Him who had so often soothed and comforted her when other aids had failed. Last night, for
the first time since she heard the dreadful news, she had
dreamed of Mark, and when she awoke she still felt the
pressure of his lips upon her brow, the touch of his arm
upon her waist, and the thrilling clasp of his warm hand
as it pressed and held her own. But that was a dream, a
cruel delusion, and its memory made the more dark and
dreary as she went slowly up the beaten path, pausing
once beneath a chestnut tree and leaning her throbbing
head against the shaggy bark as she heard in the distance
the shrill whistle of the downward train from Albany, and
thought as she always did when she heard that whistle,
"Oh, if that heralded Mark's return, how happy I should
be." But many sounds like that had echoed across the Silverton hills, bringing no hope to her, and now as it again
died away in the Cedar Swamp she pursued her way up
the path till she reached a long white ledge of rocks—
"The lovers' Rock," some called it, for village boys and

maidens knew the place, repairing to it often, and whispering their vows beneath the overhanging pines, which whispered back again, and told the winds the story which though so old is always new to her who listens and to him who tells.

Just underneath the pine there was a large flat stone, and there Helen sat down, gazing sadly upon the valley below, and the clear waters of Fairy Pond gleaming in the April sunshine which lay so warmly on the grassy hills and flashed so brightly from the cupola at Linwood, where the national flag was flying. For a time Helen watched the banner as it shook its folds to the breeze, then as she remembered with what a fearful price that flag had been saved from dishonor, she hid her face in her hands and sobbed bitterly.

"God help me not to think I paid too dearly for my country's rights. Oh, Mark, my husband, I may be wrong, but *you* were dearer to me than many, many countries, and it is hard to give you up—hard to know that the notes of peace which float up from the South will not waken you in that grave which I can never see. Oh, Mark, my darling, my darling, I love you so much, I miss you so much, I want you so much. God help me to bear. God help to say, 'Thy will be done.'"

She was rocking to and fro in her grief, with her hands pressed over her face, and for a long time she sat thus, while the sun crept on further towards the west, and the freshened breeze shook the tasseled pine above her head and kissed the bands of rich brown hair, from which her hat had fallen. She did not heed the lapse of time, nor hear the footstep coming up the pathway to the ledge where she was sitting, the footstep which paused at intervals, as if the comer were weary, or in quest of some one, but which at last came on with rapid bounds as an opening among the trees showed where Helen sat. It was a tall young man who came, a young man, sun-burned and scarred, with uniform soiled and worn, but with the fire in his brown eyes unquenched, the love in his true heart unchanged, save as it was deeper, more intense for the years of separation, and the long, cruel suspense, which was all over now. The grave had given up its dead, the captive was released, and through incredible suffering and danger had reached his Northern home, had sought and found his girl-wife of a few hours, for it was Mark Ray speeding up the path, and holding back his breath as he came close to the bowed form upon the rock, feeling a strange throb of awe when he saw the *mourning dress,* and knew it was worn for him. A moment more, and she lay in his arms; white and insensible, for with the sudden winding of his arms around her neck, the pressure of his lips upon her cheek, the calling of her name, and the knowing it was really her husband, she had uttered a wild, impassioned cry, half of terror, half of joy, and fainted entirely away, just as she did when told that he was dead! There was no water near, but with loving words and soft caresses Mark brought her back to life, raining both tears and kisses upon the dear face which had grown so white and thin since the Christmas eve when the wintry star light had looked down upon their parting. For several moments neither could speak for the great choking joy which wholly precluded the utterance of a word. Helen was the first to rally. With her head lying in Mark's lap and pillowed on Mark's arm, she whispered,

"Let us thank God together. You, too, have learned to pray."

Reverently Mark bent his head to hers, and the pine boughs overhead heard, instead of mourning notes, a prayer of praise, as the reunited wife and husband fervently thanked God, who had brought them together again.

Not until nearly a half hour was gone, and Helen had begun to realize that the arm which held her so tightly was genuine flesh and blood, and not mere delusion, did she look up into the face, glowing with so much of happiness and love. Upon the forehead, and just beneath the hair, there was a savage scar, and the flesh about it was red and angry still, showing how sore and painful it must have been, and making Helen shudder as she touched it with her lips, and said,

"Poor, darling Mark! that's where the cruel ball entered; but where is the other scar,—the one made by the man who went to you in the fields. I have tried so hard not to hate him for firing at a fallen foe."

"Rather pray for him, darling. Bless him as the sa-

vior of your husband's life, the noble fellow but for whom
I should not have been here now, for he was a Unionist,
as true to the old flag as Abraham himself," Mark Ray
replied; and then, as Helen looked wonderingly at him,
he laid her head in an easier position upon his shoulder,
and told her a story so strange in its details, that but for
the frequent occurrence of similar incidents, it would be
pronounced wholly unreal and false."

Of what he suffered in the Southern prisons he did
not speak, either then or ever after, but began with the
day when, with a courage born of desperation, he jumped
from the moving train and was shot down by the guard.
Partially stunned, he still retained sense enough to know
when a tall form bent over him, and to hear the rough
but kindly voice which said,

"Play 'possum, Yank. Make b'lieve you're dead, and
throw 'em off the scent."

This was the last he knew for many weeks, and when
again he woke to consciousness he found himself on the
upper floor of a dilapidated hut, which stood in the centre of a little wood, his bed a pile of straw, over which
was spread a clean patch-work quilt, while seated at his
side, and watching him intently, was the same man who
had bent over him in the field, and shouted to the rebels
that he was dead.

"I shall never forget my sensations then," Mark said,
"for with the exception of this present hour, when I
hold you in my arms, and know the danger is over, I
never experienced a moment of greater happiness and
rest than when, up in that squalid garret, I came back
to life again, the pain in my head all gone, and nothing
left save a delicious feeling of languor, which prompted
me to lie quietly for several minutes, examining my surroundings, and speculating upon the chance which brought
me there. That I was a prisoner I did not doubt, until
the old man at my side said to me cheerily,

"Well, old chap, you've come through it like a major,
though I was mighty dubus a spell about that pesky ball.
But old Aunt Bab and me fished it out, and since then
you've begun to mend."

"'Where am I? Who are you?' I asked, and he replied, ' Who be I? Why, I'm *Jack Jennins,* the rarinest, redhotedest secesh there is in these yer parts, so the Rebs thinks ; but 'twixt you and me, boy, I'm the tallest kind of a Union,—got a piece of the old flag sowed inside of my boots, and every night before sleepin' I prays the Lord to gin Abe the victory, and raise Cain generally in t'other camp, and forgive Jack Jennins for tellin' so many lies, and makin' b'lieve he's one thing when you know and he knows he's t'other. If I've *spared* one Union chap, I'll bet I have a hundred, me and old Bab, a black woman who lives here and tends to the cases I fotch her, till we contrive to git 'em inter Tennessee, whar they hev to shift for themselves.'

"I could only press his hand in token of my gratitude while he went on to say, ' Them was beans I fired at you that day, but they sarved every purpose, and them scalliwags on the train s'pose you were put underground weeks ago, if indeed you wasn't left to rot in the sun, as heaps and heaps on 'em is. Nobody knows you are here but Bab and me, and nobody must know if you want to git off with a whole hide. I could git a hundred dollars by givin' you up, but you don't s'pose Jack Jennins is a gwine to do that ar infernal trick. No, sir,' and he brought his brawny fist down upon his knee with a force which made me tremble, while I tried to express my thanks for his great kindness. He was a noble man, Helen, while Aunt Bab, the colored woman, who nursed me so tenderly, and whose black, bony hands I kissed at parting, was as true a woman as any with a fairer skin and more beautiful exterior.

" For three weeks longer I stayed up in that loft, and in that time three more escaped prisoners were brought there, and one Union refugee from North Carolina. We left in company one wild, rainy night, when the storm and darkness must have been sent for our special protection, and Jack Jennings cried like a little child when he bade me good-bye, promising, if he survived the war, to find his way to the North and visit me in New York.

" We found these Unionists everywhere, and especially among the mountains of Tennessee, where, but for their timely aid, we had surely been recaptured. With blistered feet and bruised limbs we reached the lines at last, when fever attacked me for the second time and brought me near to death. Somebody wrote to you, but you never received it, and when I grew better I would not let them write again, as I wanted to surprise you. As soon as I was able I started North, my thoughts full of the joyful meeting in store—a meeting which I dreaded too, for I knew you must think me dead, and I felt so sorry for you, my darling, knowing, as I did, you would mourn for your soldier husband. That my darling *has* mourned is written on her face, and needs no words to tell it; but that is over now," Mark said, folding his wife closer to him, and kissing the pale lips, while he told her how, arrived at Albany, he had telegraphed to his mother, asking where Helen was.

"In Silverton," was the reply, and so he came on in the morning train, meeting his mother in Springfield as he had half expected to do, knowing that she could leave New York in time to join him there.

"No words of mine," he said, "are adequate to describe the thrill of joy with which I looked again upon the hills and rocks so identified with you that I loved them for your sake, hailing them as old, familiar friends, and actually growing sick and faint with excitement when through the leafless woods I caught the gleam of Fairy Pond, where I gathered the lilies for you. There is a wedding in progress at the farm-house, I learned from mother, and it seems very meet that I should come at this time, making, in reality, a double wedding when I can truly claim my bride," and Mark kissed Helen passionately, laughing to see how the blushes broke over her white face, and burned upon her neck.

Those were happy moments which they passed together upon that ledge of rocks, happy enough to atone for all the dreadful past, and when at last they rose and slowly retraced their steps to the farm-house, it seemed to Mark that Helen's cheeks were rounder than when he found her, while Helen knew that the arm on which she leaned was stronger than when it first encircled her an hour or two before.

CHAPTER LI.

THE WEDDING.

On the same train with Mrs. Banker and Mark, Bell Cameron came with Bob, but father Cameron was not able to come; he would gladly have done so if he could, and he sent his blessing to Katy with the wish that she might be very happy in her second married life. This message Bell gave to Katy, and then tried to form some reasonable excuse for her mother's and Juno's absence, for she could not tell how haughtily both had declined the invitation, Juno finding fault because Katy had not waited longer than two years, and Mrs. Cameron blaming her for being so very vulgar as to be married at home, instead of in church. On this point Katy herself had been a little disquieted, feeling how much more appropriate it was that she be married in the church, but shrinking from standing again a bride at the same altar where she had once before been made a wife. She could not do it, she finally decided; there would be too many harrowing memories crowding upon her mind, and as Morris did not particularly care where the ceremony was performed, it was settled that it should be at the house, even though Mrs. Deacon Bannister did say that "she had supposed Dr. Grant too *High Church* to do anything so *Presbyterianny* as that."

Bell's arrival at the farm-house was timely; for the unexpected appearance in their midst of one whom they looked upon as surely dead had stunned and bewildered the family to such an extent that it needed the presence of just such a matter-of-fact, self-possessed woman as Bell, to bring things back to their original shape. It was wonderful how the city girl fitted into the vacant niches, seeing to everything which needed seeing to, and still finding time to steal away alone with Lieutenant Bob, who kept her in a painful state of blushing, by constantly wishing it was his bridal night as well as Dr. Grant's, and by inveighing against the weeks which must intervene, ere the day appointed for the grand ceremony, to take place in Grace Church, and which was to make Bell his wife.

*   *   *   *   *   *

"Come in here, Helen, I have something to show you," Mrs. Banker said, after she had again embraced and wept over her long lost son, whose return was not quite real yet; and leading her daughter-in-law to her bedroom, she showed her the elegant, white silk which had been made for her just after her marriage, two years before, and which, with careful forethought, she had brought with her, as more suitable now for the wedding, than Helen's mourning weeds.

"I made the most of my time last night, after receiving Mark's telegram, and had it modernized somewhat," she said. "And I brought your pearls, for you will be most as much a bride as Katy, and I have a pride in seeing my son's wife appropriately dressed."

Far different were Helen's feelings now, as she donned the elegant dress, from what they had been the first and only time she wore it. Then the bridegroom was where danger and death lay thickly around his pathway; but now he was at her side, kissing her cheek, where the roses were burning so brightly, and calling still deeper blushes to her face, by his teasing observations and humorous ridicule of his own personal appearance. Would she not feel ashamed of him in his soiled uniform? And would she not cast longing glances at her handsome brother-in-law and the stylish Lieutenant Bob? But Helen was proud of her husband's uniform, as a badge of what he had suffered; and when the folds of her rich dress swept against it, she did not draw them away, but nestled closer to him, leaning upon his shoulder; and when no one was near, winding her soft arm about his neck once, whispering, "My darling Mark, I cannot make it real yet."

Softly the night shadows fell around the farm-house, and in the rooms below a rather mixed group was assembled—all the *élite* of the town, with many of Aunt Betsy's neighbors, and the doctor's patients, who had come to see their physician married, rejoicing in his happiness, and glad that the mistress of Linwood was not to be a stranger, but the young girl who had grown up in their midst, and who, by suffering and sorrow, had been moulded into a noble woman, worthy of Dr. Grant. She was ready now for her second bridal, in her dress of white, with no vestige of color in her face, and her great blue eyes shining with a brilliancy which made them almost black. Occasionally, as her thoughts leaped backward over a period of almost six years, a tear trembled on her long eyelashes, but Morris kissed it away, asking if she were sorry.

"Oh, no, not sorry that I am to be your wife," she answered; "but it is not possible that I should forget entirely the roughness of the road which has led me to you."

"They are waiting for you," was said several times, and down the stairs passed Mark Ray and Helen, Lieut. Bob and Bell, with Dr. Grant and Katy, whose face, as she stood again before the clergyman and spoke her marriage vows, shone with a strange, peaceful light, which made it seem to those who gazed upon her like the face of some pure angel.

There was no thought then of that deathbed in Georgetown—no thought of Greenwood or the little grave in Silverton, where the crocuses and hyacinths were blossoming—no thought of anything save the man at her side, whose voice was so full and earnest as it made the responses, and who gently pressed the little hand as he fitted the wedding-ring. It was over at last, and Katy was Morris's wife, blushing now as they called her *Mrs. Grant,* and putting up her rosebud lips to be kissed by all who claimed that privilege. Helen, too, came in for her share of attention, and the opinion of the guests as to the beauty of the respective brides, as they were termed, was pretty equally divided.

In heavy rustling silk, which actually trailed an inch, and cap of real lace, Aunt Betsy moved among the crowd, her face glowing with the satisfaction she felt at seeing her nieces so much admired, and her heart so full of good will and toleration that after the supper was over, and she fancied a few of the younger ones were beginning to feel tired, she suggested to Bell that she might start a *dance* if she had a mind to, either in the kitchen or the parlor, it did not matter where, and "Ephraim would not care an atom," a remark which brought from Mrs. Deacon Bannister a most withering look of reproach, and slightly endangered Aunt Betsy's standing in the church. Perhaps Bell Cameron suspected as much, for she replied that they were having a splendid time as it was, and as Dr. Grant did not dance, they might as well dispense with it altogether. And so it happened that there was no dancing at Katy's wedding, and Uncle Ephraim escaped the reproof which his brother deacon would have felt called upon to give him had he permitted so grievous a sin, while Mrs. Deacon Bannister, who, at the first trip of the toe would have departed lest her eyes should look upon the evil thing, was permitted to remain until "it was out," and the guests retired *en masse* to their respective homes.

*   *   *   *   *   *

The carriage from Linwood stood at the farm-house door, and Katy, wrapped in shawls and hood, was ready to go with her husband. There were no tears shed at this parting, for their darling was not going far away; her new home was just across the fields, and through the soft moonlight they could see its chimney tops, and trace for some little distance the road over which the carriage went bearing her swiftly on; her hands fast locked in Morris's, her head upon his arm, and the hearts of both too full of bliss for either to speak a word until Linwood was reached, when, folding Katy to his bosom in a passionate embrace, Morris said to her,

"We are home at last—your home and mine, my precious, precious wife."

The village clock was striking one, and the sound echoed across the waters of Fairy Pond, awakening, in his marshy bed, a sleeping frog, who sent forth upon the warm, still air a musical, plaintive note as Morris bore his bride over the threshold and into the library, where a cheerful fire was blazing. He had ordered it kindled there, for he had a fancy ere he slept to see fulfilled a dream he had dreamed so often, of Katy sitting as his wife in the chair across the hearth, where he placed her now, himself removing her shawl and hood; then kneeling down before her, with his arm around her waist and his head upon her shoulder, he prayed aloud to the God who had brought her there, asking His blessing upon their future life, and dedicating himself and all he had to his Master's service. It is such prayer which God delights to answer, and a peace, deeper than they had yet known, fell upon that newly-married pair at Linwood.

CHAPTER LII.

CONCLUSION.

THE scene shifts now to New York, where, one week after that wedding in Silverton, Mark and Helen went, together with Morris and Katy. But not to Madison Square. That house had been sold, and Katy saw it but once, her tears falling fast as, driving slowly by with Morris, she gazed at the closed doors and windows of what was once her home, and around which lingered no pleasant memories save that it was the birthplace of baby Cameron. Lieutenant Reynolds had thought to buy it, but Bell said, " No, it would not be pleasant for Katy to visit me there, and I mean to have her with me as much as possible." So the house went to strangers, and a less pretentious but quite as comfortable one was bought for Bell, so far up town that Juno wondered how her sister would manage to exist so far from everything, intimating that her visits would be far between, a threat which Lieutenant Bob took quite heroically; indeed, it rather enhanced the value of his pleasant home than otherwise, for Juno was not a favorite, and his equanimity was not likely to be disturbed if she never crossed his threshold. She was throwing bait to *Arthur Grey*, the man who swore he was fifty to escape the draft, and who, now that the danger was over, would gladly take back his oath and be forty, as he really was.

With the most freezing kiss imaginable Juno greeted Katy, calling her "Mrs. Grant," and treating Morris as if he were an entire stranger, instead of the man whom to get she would once have moved both earth and heaven. Mrs. Cameron, too, though glad that Katy was married, and fully approving her choice, threw into her manner so much reserve that Katy's intercourse with her was anything but agreeable, and she turned with alacrity to father Cameron, who received her with open arms, calling her his daughter, and welcoming Morris as his *son*, taken in Wilford's stead. "My boy," he frequently called him, showing how willingly he accepted him as the husband of one whom he loved as his child. Greatly he wished that they should stay with him while they remained in New York, but Katy preferred going to Mrs. Banker's, where she would be more quiet, and avoid the bustle and confusion attending the preparations for Bell's wedding. It was to be a grand church affair, and to take place during Easter week, after which the bridal pair were going on to Washington, and if possible to Richmond, where Bob had been a prisoner. Everything seemed conspiring to make the occasion a joyful one, for all through the North, from Maine to California, the air was rife with the songs of victory and the notes of approaching peace. But alas! He who holds our country's destiny in his hand changed that song of gladness into a wail of woe, which, echoing through the land, rose up to heaven in one mighty sob of anguish, as the whole nation bemoaned its loss. Our President was dead, and New York was in mourning, so black, so profound, that with a shudder Bell Cameron tossed aside the orange wreath and said to her lover, "We will be married at home. I cannot now go to the church, when everything seems like one great funeral."

And so in Mrs. Cameron's drawing-room there was a quiet wedding, one pleasant April morning, and Bell's plain traveling dress was far more in keeping with the gloom which hung over the great city than her gala robes would have been, with a long array of carriages and merry wedding chimes. Westward they went instead of South, and when our late lamented President was borne back to the prairies of Illinois, they were there to greet the noble dead, and mingle their tears with those who knew and loved him long before the world appreciated his worth.

    *   *   *   *   *   *

Softly the May rain falls on Linwood, where the fresh green grass is springing and the early spring flowers blooming, and where Katy stands for a moment in the bay window of the library, listening to the patter on the tin roof overhead, and gazing wistfully down the road, as if watching for some one; then turning, she enters the dining-room and inspects the supper table, for her mother. Aunt Hannah, and Aunt Betsy are visiting her this rainy afternoon, while Morris, on his return from North Silverton, is to call for Uncle Ephraim and bring him home to tea.

Linwood is a nice place to visit, and the old ladies enjoy it vastly, especially Aunt Betsy, who never tires of telling what they have " over to Katy's," and whose capeless shaker hangs often on the hall stand, just as it hangs now, while she, good soul, sits in the pleasant parlor, and darns the socks for Morris, taking as much pains as if it were a network of fine lace she was weaving, instead of a shocking rent in some luckless heel or toe. Up stairs there is a pleasant room which Katy calls Aunt Betsy's, and in it is the " feather bed," which never found its way to Madison Square. Morris himself did not think much of feathers, but he made no objections when Aunt Betsy insisted upon Katy's having the bed kept for so many years, and only smiled a droll kind of smile when he one morning met it coming up the walk in the wheelbarrow which Uncle Ephraim trundled.

Morris and his young wife are very happy together and Katy finds the hours of his absence very long, especially when left alone. Even to-day the time drags heavily, and she looks more than once from the bay window, until at last Brownie's head is seen over the hill, and a few moments after Morris's arm is around her shoulders, and her lips are upturned for the kiss he gives as he leads her into the house, chiding her for exposing herself to the rain, and placing in her hand three letters, which she does

not open until the cozy tea is over and her family friends
have gone. Then, while her husband looks over his evening paper, she breaks the seals one by one reading first
the letter from " Mrs. Bob Reynolds," who has returned
from the West, and who is in the full glory of her bridal
calls.

"I was never so happy in my life as I am now," she
wrote. "Indeed, I did not know that a married woman
could be so happy; but then every woman has not a *Bob*
for her husband, which makes a vast difference. You
ought to see Juno. I know she envies me, though she
affects the utmost contempt for matrimony, and reminds
me forcibly of the fox and the grapes. You see, Arthur
Grey is a failure, so far as Juno is concerned, he having
withdrawn from the field and laid himself at the feet of
Sybil Grandon, who will be Mrs. Grey, and a bride at
Saratoga the coming summer. Juno intends going too,
as the bridesmaid of the party; but every year her chances
lessen, and I have very little hope that father will ever
call other than Bob his son, always excepting *Morris,* of
course, whom he has adopted in place of Wilford. You
don't know, Katy, how much father thinks of you, blessing the day which brought you to us, and saying that if
he is ever saved, he shall in a great measure owe it to your
influence and consistent life after the great trouble came
upon you."

There were tears in Katy's eyes as she read this letter
from Bell, and with a mental prayer of thanksgiving that
she had been of any use in guiding even one to the Shep-
herd's Fold, she took next the letter whose superscription
brought back so vividly to her mind the daisy-covered
grave in Alnwick. Marian, who was now at Annapolis,
caring for the returned prisoners, did not write often, and
her letters were prized the more by Katy, who read with a
beating heart the kind congratulations upon her recent
marriage, sent by Marian Hazelton.

"I knew how it would end, when you were in Georgetown," she wrote, "and I am glad that it is so, praying
daily that you may be happy with Dr. Grant and remember
the sad past only as some dream from which you have

awakened. I thank you for your invitation to visit Linwood, and when my work is over I may come for a few
weeks and rest in your bird's nest of a home. Thank God
the war is ended; but *my boys* need me yet, and until the
last crutch has left the hospital, I shall stay where duty
lies. What my life will henceforth be I do not know; but
I have sometimes thought that with the funds you so generously bestowed upon me, I shall open a school for orphan
children, taking charge myself, and so doing some good.
Will you be the Lady Patroness, and occasionally enliven
us with the light of your countenance? I have left the
hospital but once since you were here, and then I went to
Wilford's grave. I prayed for you while there, remembering only that *you* had been his wife. In a little box where
no eyes but mine ever look, there is a bunch of flowers
plucked from Wilford's grave. They are faded and withered, but something of their sweet perfume lingers still;
and I prize them as my greatest treasure; for, except the
lock of hair severed from his head, they are all that is remaining to me of the past, which now seems so far away.
It is time to make my nightly round of visits, so I must
bid you good-bye. The Lord lift up the light of his
countenance upon you, and be with you forever.

MARIAN HAZELTON."

For a long time Katy held this letter in her hand, wondering if the sorrowful woman whose life was once so
strangely blended with that of Marian Hazleton, could be
the Katy Grant who sat by the evening fire at Linwood,
with the sunshine of perfect happiness resting on her heart.
"Truly He doeth all things well to those who wait upon
Him," she thought, as she laid down Marian's letter and
took up the third and last, Helen's letter, dated at Fortress
Monroe, whither, with Mark Ray, she had gone just after
Bell Cameron's bridal.
"You cannot imagine," Helen wrote, "the feelings of
awe and even terror which steal over me the nearer I get to
the seat of war, and the more I realize the bloody strife
we have been engaged in, and which, thank God, has now
nearly ceased. You have heard of John Jennings, the noble man who saved my dear husband's life, and of Aunt

Bab, who helped in the good work? Both are here, and
I never saw Mark more pleased than when seized around
the neck by two long brawny arms, while a cheery voice
called out: 'Hallow, old chap, has you done forgot John
Jennins?' I verily believe Mark cried, and I know I did,
especially when old Bab came up and shook 'young
misses' hand.' I kissed her, Katy—all black, and rough,
and uncouth as she was. I wish you could see how grateful
the old creature is for every act of kindness. When we
come home again, both John and Bab will come with us,
though what we shall do with John, is more than I can
tell. Mark says he shall employ him about the office, and
this I know will delight Tom Tubbs, who has again made
friends with Chitty, and who will almost worship John
as having saved Mark's life. Aunt Bab shall have an
honored seat by the kitchen fire, and a pleasant room all
to herself, working only when she likes, and doing as she
pleases.

"Did I tell you that Mattie Tubbs was to be my seamstress? I am getting together a curious household, you
will say; but I like to have those about me to whom I
can do the greatest amount of good, and as I happen to
know how much Mattie admires 'the Lennox girls,' I did
not hesitate to take her.

"We stopped at Annapolis on our way here, and I shall
never forget the pale, worn faces, nor the great sunken
eyes which looked at me so wistfully as I went from cot
to cot, speaking words of cheer to the sufferers, some of
whom were Mark's companions in prison, and whose eyes
lighted up with joy as they recognized him and heard of
his escape. There are several nurses here, but no words
of mine can tell what *one* of them is to the poor fellows,
or how eagerly they watch for her coming. Following her
with greedy glances as she moves about the room, and
holding her hand with a firm clasp, as if they would keep
her with them always. Indeed, more than one heart, as
I am told, has confessed its allegiance to her; but she
answers all the same, 'I have no love to give. It died
out long ago, and cannot be recalled.' You can guess who
she is, Katy. The soldiers call her an angel, but we know
her as Marian."

There were great tear blots upon that letter as Katy put it aside, and nestling close to Morris, laid her head upon his knee, where his hand could smooth her golden curls, while she pondered Helen's closing words, thinking how much they expressed, and how just a tribute they were to the noble woman whose life had been one constant sacrifice of self for another's good—"The soldiers call her an angel, but we know her as Marian."

THE END.

www.ingramcontent.com/pod-product-compliance
Lightning Source LLC
Chambersburg PA
CBHW050901130726
47900CB00015B/1681